The Broken Brooch

The Celtic Brooch Series, Book 5

Katherine Lowry Logan

Copyright © 2016 by Katherine Lowry Logan
Print Edition

This book is a work of fiction. The characters and names are entirely the product of the author's imagination and there are no references to real people. Actual establishments, locations, public and business organizations are used solely for the intention of providing an authentic setting, and are used fictitiously. Any resemblance to actual events, locales, or persons, living or dead, is entirely coincidental.

All rights reserved. No part of this book may be used or reproduced in any manner whatsoever without written permission except in the case of brief quotations embodied in critical articles and reviews.

Story consultant and editor: Faith Freewoman
Cover art by Damonza
Interior design by BB eBooks

Website: www.katherinellogan.com

Cast of Characters

Order of Appearance

1. Jenny Lynn "JL" O'Grady, NYPD detective
2. Pete Parrino, NYPD detective and JL's partner
3. Austin O'Grady, high school student and basketball player at Pro Prep
4. Cate Wilson, Montgomery Winery office manager
5. Elliott Fraser and Meredith Montgomery (**The Last MacKlenna**)
6. Kenzie (Wallis-Manning) McBain, wife of David McBain and legal counsel for MacKlenna Corporation (**The Emerald Brooch**)
7. Detective Hollinger, Napa Police Department
8. Detective Michael Castellano, Napa Police Department
9. Kevin Allen, CFO, MacKlenna Corporation
10. Retired Deputy Chief Lawrence O'Grady (Pops), JL's father
11. Sammy Castellano, son of Detective Castellano
12. James Cullen Fraser, son of Meredith Montgomery and Elliott Fraser
13. Betsy Brown, Austin's girlfriend
14. David McBain (**The Emerald Brooch**) and twin sons: Henry and Robbie
15. Jack Mallory, NYT bestselling author
16. Connor, Shane, Patrick, and Jeffrey O'Grady, NYPD detectives and JL's older brothers
17. Dr. Charlotte Mallory and Braham McCabe (**The Sapphire Brooch**) and children: Lincoln and Kitherina

18. Bill Wilder, Mining sales rep
19. Chris Dalton, power forward, Golden State Warriors (fictional)

MENTIONED

1. Ryan Monahan, JL's ex-husband
2. Kit MacKlenna Montgomery, winery founder (**The Ruby Brooch**)
3. Maggie O'Grady, JL's mother
4. Julie O'Grady, JL's sister-in-law, married to Jeffrey
5. Amy Spalding, ESPN commentator (heroine in **The Diamond Brooch**)
6. Cullen Montgomery, husband of Kit MacKlenna Montgomery (**The Ruby Brooch**)
7. James Thomas MacKlenna (1700s), father of Thomas Sean MacKlenna (patriarch of MacKlenna Farm and father of the first Sean MacKlenna who appears in **The Ruby Brooch** and **The Sapphire Brooch**)

A Message From The Author

When a brooch is broken, not all its magic works.

This story is **not** a time-travel romance but it does carry the same theme found in the other Celtic Brooch books. The hero and heroine are placed in unfamiliar environments, and challenged to rise above the people they are to become the people they were created to be.

I hope you enjoy this romantic suspense. All the characters you have come to love in **The Celtic Brooch Series** are part of this love story.

It is my pleasure to introduce NYPD Detective Jenny Lynn "JL" O'Grady...

1

THE GPS IN JL O'GRADY'S rental car announced, "You have arrived at your destination." So had the police, the ABC-7 Napa Valley news van, and the medical examiner.

JL brought the vehicle to a screeching halt at Montgomery Winery's stone guard station just as the taillights of the ME's vehicle disappeared behind the closing gate.

Thank God, Napa, California, wasn't her jurisdiction. Hers was three thousand miles away.

The news van pulled to a stop on the grass, and a peppy, twentysomething field reporter scrambled out of the front passenger seat and hurried toward a cop standing near the gate. "We have a report of a shooting at the winery."

JL remained in her vehicle with an iron grip on the steering wheel, her heart pounding. Where was Austin? They had exchanged texts the moment her flight landed in San Francisco, and he confirmed he would meet her at the winery's Welcome Center in—she checked the time on the dashboard clock—five minutes.

A second cop took a position in front of the swinging gate as it automatically locked back into place. In answer to the reporter's question he said, "No comment."

"Was it an accidental shooting?"

"No comment."

"Is Ms. Montgomery at the winery today?"

"No comment."

"Was the victim a member of her family or an employee?"

"No comment."

JL's mood had gone sour during the turbulent flight from New York City, and the congested highways from San Francisco International Airport had further deteriorated her disposition. Now a shooting at the winery completely tanked it all to hell.

The no-comment cop strode toward her, tugging on the leather duty belt that creaked below his belly. When he reached JL, he said, "Montgomery Winery is closed to visitors."

"My brother works here. I need to pick him up."

"He'll have to make other arrangements."

She climbed out of the car. "Would you leave the premises if your child was locked in behind that security gate?"

"I thought you said your brother."

"He's seventeen. I raised him."

"I can't help you. Sorry. The winery is on lockdown."

She considered asking for professional courtesy. Cops loved other cops, but were territorial and resented interference by cops from other agencies. Even though she wouldn't be interfering, flashing her NYPD shield would immediately raise the cop's hackles. It wasn't worth it.

Her phone beeped with a text message. She reached inside the window and dug her phone out of her purse. The message was from Austin.

Where are you?

She typed quickly, *At the gate. Can't get in. You okay?*

Fine. Orchardist murdered. Meet me at side entrance.

She replied, *Where's that?*

"Ma'am," the cop said, "the winery is closed until further notice. Move on. Let's keep the drive clear."

"Sure. I'm going."

The reporter, smelling news to broadcast to her viewers, raced toward JL. "What does your brother do at the winery?"

"No comment."

"But your brother's in there. Is he all right?"

Her phone beeped again with another message. *Go back half a mile. Turn right on Montgomery Lane. Go quarter of a mile. Turn into back entrance to winery. I'll meet you there.*

"Was that him? What'd he say?"

JL gave the reporter her most convincing disappointed look. "He canceled lunch."

She slid back into the driver's seat and turned the car around, keeping an eye on the rearview mirror. If the reporter followed her, she'd have to take an alternate route to the side entrance.

Austin had invited her to be his plus-one at the winery's October End of Harvest Gala and attend his basketball tournament. Of all the things that could have gone wrong, why did it have to be a shooting? Why couldn't the perp have stolen bottles of wine or olive oil? Snagged in this kind of swirling turmoil, she couldn't introduce more trauma into his environment. Telling him about the divorce might have to wait.

Whatever was going on at the winery, at least he was safe. She worried about him 24/7, and had since her mother died when JL was seventeen and Austin was two months old.

Decisions about his welfare were weighty ones she took more seriously than her job. How long had it taken her to agree to his transfer from a high school in Pearl River, New York, to an elite basketball high school in Napa? A month? No, two. Her father and her four older brothers had intervened. They handed her a pair of scissors and demanded she cut the apron strings.

"You've got to let him go, JL," her father had said.

When faced with five men, all standing at least six-one and each weighing close to two hundred pounds, you had to pick your battles carefully. That was one she couldn't win, and she had finally acquiesced.

Months later, she had helped Austin pack his bags and shipped him off to spend his last two years of high school at Pro Prep in Napa. The move almost guaranteed a college scholarship to a top, nationally ranked program, but she missed her baby like crazy. At six-three and one ninety-five, he hadn't been her baby for a very long time, but it was hard to see him any other way.

She turned onto Montgomery Lane. Whatever had happened, Austin needed her to be a calming influence.

In his last phone call before she boarded the plane in New York, he had reminded her that the mad rush of crush had descended upon the valley. He had never before been evocative with his language, unless he was describing the physicality and emotional intensity of a basketball play. He had been, though, when he described the vivid orange, yellow, and lime green vineyards.

"The winery-hopping tourists have created a nightmare, JL," he said. "While you're sitting in bumper-to-bumper traffic, relax and enjoy the beauty. I've never seen anything so—" He had paused for several seconds before finally saying, "...vibrant." She almost laughed. For a gray prose sort of a guy, he purpled it up pretty well.

She stopped at the side entrance and waited at the gate. With each passing minute, she tapped her fingers faster on the steering wheel. She reread the directions on her phone to be sure she had made the correct turns and stopped at the right gate. Confident she was where she was supposed to be, she went back to tapping her fingers on the steering wheel.

Five minutes later, she sent a text to Austin. He didn't answer, which wasn't that unusual. At the ten-minute mark, she sent another one. He didn't answer that one either, but he did show up driving a golf cart. He opened the gate, and she drove through the entrance.

"I was getting worried," she said, climbing out of the car.

"Sorry. I got held up at the security office." He pulled her into a hug, dwarfing her, and she had to crane her neck to look up at him. Lines of concern cut into his chiseled face.

She stepped back to get a good look at him. He hadn't shaved in two or three days, and his auburn hair hung over his ears, but his clothes were clean and pressed, and she didn't see any ink. As long as he didn't get a tattoo, she didn't care about the length of his hair or how many days he went without shaving. "I think you've grown an inch since I saw you in Kansas this summer."

His head popped up and his chest seemed to swell. "They've

listed me as six-four in the tournament program."

Her belly ached right along with her heart. He was growing up, and she wasn't around to watch it happen. "That makes you taller than Pops. You'll have to wear your jeans halfway down your ass or they'll be too short."

"Funny." Subconsciously, he tugged at his pants even though they weren't hanging below the hem of a Montgomery Winery T-shirt. "I've got to take the cart back to security. Follow this road until you reach the Welcome Center. Meet me there, okay?"

"Do you want me to wait in the parking lot?"

"No, go inside. I'll be there in ten minutes. If the door is locked, the code is eight-seven-seven-two-hash." Austin jumped back into the cart and drove off before she could ask the identity of the victim. He probably planned it that way. He always left the room when she and her brothers talked shop. He didn't like to hear gory details of the cases they worked, and he liked listening to complaints about departmental politics even less.

She returned to her car and continued down the road. Coming out of a curve, she hit the brakes before piling into a line of parked patrol cars with blinking blue lights. A cop wearing a yellow vest was setting up collapsible traffic cones.

He straightened, his dull brown eyes glaring. "All employees were told to shelter in place. You're not supposed to be out."

"I didn't get the memo." She didn't need to be snarky, but the cop should have placed the cones before the curve, not after it.

"Let me see some identification."

She reached into her purse and grabbed her shield, but reconsidered and handed over her passport instead.

He opened the document, thumbed through the pages, and handed it back. "What're you doing here?"

"Visiting for the weekend. I'm on my way to the Welcome Center."

"We were told there weren't any visitors on the premises."

"Well, I'm a visitor and I'm here."

"The Welcome Center is directly ahead, but you'll have to take the dirt road on the other side of the curve. Back up and turn around."

She pointed over her shoulder with her thumb. "Before the curve? Where you should have placed the cones, right? That's the curve you're talking about?"

A crooked bottom tooth scratched his upper thin lip, and his thick brows collided above his nose. "There's an investigation in progress. Do not exit your vehicle until you arrive at the Welcome Center."

She considered another snappy retort, but bit her tongue before turning around and backtracking. Whatever was going on, she wasn't part of it, and that didn't hurt her feelings at all. For the past few months, she had questioned whether she still wanted to be a cop, but the badge defined her, and at this point she wasn't sure who she was without it. Part one of her weekend plan was to figure that out. Part two was to tell Austin about her divorce. Or vice versa.

The final decree had been signed twenty-six hours ago, and Austin didn't even know she and her now-ex-husband, Ryan, had separated more than a year earlier. The news would upset him. He might even be more hurt than she had been when she discovered Ryan was a lying, cheating son of a bitch. It had taken her way too long to figure that out. What kind of detective was she that she hadn't noticed the signs of a cheater: a hastily made bed, the scent of a strange perfume, a password-protected email account?

A dumb detective or a blind one.

Beating herself up served no purpose. Working undercover had changed Ryan, and she didn't like the man he had become. Although O'Gradys didn't get divorced, she refused to waste her life in an unhappy marriage.

Her phone beeped again. She glanced at the face to see another text from Austin.

Delayed. Be there in fifteen.

The visitors' parking lot faced two one-story buildings constructed of dove-gray fieldstone and connected by a glass-enclosed pass-through. The sign on one building said CORPORATE OFFICES.

The sign on the other said WELCOME CENTER, TASTING ROOM, AND STORE.

The only other vehicles in the lot were two luxury sedans, three golf carts, and a minibus with the winery's logo on the side. She backed into a spot and eased out of the car, stretching her back and shoulders. Traveling made her tense, but watching Austin play ball made her even more so. If she could run three or four miles before the tournament started at seven o'clock, and release some of the tension she had brought along from rain-soaked New York, she might not beat up the game's refs until after halftime.

She coaxed the rubber band off her ponytail and carefully tousled her below-the-shoulder dark auburn hair. Her fashion-conscious sister-in-law had done a Pinterest search of boards titled WHAT TO WEAR IN WINE COUNTRY and emailed her a list of suggestions. JL had settled on a sleek, mostly black outfit of skinny jeans, a golden-yellow turtleneck sweater, and a fitted black leather jacket. The three-inch Jimmy Choos she found on sale added a bit of glamour, or—as her sister-in-law claimed—pizzazz.

At the last minute, her partner, Pete Parrino, had canceled an appointment and insisted on driving her to the airport. He was a first-generation Italian-American, and although he didn't have a strong accent, he slipped into one easily. He often punctuated his comments with elaborate gestures, befitting the Italian operatic tradition. Most of the time, she didn't understand what he was saying.

"You look *molto caldo*. Don't come back to New York until you *fottere* one of those rich wine guys. I'm tired of you biting my head off for *cazzate*."

Fottere and *cazzate* were two expressions she did understand. "Tell me how you really feel, Pete."

"Okay, here it is, *ragazza tosta*. I'm going to ask for a new partner if you don't get screwed."

Had she really been that bitchy lately? Probably. It wasn't natural for a thirty-four-year-old woman, or "tough chick" as Pete called her, to go without sex for long periods of time. She should be in a satisfying relationship, not flying across the country to watch high school basketball and be Austin's plus-one. Except for giving up on her marriage, she had always played the cards she had been dealt. Now it was time to reshuffle the deck and play a new hand. It might be better or it might be worse, but at least she was playing.

As Yogi Berra used to say, "When you come to a fork in the road, take it."

2

JL SHOULDERED HER oversized purse and pulled on the doorknob, but the Welcome Center door wouldn't open. As soon as she entered 8772# on the keypad, the door buzzed and opened.

The scent of fermenting grapes, while not as strong inside the building, permeated the air. The contrast between her old, gray precinct house in NYC and the Welcome Center couldn't have been greater if she had traveled through a time warp. The oak beams and vistas of crimson vineyards gave the room a pulsating life of its own, and the crackling fire encouraged visitors to get comfortable and savor fine wine. She glanced around, looking for the wine tasting event she had read about on the website. Locked display cases held the only visible bottles—old, valuable bottles that probably tasted like vinegar.

Rarely, did the stupid shit people did out of greed and anger surprise her. In over ten years on the force, she had seen the good, the bad, and lots of the ugly. Give someone money and power and nine times out of ten they abused it.

According to the *Forbes* "Richest People in America" article she read, Dr. Elliott Fraser and his wife, Meredith Montgomery had a combined net worth ranking them three hundred ninety-eighth on the top four hundred list. Austin had good instincts about people, and believed the power couple were two of those rare good ones. A Google search had confirmed his opinion, but in her experience, good people often did bad things—and that included good cops.

JL planted herself in front of the fireplace and the heat siphoned off the chill of bad memories and failures. That sounded like the first line of a country music song. She wasn't a country music fan per se, but she had listened to George Strait's entire collection on the jukebox at the Pearl River Saloon, a pub two blocks from her house, while drowning her sorrows in pitchers of cold beer. The owner got sick of hearing the sad songs and removed all country music from the coin-operated machine. The day she went in for a beer and discovered she could no longer drink and cry to George's heart-wrenching music, was the day she committed to saving her money and jumping back into the dating pool.

Unfortunately, whenever a friend suggested a setup, the guy was either a cop or a private detective. Ryan had left a bad taste in her mouth, and she wasn't ready to date another man who worked in law enforcement. She loved her dad. She loved her brothers. She loved her partner, but she wanted a personal life away from that world. Pete warned her that men outside of law enforcement wouldn't understand her job, and would put pressure on her to quit. Maybe that was true, but she wanted—no, she needed—to find out for herself.

The portrait of a beautiful woman hung above the mantel. Her mesmerizing eyes were an extraordinary shade of green, and her enticing smile was a tease. The woman had a secret she didn't plan to share. A brass plate beneath the painting identified her as KITHERINA MCCABE MACKLENNA MONTGOMERY (1826 TO 1913).

Pinned to her décolletage was a ruby brooch. JL's eyes narrowed as she looked more closely. The pattern in the silver tracery resembled a brooch of her mother's, but the stone in her brooch had been purple. Triggered by a sensory memory, JL's fingers grew warm and tingly.

It's old. It's fragile. It's broken.

Her mother said those words when she found JL playing in her jewelry box. How old had she been? Three or four? What had her dad done with her mom's jewelry? JL wasn't much of a jewelry person, but if he had sold her mother's brooch, maybe she could track it down and buy it back. JL zoomed in on the brooch with her cell phone and snapped a picture of the painting. When she returned home, she would show it to her dad and ask him what had happened to her mother's brooch.

The click of heels on the stone floor preceded a woman's voice by mere seconds. "Detective O'Grady. Hi. I'm Cate Wilson, the office manager." She extended her arm to shake hands, and the charms on her silver bracelet tinkled softly. "I'm sorry I wasn't here to greet you. I was on a call, but Austin sent me a text and said he gave you the code. I'm glad you didn't have to wait outside."

JL shook hands with an attractive woman in her late forties. "Austin has mentioned frequently how helpful you've been."

"He's such a great kid. I'm glad to help out."

"Taking pizza to him while he's studying for exams goes above and beyond," JL said.

"I've got two preteens. I know how they are when it comes to studying. As long as you feed them, they'll stay at it."

A sting of tears surprised JL. She glanced away for a moment. This sweet woman had filled a need in Austin's life that JL couldn't from thousands of miles away. It was much more than what Cate had done for him that prompted the tears, though. The reality was that Austin would never return home to live. After high school, he would play college ball, and then, if all went according to his plan, he would play in the NBA.

"I'm glad you got through the gate," Cate said, interrupting JL's thoughts. "The police announced they were locking down the winery."

"They wouldn't let me in. If Austin hadn't opened the side gate, I'd still be sitting on the side of the road."

"Couldn't you flash your badge or something?"

"The cops wouldn't tell me what was going on. I sent Austin a text, and he responded that there had been a shooting."

"They haven't told us much. All we know is that poor Salvatore was shot and found in the orchard about an hour ago."

"Do they have a suspect?"

"We don't know." Cate glanced at her watch. "The policemen who came by to tell us not to leave the building said a detective would come talk to us."

"Cate, lass. Where are ye?" a man with a Scottish accent yelled.

Cate rolled her eyes. "Elliott never uses the intercom. With these stone walls, sound carries inside both buildings."

A door slammed, and a moment later, a man strode into the room. "There ye are."

Photos on the web didn't do Dr. Elliott Fraser justice. He was a man to turn heads, and with his gray hair and dark brown eyes, he certainly turned hers. He was a silver fox dressed in a dark green polo shirt and pressed khakis.

"Elliott, this is Austin's sister, Detective O'Grady."

"Good. I'm glad ye're here. Maybe ye can find out what's happening. We were told not to leave the premises."

"I rescheduled the meeting at the bank for three o'clock this afternoon," Cate said. "I told the president we might have to cancel at the last minute."

"We don't know what the police will need from us, and we have to make arrangements," Elliott said.

"Maybe you can find out what's going on," Cate said to JL.

"All I know is that the ME's van was driving in when I arrived."

"They'll take him to the funeral home. We can then make plans. The family will probably want him back in Sicily," Cate said.

"It doesn't work that way," JL said. "They'll remove the body as soon as they've decided there's no evidentiary value relative to the body's position. It's important to keep…Salvatore, right?"

"Salvatore Di Salvo," Elliott said.

Di Salvo?

She swallowed, only to find there wasn't a drop of saliva in her mouth. She pressed her fingers against her throat, clearing it softly. "Could I trouble you for a drink of water?"

Cate disappeared and returned almost immediately with a bottle of spring water. JL untwisted the cap and took a long drink. Surely, Salvatore wasn't connected to the Di Salvo family she had sent to prison four years ago? She took a breath and knitted a thread of steel into her voice.

"As I was saying, it's important to keep the body in a cool environment to stabilize the decomposition rate." Why was she telling them this? They didn't need to hear gory details.

"Will ye go to the scene and find out what's going on?" Elliott asked.

"I don't have jurisdiction, sir. The Napa police wouldn't want my help. And I wouldn't want theirs."

"Ye're a decorated detective with the most recognized law enforcement agency in the world. Why wouldn't they want yer assistance?"

She wasn't surprised Dr. Fraser had done a background check on Austin's family. She had done one on him. "The cops are working an active crime scene investigation. They'll get to you as soon as possible. If they ask for my help, I'll be glad to do what I can, but I can tell you right now, they won't want me interfering in their case."

He ran his fingers through his hair and every strand fell back into place. Perfect man. Perfect hair. Was he a perfect husband, too? From the news reports she had read, he appeared to be. His wife was lucky.

A door on the opposite end of the room banged open and Austin thundered in, breathing hard. "Good," he said to JL, panting. "You met Dr. Fraser. Have the cops been here?"

"No," JL said. "You must have run all the way here. Catch your breath, and then tell us if you heard anything else."

Austin shook his head, his shoulders slumping.

"Sit down and tell us what ye know, lad," Elliott said.

Austin dropped into a leather chair, and, with his voice barely audible said, "I found him in the orchard. Salvatore, I mean. He had a bullet hole in the center of his forehead. One eye was wide open like he couldn't believe what was happening to him."

JL sat on the edge of the chair and squeezed Austin's long, powerful arm affectionately.

"I've heard you and Pops talk about cases, and how you're not supposed to touch anything. So I didn't get close. I didn't want my big footprints with these funky treads near the body."

"Have you already given your statement?" JL asked.

"Not yet."

"Then don't say anything else right now."

Elliott typed on his cell phone. "Where's Meredith? Have you seen her?"

"I called security to tell them I found Salvatore," Austin said. "They told me to wait for them to get there. As soon as the security chief arrived, he sent me to find Ms. Montgomery at the cave. I found her, told her what happened, and she jumped in a golf cart and drove away."

A striking redhead in her mid-thirties with long, muscular legs entered the room. The woman matched Austin's description of Kenzie McBain, MacKlenna Corporation's in-house counsel. Two other things caught JL's eye: a West Point class ring instead of a wedding band on her left hand and a second-trimester baby bump. With five nieces and nephews, JL knew baby bumps.

"Elliott, have you heard anything?" she asked, with a barely suppressed twinkle in her eye.

He peeled his glare from his cell phone and focused on the redhead. "*No.* I even reached out to the police chief and the mayor. They wouldn't take my calls or respond to my texts."

"What? Everybody takes your calls. Have you lost your influence?" Kenzie asked.

"God, I hope not," he said.

"JL, do they think the shooter is still on the property?" Cate asked.

Austin's eyes probed JL's, green and hard, and she knew what he wanted to hear, but she couldn't give him the assurance he needed. "If the shooter is another employee, more than likely, yes. If he or she came onto the property to shoot Salvatore, then they probably left immediately. At any rate, I don't think the rest of us are in danger."

The redhead turned her attention to JL. "You're Austin's sister, right? I'm Kenzie McBain. I heard you were coming for the weekend. Since you're a cop, will you talk to them and find out what's going on? I just got off the phone with my husband. He's furious that we can't get any information. He's going to get on a plane in Kentucky, and come here with our two sick three-year-olds if I don't call him back with news immediately."

"The boys are sick. They don't need to travel," Cate said.

"I know that. But we're talking about David McBain and a murder."

"We need David here," Elliott said.

"If I tell him you need him, he'll leave the boys with their manny, Mike." She punched keys on her iPhone. "I'll leave this afternoon and trade places with him."

"If ye leave the negotiating table the acquisition for the new winery could fall apart. I need ye here more than I need David."

"What about the gala, Elliott? We need to notify people today if we're going to cancel," Cate said.

"Meredith will have to make that decision based on her conversations with the police."

"Your event is more than forty-eight hours away," JL said. "If the location isn't near the crime scene, you shouldn't have to cancel unless it would be bad PR to have it under the shadow of a murder." JL immediately regretted opening her mouth. "I should have prefaced that by saying 'in New York City,' we wouldn't suggest an event be canceled unless it encroached on the crime scene."

The door opened again and another woman entered—Meredith Montgomery. JL had seen her picture on the winery's website, too. She was as beautiful as her photograph. She and Kenzie were the same height, but Meredith was smaller-boned, and while both women had a sophisticated, classy look, Meredith had something more intangible—a presence.

When Elliott embraced her, they seemed to meld into one. JL's heart leapt to her throat, and she glanced away. It wasn't Christian of her to be jealous of their relationship, but she was. Chalk up another sin. Her confession list was starting to compete with the length of her arm.

"Did ye talk to the police?" Elliott asked.

"No. I thought we could do that together. Salvatore was the sweetest man. Why would anyone kill him?"

Elliott hissed. "If the police ever show up we might find out."

"They're on their way. I saw two men in suits walking in this direction." She found a tissue in her jacket pocket and used it to dab at her nose.

Someone knocked on the same glass door Austin and Meredith had used. Cate rushed to open it, inviting two men into the room.

"I'm Detective Hollinger and this," he said, pointing to the other man, "is Detective Castellano."

Hollinger reminded JL of her ex-husband Ryan, a by-the-book former Marine. Five-ten, sandy blond, blue eyes, muscular, probably annoyingly punctual, and, like Ryan, tied his tie in a double Windsor knot. No off-the-rack suits for either of them. The shorter, swarthy Castellano packed a few extra pounds and had a loneliness about him that he carried in his deep-set eyes, visible behind dark-rimmed glasses.

Hollinger consulted his notebook. "We need to speak to Dr. Fraser and Ms. Montgomery."

"I'm Fraser," Elliott said. "This is my wife, Meredith Montgomery."

"I'm Kenzie McBain, in-house counsel. I'll be present during interviews with the Frasers and their employees."

Hollinger made a swiping motion with his index finger. "Let me have the names and positions for the rest of you."

"Austin O'Grady. I'm an intern."

The cop checked his notebook. "You found the body, right?"

JL placed her hand on Austin's arm. "I'm JL O'Grady, Austin's sister and guardian. I'll be present during his interview. And, yes, he found the body."

"Have you talked to your sister or anyone else about what you saw?" Hollinger asked.

"She told me not to talk about it until I'd given my statement."

"Good advice. We'll need a room to conduct interviews. Is there an office we can use?" Castellano asked.

Kenzie spoke up. "My office is available."

Hollinger nodded. "Fine. We'll interview Austin first, then Dr. Fraser and Ms. Montgomery."

JL followed Kenzie, the two detectives, and Austin out of the Welcome Center, through the covered pass-through, and into the Corporate Offices building. The building had the same feel as the Welcome Center, with its oak beams, glass walls, and earth tones in the fabrics and carpets. The interior, although designed to evoke a sense of tranquility and order, did nothing for JL. Kenzie continued down a corridor and turned into a corner office.

On one wall behind Kenzie's desk were several photographs of her with an older man in a wheelchair who wore a leather jacket with military insignia. In the background was a restored World War II airplane. On the opposite wall were pictures of her with her army buddies. They were all dressed in combat uniforms. Based on the background in the photographs, JL guessed the pictures were taken during a deployment in Afghanistan or Iraq. On her desk were pictures of a man who resembled the sexy actor Gerard Butler, along with pictures of twin boys.

One picture on the wall tugged on JL's heartstrings because she had a similar one. It was Kenzie wearing a dress uniform standing next to an older man, also in dress uniform. If JL had to guess, she would say the man was Kenzie's father. JL had a picture on her wall at home of her and her dad when she graduated from the academy. Both men wore that proud father look.

"Take a seat, gentlemen," Kenzie said, pointing to a round conference table with six chairs. She sat on one side of Austin, JL on the other. The two detectives sat together, leaving an extra chair between JL and Hollinger.

"Spell your name, please," Hollinger said.

"A-U-S-T-I-N K. O-apostrophe-G-R-A-D-Y."

"What's the K stand for?" Hollinger asked.

"Klenna," Austin said and then spelled it. "K-L-E-N-N-A."

Kenzie raised an eyebrow. "Is that a family name?"

"It was our great-great-great grandmother's name. Three greats. Right, JL?"

"I think it's four."

Austin gave a nervous laugh. "Thank goodness it wasn't O'Klenna, or I'd be Austin O'Klenna O'Grady."

JL patted his hand. "It's okay, sweetie. Don't be nervous. Just answer the questions." She wanted him to stay focused and answer only what was asked. She wasn't trying to hamper the investigation, but she was intent on protecting him and avoiding pushback from the detectives.

"What time did you arrive this morning?" Hollinger asked.

"I had class until 11:30—"

"Where do you go to school?"

"Pro Prep."

Castellano's eyebrows shot up. "You're an elite basketball player."

Austin glanced at the wall clock. "Yes, and I have a team meeting in an hour."

"We won't take long. You'll get there," Castellano said. "What time did you arrive at the winery?"

"As soon as I got out of class, I drove here."

"And what did you do when you arrived?"

"The security chief asked me to join the search for Salvatore."

"Where did you start?" Hollinger asked.

"I was sent to the orchard to look for him."

"To be specific, you're talking about the orchard where the olive trees grow, not the vineyards where the grapes grow?" Hollinger said.

Austin gave the detective a look that JL had seen hundreds of times. It was his what-the-hell look. "I know the difference between an orchard and a vineyard. Yes, I'm talking about the orchard. It covers eight acres. The vineyards cover ten thousand. That's a lot of ground to search, and no one knew where Salvatore was."

"Is it normal for security to have such a massive search for an employee?" Hollinger asked.

Austin shrugged. "I don't know."

"I can answer that," Kenzie said. "A comprehensive protocol was adopted several years ago after the death of Meredith Montgomery's first husband. It ensures all members of the senior staff are accounted for whenever they're on the property."

"How many people are on the senior staff?" Hollinger asked.

"About twenty," Kenzie said.

"We wear monitors." Austin pointed to the small pager on his belt. "I'm not on the senior staff, but Kenzie insisted I wear one, too, for ah…"—he glanced at Kenzie—"liability, right?"

She smiled, nodding. "We want to be sure you're safe."

"Did Mr. Di Salvo wear a monitor?"

"Yes," Austin said, "and this morning it was working, but after two hours his location hadn't changed. That was unusual for him. When he didn't answer his cell phone, a security guard went looking for him. The monitor was found on the ground near the mill, but Salvatore wasn't there. That was when an alert went out. Everyone stopped what they were doing and joined the search. I was sent to the orchard on the north-facing hillside."

Castellano removed his glasses and wiped them using the bottom of a navy silk tie. "How'd you get there?"

"I drove a golf cart. I rode up and down the rows of olive trees until I spotted him crumpled on the ground. There was blood everywhere. I knew he was dead."

"Did you touch him?" Hollinger asked.

Austin shook his head. "I didn't get out of the cart. I didn't go near the body or touch anything. I could only see one of his eyes. It was empty and staring back at me." Austin rubbed his knuckles across his chin, scraping the stubble. "Salvatore was a snappy dresser, as Gramps would say. His hair was always perfect, like Dr. Fraser's, but when I looked at him, all I could see was blood. It matted his hair. I got…" Austin stopped and took a few deep breaths while he fidgeted in his chair. He glanced toward the closed door, pointing his feet in that direction.

"Go on," Hollinger said.

JL glared at the insensitive cop while she rubbed Austin's shoulder. "Give him a minute." She handed over her bottle of water and he took a big gulp, followed by several deep breaths. "Take your time," she said. "If you need a break, say so."

Austin shook his head again. "I felt sick to my stomach, so I put my head between my knees. That was the real reason I didn't get out of the cart. I didn't think my legs would hold me up."

"Then what did you do?" Hollinger asked.

JL knew the detective was only doing his job, but his insensitivity pissed her off. She didn't act like that when she interviewed witnesses. No? Well, not usually. If Pete were in the room right now, he would tell her she was being hypocritical. Maybe she was. She made an effort to relax her lips, but got nowhere with that. They remained tightly drawn. This was Austin, not a random witness, and her need to protect him sometimes bordered on the obsessive.

"I called security on the walkie-talkie mounted in the cart," Austin said. "They told me to wait until they got there, and to make sure no one touched anything." He tugged on his fingers, popping the joints in his right hand. "It didn't take them long. One of the guards told me Ms. Montgomery was at the Wine Cave, and they wanted me to go get her."

After tapping his clean glasses against his fingertips, Castellano finally settled them back on his nose. "Why send you? Why couldn't one of the guards call her with the news?"

"The front section of the cave system, which we call the Wine Cave, is where the parties are held. Behind that is a storage section, and behind that is the old section. Security keeps the door to the old section bolted, and no one goes in there. At the front of the cave you can get cell reception, but as you move farther back, there's none at all. The same goes for the monitors. Ms. Montgomery was in the storage section, where there's no reception."

Hollinger made notes in a pocket-size notebook. "What'd you do next?"

"I drove to the cave, but it took a while to find her."

"How long?" Hollinger asked without looking up from his notebook.

"Ten minutes, maybe. I gave her the news. She ran out and took the cart I'd been driving. I don't know where she went."

"What'd you do next?"

Austin glanced at JL. "I got a message from my sister. She said she couldn't get in through the front gate. I told her to meet me at the side entrance so I could let her in."

Hollinger dropped his pen and glared at JL. "Did your sister tell you why she couldn't get in?"

"She said the police wouldn't let her."

"You knew the winery was on lockdown, but you thought it would be all right to let in a family member when a murderer might be loose on the property?"

"I didn't know there was a lockdown, and besides, I thought she could help. Why wouldn't I let her in?"

JL almost choked, but composed herself.

Hollinger's guarded eyes narrowed. "And what made you think, if you thought at all, that your sister could be of any help to the Napa police?"

JL stiffened her back. Austin would be affronted by Hollinger's question, and even more so by his attitude. She considered giving Austin a warning kick under the table to back off, but the tic in his jaw told her he wouldn't listen, even if she got up in his face.

"She's a damn good detective, and you could use her experience."

Although the note of pride in Austin's voice made her heart swell, the frown deepening on Hollinger's face while he glared at her did just the opposite. He could make Austin's interview difficult if he wanted to, and pissing him off was a sure way to do it.

"Detective? From where?"

Keeping it vague, she said, "New York."

His dark eyes glittered with undisguised contempt. "I don't need to remind you that you have no jurisdiction here."

"You just did," she said calmly.

Hollinger made a pretense of checking his notes again. "When you found the body, did you touch the deceased or the gun?"

"I already told you I didn't get out of the cart. And no, I didn't see a gun."

Hollinger made another note in the notebook. "And what time was it when you found the body?"

"I checked my watch after I called security. It was twelve-thirty-five."

"How long have you been interning here?" Hollinger asked.

"A year." Austin glanced at the two officers. "Am I finished? I have a tournament starting tonight, and I can't miss the team meeting."

"We're almost done," Castellano said.

"Have you worked at the mill before or spent much time around Mr. Di Salvo?" Hollinger asked.

"In the last two weeks, most of my hours were spent at the mill, shadowing Salvatore and learning about olive oil."

"Did you see any visitors hanging around the mill or talking to Mr. Di Salvo?" Hollinger asked.

"There are visitors every day. If Salvatore was there, he would stop what he was doing and talk to them."

"Did he ever have a disagreement with a visitor?" Hollinger asked.

Austin shook his head. "Not that I saw. He was always friendly."

"Did you notice anything different about him in the last few days or so? Was he short-tempered, distracted, or was there any change in his habits?" Hollinger asked.

Austin pursed his lips. "He was late Monday or Tuesday. I don't remember. Security called the mill to check on him because his monitor hadn't been switched on. Salvatore arrived shortly after that."

"How did he seem to you?" Castellano asked.

"I don't know." Austin squinted, looked up, and then returned his gaze to Hollinger. "He was tense, looking over his shoulder, a lot like he was expecting someone. He left for the orchard shortly after that."

"When did you see him again?" Hollinger asked.

"Yesterday. He seemed fine, joking with a couple of the men."

"And that was the last time you saw him?" Castellano asked.

"Yes, sir." Austin looked at his watch again. "I need to go. If I'm late, I'll sit on the bench tonight."

"Where can we reach you if we have additional questions?"

Kenzie slid business cards across the table. "You can call me."

They pocketed the cards, then Hollinger asked, "Is there anything else you'd like to add?"

"No, sir."

"One more question." Castellano directed the question to Kenzie. "Your head of security said Salvatore Di Salvo was from Sicily, and was in this country on a temporary agricultural work visa. How long has he been here?"

"Five years, I believe. Cate, the office manager, can give you an exact date."

"I'll ask her. That's all I have for now. If we have more questions, we'll call to arrange a time," Castellano said.

Hearing the Di Salvo name made JL's side ache, thanks to a souvenir from one of the Di Salvo brothers, who had put a bullet in her when she busted their narcotics operation. They were bad people—really bad—and they were all supposed to be in prison. Austin had conveniently forgotten to mention that a Di Salvo worked at the winery.

"How old was Salvatore?" JL asked.

Hollinger flipped back through his notebook. "Thirty-two. Why?"

She pressed her hand against her side again to silence the echo of long-ago pain. "Curious." She pushed away from the table and made a move to stand.

"How long will you be in Napa?" Hollinger asked.

JL flashed a snarky smile—the kind she gave her brothers when they were kids. The kind that said, *don't tempt me because I can beat you up*—whether it was true or not. "Four days, but I'll be glad to extend my vacation if you need my help."

"I wouldn't change your return flight, if I were you," Hollinger said. "We're done for now."

JL pushed her chair back under the table. "Good luck with your case, detectives. If you're dealing with the Di Salvo family, you'll need it." She slung her purse strap over her shoulder. "Come on Austin. You don't want to be late." She didn't rush out of the room, but she didn't linger either. As soon as the door closed behind them, she swatted his arm. "Why'd you piss off that detective? You know cops are territorial. Telling him I was a detective was a surefire way to get on his bad side."

"I didn't like him. I knew it would piss him off, and I knew you were big enough to take him."

"Thanks for the vote of confidence, but he could have hauled your ass down to the station to look at mug shots just so you'd miss your meeting."

"Nah, he doesn't want to tangle with you. Did you see his face when I said you were a detective? He looked like he was constipated. He got all scrunched up." Austin screwed up his face imitating Hollinger's expression.

JL punched Austin's arm again. "Stop that. Your face will turn to stone and pigeons will roost on top of your head."

"I'm not three years old." He made another face to tease her. "Bet he goes right back to the station house and Googles you."

"This isn't a game. A man was murdered. A man with the same last name as those involved in a drug cartel I busted. A man…"—she glared at Austin—"you neglected to mention during any of the phone conversations we've had in the past several months."

Austin held the door, giving her a little shrug. "I knew if I said anything, you would worry."

"You're right about that, but you should have. I could have checked him out." Using her hand as a visor to block out the sun, she glanced up at him. "Look, this could get very nasty. Until it's solved, you shouldn't be here."

"Why? I haven't done anything."

"No, you haven't, but I have, and we have the same last name. If I can connect the dots, so can the Di Salvos. Until I find out whether there is a connection to the mob family, you need to stay away. Okay?"

Austin directed her through a side garden that spilled into another parking lot where three identical trucks were parked side by side. They sat on a wrought iron bench and continued their conversation.

"I won't miss the gala."

"Deal. Now tell me about the gun."

Austin kicked out his legs and crossed his ankles. "There wasn't a gun. Hollinger was messing with me. I probably know more about police procedure than he does."

"I doubt that. You always leave the room when we talk about police matters."

"I might leave the room, but I can still hear the gross stories." He glanced around the parking lot. "Where's your rental?"

JL finished off her bottle of water and slipped the empty bottle into her purse. "Around the front. We should have gone out the other door."

"Nah, I'm driving a truck." He pointed to the first of three Ford F-450s with Montgomery Winery logos painted on the doors.

"They gave you a truck to drive? It's an expensive one, too."

"They're good to me. I couldn't ask for a better home away from home. Whatever I need, Dr. Fraser, Ms. Montgomery, or Kevin makes it happen. They don't spoil me with things, you know. They give me their time. I didn't want to take the truck, but Dr. Fraser told me I had to have reliable transportation."

"You got lucky with this job."

"Dr. Fraser told me last night that Coach Calipari from the University of Kentucky was coming to the gala Sunday night. That's why I have to go."

JL placed her arm on the back of the bench and turned toward Austin, her heart beating a little faster. She had been praying he would get a scholarship from a northeastern school, but it didn't look like that was going to happen. "Kentucky? Really? That's great." She had to work hard to load a pile of enthusiasm into her voice. "The NCAA recruiting rules won't allow you to talk to him, yet, will they?"

"No, but I can nod from the other side of the room."

"If you go to Kentucky, will you be able to make a contribution right away, or will you have to sit on the bench your freshman year?"

"I can't give them more physicality in the paint, but I can hit clutch threes, something they lack right now with their incoming class. I know Coach has watched my tapes. We'll see what happens."

"Fraser's a man with connections."

"Kenzie has the basketball connection. Her half brother Jim Manning played at UK for Joe B. Hall. Mr. Manning has been my biggest promoter, but I could use another connection. Know anyone?"

For a moment, she didn't answer, and then she shrugged. "I'm just a cop from New York City."

"Pete's a cop, too, and he knows a couple guys who play for the Yankees."

"Then ask him. Maybe he knows someone who knows someone. But tell me this—would you really like to go to school there, in Kentucky, I mean?"

"It's at the top of my short list. And the Frasers spend as much time at their farm in Lexington as they do in Napa."

"Then I'm very excited for you."

"Don't tell Ryan. I'll call him after the gala. He'll be blown away."

She didn't want to tell Austin about Ryan before Sunday night, but she had to tell him before she returned home. It wasn't fair to keep the news from him.

"I won't tell him," she said, "but let's talk about what's happening here. Tell me about the gun, or why you think Hollinger mentioned it."

"I didn't see one. It could have been under Salvatore's body, but you can see for yourself. I have pictures."

"*You what?*"

"I took pictures of Salvatore in case anyone...I don't know...walked through the crime scene. I wanted to preserve it."

"And you didn't tell the cops you took them?"

"I didn't think about it."

"You have to tell Hollinger."

Austin made a move to stand. "Okay."

"Wait a minute." She tugged on his arm and pulled him back down to the bench. "Give me your phone." He handed it over and she used the AirDrop app to send the photos to her device. "Go knock on Kenzie's door and tell Hollinger you need to talk to him."

While Austin returned to Kenzie's office, JL scrolled through the crime scene photos. They looked eerily familiar. Gunshot to the forehead. The residue around the entrance wound indicated the shooter placed the muzzle in close contact. The vic was lying partially on his side. He could have been kneeling at the time of his death. Hard to tell, since the body would have responded to neurological spasms and not to the force of the bullet. The one eye she could see in the photo was open, and blowflies were actively laying eggs around the wound and in the eye. She enlarged the picture. No other insects were visible. Decomposition was fresh. Salvatore had only been dead an hour or two at the time Austin took the pictures. If he had arrived earlier, he could have run into the perp. That shook her up—a lot.

She forwarded the crime scene pictures to Pete with a message to compare them to the Di Salvo case and to keep quiet about it. She would call him later, after he had a chance to compare the photos.

A few minutes later, Austin slammed the door to the building and stomped over to her. *"They kept my phone."*

"There's evidence on your phone, kiddo. You'll get it back. Calm down."

A spot of color appeared on his cheeks. He was good-natured, and rarely displayed his temper. Something else was going on with him.

"*When?*" he demanded.

"Probably tomorrow."

He pulled on each finger, cracking his knuckles. "Damn. I'm expecting a text. If I don't answer, she'll—"

"Aha," JL said, smiling. "So there is a girl in your life. Pops asked me to find out if you were dating."

Austin sat down again, and the spots of color on his face darkened. "We have been for a while." He popped the fingers on the other hand. "If she sends me a text, I won't be able to answer. She'll think I'm mad for some dumb reason."

JL smacked his hand. "Stop that. You're going to get arthritis in your fingers."

"No, I'm not, and it makes them feel better."

JL reached into her purse for her phone and held it out to him. "Send her a message. Tell her you lost your phone and you'll meet her in the gym after the game." When he didn't take it, she thumped his chest with it. "Go on. Send her a text."

He shoved his hands under his armpits.

"Why are you being such a jerk?"

He snatched the device, pounded the keys, waited a few seconds until the phone dinged with a message, and then he sent another one. "There. You satisfied?" He dropped the phone into her purse.

"Only if you are. So what's her name?"

"Betsy Brown." A smile curled at the corners of his mouth. "She's going to dinner with us after the game." The grin slipped, and he drew his brows in. "And *don't* embarrass me by telling family stories."

She placed a hand over her heart. "I'm crushed. Would I do that to you? I think you've confused me with your sister-in-law."

"Don't get me started, JL. I gotta go. Come on. Walk me to the truck." They crossed the parking lot, and he climbed into the driver's seat. "I'll see you at the game."

She gripped the edge of the partially rolled-down window. "You're going to get out of your head and into the game, aren't you?" At seventeen, Austin had an uncanny ability to focus, but he had never found a dead body before.

"It's rough, you know." He didn't meet her gaze. Instead, he stared off into the void for a minute saying nothing. "When I get the ball in my hands, I won't think about anything except the game."

"I'm glad I'm here, sweetie—"

"Please don't call me that around anyone, especially Betsy."

"Okay, I won't, but if you need to talk later—"

"I'll use my roommate's phone and call Ryan tonight to tell him about the game and what happened here. He won't try to baby me."

She gasped. "Seriously? I don't baby—" She stopped herself. "Maybe sometimes I do." She shrugged. "I'm going to go have a drink now."

"Drink? It's not even five o'clock," Austin said.

"It is somewhere, and besides, vacation rules apply." She tapped the door with her palm, signaling him to drive on. "Call Ryan and stay safe." While she watched Austin drive away, she sent Ryan a text. *Expect call from Austin tonight after the ball game. Do not tell him about the divorce.* A few seconds later, she got a one-word reply. *Ok.*

One of her older brothers, she wasn't sure which one, had told Ryan she was going to California. Ryan had sent a text and asked her to send pictures from the game. If he was going to play nice and not tell Austin, she could play nice, too, and send him a few pics.

Thinking about Austin's traumatic day, she wished she didn't have to tell him about the divorce, wished she could cut the memory of finding Salvatore out of his mind, and wished he wasn't growing up so damn fast. Then she remembered she hadn't asked about the hotel reservation he had promised to make for her. She slapped her palm on the hood of the truck next to her. "Damn." He no longer had a phone. She scrolled through her contacts until she found the phone number for the front desk at his dorm, and left a message for him to return her call.

If he hadn't made a reservation, she'd have to stay in his room. She seriously doubted she could find a vacancy on a Friday afternoon, at least in a decent hotel. However, even a one-star hotel in Napa was probably cleaner than Austin's dorm room.

3

JL PUNCHED IN the door code and reentered the Corporate Offices building, gnawing on her lower lip. She needed a shot of whisky, a glass of wine, or a beer. Maybe one of each. She strode down the hall, following the signs to the Tasting Room. Just as she reached Kenzie's office, the lawyer stepped out, and JL almost bumped into her. They sidestepped in the same direction and then the other. Finally, laughing, they both planted their feet.

"You're just the person I wanted to see," Kenzie said.

"What's up?" JL asked.

"I want your opinion about the shooting and the obnoxious Detective Hollinger."

Remembering the cop's questioning of Austin and his resemblance to Ryan, JL made no attempt to sugarcoat her opinion. "Hollinger's a *jerk*. He reminds me of my ex-husband." She flinched, immediately regretting her loose tongue.

A surprise *wham* flashed across Kenzie's face, and then quickly vanished. However, a note of puzzlement was detectable in her voice when she said, "Ex? I didn't know you were divorced."

"Yeah, I am, but Austin doesn't know." JL pointed toward Kenzie's office. "Let's take this discussion out of the hall."

"Sure." Kenzie gestured for JL to enter the office first, and then Kenzie closed the door behind them.

JL plucked her phone from her purse and set it down on the conference table. She didn't want to miss Austin's return call. Then she reclaimed the chair she had used earlier. "Here's the deal. Ryan and I split up a year ago, but we agreed not to tell Austin until the divorce was final. I didn't want him to hang onto a false hope that Ryan and I would get back together. But the jerk wouldn't sign the papers. This should have been finished six months ago, but he dragged his ass to piss me off. Here we are a year later, and Austin doesn't have any idea there's trouble in paradise. The divorce was final this week, and I don't know how I'm going to tell him."

Kenzie sat down next to her. "Austin talks about Ryan all the time."

JL second-guessed her year-old decision. In hindsight, not telling Austin had been a bad one. "I know. The news will upset him, and I won't be around to help him deal with it."

"He's not a kid. He'll be okay, and Elliott and Kevin will be around if he needs them."

JL swallowed an uneasy sense of guilt that rose into her chest and hung there. "I'd appreciate it if you could keep the news to yourself, at least until I tell Austin."

"Sure," Kenzie said. "No problem."

"That's enough about my troubles. Let's talk about the case. You work here. What are your thoughts?"

"Why didn't you tell Hollinger you were a detective in New York City?"

"I don't have jurisdiction here, and I didn't want him to see me as a threat. You know the whole my-force-is-bigger-than-your-force kind of thing."

Kenzie laughed. "So you think he's got a small dick and a big ego."

"Exactly," JL said. "His ego will get in his way. If he thinks he has something to prove to the hotshot detective from New York, he could be dangerous. Nothing illegal, but he could harass Austin, and I don't want that."

"My husband might be able to do something about Hollinger. I'll ask him. In the meantime, I'm sure you looked at Austin's pictures. Could you tell anything about the murder?"

JL put her elbows on the table and clasped her hands. "Blowflies are the first insects to attack a body. After a couple of hours, more insects arrive. Salvatore only had blowflies on him."

"Which means he hadn't been dead long when Austin found him."

"That's right," JL said.

"What was he shot with? Pistol or rifle?"

"Small-caliber pistol. Judging by the appearance of the entry wound visible in the photograph, the shooter fired from very close range. Either the perp pressed the gun to Salvatore's forehead, or the muzzle was only a few inches away."

"Executions are usually to the back of the head. How would you interpret the forehead shot?" Kenzie asked.

"Very controlled. Not many men could shoot a vic who's standing there looking at them, and in the forehead."

"I need to call David. He'll want to know." She punched in a number on her phone and waited only a moment before she said, "JL and I are in my office talking about the case. She believes Salvatore had only been dead a couple of hours when Austin found him…Bullet to the forehead…No…close range…Okay, hold on. Here she is." Kenzie held the phone out for JL. "He wants to talk to you."

"Detective O'Grady."

"David McBain. I have one question. Is there anything about the murder that looks familiar to ye?"

For a moment, she thought she was speaking to Elliott. Kenzie obviously married a Scot, too. "Why do you ask?"

"Detective, ye don't know me, but I know ye. Ye were the lead detective on the Di Salvo case four years ago in New York. Ye were shot and barely survived. I want to know if there are similarities between the murder in that case and Salvatore's murder."

"You get right to the point, don't you?"

"Get used to it. Kenzie and I are protective of the Frasers and their circle of friends. Ye and Austin are in that circle now. I know the Napa cops don't want yer help, but I do. If the cartel is using winery property to distribute cocaine or any other illegal substance, I intend to shut them down."

"You've made a big leap here," she said.

"It's not a leap. The Di Salvo family was using the olive oil business as a cover for a cocaine operation in New York. Ye cut off the head, but the body might have continued to grow and set up an operation in Napa. I don't know what Salvatore had to do with it, if anything, but I intend to find out."

"That's quite a supposition," JL said. "If the Di Salvo family has been on your radar, why haven't you investigated them before now? It might have prevented a murder."

"It wasn't on my radar. Not until Kenzie put Detective O'Grady and Salvatore Di Salvo in the same sentence. Now I need the crime scene photos Austin took."

"You've put me in a difficult position. If I share the pictures, Hollinger could accuse me of interfering with the investigation. Granted, it's not my investigation, but..."

"We have a murderer running loose, and the longer we debate ethics, the colder the trail gets. Will ye send me yer photographs?"

She puffed out her cheeks, the way she always did when something concerned her and she needed to stall for a few seconds so she could think. "I can't do that. The next time I see Detective Hollinger, he'll ask me if I looked at them, and then he's bound to ask me if I showed them to anyone. If I say yes, my detective sergeant will hear about it, and I don't want that mark on my record. If you have anything else, I'll be glad to do what I can." She handed Kenzie's phone back to her. "Is the Tasting Room open? I'd like a drink."

"Should be. If not, help yourself. The Tasting Room is on the far side of the Welcome Center. I'll join you there as soon as I finish talking with David."

"Great." JL picked up her phone from the table, and her hand hovered over her purse. Did she really care what Hollinger did or didn't do? Wasn't she more concerned about the possibility the Di Salvos were back in business? Did she believe Hollinger had the balls to deal with the cartel? She glanced at Kenzie and took her measure again. She didn't know much about the lawyer, but based on the ring on her finger, she had guts, or she wouldn't have made it through the academy and her deployments afterward. A gutsy woman would have married an extraordinary man. If David McBain was that extraordinary, JL had to help him. She and Kenzie made eye contact briefly. Words weren't necessary. JL placed her phone on the conference table, snuggled her purse under her arm, and left the room.

She was doing the right thing. It might not be the smartest step for her career, but the right thing. If Austin called her personal phone and couldn't reach her, he'd call her service phone.

Signs on the wall had arrows pointing to the Tasting Room. Selling wine was Meredith's number one business, and JL intended to taste several of the winery's labels, and to drink even more. According to the tips on the HOW TO IMPROVE YOUR WINERY EXPERIENCE Pinterest board her sister-in-law forwarded to her, JL was to say, if asked what kind of wine she enjoyed: *I enjoy all kinds of wine. Which would you recommend?*

This was her first trip to Napa, her first wine tasting, and Sunday night would be her first celebrity event attending as a guest and not a working cop. As formfitting as her dress was, she hoped she could get away with a concealed-carry rig without it bulging in the wrong places. Her all-knowing sister-in-law, Julie, assured her she would look beautiful, but hadn't mentioned where she was supposed to carry her gun.

How Julie got to be worldlier than JL was simple. Her sister-in-law read fashion magazines and kept up with the latest celebrity gossip. She tried sharing girls' stuff with JL during Sunday brunches at Pops house, but JL rarely stayed in the kitchen and listened. She preferred to drink beer with the guys and yell at the refs while watching the Giants, Yankees, Knicks, or Rangers, depending on the season. She had evolved into one of those fans who threw things at the TV—soft things like pillows—and who stomped around the room yelling like her life would end if her team lost a game. She lived and worked around too much testosterone.

When her mother was alive, she had instilled enough poise, presence, and public speaking skills that, when dressed up, JL looked like a gazillion bucks. At least that's what her brothers said, and nobody argued with the O'Grady boys.

The Tasting Room was empty when JL arrived. The room had a generous sitting area, with four oversized chairs in front of a snapping fire, but no bartender. Kenzie said to help herself, and that was exactly what JL intended to do.

She stepped to the other side of the bar and opened the under-the-counter refrigerator. There were a dozen bottles of white wine. Without a recommendation, she went *eney, meeny, miny, moe* and caught a half-full bottle of chardonnay around the neck. Since the bottle was half-empty, she considered that enough of a recommendation. She poured a glass and sipped. "Hmm. A hint of toasted oak and butter." She liked it.

Her feet created a gentle rhythm as they glided across the stone floor toward the fireplace. Her mother would have enjoyed this room. Its textures and colors would have engaged her senses and imagination, and the whispering silence would have inspired her. Would she have recited Shakespeare or hummed a number from one of her favorite musicals? JL considered how odd it was that she had thought of her mother more in the past hour than she had in the past few months.

Her service phone beeped, scattering thoughts of her mother.

She eased into one of the chairs in front of the fire, placed her wine glass on a nearby table, and rummaged through her purse for her phone. Pete had left a message. *Reviewing old case file. Photographs look similar to your current case. Call to discuss.*

A sharp pain stabbed her in the middle of her chest. Pete had all but confirmed the Di Salvo cartel connection. She flipped her phone back and forth in her hands, thinking. Should she tell Pops? If she did, what would his response be? Would he tell her to share her suspicions with Hollinger, or tell her to walk away?

Kenzie entered the room. "Did you find everything you need?

Cate just told me she advised the bartender not to come in today."

"I found an open bottle of chardonnay. Thought I would start with that one. Saved me the trouble of looking for a corkscrew."

"You can't go wrong with any of Meredith's labels. They're all delicious." Kenzie poured sparkling apple juice into a champagne flute before crossing the room and returning JL's cell phone to her. "You left this in the conference room."

JL dropped it into her purse. "Thanks."

"No. Thank *you*." Kenzie dug into a bowl of nuts sitting on the table and popped a handful into her mouth.

"I've met most of the people Austin talks about, except Kevin. It's Kevin, right?"

"Kevin Allen," Kenzie said. "I saw him earlier. If he doesn't drop in soon, you'll meet him at the game. He's probably schmoozing with the cops. If you want to know what's going on, ask him." Kenzie dug into the bowl for another handful of nuts. "David calls him a wee gossip. James Cullen, Elliott and Meredith's son, is almost as bad. Kevin has had too much influence over him."

"How old is he?" JL asked.

"Who? James Cullen or Kevin?"

JL laughed. "James Cullen."

"Thirteen going on twenty-one. His parents have homeschooled him, and he's traveled extensively. He's way ahead of what normal thirteen-year-olds know of the world. Plus, he's highly intelligent, a great conversationalist, and charming as hell. My twins worship the ground he walks on, and so does Lincoln."

"Who's Lincoln?"

"He's the son of Braham McCabe and Charlotte Mallory. He's nine going on eighteen. The twins worship the ground beneath his feet, too."

"Are the McCabe/Mallorys coming to the gala?"

"Charlotte is a surgeon, and they live in Richmond, Virginia. She had an emergency surgery this morning, so they'll be here tomorrow."

"The portrait of the woman hanging over the fireplace in the

Welcome Center was a McCabe. Is that Braham's family?"

"We're all related. The connections go back many generations."

"Are you related, or is your husband?"

"Interestingly enough, it turns out we're both distantly related to the MacKlennas."

"And Elliott is, too?"

"Elliott's line goes back to an illegitimate child of James Thomas MacKlenna I in the mid-1700s."

A man's deep, smoky voice came from the hall, and a small grin flickered at the edge of Kenzie's mouth. "Kevin's here. Beware. He comes with a warning. 'Heartbreaker: Proceed with caution.'"

"Urggg," JL said. "So was my ex. Thanks for the warning." JL emptied her glass and returned to the bar for a refill. "Will your husband make it here in time for the gala?"

"I'll be surprised if he's not here in the next twelve hours."

"What about your boys?"

"You know how supervisors have to rely on the cop on the street for the best information? It's the same way at our house. David and I travel a lot, usually together, but occasionally we go in different directions. We decided when the boys were babies that the parent with the children would make decisions about their care. I might not like what he does when they're with him, and he might not like my decisions, but we don't second-guess each other."

"I didn't trust anyone to make decisions about Austin's care when he was a baby."

"I trust David with my life, my heart, and my babies. He's an amazing man."

JL returned to her chair with another glass of wine. "Trusting a man with my life is much easier than trusting one with my heart. Some men don't realize how fragile the gift of a heart can be."

"I think it works both ways. As strong as David is, his heart had cracks when I met him. The boys and I have healed those cracks, but it didn't happen overnight."

JL met Kenzie's eyes, and she found herself wondering about Kenzie's thoughts and the man at the center of them. "How long has it been since you've seen your boys?"

"I flew up Tuesday. David and I try not to be apart more than a couple of days, but this was a special situation. Actually, this is the longest we've ever been separated."

JL thought back through her marriage. When Ryan had worked undercover, they would go weeks without seeing each other. When they finally reconnected, the sex had been hot but unemotional—a side effect of living a lie.

"How long have you been married?" JL asked.

"Four years. We met in London during my last year in law school. I was planning to practice international law, but that all changed when I met David. My half brother has been Elliott's friend and attorney for thirty years. He was ready to cut back on his workload, so Elliott created an in-house counsel position as part of a corporate restructuring, and offered the position to me. I couldn't say no."

"What's David's job?"

"He's president of MacKlenna Corporation."

"Looks like Elliott's keeping it all in the family."

"He keeps his family close," Kenzie said.

"And his enemies closer?"

"If Elliott has enemies, I've never heard of them."

"If he has no enemies, then Salvatore's murder wasn't in retaliation for something he's done."

"I don't see how it could have anything to do with Elliott. The winery is Meredith's interest."

JL sipped her wine. If the murder didn't have anything to do with Elliott, then maybe it was connected to Meredith. "Could the murder have something to do with her, or with her work?"

"I doubt you could find a winery owner in California who doesn't respect what she's accomplished. Her father left her a good business, but she's more than doubled it."

"No enemies, then?"

Kenzie stared at JL, and the only nod to time passing was the soft ticking of a clock on the wall near the bar. "You know, you're good at this. You're very disarming. You appear to be demure, but you aren't. You probably use that to your advantage. You've been interviewing me for twenty minutes, and I wasn't even aware of it until you asked me if Meredith had enemies."

JL took a handful of nuts from the bowl and popped a few in her mouth. "You would have been aware of it if you had something to hide."

Kenzie laughed. "I see a lot of Austin in you. You're both very honorable. There's not a gray area with you. It's either black or white. Good or bad. Right or wrong. No in between. No maybes. You and David will get along like oil and water." Kenzie clapped her hands. "I can't wait to see it. I predict that by tugging from opposite ends, you'll pull each other to the center. And that's a good thing."

"I don't think I'll be around long enough to see that happen," JL said.

Kenzie's dimples appeared in her cheeks when she grinned. "We'll see." Her cell phone beeped, and she checked her message and entered a reply while JL sipped her wine and gazed out at the vineyards. Kenzie put down her phone and snatched another handful of nuts.

"Do you spend a lot of time here?" JL asked.

"We spend fifty percent of our time in Scotland. The rest we split between the farm in Kentucky and here."

"So Meredith could have some enemies and you wouldn't know them."

"I might not, but David would. He has a large network with feelers all around the world. He's like the all-knowing Wizard of Oz."

"And don't arouse the wrath of the great and powerful..."

Kenzie laughed. "That's truer than you know."

Call it a hunch. Call it her sixth sense, but JL believed the Frasers didn't murder Salvatore. Could the murder have been in retaliation for something the Frasers did? She didn't think so, but she couldn't rule it out yet.

"I've seen pictures of the farm on the Internet, and now looking out over the vineyards, I couldn't choose between the two. Compared to the seedy parts of NYC I see every day, this is heaven."

"You should see Fraser House in the Highlands. You'd know for sure you were in heaven. The house is actually a six-hundred-year-old castle. Cold in the winter, but beautiful. If David had a choice, he'd stay in the Highlands year round. He prefers the cottage behind the main house. As long as I'm with him and have Internet, I don't care."

"Sounds like you can work anywhere."

"Usually I can, but the corporation is in the process of buying a farm to start a winery in Kentucky, and the owners are located here. They wanted face-to-face meetings, so here I am."

"What do the sellers think of Meredith?"

"I haven't heard anything negative," Kenzie said. "In fact, they'd like to trade Montgomery Winery for the property in Kentucky, but Meredith won't budge on that."

"How badly do they want it?"

Kenzie looked at JL, and after a long moment said, "I don't know."

"If David's network's tentacles stretch to the wine industry, ask him to check out the sellers for ties to organized crime."

"He's done due diligence, but I'll ask him to take a deeper look." Kenzie punched keys on her phone, and a few seconds later, it beeped. "David said he'd like to have a conference call tomorrow with you and Elliott."

"Sure. Will you and Meredith be there, too?"

"Meredith has her hands full with the gala, and Elliott will tell her what she needs to know. If David wants me there, he'll ask. If not, he'll fill me in later. I have plenty on my plate right now."

"Fill you in about what?" a warm baritone voice asked.

"Are you eavesdropping, Kevin?" Kenzie asked.

JL glanced at the newcomer over her shoulder, and gave herself a mental shake. Unless she was looking for trouble, she needed to stay clear of this heartbreaker. His eyes were the color of the darkest piece of chocolate in a Ghirardelli Sampler and fringed with long, thick lashes. Women had to be drooling at his feet. Not her, though. She didn't drool at anyone's feet.

Her power gaze did a slow glide down his lean runner's body with nary a jiggle in sight, and then back up to very sensual lips. She caught herself imagining what they would taste like coated with dark chocolate. While that was a turn-on, his expensive salon-styled hair wasn't. He had finger-licking thick and luxurious hair, but the price tag to maintain the look was, in her opinion, extravagant.

A short-sleeve polo shirt stretched taut across broad shoulders, outlining curves and forms of well-defined muscles. The creases down the front of his khakis were as sharp as her persnickety father's trousers. JL often complained that she got paper cuts when she picked up his dry cleaning.

A look of mischief danced in Kevin's eyes as he strode across the room, and his scorching gaze landed on her with a gleam of male interest. A cheeky little quirk appeared at the corner of his mouth while he studied her. "You must be Austin's sister."

"And you're Kevin. Austin's mentioned you." Other than being sinfully hot, her first impression was that he was arrogant and self-absorbed.

He took her outstretched hand in his cool, dry palm, giving her a firm squeeze while maintaining eye contact and a broad grin. "You don't look like Austin, and you definitely don't look like a cop."

She cocked her head, sending her hair swinging against her chin. "I'm not sure how to take that."

"I've never seen a detective who should be on the cover of *Vogue*."

JL rolled her eyes. "Does that pickup line usually work for you?"

Kenzie snorted. "Kevin, stop hitting on her."

JL detected a sort of tightening up, so subtle that if he had been even an inch farther away, she wouldn't have caught it. "I wasn't hitting on her."

"I hope you're not teaching Austin lines like that," JL said.

He pressed his hand against his chest, fingers spread wide. "Are you kidding? I got that line from him."

JL laughed. "Aw, crap. Don't tell me that. I thought my older brothers had given him better material."

Kevin dropped into a chair and threw one leg over the other. When he did, the crease in his trousers stayed straight. His sockless foot sported a polished Italian loafer. He stacked his hands behind his head, showing off nicely shaped muscles. He might still be self-absorbed, but not arrogant. He seemed more charming and goofy than anything else. Compared to the men she knew, she found him refreshingly different.

"Have you talked to the police?" Kevin looked first to Kenzie and then to JL.

"They interviewed Austin, Elliott, and Meredith," Kenzie said.

Kevin dropped his hands and leaned forward. "Why Austin?"

"He found Salvatore's body in the orchard," JL said.

"How the hell did that happen? Is he okay?"

"Security sent him to the north orchard to search. He found Salvatore there. Austin's upset, but he'll be fine." JL hugged herself, feeling a chill ripple through her. Her pride in Austin clashed with fear for him.

Kevin glanced at his watch—a Fitbit Surge. The chunky plastic band didn't make a serious fashion statement, but it said a lot about his athleticism. "He's got a team meeting in a few minutes. I could go to the school to check on him, or send him a text."

"The cops have his phone. He took crime scene pictures, and they confiscated it," JL said.

"He needs a phone. I'm definitely going to the school. Kenzie, I need one of those burner phones you keep in your file cabinet."

"I'll give you one, but don't you think Austin can survive a few hours without one? Give it to him after the game."

"I wish he had one right now," JL said. "I forgot to ask him about my hotel reservation. I left a message at the dorm for him to call me. If he does, I'll mention the burner phone."

"You don't need a hotel," Kenzie said. "You can stay at the lodge. There's plenty of room."

"It's full," Kevin said. "But there's still room at the cottage."

"No one's checked in yet. We can move people around," Kenzie said.

"That's too much trouble. All the guests have their confirmations and room numbers," Kevin said.

JL noticed the tension between Kevin and Kenzie, and decided to make her own arrangements. "I don't want to impose. If Austin hasn't made reservations, I'll stay with him."

"*God*, you can't stay there," Kevin said. "Not only does it smell like a locker room, but it hasn't been cleaned in weeks."

Kenzie leaned forward in her seat, outwardly composed, but she couldn't hide the tension around her eyes. "Elliott will be glad for you to stay here. You can snoop around without interference from local police."

Whatever was going on between Kenzie and Kevin, JL was staying out of it. "Thanks. I appreciate the invitation, and I would like to see the crime scene, but I doubt I could get close enough today."

"Do you run?" Kenzie asked.

"Yes."

"There's a running path near the area where Salvatore was killed. You could run an out-and-back and see the site from both directions. I've got work to do, or I'd go with you."

"I'll go," Kevin said.

"Thank you, but—"

"—Meredith and I were supposed to run this morning," he said, "but she couldn't get away. How many miles do you want to run?"

JL did a quick calculation of how much time she had until the game started, and what she needed to accomplish beforehand. She didn't want to be rushed during the calls to Pete and Pops. Warm up, run, cool down would take an hour. Another hour for phone calls and organizing her notes, plus an hour to get ready, and time to settle into her room.

"What time do I need to leave for the ball game?" she asked.

"We'll leave at five fifteen. Elliott likes to stop at a local restaurant and have appetizers before games," Kevin said.

It was now one thirty. That would give her enough time. "Five to six miles. We probably can't get close to the crime scene, but I'd like to see as much of the general area as possible. Can we do that?"

Kevin pushed to his feet, giving a soft groan. "Sure can."

"JL can, but I'm not sure you can," Kenzie said. "If you're going to pace Meredith in the New York City Marathon, you have to rest your knee."

"We don't have to run," JL said. "Or we can start out running and slow the pace if your knee acts up."

"Like that's going to happen," Kenzie said. "You'll only make it worse and not be able to run."

He winked at JL. "We'll take it easy."

He made no effort to hide the fact that he found her attractive, and she doubted she managed to hide her interest in him, either. The weekend was off to a good start, proving to be full of possibilities.

Kevin glanced at his watch then said to JL, "If you're ready, we'll head out."

She gave Kenzie a see-you-later wave, returned her glass to the bar, and left the Tasting Room with Kevin. Remembering that she had parked in a different lot than Austin, she said, "I'm parked in the front lot. What about you?"

"I drive whatever's available. A cart, a truck, Kenzie's Mercedes."

"Ouch. I'd leave her car alone today. She's got a lot going on."

Kevin held the front door of the Welcome Center open for JL, giving her a crooked grin. "She'll take Elliott's car, and if there's not a car or a cart available to drive to the villa, Elliott will call me for a ride. The only one inconvenienced, ultimately, is me."

"Why don't you save yourself the trouble and ride with me?" Kevin walked her to her rental car and opened the driver's door. She slid in behind the wheel, then—remembering the ongoing investigation—she asked, "Have you talked to any of the cops today?"

"A few."

When he slid into the passenger seat, she got a whiff of him for the first time. Underneath an earthy scent from wandering around the vineyards was an immaculately clean, fresh, and natural smell, and something else, something even yummier—musk and cedar, both pure and virile.

"What questions did the cops have for you?" she asked.

"Are you asking as a detective or because you're curious?"

"I'm a detective. You can assume my questions are related to the investigation."

Kevin looked all around him, especially over his shoulder. "Then I should watch what I say."

She canted her head and mentally weighed the evidence she knew thus far, which was very little. "Only if you're guilty."

4

KEVIN DIRECTED JL down a vineyard-lined interior road that dead-ended at a three-story Victorian house with a wraparound porch, complete with a swing, wicker rockers, and lush, deep green ferns.

"Is this the lodge?" she asked.

"No. This is the cottage," Kevin said. "The name is a misnomer, I know. Compared to the size of the villa, it's a cottage."

"Cottage. Mansion. Whatever. It's beautiful. I'll have to give the porch swing a try. I love drinking coffee and watching the sun come up. It's the most peaceful time of day."

"So is sunset with a glass of wine. The colors in the vineyards are even more vivid."

"I'll try both tomorrow and let you know which one I enjoy more."

"I'll put my money on sunset."

JL grabbed her purse while Kevin handled her suitcase. He led the way up the steps to the porch. "You're not at all what I expected."

She stopped mid step, cocked her head, and looked up into his widening eyes. "And what was that?"

"I thought you'd look more like a cop than a…well…a movie star who plays one."

"If that's another pickup line, it's not working for you, either," she teased.

"I'm not hitting on you. Honest. You surprise me. That's all."

She climbed the rest of the steps and joined him at the door. "If the only family member you've met is six-three and almost two hundred pounds, it's natural to be surprised to meet another member who is only five-two in her stocking feet."

Kevin fanned a key ring with a dozen or more different-sized keys, selected one, and unlocked the door. "I saw a picture of you with your dad and older brothers. You were all in uniform. You looked tough, like—don't mess with me."

"If I didn't look tough, I'd get stomped on. I'm built like my mother. She sang and danced on Broadway for years. Austin got her coordination and agility."

"What about you? What'd you get?"

"I got to take care of him."

"That's better than a pair of old dance shoes and the moves to go with them." He gestured for her to enter the house. "Welcome to Montgomery cottage."

Natural light fed an open and airy formal entryway, and it took a few seconds to take it all in. "Beautiful. If this is a guest house, what in the world does the villa look like?"

"I'll take you over there tonight or tomorrow," Kevin said. "It's nice, too."

"Nice? Are you kidding? This is a dream house." A spiraling grand staircase led to the second floor with an open landing. On the left side of the foyer, French doors led into a sitting room. The hall straight ahead peeked into a living room through a wide archway.

The flowers, fabrics, and furniture blended with the colors in the vineyards, clearly visible through dozens of windows. She had been in hundreds of gorgeous homes in the city, but only after violence had struck, leaving behind empty safes and blood trails. Not one of those homes, even if violence hadn't invaded, felt as welcoming as Montgomery cottage. It was more than welcoming. It felt like home.

"The downstairs master is this way." Kevin pointed past the staircase. "There are also four suites upstairs, and we have ten suites at the lodge."

"Where is that?"

"About a quarter of a mile from the Welcome Center in the other direction. The winery has a constant stream of out-of-town guests. For their convenience, Meredith staffed the lodge with a full-time chef. You can go over there to eat anytime. If you want a snack before you run, there is food in the fridge here. Make yourself at home."

"Has Austin stayed here before?"

"The lodge has a pool and weight room. When he sleeps over, he stays there."

"Nah. He stays there because it has a full-time chef. He has his next meal planned before he finishes the one he's eating."

"If I was his size, I would, too."

She had a glimpse of the large living room and a doorway that led to the kitchen. "Is anyone else staying here this weekend?"

"Just me so far. The rooms will fill up with last-minute guests. My suite is upstairs."

Now she understood the subtext of Kenzie and Kevin's earlier lodge/cottage discussion. Kenzie must have been trying to protect her. "I'm surprised you don't have a home of your own."

"I'm sort of a wanderer, going from town to town…"

"Let me guess. You go where the pretty girls are and you never settle down." She laughed. "That Dion song is one of my old favorites."

"My mom came of age in the 1960s, so I grew up listening to music from that era. My tastes are more eclectic now. Jazz tops the list. But to answer your question about where I live—I follow Elliott and Meredith. Where they go, I go. When we close on the new winery, we're building a house there. It'll be my main residence. I'll still travel between the farm and Napa—"

"And Scotland."

"Fraser House, too, but not as much as I do now."

"I bet you rack up frequent-flier miles."

"The corporation has a jet. If I'm going somewhere on the West Coast, I'll rent a plane and fly myself, but if I'm going cross-country,

I'll fly as a passenger on the corporate plane."

"Getting a pilot's license has been on my bucket list since I was a teenager. I think I can delete it now. It's not going to happen."

His smile created brackets on both sides of his mouth. "You never know. It wasn't on mine until opportunity butted up against necessity, and the rest, as they say, is history." He opened a door off the hall and stood aside so she could enter first. "Here's your room. You'll find everything you need in the closets. There are even cowboy boots in different sizes."

"Hats, too?"

"Even hats."

The bedroom was painted pale gray, a color that almost matched the sky visible through the bay window. A vase of flowers filled with light orange roses and hot pink miniature carnations seemed to float between the view and the room's interior.

She dropped her purse on a chair near the door. "This is a guest room? It's gorgeous. Do you have to kick guests out? I can't imagine anyone wanting to leave."

"It's important to Meredith that visitors have a first-class experience while they're here. The decorator played off the colors in the vineyards. I never noticed it until Kenzie mentioned it, and I generally notice color."

"Is that because you're a pilot?"

"It might be. I've never thought about it."

"Austin can walk in and out of a room and never notice anything except the size of the TV."

"We watched the NCAA tournament here last March. He kept saying he felt like he was sitting in the stands," Kevin said.

During the tournament, she had called Austin at halftime in the Kentucky game, and he had told her he was watching the game with Kevin, but he hadn't mentioned the TV. It was so like him not to brag.

Kevin set her suitcase on a folding luggage stand with canvas straps. "Austin was disappointed your husband didn't come. I guess he had to work, huh?"

The heat of Kevin's gaze warmed the crown of her head. "Well, about that..." She crossed the room to the window and, while gazing out at the vineyards, said, "He wasn't invited. My...our divorce was final this week."

"Divorced?" Kevin blew out a hissing breath. "Really? Austin doesn't know, does he?"

"Nope." A pause followed, long and somewhat uncomfortable. She dropped on the window seat and knotted her hands in her lap. "I don't know how I'm going to tell him. Ryan's his hero." She kicked off her shoes and pulled her knees to her chest. "When Pops and my older brothers found out Ryan cheated on me, they wanted to beat him up. I asked them not to, because we all had to work together. It wasn't easy, but we got through it."

"You're their little sister. They should have beaten him up." Kevin's phone rang, and he checked the face to see the caller's name. "I've got to take this. We'll figure out a way to tell Austin so he's not too upset."

"Good luck with that."

His finger paused over the surface of the phone. "I'll meet you on the porch in fifteen minutes." He turned and left the room, saying, "Kevin Allen...I can't today...I'm open tomorrow..." His voice faded as he trotted up the stairs.

She had now shared her story with two people at the winery. Austin wouldn't appreciate being the third person to learn the truth. He would ask if anyone else knew, and she couldn't lie to him. Really? Lying by omission was just as bad as outright lying, maybe more so.

She shrugged off the thought—for now.

Time was slipping away. If she didn't hurry, she'd be late. Kevin had been very accommodating with his offer to run with her, and she didn't want to keep him waiting. He had manipulated her into staying at the cottage, though. She wasn't sure what she thought of that. Time would tell which first impression would be more accurate: arrogant and self-absorbed or charming and goofy.

She dressed quickly and returned to the porch to find Kevin in the middle of a hip flexor stretch. It took a moment to force her gaze away from his great legs, broad shoulders, and muscular arms, and focus on the vineyards instead. Not a bad substitute, but she would much rather stare at his shoulders.

"Do you want me to stretch you out?" he asked.

A very robotic voice played in her head—*Proceed with caution. Warning. Warning.* The message was clear, but she was a big girl and could take care of herself.

And she'd already decided vacation rules applied.

She removed the rubber band from her wrist, pulled her hair into a ponytail, and secured it tightly. "I don't think anyone has ever offered to do that for me."

"You must run by yourself."

"I'm a member of the NYPD Running Club, but my schedule's so crazy it's hard to coordinate with other runners."

"Lie down on the mat, and I'll stretch your hamstrings."

She couldn't think of a better way to start a run than having a hot guy stretch out her legs. Beneath her running tights, she wore a pair of handgun holster shorts concealing her pistol at the small of her back. She drew the weapon and laid it on the towel beside her. Since the shooting in the Di Salvo case, she carried 24/7, and the department had even granted her special permission to fly armed.

"Do you always carry?" Kevin asked.

"Always. Does it bother you?"

"I guess not. It's weird, though." He placed one warm hand on her ankle and the other at her knee and lifted her right leg. "You're so small and non-threatening." He pushed her leg toward her head. "You'd never know you could take someone down."

She grimaced with the stretch—a pain that hurt so good. She moistened her lips with a flick of her tongue. "I'm really tight."

"If you're interested, I'll set you up with a massage later tonight."

"Is that another one of your pickup lines?"

He chuckled almost soundlessly. "It sounded like one, didn't it? I meant a real massage with a sports therapist. Elliott has a great one. Anne will bring her table here and fix you right up."

"How could I say no to that?"

"You can't, especially not as tight as you are." He lowered her leg, picked up the other one, and did the same stretch while his gaze traveled up her body slowly, leisurely. "Is that better?"

The look in his eyes was hotter than an R-rating. Time paused for a moment, for a heartbeat, and her leg tingled beneath his hands. The tingle continued all the way up to her breasts and then spread down through her entire being.

"Put some oil in your hands," she said breathlessly, "and you're probably as good as Anne."

He jumped to his feet, but she could barely move, as if her joints had frozen solid where she lay. He arched a brow slowly. "Are you hitting on me, Detective?"

"I should be asking you that question. You're the one who's had his hands all over my legs."

"Not all over. If I'd done that, you wouldn't be asking if I was hitting on you. You'd know for sure. You ready to run?"

She was aware of him as a virile, breathing man, and the heat of his energy was palpable above the scent of fermenting grapes blowing across the wraparound porch. He reached for her hand and pulled her to her feet, and she landed only a breath away from him, a nice kissable distance. Now it was his turn to cock his head and grin.

"What're you grinning at?" she asked.

"You surprise me, that's all."

"You've said that three times now."

A playful smile teased the corners of his lips. "Then stop surprising me."

For a moment, she didn't reply. She couldn't. His gaze locked her in. A dog barked in the distance and broke the spell. "You surprise me, too. And I'm rarely surprised. We'd better go run, or—"

"Or what?" he asked.

"We'll be late for the game." She broke eye contact and readjusted her weapon, only because she needed something to do other than gaze into Kevin's eyes.

"We can't have that, can we?" He pointed toward a hill in the distance. "We'll head in that direction. There were three cruisers parked off the road earlier. If they're still there, we'll see them when we hit the orchard."

"How far from here?"

"As the crow flies, a quarter mile. If we take the running path, it's about two."

Falling into step with him was as easy as falling into the depths of his eyes. The gravel crunched beneath their feet until they left the driveway behind and turned onto a level, firmly packed trail cleared of rocks and roots.

With the pace Kevin set, conversation came easily. "Nice trail."

"Meredith's been a runner most of her life. There are eight loops around the winery, and all but one of them are like this. She wants to run without obstacles slowing her down, so the trails are maintained like the rest of the property."

"Do the loops intersect?"

"They all have a cutoff that leads to another trail. So you could run twenty miles and never be far from home. The trail we're on now is an eight-mile out and back. We can run out two and back two. Or four and four if you want to run the whole trail, or we can take a side trail and run more than eight."

"Let's do the first two and see how your knee feels."

The trail narrowed as it curved around an oak tree. She slowed to avoid the only roots she'd seen so far, and to let Kevin take the lead. "Who else uses the trails besides Meredith?"

"Kenzie, Elliott, me. That's it."

On the other side of the tree, they once again ran side by side, and she listened to their footfalls. Kevin was a light runner, passing silently through the mini-forest. The wind rustled the leaves that had yet to fall, and the sun peeked through the canopy. She heard every twig break, every chirp, and every squirrel scampering through the underbrush. Funny how the same sounds went unheard when she ran in Central Park. The absence of street noise made it easier to hear the subtle sounds of the Napa woods.

She became intimately aware of the rise and fall of his chest, the way he held his head naturally and his shoulders low and loose. He had a slight knee lift and quick leg turnover, and his fingers lightly touched his palms. Perfect form. And while she thought about his perfect form, her body remembered his warm, gentle touch, and she heated, not only from the exercise but from wanting his hands on her again, and in more intimate places next time.

And with that thought, her step faltered. She refocused on running and picked up her pace again. "Does the trail leave the woods up ahead?"

"It's a mile through the woods, two miles through the vineyards, and a mile through an olive orchard."

"Does it stay this flat?"

"The last mile is a steady incline to the top of the hill."

"If we only do six, we'll miss that. Shucks."

"I can tell you're disappointed."

"If no one else uses the trails, the shooter could have taken one of them—this one even—knowing he or she wouldn't be seen."

Kevin slowed and glanced around. "You don't suppose…nah, the shooter would be gone by now." He picked up his pace again. "Not only could he, assuming the shooter was a man, but he probably did. It's the quickest way to go by foot from one part of the property to another. But nobody walks. The workers ride in trucks and the staff takes carts. Meredith discourages the use of all vehicles on the trails."

"Because she doesn't want her running paths disturbed?"

"No, that's not it at all. She's afraid someone will get hurt and won't be found until it's too late."

"She's serious about security, isn't she?"

"If you had to turn off a respirator and watch someone die you would be, too, I think."

"My dad, we call him Pops, had to do that. Mom had a stroke when Austin was six weeks old. She fought so hard to recover the use of her left side. Then, just when we thought she was making progress, she had another one. She was brain-dead after that."

Kevin stopped running and stood still as stone. His heart might even have stopped. She couldn't tell, he was so still. "I'm sorry. I didn't know."

She ran in place, waiting for him to catch up, but he didn't move. Finally, she stopped and walked back to him. "It's okay. It was a long time ago. It was harder on Pops and the older boys, but I had Austin. I didn't want him to ever feel the loss I did.

"After high school, I went to college at night so I could be with him during the day. It took longer to graduate, but I wouldn't have missed one minute of my time with him. Ryan and I started dating when Austin was eight, and Ryan became like a dad to him."

"Now I understand why Austin's so close to him. Do you think that will change now you're divorced?"

JL shook her head. "Ryan loves him. His feelings won't change."

"It all makes sense now," Kevin said. "Come on, let's run."

They reached the vineyards and picked up the pace, running full out, exorcising whatever demons they had picked up along the route. The faster they ran, the less they talked, until they reached the border between the vineyard and the orchard. JL slowed first, and then Kevin, and their breathing rhythm changed to a moderate-paced pattern. They could talk now.

"Tell me about Salvatore," she said.

"He was brilliant. Everyone liked him. He had a thorough knowledge of growing and harvesting olives and making oil. This year Montgomery Winery rose to the top of the list of Napa olive oil-tasting tours. To turn the business around in five years was quite an accomplishment."

"Where was the winery five years ago? Before Salvatore arrived."

"We weren't even on the list."

"You're right. That is major. He had to have been very busy."

"And he never took time off. His goal was to get the winery on the list within four years. Missed it by a year, and now this. It sucks."

"Do you think he could have been involved in anything illegal?"

"Like what?"

She slowed a bit, thinking. "Selling trade secrets, stealing olive oil, murdering coworkers. Anything."

"Not Salvatore. He was a gentle giant."

"Giant, huh?"

"He was a big man for a Sicilian. Almost as tall as Austin, but Salvatore had twenty to thirty more pounds on him. So, tell me, Detective, how does someone your size take down a person that big?"

"It's not easy," she said.

"Let's cut through the orchard. See how far we can get before the police turn us away."

They ran down a row of olive trees about a hundred yards until they came to the crime scene tape, and a cop guarding the perimeter. About ten yards behind him, three other cops were sticking small evidence flags in the ground. JL used her cell phone to take a movie of the area enclosed in the yellow crime scene tape. The cop guarding it stood with arms on his hips, glaring. There wasn't a damn thing he could do about her being there or taking pictures.

"Let's go," she said. "They'll be here until dark, and possibly through the night. We can't get close enough to see anything."

"We can come back in the morning," Kevin said.

JL glanced up into the sky. "You know what we need? A drone."

"A drone, huh? Consider it done."

"Really? You have one?"

"I'm not sure if it's here or in Kentucky, but I'll find out." He whipped his cell phone out of the pocket in his shorts and placed a call. "Hey, Boss. We need the drone. Is it here or in Lexington? JL wants a good look at the crime scene, but we can't get close enough. Are you at the security office now?...Great. Will you ask him to bring it up here?...No...We're on the running path near the scene...Sure. Thanks." Kevin disconnected. "Security is bringing the drone up."

"If you're wearing your monitor, they'll be able to find us," she said.

"I always wear it. Do you want to wear one while you're here?"

"No, thanks." The last thing she wanted on vacation was to have her comings and goings monitored. It was beginning to sound too much like Big Brother watching, which made her wonder: If security was so tight, how did a murderer get on and off the premises? "Are there cameras stationed around the winery?"

"Yes, and before you ask, the police took the surveillance tapes earlier."

"Are there backups?"

Kevin looked around and then leaned in close. "There's a backup, but security doesn't know about it. If you want to see the tapes, you'll have to get access to the feed from David."

"Why the secrecy?"

They jogged back to the path, where they stopped so Kevin could re tie his shoelace. "An outside vendor manages security for the winery, but Meredith doesn't trust the company." While Kevin was bent over, he double-knotted his other shoe. "David put in a second system so he could monitor the feeds."

"Then he should be able to look at the tapes and see who was in the orchard," she said.

"Unfortunately, the orchard isn't covered by the surveillance cameras yet."

"Any other locations not covered?"

"The cottage, lodge, and villa. Meredith doesn't want eyes on her home, and I don't want them on mine. There should be some expectation of privacy around here."

"When will the orchard be covered?"

"Who knows? Elliott's plan right now is to hire a VP of global corporate security who will come in and set up systems at all four locations."

"I thought there were only three."

"After we close on the new winery, there'll be four, and Elliott has his eye on a ranch in Colorado. The corporation will continue to grow."

"What exactly do you do?"

"I'm CFO." Kevin lifted his gaze and pointed with his chin. "We've got company."

A golf cart pulled to a stop beside them, and Hollinger jumped out. "Detective O'Grady, I'd like a word with you."

"Terrific," she mumbled low enough for only Kevin to hear. He stepped aside, and Hollinger moved in closer, holding up Austin's iPhone.

"Did you look at the pictures your brother took of the crime scene?"

There was no point denying it. "Yes. All the pics were in focus, too. He did a good job under the circumstances."

"Do you know why he took them?"

"To preserve the crime scene," she said. "And I have no reason to doubt him. He has too much integrity to post them on social media, if that's what you're afraid of."

"Did you show them to anyone?" Hollinger asked.

To say that she didn't *show* them to anyone made for a very fine distinction between what she did and what she allowed to be done. She decided to confess to giving the pics to her partner. He could take care of himself, and he was in law enforcement. David wasn't. Although, from what she'd heard of Kenzie's husband, JL wasn't so sure exactly what David did do.

"I sent them to my partner in New York," she said.

Kevin was standing in her periphery and looked at her, one eyebrow slightly raised.

Hollinger's eyes moved along her face, probing her for God knows what. "I could have you charged with interfering with an investigation."

She put her hands on her hips and didn't back down, even though Hollinger had a good six inches on her. "Go ahead. Give it your best shot."

"I could charge your partner, too."

A vein in her forehead throbbed. "His name is Pete Parrino. P-A-R-R-I-N-O. Be sure to spell it right. He gets pissed when his name is misspelled. He's at the Midtown North Precinct."

"I'll spell it right. Don't worry." JL and Hollinger stood two feet apart and glared at each other. Finally he said, "Stay out of this investigation."

She gave him a suit-yourself shrug. He slapped Austin's phone into her hand, turned on his heel, stomped over to the golf cart, and drove off, weaving along the path.

She stood there watching him disappear down the hill, shaking her head. "Pops would howl at that. He has the most infectious laugh, and he has no tolerance for assholes like Hollinger."

"What's up with him? Did he really think he could scare you? If he did, he has no idea who he's dealing with."

She wiped sweat from her forehead with the tail of her T-shirt. "Thanks for the vote of confidence." The breeze picked up, and since she was cooling off, she shivered. "Let's go. I've got to get my heart rate back up."

He made a go-ahead gesture with his hand, and they took off in the opposite direction of the retreating detective. "Was that the same detective who interviewed Austin?"

"Yes, but he wasn't that unglued earlier. Something's happened since then."

"Like what?"

"I don't know. Maybe he's up for a promotion and his supervisor reminded him of how beneficial it would be if he solved the case quickly."

"Ouch. If you put the shooter behind bars, what would that do for Hollinger's promotion, assuming there is one?"

"Tank it. We need to tread carefully."

"What do you care? You're only going to be here four days."

"Austin will be here for several more months. I can't leave a mess for him to deal with."

"David can put out feelers and find out what's going on. If Hollinger's promotion is dependent on solving this case, he could get harder to deal with, and not only for Austin, but for all of us."

As the incline grew steeper, JL shortened her stride. She was now slick with sweat, and her lungs burned with every labored breath. She pumped her arms and raced Kevin to the top, but he beat her by a few seconds. She hunched over, propping her hands on her knees, panting, gasping. "That felt great. How are your knees? Okay?"

Trying to catch his breath, Kevin walked in tight circles with sweat dripping off him. "Fine."

The lung-bursting effort to power her way up had been a challenge, but the panoramic view of the winery from the top of the slope was extraordinary. The brilliant fall colors were magical, and the company was certainly entertaining and much more.

"Don't tell Kenzie and Meredith, but if the three of you raced, you'd beat both of them by a few minutes."

"Meredith is twenty years older, and Kenzie is in her second trimester. I'm not sure beating them would be much of a victory."

"They can both do a half marathon in one-forty-nine-o-five. What's your PR?"

"One-forty-five-fifty-five."

"See? I told you."

"But remember, running is ninety percent mental and the other half is physical."

"That sounds like a play on a Yogi-ism."

She smiled. "You know baseball."

"Baseball, basketball, football, volleyball, golf. If it's played with a ball, I know the game and the players." He pointed down the hill. "Here comes the security cart with the drone."

"Hollinger will go ballistic when he sees that thing buzzing overhead," JL said.

"Yep." Kevin punched numbers on his phone again and put the call on speaker. "David, I've got JL with me. We had a run-in with Hollinger, the detective who interviewed Austin. He's pissed. JL thinks something's going on with him."

"Like what?" David asked.

"He's a badass with attitude," she said. "He threatened to charge my partner and me with interfering with his case. I told Kevin that it's possible there might be a promotion for Hollinger if he solves this case quickly. He's definitely under some kind of additional pressure. You can feel it when you talk to him."

"I'll see what I can find out. Anything else?"

"We're going to use the drone to video the crime scene," Kevin said.

"Not if Hollinger is around," David said. "Let security handle the drone. I'll make the call. Stay clear of the detective. I don't want to get there tomorrow and find both of ye behind bars."

Kevin clicked off the call. "You ready to head back?"

"I'll meet you at the bottom," she said. "I can't keep up with you running downhill."

Sweat trickled down the sides of his face, and he wiped his forehead with the sleeve of his T-shirt. "You sure?"

She nodded.

"Be careful. There might be a murderer hiding in the orchard," he said.

"Don't worry. I'm armed. Remember?"

He backed up a step and checked out her back where she had holstered her gun. "How could I forget?" He winked then took off down the hill.

Her stride was slightly longer as she ran downhill, but it wasn't long enough to keep up with Kevin, who was now at least twenty yards ahead. She let her mind float free, or as free as it could with the view of him running in the distance. She couldn't remember ever seeing a sexier man running the streets of New York City.

The trail leveled off and she was once again in the vineyards. Where was Kevin? He should be in view by now. She picked up her pace, but slowed when she spotted him relieving himself behind a tree.

"Men have it so easy," she said.

He tucked himself back into his shorts and came striding across the path toward her. "Sorry about that."

"Doesn't bother me. I grew up with brothers and very little privacy, and I work around men who think farts, burps, and nose picking are socially acceptable behaviors. If I ever catch Austin acting like he grew up in a barn, he'll get his ass chewed."

"You *are* tough."

"I have to be, or any badass who thinks he can take me down

won't stop until he does."

"Is Hollinger in that category?"

She gazed up at Kevin. His brown hair, wet around the fringes, only made him more appealing. "He'll threaten, but underneath that bluster, he's a good cop."

"How can you tell?"

"Instinct. He won't cross the line, but that doesn't mean he won't try to make life miserable for the O'Gradys. I've got to be sure Austin's protected before I leave town."

Kevin's brow furrowed. "How do you plan to do that in three days?"

She raised one eyebrow slightly at his intense scrutiny of her face. "The only way I know. Find the murderer."

5

JL TURNED OFF the water in the shower and wrapped a towel around her freshly washed hair. She and Kevin had taken longer to run than she planned, which put her almost an hour behind schedule. Was it more important to talk to Pops and Pete about the investigation, or go to a pregame meal with the Frasers? No contest. The investigation was a higher priority.

A thick Turkish bathrobe hung on the back of the bathroom door. She swaddled herself in the warm cotton and cinched the belt around her waist. The guest room's amenities were equal to a five-star hotel. Not that she had ever stayed in a five-star, but she had investigated robberies and murders in some of the finest hotels in New York City. She knew what they offered, and she knew what she would never be able to afford on a cop's salary. She could live happily without all the trappings of wealth, but she wanted more for Austin.

Before she dried her hair and put on makeup, she went in search of a drink. A beer was preferable, but she would settle for a glass of wine.

Her cozy slippers slapped against the hardwood floor as she wandered through the house. She would start in the kitchen, then work her way through the main floor. A guesthouse at a winery that supplied guests with Turkish robes and Tempur-Pedic slippers would surely have a well-stocked bar.

Besides eggs, vegetables, and assorted cheeses, the refrigerator had sports and diet drinks, juice, water, and a dozen bottles of white wine. The wine she had in the Tasting Room was good, but she couldn't remember the name.

"If you want a recommendation, I'd go with the *Cailean*."

Kevin's voice was an intimate touch and made every muscle in her body tighten in anticipation. Then she remembered the towel wrapped turban-style around her head. It was too late to yank it off, and if she did, her wet hair wouldn't look any better. Her safest bet was to stay hidden behind the door.

"It's a refreshing chardonnay," he continued, "with layers of pineapple, green apples, and juicy pears. It's lighter than the oaky wine you had earlier in the Tasting Room."

He had noticed what she had been drinking. What did that say about him? What did that say about her choice of wine? She didn't do nonchalance well, but she gave it a shot and glanced over her shoulder. "How do you know what I was drinking?"

He stood in the doorway—shirtless and chiseled—as if undecided whether or not to come into the kitchen. Decision made, he ranged toward her, all rippling muscle, his bare feet padding across the hardwood floor. "I saw the open bottle on the bar."

Black wicking jogging pants with a streamlined fit through the butt rode low on his hips. The peaks of his hipbones hit above the waistband, and muscles that wrapped his abdomen flexed when he moved. She peeled her eyes off him and stared into the fridge at the collection of white wines, but the labels on the bottles all blurred together. All she could see were his pumped pecs and ripped abs. His gym workouts must be a part-time job to chisel a body into that kind of shape.

He placed his hand above hers on the edge of the door. Sensual energy radiated from him in soundless, heated waves. The bottles on the shelves were in danger of boiling instead of chilling. "Let's open this one. It has a long, pure-fruit finish. Meredith's done well with this label."

He reached over her head and pulled a bottle off the shelf. Whatever he had spritzed on his skin gave him the perfect man-scent with a twist: fresh, woodsy, and spicy. She ran through all the erotic things she would like to do with him.

It was perfectly normal to have those feelings, wasn't it? After all, she hadn't had sex in over a year, and she hadn't had good sex since...well...she couldn't remember. Plus, and this was the biggie, vacation rules applied. She could drink before five o'clock, and she could have sex with a hot guy without feeling guilty.

He opened the bottle and poured a glass. "Tell me what you think."

Think? It was hard to think about anything other than him. But she sipped, and she thought. The taste was nice enough, but she couldn't smell the wine because her nose was so full of fresh-from-the-shower Kevin. "Hmm. Tasty."

He corked the bottle without pouring a glass for himself and returned it to the shelf.

"You don't want any?" she asked.

A look of surprise came over his face, changing quickly to a delighted smile. "I always want some, but I have a beer opened in the other room."

Despite her best efforts at maintaining self-control, being near Kevin, her best efforts weren't good enough. "Where is the beer?"

He set her wineglass on the counter. "Come with me."

"Give me the glass. I don't want to waste the wine."

"Leave it. You might want it later." He led the way through the kitchen into the living room, where a ninety-inch TV hung over the large fireplace. Watching a ball game on a TV that size would be like having front-row season tickets. This must have been where Austin watched the NCAA tournament.

Two remotes sat on the coffee table along with an open half-read book by David McBain. Books by McBain and several by the author Jack Mallory filled the corner bookcase.

"Did Kenzie's husband write those?"

"Yes. You'll find David's and Jack's books everywhere around the winery."

"I've read Mallory's books but not David's."

"Don't tell them. They're good friends, but they're very competitive when it comes to their books."

She laughed. "I'm glad you told me. I'll start on David's book tonight. Do you have a recommendation?"

"All of them are very good. I started on that one last night and read until I couldn't keep my eyes open. I was hoping to finish it before I saw him tomorrow. He accuses me of never reading his books, and that one came out recently."

"You've gotten halfway. That's a good start. He'll appreciate that."

"Unless I finish it," Kevin said, "he won't believe I ever picked it up." He stepped behind a long mahogany bar polished to an impossible shine, and opened the refrigerator. She perched on a barstool and leaned over the bar to check the contents. "Ales, malts, and lagers? Hmm. I'll take a Guinness."

"How'd I know that?" He twisted off the cap.

"Add clairvoyant to your list of talents," she said.

He slid the white-necked bottle across the bar right into her hand.

"Impressive. I bet that took practice." She wrapped her fingers around the neck and lifted the bottle to her lips, smelling the rich, roasted barley.

"I've missed a few times and had to mop up the beer and sweep up the glass, but you have excellent reflexes. I figured I'd be safe."

"You're safe with me." Her thighs wanted to cradle his head like her hand cradled the neck of the bottle. She dragged her gaze from his lips to his eyes, feeling like a predator waiting to pounce on a toothsome morsel. She smiled from the inside out, pleased she could put aside her by-the-books persona and enjoy being a woman with needs and desires.

"The label says to drink straight from the bottle, but if you want a frosted mug there are some in the freezer."

"I'd never ruin a beer by pouring it in a glass." She took a long pull on the bottle. The beer was icy cold and perfect. "Hmm."

"That good, huh?"

"That good. If you ever meet my sister-in-law, please don't tell her I drank beer at a winery. I'd be shunned for the rest of my life."

He gave her an irresistible, roguish wink. "We don't mind if you drink beer as long as you buy wine to take home."

"I'll remember that." She took another greedy swig and savored the taste of the delicate brew while it slid down her throat. She knew her eyes were eating him up, and she saw no need to be discreet about it, either. A small sheen of beer glistened on his lower lip; a lip that held more than her eyes captive.

"You have five brothers and only one of them is married?"

"My sister-in-law is great. I love her. If she ever gets a look at you, though, she'll try to fix you up with every one of her single friends." If that happened, JL would insist on being at the top of the list.

Kevin walked to the other side of the bar and leaned one hip against the stool next to hers while he drank from a bottle of Coors. "As long as one of the friends is you."

"Your pickup lines aren't getting any better." She glanced at the mirror and cringed at her reflection. "I'm sitting on a barstool drinking beer with a hot guy, looking as frumpy as I could possibly look, and I'm complaining about pickup lines when I should be very grateful they're directed at me."

His eyes never left hers, and a little tic jumped at the corner of his lip. "You could still be wearing sweaty running clothes and you'd look as beautiful."

The lines were corny, and he didn't need to practice them on her. She was a sure thing. If she wasn't telegraphing that message, then she was so far off her game she wasn't even listed as a second-string player. The only question left to answer, as far as she was concerned, was when and where.

"What time is it?" she asked. "I've got to call Pops and my partner before I go to the game."

"It's five o'clock," Kevin said. "If we're going to meet Elliott and Meredith, we need to leave in fifteen minutes."

"I can't make it. Will you tell them I had calls to return, and I'll see them at the game?"

"No problem. I'll wait and drive you."

"You don't have to. I can drive."

"I know I don't, and I know you can, but parking is a bitch, and I have a special spot. Besides, I have a call that might take a while. I'd rather make it here than in the car."

"Well, if you have a special spot..."

"Don't worry. I know all the special spots." He grinned, clinking his bottle against hers. "I'll meet you at the front door at six-thirty."

She shook her head as she watched him walk away. If he weren't so charming, she'd be rolling her eyes at his innuendos and double entendres. But he was sizzling hot. The wide expanse of his back muscles narrowed at the waist, then down further to the dimples right above the band of his low-slung sweatpants. The view was an aphrodisiac.

"Kevin," she whispered. "Don't go." Relief that he didn't hear her warred with disappointment, and disappointment won, hands down.

Her sister-in-law would call Kevin a metrosexual. JL didn't care. She lived and worked with alpha males and was tired of them. Kevin was charming and accommodating. He wasn't out to prove anything or beat up bad guys. He only wanted to enjoy her company—in bed, out on the trail, or going to a ball game—and that sounded like a great way to spend the weekend. It wasn't like she wanted to marry the guy. She wanted something different, someone different, and Kevin was all that and more—much more.

She left the room smiling, and she was still smiling when she reached her guest room. Her phone showed a missed call from Austin. She listened to the voice mail. He apologized for not making a reservation and that he would see her after the game.

"And where do you expect me to stay?" she asked Austin in absentia. "In your room?" She was positive he had given her situation no thought at all, and she couldn't blame him. He was seventeen, getting ready for an important tournament, and he had found a murder vic only a few hours earlier. That alone would have distracted any seventeen-year-old. Her needs were not even on his radar.

She nestled into the window seat, tucked her legs up under her hip, and called her father. "Hey, Pops. Can you talk?"

"Sure, sweetheart. Have you seen Austin yet?"

"Yes, and he told me he's listed as six-four on the tournament roster. He's put on a few pounds and looks great. Oh, and get this. He has a girlfriend."

The excitement was audible in the senior O'Grady's voice when he asked, "Have you met her?"

"I will tonight. I'll be sure to take a picture of them."

"Send it to your brothers, too."

"I will." She paused a minute and took a breath. She wasn't sure what Pops' reaction to the Di Salvo murder would be. "We've got a situation here. The Frasers' olive orchardist, Salvatore Di Salvo, was murdered this morning, and Austin found the body."

"*Jesus Christ.* Di Salvo? Are you sure? How's Austin?"

"He was shook up a bit, but he's okay."

"You're not involved in the investigation, are you?"

"The Napa cops don't want any help from me."

"Of course they don't, and you wouldn't want theirs. You're a threat. Stay away from their investigation, or they'll charge you with interference."

"The lead detective's already threatened to do that."

"Then pay attention. Your detective sergeant doesn't want you involved, either. You're there to spend time with Austin, not work a case."

"What am I supposed to do? Ignore what happened here, even if it might be connected to my case?"

"Your case ended four years ago."

He was right. Her case had ended, but her gut told her Salvatore's death was connected, and she couldn't walk away. "Austin took pictures of the crime scene. I forwarded them to Pete. He said they looked familiar—olive grove, small-caliber pistol shot to the forehead, and no signs the vic struggled."

"You don't have jurisdiction."

"I could go undercover again. If the family has set up a narcotics operation on Montgomery Winery property, I can find it."

"Not in a weekend."

"Then I'll get more time off."

"It won't be approved. If there's a cartel setting up shop on Montgomery Winery property, once they hear the O'Grady name, they'll come gunning for you. Austin, too. Do you want to put his life in danger?"

"Of course not."

"The local detectives will run Salvatore's name through the system. They'll connect the Di Salvo name to your case. If they want your help, they'll ask."

"They won't connect the case to me. That happened soon after I got married, when I was using my whole name and Ryan's name."

"That lasted, what, six months? If you'd kept his name, the marriage might have lasted."

"It wouldn't have made any difference, and you know it. Besides, everyone on the force knew me as JL O'Grady. Who the hell was Jenny Lynn O'Grady-Monahan?"

"Ryan's wife."

"He didn't believe it for long, or he wouldn't have cheated on me with every single woman in Pearl River."

"Don't tell Father Paul I said this, but you deserve to be happy, even if that meant divorcing your husband. Ryan is a bastard. He doesn't deserve you. You'll find a man who does. I'll get the marriage annulled so you can marry again in the church. Find a good man, JL. A man who will treat you right. Now get off the phone and enjoy your time with Austin. I love you."

"Love you, too, Pops."

Her father's advice to stay out of the investigation rankled her, but she had called for advice. If she wasn't going to listen to it, then why bother to call? Simple. She respected his opinion. He had risen through the ranks of the NYPD until the police commissioner appointed him deputy chief, a position he had held until his retirement. Throughout the NYPD, he was highly thought of, and so were her four older brothers. The youngest of the four, also a cop, was attending law school at night. When the O'Gradys were together, they made a formidable team.

She needed another beer before she called Pete. She padded down the hall again, scrolling through a long list of emails on her cell phone. There wasn't anything that couldn't wait until she returned to work on Tuesday.

"Back for another one?"

She glanced up from her phone to see Kevin at the bar flipping pages in a spiral notebook. He still hadn't found a shirt.

"I thought you went upstairs for a conference call—"

"—I thought you were calling your father."

"I did—" she said.

"I did—" he said, and they both laughed. "I needed this notebook for the call, and left it here earlier. Now I'm trying to jot down a few notes before I make another call. What about you?"

"Pops advised me to stay out of the investigation."

Kevin reached in the fridge for another Guinness, twisted off the lid, and handed it across the bar to her. "Are you going to listen to him?"

She put the bottle to her lips and then lowered it, thinking. "I love him. I depend on his advice—"

"But you rarely take it?"

"I wouldn't say that. I didn't like the advice he tossed out this time. He was unbending about it."

"Unbending as a stone. Sounds like my father."

She took a long pull on her beer. "It must go with the territory."

Kevin tugged on the end of her hair towel. "If you don't take this off, your hair will never dry."

"There's a hair dryer in the bathroom."

He untwisted the towel and her hair fell to her shoulders in damp waves. "Are you going to listen to his advice this time?"

"I'll decide after I visit the crime scene and take a tour of the property. Austin mentioned a wine cave. I want to see that, too.

Then I'll decide."

Kevin folded the towel in half and then in half again. "You only have a few days. What can you accomplish?"

"Sometimes a lot. Sometimes very little. It depends on how sloppy the perp was."

"I'll give you a tour tomorrow. Riding horseback is the best way to see the vineyards. Are you up for that?"

"I'll ride anything as long as it has a calm disposition, an even temperament, and doesn't spook easily."

He folded the towel in half again, his eyes twinkling. "I don't spook easily."

She couldn't help but laugh. "Did you really say that? You're incorrigible." She took a long pull on her beer, thinking that maybe he didn't have any filters and said whatever was on his mind.

"Well, I don't spook easily. You can ask anyone. And as for horses, Meredith has two quarter horses that fit your qualifications."

"I bet you're an experienced rider."

He lowered his head, shaking it. "You're having fun feeding me lines, aren't you?"

She held up her hands, surrendering. "Not me."

"Okay, here's a straight answer. I got my first horse when I was four. I played polo for several years, and then I started show jumping. That's how I met Kit MacKlenna. We were both jumping in a three-day event in Lexington during our junior year in high school. We became good friends. She invited me out to her family's farm to ride. That's where I met Elliott."

"I thought Elliott owned MacKlenna Farm."

"He does now. When Sean and Mary MacKlenna died, Kit moved away, and Elliott bought the farm."

"Where is she now?"

Kevin picked up the folded towel and swept it across the bar's surface, wiping up the beads of condensation that had dripped off the beer bottles. He was obviously stalling. He avoided eye contact when he said, "She's in…Scotland."

"Is she related to Elliott?" JL asked.

He tossed the wet towel into the sink as if he were shooting a basket. "There's a direct connection between Elliott and the MacKlennas, but you have to go back a dozen generations to find the link."

"What about you? Are you related?"

He shrugged. "I'm the only one around here who isn't."

"I'm surprised. You and Elliott look so much alike."

"I've been told that before. I've worked for him for almost two decades. I use the same hair stylist. We dress alike and use the same trainer. The longer we're together, the more I look like him. It's weird. My parents have been together so long even they look alike." Kevin rested his forearms on the bar and leaned forward, moving into her personal space. "What the hell was wrong with your husband?"

"That was a non sequitur if I've ever heard one."

"I'd much rather talk about you than the MacKlenna/Fraser clan." He leaned even closer and touched a finger to her jaw. "You're smart, beautiful, fun, courageous, and honest. Why'd your husband cheat on you?"

She couldn't take her eyes off his masculine lips…picture-perfect, kissable lips. "He didn't love me. Maybe he did at first, but it didn't last. Once he started working undercover, his hours were crazy, and we rarely saw each other." She looked into Kevin's eyes then and what she saw there made her breath hitch.

"Breathe." His voice was as stirring as the way he looked at her, and the way he said *breathe* made the process sound doable.

"I'm standing across from a sexy guy who's not wearing much. It's kind of hard to breathe."

"And I'm standing across from a woman who's only wearing a robe." His hands slipped within the folds of the terry cloth, and there was far more tenderness in his touch than there had been earlier when he stretched out her leg muscles. His mouth gently fit over hers, moving slowly, like a warm light, until the entire room spun on its axis.

She had kissed men before. Plenty of them, but there was something unique with Kevin. He wasn't tentative when he kissed her; rather, his kiss was a promise that his leashed passion was hers to explore.

"We have an hour," he said. "That's enough time to do what we both want." His expression wasn't serious, but there was nothing wishy-washy about it either. He wanted her, and she read the depths of that in his eyes.

"Or we could finish our calls and get ready for the ball game." Her heart was beating hard now, and she could feel it all the way down to the soles of her feet. The steady hand of time stilled again for the second time that afternoon. He kissed her again. His mouth was soft and warm, and she leaned in to it eagerly.

"I would have run twenty miles today to be with you," he said.

"I'm a sure thing, Kevin. You don't need to try out any more lines on me."

He gave her a sheepish grin. "I've been telling the truth."

"Then tell me this. If we have quickie sex, won't everyone see it on our faces?"

He gave her nape a squeeze with one hand. "Elliott and Meredith will, and I'll get reamed, but…"

"Then I won't put us in that position." JL slipped off the barstool. "I'm going to go call my partner and get ready for the game."

"Wait." He came around to the other side of the bar. "Before you go…" He pulled her into his arms and threaded his fingers up underneath her hair to cradle her head. He laid his lips on hers, easily sliding her into a kiss the way they would slide into bed later. His tongue was soft as it slipped into her mouth, but he was unbelievably hard everywhere else. The skin beneath her hands was smooth and taut over broad shoulders, and the play of muscles rippled down his back.

She couldn't remember ever wanting a man more than she wanted Kevin at that moment. Although she wanted more of him, she had to break away. He changed the angle of the kiss and nipped at her bottom lip. At her low, throaty moan, he grew harder against her. He kissed the top of her head. "I'm walking away only because it's important to you, but as soon as we're alone again…"

She looked up at him. "I won't let you go until we're both satisfied. But right now I don't have the strength to resist you."

"You can face down drug dealers and murderers, but you can't walk away from me? How's that possible?"

"I wish I knew."

"I'll meet you on the porch in forty-five minutes." He turned and walked away again, but this time she studied the beer bottle label and not his physique. If she had to look at the dimples in his lower back, she would call to him, and this time she wouldn't whisper his name.

6

JL'S CONVERSATION WITH PETE took fifteen minutes. No matter what she said, he wouldn't back off his opinion that she should stay clear of the investigation. That pissed her off, and she told him so. Before she hung up, she made him promise that if Hollinger or Castellano called, he would let her know.

Another beer would have been nice, but she didn't dare return to the living room. If she ran into Kevin before she was dressed and ready to go, they wouldn't make it to the ball game, and that would be a disaster on many levels.

Her normally steady hand had a slight tremor, and it took twice as long to fix her hair and apply makeup. Deciding on what to wear took even longer. She stood in front of the closet and considered the same outfits repeatedly before making a decision. Finally, while the clock ticked down to the witching hour, she settled on skinny jeans and a bluebell-colored ribbed pullover with cuffed elbow sleeves. Gyms were notoriously hot, and the excitement of watching Austin play guaranteed she would be sweating before halftime. She grabbed her leather jacket, concealed her gun in an SOB (small of back) holster, and headed for the porch.

Kevin was already there, standing near the railing, hands in his pockets, thumbs out, staring at the vineyards. He turned as she opened the door.

"Sorry I'm late."

He smiled before glancing at his watch. "You're right on time.

I'm perpetually early."

"I've noticed." The intensity and heat in his eyes was enough to bring a flush to her face. She resisted the urge to pat her cheeks to cool them. Not that it would help.

"Before we leave, there's something I have to do."

"Okay," she said. "I'll wait."

He slid his arms around her and captured her mouth in a scorching kiss that shared breath and taste, and primitive excitement suddenly turned explosive. If she didn't push away from him, she'd lose it completely.

"We've got to go," she said.

"You know how to hurt a guy's ego." He dragged his mouth back to hers for longer, deeper, hotter kisses, letting his hand linger on her back, pressing her lightly to him. "Your bed or mine?"

"Later. Not now. Yours," she answered between kisses.

"So you can leave me in the morning?" he asked, nibbling on her lip.

"Only to take a shower before we go riding. Outside, I mean."

He brushed back a loose strand of her hair and tucked it behind her ear. "You've got it all planned out."

"Not really. I'm having trouble moving off this porch." She shuffled her feet side to side. "See? They won't go forward."

Kevin threw his head back, laughing. "Come on. I'll help you." He took her hand and led her around to the garage. Using a remote on his key chain, he opened the door. Parked side by side were a black Land Rover and a silver AMG Roadster.

"Why would you drive Kenzie's Mercedes when you have one of your own?"

"It's a game we play."

"Do they drive your cars, too?"

"Hell no. Mine stay in the garage."

She smacked his arm, a demonstrative gesture she used only on her brothers. Not anyone else. Not even Pete. Until today.

"Ouch," Kevin said.

"Sorry. Habit."

"Beating up on guys is a habit?"

"Yeah, when they say dumb stuff."

He hit the unlock button on his key fob and opened the passenger side door for her. She slid into a luxurious leather seat. This would be the most expensive ride she had ever taken, and she was going to a ball game wearing jeans, not to a fancy ball in a red-carpet-worthy dress. What a waste.

"Do you want the top down?"

"Sure," she said.

He lowered the top and put up the wind blocker. The mesh screen would help calm the draft. He pulled out of the garage and sped down the drive toward the side entrance to the winery. As he drove through the security gate, he asked, "Are you going to tell Austin about the divorce tonight?"

"No, not even if a perfect moment arises. He's excited about the tournament and the gala Sunday night. I'm not going to ruin the weekend for him."

Kevin put on the blinker and merged into traffic, heading into Napa. "Have you ever thought about doing anything else for a living?"

"Why're you asking?"

He glanced at her then turned his eyes back on the road. "Your job scares him."

"I know, but it's what I do." She wasn't so sure she wanted to continue doing it, but that wasn't something she was ready to share, especially with someone who talked to Austin regularly. She closed her eyes and enjoyed the hot air blowing on her neck from the air vent built into the headrest. Comfort and warmth lulled her to sleep.

"Wake up, we're here."

She opened her eyes to see the high school gym straight ahead. "How'd we get here so fast?"

"You fell asleep."

"I did?"

He zipped into a parking spot marked PRINCIPAL. "A long flight, a three hour time difference, two glasses of wine, two beers, and an eight mile run would exhaust anyone. I'm glad you took a nap. You won't get much sleep tonight."

"Then I'm glad I rested. So tell me, what happens if the principal shows up and can't use his or her spot?"

"We have an arrangement." Kevin raised the roof and got out of the car. JL opened her own door before he could come around to help her.

"I'm not sure I want to know the arrangement."

Kevin popped the trunk and grabbed a package wrapped in brown paper. "He gets a couple of bottles of his favorite wine, and I get a parking spot."

"With so much wine around, it doesn't seem like a bottle would be such a prized commodity."

"Not all wine is, but this," he said, gesturing to the package, "is the MacKlenna Winery Reserve Chardonnay, a fifty-dollar bottle of wine."

"So you're paying a hundred dollars for a parking spot? That's outrageous."

"Maybe. But I wanted to drive this car tonight, and a high school parking lot isn't the safest place to park. The police have a bigger presence on this side of the building."

"Let me guess. The administrative offices are accessed through that door straight ahead, and they've had break-ins on game nights."

"Several." Kevin led the way around to the front of the building. "I'll meet you in the gym. I need to deliver my"—he glanced down at the package, then back to JL—"payment."

She made her way through the popcorn-scented lobby and the crowd converging on the concession stand. Just as she entered the hot, electric atmosphere of Justin-Siena High School's gymnasium, Austin approached the basket for a practice layup. He had Maggie O'Grady's agility, and watching him on the court held JL's attention in as tight a grasp as her mother's Broadway performances had all those years ago.

Kevin walked up behind her and put his hand on her shoulder. She glanced up, smiling. "I hope business was transacted successfully."

"It was, yes."

His breath fanned her cheek, and the musky scent of his soap paired erotically with the smooth, seductive sound of his voice. She had to remind herself that she was in a high school gym, not in Kevin's bedroom. For the next couple of hours, she had to focus on basketball.

"And I have a guaranteed spot for the next game," Kevin continued.

They stood on the sidelines and watched the team warm up. "I haven't seen Austin on the court in months," she said. "Watching videos isn't the same. I've missed a lot that I can never get back."

"We make decisions based on what's best at the time. If we had the benefit of hindsight, we might not make them. We can't live with regret. If you don't like the way a decision turned out, make changes now."

"I can't."

"Have you tried?"

She shook her head.

"Maybe it's time, then."

Had he been eavesdropping on her thoughts? How did he know she had reached a crossroads? It was time to make a change. The question was—did she have the courage to do it? Could she leave her family? New York? The NYPD? For what? To follow Austin for a couple of years? That didn't make much sense. Maybe when he settled in a location for more than two years she would consider moving.

What about her career? She had to think of herself, too. And that brought her full circle. She still didn't have an answer, at least to the bigger questions. The smaller ones were easier. To start with, she intended to sleep with Kevin, and for tonight, she wouldn't think any more about Austin, her career, or the investigation.

She jumped back into the here and now and asked, "Have you been to many of Austin's games?"

"We've missed a few, but we try to arrange our schedules so we can bring James Cullen to see him play."

"He's Elliott's son, right?"

"Thirteen going on twenty-one."

She chuckled. "That's what Kenzie said."

Kevin pointed toward the center of the visiting team's bleachers. "Elliott and Meredith are over there. Looks like there's room for us."

One of Austin's teammates missed a pass and the ball careened toward her. Before she had time to react, Kevin reached in, caught it, and threw it back.

"Let me see those hands," she said. Kevin spread out his fingers, and she placed her palm against his. Her fingers barely extended beyond his palm. "Did you play basketball? You have perfect hands for the game."

"I spent too much time in the barn taking care of my horse and going to shows. I didn't have time to play ball. That's why I enjoy coming to Austin's games."

"Because it shows you what you missed?"

"I missed more than playing the game. I missed learning how to play well with others. Being part of a team teaches you how to do that."

"You're part of a team now, aren't you?"

"A team of one with four bosses. That's not much of a team."

A teenage boy wearing a Pro Prep T-shirt limped past carrying a bag of balls. "Hi, Mr. Allen. We're going to kick butt tonight."

Kevin and the boy did a horizontal high-five/fist-bump combo. "We sure are, Sammy." Then to JL, he said, "Sammy's a volunteer team manager. Pro Prep solicits volunteers from other schools to fill support positions for the team. Sammy takes care of the equipment during games."

She smiled at Sammy, and then she noticed him waving to a man standing by Pro Prep's bench. She did a double take. It was Detective Castellano, and his eyes were a laser focused on her.

"Don't look now," she said to Kevin, "but one of the detectives working the case is standing behind our bench, and I think he's related to Sammy. Do you know if he is?"

Kevin's eyes crinkled at the corners. "You told me not to look."

She smacked him below the shoulder.

"Ouch." He let his arm hang loosely at his side while he rubbed his bicep, exaggerating his injury, and said in a low growl, "I love it when you hit me. It's so damn sexy."

Although desire for him burned through her, she made a face that feigned exasperation. "You're sick." She glanced toward the bench again. Castellano had turned to talk to a man wearing the other team's jacket. "Look now."

"Yeah, that's Sammy's dad. Is that good or bad?"

"I don't know yet. I'll try to talk to him during halftime." So much for not thinking more about the investigation tonight.

As they continued to make their way toward the bleachers, a dozen people spoke to Kevin. Adults slapped him on the shoulder, and kids ran up to him, giving him high-fives.

Kevin was more in tune with Austin's life in Napa than she ever hoped to be. Austin had made a home in California without her, and she couldn't compete with the Frasers. If the University of Kentucky offered Austin a scholarship, he would move there, and the Frasers would be in Lexington, too. So much for not thinking more about Austin tonight either.

A student ran by and shouted, "We're going to kick Justin-Siena's ass tonight, Mr. Allen."

"You know all the players and supporters, don't you?" she asked.

"All the players. Most of the supporters. We have the players out for dinner once a month. It gives Austin some ownership."

She stopped mid stride. "Why? Are you grooming him for something? If so, I want to know what it is. Why are you investing so much time in Austin and his team?"

Kevin pulled her over next to the wall and out of the flow of fans heading to the bleachers. "Meredith, Elliott, and I know what it's like to be alone. We care about Austin and hope one day he'll come to work for us."

She held her arms tight to her body and looked up at him, glaring. "In what capacity?"

"He won't play basketball forever. You know that. He could suffer an injury that would end his basketball career. If that happens, we want him to consider working for MacKlenna Corporation in a role that fits his special talents. We're not sure what role that is, and frankly, it might not be created until he's ready to hang up his jersey."

"He's going into the NBA."

"Do you know how many young men have that same dream? There are dozens of outstanding players every year who don't make it into the first or second rounds during the selection process. Austin can't count on making millions in the NBA. That happens to a lucky few. It might happen. Hell, it probably will happen, but we want him to have a fallback plan that doesn't—and I don't mean to offend you—include becoming a police officer."

Although the truth didn't offend her, his words did hurt. "I don't want him on the force, either. But I still can't figure out why you picked him out of all the players and are willing to invest so heavily in his future. It doesn't make sense to me."

"I didn't pick Austin. James Cullen did." Kevin paused a moment and looked out over the crowd, then returned his gaze to her. "James Cullen said his fingers tingled when they shook hands. He thought that was a sign and told Elliott to offer Austin an internship, and if he didn't want one, then Elliott should become his sponsor."

"That's crazy. Austin's grip is so firm he probably cut off James Cullen's circulation when they shook hands."

A slight wry smile crossed Kevin's face. "It wasn't his grip. James Cullen believes he has a sixth sense. Don't you believe you have one?"

She had a cop's intuition or hunches. Different names for the same thing. She thought back to the moment she was staring at the portrait in the Welcome Center and how her fingers tingled when she noticed the woman's ruby brooch. "Yes, I have a sixth sense, and I depend on it to survive."

"There you go," Kevin said.

The Frasers' interest in Austin still confused her, but when the buzzer sounded and the players returned to the bench for final words with their coaches, she let the conversation go, for now.

"We better get to our seats. The game's about to start," Kevin said.

For the next hour, JL sat on the edge of the bench screaming for Austin, and so did Kevin. What really surprised her, though, was Kevin's mini-me. James Cullen sat on the other side of him and mimicked every move and reaction. That level of mimicry evolved only from spending a considerable amount of time together—like brothers and sisters.

At halftime, JL went in search of Detective Castellano, finding him outside the visitors' locker room. He had loosened his tie and folded his suit jacket over his arm with his glasses poking out of the breast pocket. His face was shiny with sweat. The gym was hot, but she didn't think it was that hot.

"Your brother's having a good game," he said.

"Yes, he is. Sammy is doing a good job, too. Why didn't you mention his position with the team this afternoon?"

Castellano folded his jacket over his other arm and smoothed it down. He was nervous, and JL wasn't sure why.

"It wasn't the right time."

Right time? It was more than that, she could tell from his tight smile, but she didn't push it.

"Look," he said. "My uncle spent thirty years with the NYPD. The department was good to him."

"I didn't say I was with the NYPD."

"I checked you out." He looked past her toward the floor and then returned his gaze to her. "What I'm getting at is that I'm not as closed-minded about outside help as my partner is, especially help from a New York City cop."

"But you can't tell Hollinger that."

Castellano chewed his long upper lip and nodded reluctantly. After a long pause, he said, "My uncle told me you were involved in the Di Salvo racketeering, money laundering, and illegal drug case four years ago. He asked me if the New York case was related to the one here. What do you think?"

She shrugged. "I thought we put the Di Salvos out of business. Maybe we only put them out of New York. You might want to do a background check to see if there's a family connection. But don't worry. I'll stay out of your way."

Castellano looked over her head again. "Hollinger doesn't want you anywhere near the investigation. If he knew I was talking to you, he'd go ballistic."

"But you're willing to risk it. Why?"

He returned his gaze to her. "I don't care about the press or a promotion. I want to catch a killer. And I think you can help."

JL liked his attitude and appreciated his honesty. If there was anything she could do, she would, especially if it gave him a lead that would help him solve the case before Hollinger.

Sammy limped out of the locker room. "Hi, Dad."

"Hey, son. Have you met Austin's sister, Detective O'Grady?"

Sammy's dad nudged him in the arm, and the boy's hand shot straight out. "Nice to meet you, ma'am. Are you with the Napa Police Department, too?"

"No, I'm just in town visiting Austin."

"He's an awesome player, and he's nice, too," Sammy said.

JL shook his sweaty hand. "Thank you, Sammy. Are you enjoying your job?"

"Sure am. The second half is about to start. I've—"

"Go on, son," Castellano said. "Do your job."

Sammy followed the players toward the court, leaving JL alone with his dad again. "Nice kid. You're doing a good job with him. Very mannerly."

Castellano shoved his hands into his pockets and shuffled his feet. "Sammy lost his mother three years ago. He struggles with his handicap, but we manage."

She could empathize with Castellano. Under different conditions she would share her story, but not tonight.

The rest of the team came out of the locker room, and after high-fiving Austin, she said to Castellano, "I'll give you this much. Your murder scene looks very similar to the one I investigated. If you're asking me if both murders were committed by the same perp. I don't know. I thought we caught the sons of bitches." The buzzer went off, indicating the start of the game. "Give me your card. I'll call if I learn anything that might help you."

"Thanks. My uncle said you'd help."

She stuffed the business card into her pocket. "Do I know him?"

"No, but he knows your father."

"Is he a Castellano, too?"

The detective hunched his shoulders and gave her a slow nod. "Yeah, he's a Castellano, too. Highly decorated, by the way."

She left to rejoin Kevin for the second half. He and Elliott were easy to pick out in the bleachers. They looked like movie stars in a sea of fans.

"Excuse me. Excuse me," she said, as she made her way down the row toward Kevin. When she reached him, he held out his hand. When they touched, a shiver of pleasure went through her, and she smiled broadly.

"How'd it go?" he asked.

"I'll tell you later."

Elliott watched her with almost a predatory glare. She smiled, not because she wanted to appear friendly, but because she wanted to set him off balance. He didn't smile back. Without looking at Kevin, she said, "Elliott's got his eye on us."

"Elliott can be too critical sometimes. Don't worry about it. I'll straighten him out later."

The game started, and JL forgot about Elliott's displeasure. More than once, during a tense play, she tugged on Kevin's arm. After the ref swallowed his whistle on several instances of contact, he finally called a charging foul on Austin. JL screamed, *"Get some glasses, ref. That wasn't charging. Are you freaking blind?"*

When the game went into overtime, her blood pressure shot up, which caused her heart to beat faster and her muscles to tense even tighter. Then, as the clock ticked down to the final minute, Justin-Siena's point guard passed the ball. Austin pushed it away and dribbled to the front. Guarding him was one of Justin-Siena's perimeter defenders. Austin drove inside the three-point line, executed a quick crossover, and made a twenty-foot jumper to give Pro Prep an 87-86 lead with 5.2 seconds. JL came to her feet and counted down the seconds as Justin-Siena's guard drove to his basket. He threw up a shot a split second before the buzzer sounded. The ball seemed to hang in the air, and she watched with one eye closed. Finally, the ball came down, hit the rim, and bounced off, giving Pro Prep the win.

"*What a game.*" She hugged Kevin. "*What a game.*" She released him quickly and hugged James Cullen. "*Oh my God.* What a game. Wasn't that the best game *ever?*"

James Cullen glowed. "Yes, ma'am. Best I've seen."

The teams lined up and shook hands, and she remembered she was supposed to take pictures. She grabbed her phone and snapped a few before the team left the floor for the locker rooms. The fans fled the gym to take their celebration off campus.

"Come on," Elliott said. "Austin will meet us at the restaurant. JL, ye can ride with us."

She resisted the temptation to glance at Kevin, and instead hurried to catch up with Meredith.

"Austin played a great game," Meredith said. "If he was upset over Salvatore's murder, you couldn't tell."

"He's always been able to focus and block out things and situations that upset him."

"I guess he's had a lifetime of listening to police talk about murders and tragedies," Meredith said.

"He always left the room during get-togethers when we talked about work. Our jobs scare him. He's afraid he'll lose one of us. He doesn't have any memory of Mom, but he knows her loss has impacted us in lots of ways. He thinks he can hide from that kind of grief."

"It'll be a rude awakening when he discovers he can't," Meredith said.

JL followed her outside. Elliott had an even better parking space for his Mercedes—parked illegally near the front door. "Why didn't they tow your car? Did you pay off the cops with a case of wine?"

Elliott opened the passenger side door and the backseat door. "Not wine. A large donation to the police benevolent association. As long as I don't do anything too egregious, they look the other way."

JL climbed into the backseat. "And parking in front of a fire hydrant isn't considered egregious?"

"Tonight it wasn't. Tomorrow it might be. I never know."

"But you take the chance anyway?"

He closed the doors and walked around to the driver's seat. "To answer your question, JL, some things are worth taking a chance on. I didn't want my bride and my son walking through a parking lot full of teenage drivers. Surely you know all about taking chances."

Looking at her in the rearview mirror, his glare burned through her, but she held his gaze. She wasn't backing down. "I consider all decisions through a prism colored by danger to myself, my partner, and my family."

"If yer actions will hurt someone, a spouse for instance, do ye take the risk?" he fired back.

As tempted as she was to drop her gaze, she refused to show any weakness. He was referring to her and Kevin, but she wasn't going to let him box her in. Instead, she said, "There's always a chance when I chase a perp down a dark alley and my partner follows me that one of us could get shot and killed, but if the perp gets away, there's a good chance someone else will." She wasn't sure, but she thought Elliott's mouth quirked up slightly at one corner. It had been a test, and she must have passed.

Elliott pulled into the parking lot at Cordeiro's Steakhouse located at the base of the East Hills of the Napa Valley. James Cullen jumped out. "My friend Craig said he'd be here after the game. I'll meet you at the table." He ran into the restaurant and disappeared.

Meredith watched him, shaking her head. "I've got a couple more years before I have very little control over what James Cullen does. I hope he's learned half of what we've tried to teach him."

"My mom raised four sons and a daughter before Austin was born. She ruled the house. Manners, education, and the church were all number one priorities. I've tried to raise Austin the way I was raised, but I've lost my influence now."

"In many ways, you and Austin grew up together. I don't think you'll ever lose your influence over him. He adores you. Every conversation I have with him, your name comes up. He's proud of you. He doesn't like that you put your life on the line, but he's proud that you do."

The host showed Elliott, Meredith, and JL to their reserved table. "Is Kenzie joining us?" JL asked.

"I just got a text. She said to go on and eat," Elliott said.

Kevin was waiting at the table. He stood and held a chair for JL.

"How'd you beat us?" she asked.

"You've ridden in my car, and you've ridden with Elliott. Are you sure you want to ask that question?" Kevin said.

"Oh," she said.

James Cullen hurried over to the table. "Dad. I heard on the news that Amy Spalding—you know, that pretty ESPN reporter, the one who became the first baseball commentator—"

"I remember," Elliott said. "What about her?"

"She inherited a big house on Riverside Drive in New York City," Kevin said.

"From her great-great-aunt," JL said. "I heard that this morning. The woman was a recluse and very wealthy. Amy was her only relative."

"She's gone missing," James Cullen said. "She didn't show up for work. And no one has heard from her."

"I saw a report on CNN at the airport. Spalding was last seen going into the house," JL said.

"Can you ask your brothers for an update?" James Cullen said.

"It's not their case," she said. "But I'll ask."

James Cullen sat and put his napkin in his lap. "Do you think she could have gone away like Aunt Kenzie, Aunt Charlotte, and

Aunt Kit?"

Elliott folded his arms on the edge of the table and leaned toward James Cullen. "People go missing every day, lad. They don't all go on adventures. Now, look at the menu and decide what ye want for dinner."

"I'd like the salmon, please, with a nice red wine," James Cullen said.

"Red wine? Really?" Kevin said.

James Cullen's mouth turned up in the corner with the same little quirk visible in Elliott and Kevin's grins.

"The way you like your salmon cooked, you never pair it with red wine. I taught you better than that," Kevin chided.

Elliott rubbed James Cullen's head, mussing his hair. "Good try, lad."

JL studied Meredith and Elliott's faces during the conversation with James Cullen. There was a subtext to the conversation, but Elliott and James Cullen hadn't provided enough clues for JL to figure out what. Even Kevin fidgeted at the mention of adventures. She sent Pete a text asking for news of Spalding's disappearance. A minute later, her phone beeped with a message: *Last seen going inside aunt's house. Entire premises searched. Videocam reviewed. Spalding vanished. No explanation. No leads. No sign of foul play.*

James Cullen looked at her, eyes wide. "Any news?"

"Nothing," she said.

"I'm going to ask Uncle David to look into it," James Cullen said.

"The police are working on it," Elliott said. "Give them time to do their job."

"They won't find her. She's gone where they can't go."

James Cullen's comment hung in the air when the star of the evening walked over to the table. He was escorting a striking blond-haired woman almost six feet tall. Kevin and Elliott both stood.

"Hello, Betsy. Nice to see ye again," Elliott said.

Kevin and Austin did a fist bump, and then Austin came to JL, kissed her cheek, and said, "JL, this is Betsy Brown. She's a senior at

Justin-Siena, and has applied early decision to Duke. She wants to go to medical school." Then he leaned over and whispered, "Remember. Don't embarrass me."

A knot lodged in JL's throat. She pushed her chair away from the table and stood. Even wearing three-inch heels, she barely reached Betsy's shoulder. "I'm glad to meet you. Duke's far from home."

"Yes, ma'am," Betsy said. "But I'm an army brat. We've moved a lot. I spent my grade school years in North Carolina. It's only my dad and me now, and he's close to retirement. If I go to school there, he'll move closer so he can watch me play."

James Cullen's eyes lit up. "Basketball or volleyball?"

"Either one."

"I'm trying to get her to apply to UK, too," Austin said.

"Forget doctoring people," Elliott said. "Animals are much easier to get along with."

"Don't listen to him," Meredith said. "People don't weigh a thousand pounds, kick, bite, or slam you into walls and break your arms and legs."

"They also don't quit ye and go to another doctor because they don't like yer advice."

Meredith licked her finger and made an imaginary mark in the air. "I'll give you that one."

James Cullen twitched as he giggled. He elbowed JL. "Dad usually doesn't get marks for winning points."

"He doesn't? What does he get?" JL asked.

"Funny faces, like this…" James Cullen scrunched up his nose and lolled out his tongue, making JL laugh.

"Don't encourage him," Meredith said. Then, to her son, she said, "Do you know what you want to eat?"

"Same as always," he said. "Salmon."

JL was aware of every move Kevin made, every comment, every breath. Their legs bumped several times until she finally gave up trying to control her wayward knee and left it to rest against his. She doubted they were fooling Elliott and Meredith. While they didn't say anything, Meredith did give her a few speculative glances.

JL laughed and told funny stories about characters she had met on the streets of New York City, and, to please Austin, she didn't tell any family stories. After the wait staff removed the dessert dishes, JL remembered that Hollinger had returned Austin's phone. She reached into her purse to get it just as the server walked by. She grabbed her wallet instead. "I'd like to pay for my dinner, my brother's and his date."

The server said, "The check's been taken care of, sweetie."

JL's shoulder twitched. Anytime she needed calming or a reminder that graciousness should always come before pride, she sensed her mother's presence. JL glanced at Kevin, who pointed at Elliott.

"Elliott, thank you. You've given me a room for the weekend. You don't have to buy my dinner, too."

Although he smiled, it didn't reach his eyes. "It's my pleasure, lass."

JL snapped her wallet shut and dropped it into her purse while willing her lips to maintain a gracious smile, which probably didn't reach her eyes either. She was from a working-class family, and not accustomed to going out for dinner and spending a day's pay. Elliott had either tossed down an Amex or handed over hundred-dollar bills and bought dinner for seven. She didn't see the tab, but based on the prices advertised in the menu and what everyone ordered, dinner had to have cost between three and four hundred dollars. And Austin hadn't batted an eye when he ordered a large New York strip. Growing up, he had learned the value of a dollar. What was he learning now?

Kevin stood and put his hand on JL's chair. "Boss, I'll take JL back to the cottage."

"Meredith will drive her. I want to go over my notes with ye from the meeting at the bank this afternoon. If we wait until tomorrow, I'll have forgotten what's important."

"That's unlikely. But you're the boss."

"Thanks for dinner, Dr. Fraser," Betsy said. "I'm looking forward to the gala Sunday night."

"I'm glad ye're coming. It's been a while since I've seen yer dad."

They all walked out of the restaurant together, and JL followed Austin and Betsy to the truck he was driving. "Will I see you tomorrow before the game?"

"Come to the dorm about noon," Austin said. "We'll have lunch."

"At the dorm?" Her stomach flip-flopped at the thought, but she'd deal with it if that's where he wanted to eat.

"Hell no. I want to go somewhere nice. And not McDonald's or Pizza Hut either."

"If you'll watch your language, I'll take you wherever you want to go." She hugged him good-bye and watched him drive off. Meredith drove up beside her. Before JL climbed into the passenger's seat, she glanced over to where Kevin had parked. He waved, but he didn't look happy. She wasn't either, but she gave him a thumbs-up and slid into the seat.

Watching Austin drive away with Betsy, JL said to Meredith, "I had this horrible thought that my older brothers screwed up Austin's sex education as badly as they did teaching him pickup lines."

Meredith laughed. "I don't think you have to worry about Austin and Betsy. They're responsible. I'm sure they're sexually active, but I'm also sure they're taking precautions."

JL stared in open-mouthed shock. "How do you know? Has he said something? God, I should talk to him. I'll do that tomorrow."

Meredith continued laughing. "Relax. He hasn't said anything to me. He might have talked to Kevin, or even to Kenzie, but not to me."

"Kevin I can understand, but why Kenzie?"

Meredith drove the car out of the parking lot, following Kevin and Elliott. "Kenzie did two tours in Afghanistan, and she graduated from West Point. She's spent more time with men than women, and she has two boys of her own. Granted, they're only three, but still—"

JL turned in her seat to face Meredith. "You're saying a kid like Austin, away from home, would see Kenzie as a mother substitute and be comfortable asking her life questions?"

"That's it in a nutshell."

"Gee, thanks. That makes me feel great."

Meredith reached out and patted JL's hand. "I didn't tell you that to hurt your feelings. I told you so you'd know Austin has people around him who care about him."

"What I don't get is why. Kevin said James Cullen chose Austin based on a tingly feeling he had. Can you see why that is hard for me to grasp? I see black and white. There's very little gray in my life. You don't invest time, energy, and money in another person because of a tingly feeling, or because you hope one day they'll come to work for you."

Meredith returned her hand to the steering wheel and put on her blinker to turn left. "Let me see if I can help you understand. Elliott grew up as an only child. When he was young, his mother ran off with another man and died in a car accident. The week before she left home, he had disobeyed her and gotten into trouble. He believed his bad behavior caused her to leave and that she no longer loved him. Crazy, I know, but kids can grow up with a set of beliefs often based on lies. It messes them up.

"Elliott didn't think he was worthy of love after that. He had inappropriate relationships that were doomed from the beginning. Every time one failed, it confirmed his belief that he wasn't worth loving."

"A self-fulfilling prophesy," JL said.

"Exactly," Meredith said. "It took a while to get him straightened out, but Kevin, David, and I walked over broken glass to help him.

"The thing about Elliott is that he truly loves people, and he enjoys having a circle of friends and family to care for. Most of the people in his circle don't have other family. You and Austin do, so you bring unique characteristics with you. You understand the give and take that comes from an emotionally healthy family.

"I know you lost your mother, and that has impacted your life and your brothers', but Austin got a hundred percent from you. He wouldn't have gotten a hundred percent from his mother. He would have had to share her with his dad, his brothers, and you, the only girl in the family."

"So you think he got a better deal with me than he would have had with Mom?" JL wasn't sure she wanted to hear this.

"I didn't say that. He got a different deal. That's all. Elliott got a different deal because he was raised by a troubled man, but he had a grandfather who meant the world to him."

The conversation died, and they rode in silence for a few moments. Then Meredith said, "Earlier tonight, you didn't back down from Elliott. You challenged him. I can get away with that, but nobody else can, except you. That told me a lot about your character."

"Are you talking about the discussion on taking risks and hurting others?"

"I saw the way he was looking at you in the mirror. He was pushing to see what you'd say and how far you'd go. I don't think I've ever seen him do that before."

"It gives me no satisfaction to be the first."

"Oh, I doubt you are. You're just the first I've seen." Meredith drove up to the gate, and it opened automatically.

"Do you have a sensor on your car?"

"Elliott and I have sensors on our cars. All other vehicles have remotes." Meredith drove down the lane and pulled the car to a stop in front of the cottage. "I'm sure you noticed how quickly Kevin capitulated at the restaurant. One of these days, he'll tell Elliott he's had enough. I've told Elliott that, but he continues to push Kevin. I don't know what he expects to happen, but I worry about it. They're so close, and so much alike. It's scary."

JL opened the door. "Thanks for the lift. Kevin and I are going horseback riding tomorrow. I want to have a good look at the property's nooks and crannies you can't see while riding in a car."

"Is this for pleasure or business?"

"It's hard for me to separate one from the other. I guess the ride will be both."

"Kenzie told me about a possible connection to your case in New York. If the cartel is using the winery property to make or distribute illegal drugs, I want them shut down with as little publicity as possible. But, and I'm serious about this, I don't want you to put your life or Austin's life in jeopardy. Got it?"

"Got it. Thanks for the ride," JL said.

"Hey, get some sleep. Those dark circles will look worse in the morning if you stay up all night."

"Is there a reason you think I will?"

"I've known Kevin for fifteen years, and I've never seen him look at a woman the way he looks at you. Please don't break his heart."

Obviously, Kenzie hadn't told Meredith about the divorce. JL came within a breath of telling the woman about it, but she couldn't. Not until she told Austin. The more people who knew, the bigger the chance he would learn the truth before she was ready to tell him. But she had to tell Meredith something.

"Kevin's heart isn't mine to break. Good night." JL closed the car door, walked up the steps, sat in a rocker, and watched Meredith's taillights disappear down the lane.

Your heart isn't mine, Kevin. This is only a weekend fling.

7

THE ROAR OF a downshifting sports car woke JL from a deep, dreamless sleep. Her eyes popped open as the taillights faded behind the side of the house. The garage door opened on well-lubricated rollers, without rattles or creaks. Streams of light poured out onto the driveway then went dark when the garage door closed. Kevin was home.

She sat straight in the rocker on the wrap around porch, rubbing her gritty eyes. She sniffed the sweet, pungent zing of ozone in the air. It was going to rain and soon. The water would wash away any remaining fibers and tracks leading to and from the crime scene.

Landscaping lights dotted the path from the garage to the front walk and backlit Kevin's silhouette as he jogged to the porch, jingling his keys. "I didn't think you'd still be awake."

He sounded relieved. Good. She didn't want to look like an idiot for waiting in the dark for him. She pulled to her feet, yawning. "What time is it?" He wrapped her in an embrace, and his arms held urgent tension. Or was that hers?

"One o'clock." He gave her a teasing kiss on the mouth, then they settled into a slower, softer one. "For the last few hours, all I've thought about was kissing you again."

That was what she wanted, too. She could have stood there for the rest of the night in his arms with his lips against hers, the sweet taste of whisky on his breath, and his hands stroking her back, but his erotically swirling tongue was igniting sparks of desire so intense she wanted to drag him down to the yoga mat they'd used before their run. She cupped the side of his face and stroked his slightly bristled cheek with her fingertips. "I didn't want to miss you. I was afraid you'd be late and decide to go on to bed without waking me."

"I'm going to bed, but not without you."

She nibbled on the corner of his mouth, lightly tugging on his lower lip. "Did Elliott warn you away from me?"

Kevin's hands moved down her sides, stopping at her hips, and the full length of his erection pressed against her. He gripped the back of her thigh, coaxing her even closer, his hand cupping her ass, and she ground her hips along the hard length of him. The thunder of her heart bellowed in her ears, and she couldn't deny what his nearness did to her. Whatever this was, it had the potential of being much more than vacation sex.

"We both sidestepped the question," Kevin said.

"You got lucky, then. Meredith didn't sidestep." JL gazed up at him. "She told me not to stay up all night, and not to break your heart."

He flinched slightly, his lips compressed. "Ouch. She can be brutally honest."

Streaks of lightning, like gnarled veins, temporarily lit the sky, but they didn't frighten or distract JL. Storms had never bothered her, except one night many years ago. "Meredith loves you. That was clear. I even considered telling her about the divorce, but I couldn't trust that she wouldn't tell Elliott. That would make four people in Napa who learned the truth before Austin. That would piss him off even more."

"Let's go to bed. You smell so good I want to eat you."

"You're smelling the harvest or the ozone."

His chuckle rumbled through his chest and vibrated against her face. "I know the smell of rain and the smell of grapes. Your scent is driving me mad now. Come to bed and let me make love to you."

"Are you pitching more lines at me, Mr. Allen?"

His fingers brushed her lips, light as the touch of a raindrop in a gentle storm. "You told me you are a sure thing and I don't need to ply you with clever lines."

"Clever, huh?" She trembled slightly. Yes, she was a sure thing, but was that all she was to him? Was that all he was to her? "Did I really say that?"

"You're recently divorced, three thousand miles from home, no responsibilities, and you have opportunity. Sounds like vacation sex to me," he said.

It might have started out that way, but that wasn't how it was going down. At least for her. "I've never had vacation sex before. If that's what this is, I'm not complaining."

He held the door for her. "I want to strip you naked, lick every inch of you, and make love until the sun comes up…and then start all over again."

She stepped into the foyer. "Sounds like you have it all planned out. Is there room for any spontaneity?"

Kevin closed the door and locked it. "How about a quickie up against the wall between basketball games, or a roll in the orchard during our trail ride? I'm open to possibilities."

She experienced some light-headedness, and realized she had been holding her breath in anticipation of what was to come. She breathed in and out slowly and changed the subject. "Did Elliott really need to see you tonight, or was he trying to keep us apart?" She reached for Kevin's hand, and this time she led him through the house toward the staircase.

"Hard to tell. He wasn't feeling well. He went to the bathroom several times. We talked about the vineyards, and a couple of horses he's interested in buying. He usually talks to David about acquiring new stallions. I think he had a lot on his mind and didn't want to worry Meredith with it."

Kevin and JL climbed the steps arm in arm. "So he worried you instead?"

"Until a couple of months ago, I was with him 24/7 for almost two decades."

"That didn't give you much time for a life of your own."

"I haven't had much time of my own, that's for sure, but traveling around the world first class, meeting royalty, actors, musicians, and staying in the fanciest hotels, has been worth the sacrifice. To be honest, though, I didn't think I was sacrificing anything until I came out here to work on the new winery."

"What made the difference?"

"I didn't have to schedule my day around him."

"If tonight was any indication of the demands he's put on you, I don't know how you ever had time for an evening out."

Kevin laughed and pulled her closer to him. "I always had to make sure he was settled for the night before I scheduled time for me."

"Well, I'm convinced tonight he tried to ruin your evening on purpose."

They walked down the hall, passing several closed doors, until Kevin pointed to a room at the end. "For a long time I thought Elliott was grooming me to take over the operation, but then he appointed David to the president's position."

JL found a stained-glass table lamp and switched it on. The large bedroom was stunningly masculine, and furnished with oak furniture and oriental rugs. The walls were a yellowy olive green, a more contemporary color than a dark hunter she had seen other men use. The honey-colored furniture brought the outside into the room, making it warm, comfortable, and elegant.

She kicked away her shoes, peeled off her jacket, and tossed it onto a chair, reining in the desire that had built up until she was already on the verge of exploding. "Maybe David will go back to writing and the job will be yours."

Kevin removed his loafers and set them side by side at the foot of the bed. Then, using an app on his iPhone, he turned on R&B music that played softly in the background. "My prediction is that David will stay in the job until James Cullen is ready to take over."

She placed her holstered gun on the dresser near the bed. "He's Elliott's son. That makes sense, but has Elliott ever indicated he wouldn't have a place for you?"

Kevin stripped off his shirt and dropped it on the bench at the end of the bed, looking hungrily at her. "No, but there's no other position for me in the corporation." He pulled her into his arms and kissed her neck, finding his way slowly to her lips and sweeping his tongue against hers, stroking in an irresistible and erotic rhythm. "I don't want to talk about Elliott or the job." He tugged her sweater over her head and flung it on the bench with his shirt.

She ran her hands over his abs and muscular chest, and the muscles twitched and flexed as her slow, curious fingers danced over his perfect, almond-shaped nipples. "I don't have any contraception."

His smoldering eyes looked deep into hers, and her nipples hardened. He slid her cami straps down her shoulders until they anchored at her elbows. "I'll protect you," he whispered, pushing the silky garment down over her breasts.

The hardened tips grazed his bare chest, and she savored the feel of his skin brushing against hers. A groan vibrated his chest while he delved deep in her mouth, their tongues tangling sensually. She slipped her arms out of the straps and gripped his hair, combing through the strands while she clung desperately to him.

Thunder rumbled through the sky, and strobes of lightning brightened the dim room. The desire pulsing through her was too potent, and she blocked out the sounds of the storm, the R&B music, and the creaks in the old house.

His mouth covered a nipple, and he rolled it between his teeth, sucking until she shivered. His hands tightened on her undulating hips. She unzipped his pants, and he reached for hers, pushing her jeans and panties down over her hips until she shimmied out of them.

He opened a foil package and rolled on a condom before picking her up. She wrapped her legs around him, and with an urgent thrust, he entered her. She cried out at the overwhelming sensation. Here was the man who could give her back her lost youth. The man who could make her feel young and loved. She snuggled in his arms, and her heart was profoundly touched.

"My God, JL. What are you doing?"

Her eyes shot open to see Austin standing in the doorway.

Kevin looked over his shoulder. *"God dammit, Austin. Get out and close the door.* We'll meet you downstairs in a minute."

JL dropped to the floor and stood on wobbly legs, grabbing the throw at the end of the bed. How was she going to explain this? "It's not what it looks like," she said.

"I can't believe you'd cheat on Ryan. *How could you?"*

"I'm not cheating on Ryan."

"Well, you could've fooled me. Screwing another man is cheating in the book I was raised with." Austin turned away from them and rammed his fist into the wall, punching a hole in the drywall. Then he ran out of the room. The crumbling, crunching sound of a wrecking ball followed his clomping down the stairs.

JL snatched up her clothes and dressed on the run. "Austin, wait. Wait, please. Let me explain."

She reached the top of the steps as the front door slammed. *"Austin."* She tore down the stairs, jumping over portions of the railing he had ripped from the wall.

Kevin raced past her toward the door, flung it open, and ran out into the rain.

JL ran after both men, zipping her jeans. She reached the porch in time to see Kevin grab the passenger side door handle, but Austin had locked it. She ran to the driver's door, shoeless in the downpour. "Austin. Get out of the truck and come inside. We have to talk about this."

"There's nothing to say. Go home." He put the truck into gear. "Let go of the door, Kevin. I'll have a friend return the truck tomorrow. I quit. I thought there was a friend code, that you didn't date sisters. Oh, my bad. A code that you didn't screw your friend's sister."

"You don't know the whole story, Austin." She wiped rain off her face with both hands and pushed back her dripping hair. "Get out of the truck and let's talk." She could shout out that she was divorced, but she knew he wouldn't be able to move past the betrayal to see that she and Kevin had done nothing wrong. *"Please."*

"There's nothing to talk about," he said. Lightning split the night sky and lit up the yard. The pained expression on his face severed her heart in two. "*Go home.*" His tires spun as he squealed away from the house.

She ran after the truck, screaming his name. Her tears, steaming from the heat of fear radiating off her body, mingled with the rain. When the taillights disappeared, she dropped to her knees, crying. Austin's pain ripped out her insides, leaving her feeling raw and abandoned. In a flash, JL was once again a teenager reliving her mother's death—a death she believed was all her fault.

Kevin pulled her to her feet. "Let's get dry and go after him."

She turned and buried her face in Kevin's shoulder. "He's gone. He won't come back. They never come back."

"We need to find him. He cut his hand when he punched the wall. I don't think it's serious, but there was a little bit of blood on the wall."

"Blood? Oh God." She clutched Kevin's shirt. Despair speared through her, leaving her shaking and sick to her stomach.

"You have to be in control by the time we find him. He won't respond to you if you're not. Come on. Let's go."

Kevin was right. She had to do what she did so well—manage a crisis to a favorable outcome. She spooled her fear and shut down her emotions.

They hurried back to the porch, dripping wet, and stood there long enough to shake off the worst of the water.

"College coaches are coming to see him play today. If he cut his hand, he'll need stitches and might miss the next game. If I had set out to ruin his life, I couldn't have come up with a better plan."

"We'll fix it. First, though, we have to find him. Go change. We'll leave in five minutes."

Kevin's compulsive need to schedule amid the chaos comforted her. She didn't have to think of what to do next. He already had.

She left wet clothes on the floor in the bathroom and dressed in a clean pair of jeans and a sweatshirt.

Kevin knocked on her open door. "Are you ready?"

"Almost." She grabbed a pair of socks to wear with the cowboy boots she found in the closet, and sat down to put them on.

"Call Ryan and ask him to contact Austin. Maybe he can talk some sense into him."

She shoved her foot into a boot and adjusted her pants leg. "I still have Austin's phone. I forgot to give it to him at the restaurant."

"It would really help if Ryan could tell him about the divorce."

She pulled the boot onto her other foot. "No it wouldn't. Austin would punch a hole in another wall. At this point, he wouldn't care that we're consenting, unmarried adults."

"He's old enough to understand life isn't always perfect. He's a good kid. I think you're underestimating him. He'll get over it."

"You don't know him, Kevin."

"I think I do." He held her gun in his hand. "Do you want this?"

She stood and looped the holster through her belt. "Let's go to the dorm."

"Okay, but I'll go in and explain this is my fault."

"Yeah, right. He won't believe that."

"How about asking Kenzie to talk to him?" Kevin said.

JL grabbed her shield and cash out of her purse and forced them into her jeans' tight rear pockets. "I'm not waking her up to deal with this." She reached for a cowboy hat from the closet and adjusted it to fit snugly on her damp head. "How did Austin get inside the house? I saw you lock the door."

"I gave him a key this summer when I went to Kentucky for a couple of weeks. I never asked for it back. But what I don't get is why he was here at one-thirty in the morning."

JL hit the light switch, turning off the one light she had turned on, and they left the room. "He probably wanted to have a guy talk with you about Betsy. At this hour, my best guess is that they had sex without protection."

"He's too responsible. He wouldn't do that."

She headed toward the front door, but Kevin pointed in the direction of the kitchen. "Let's go out the laundry room. We'll take the Land Rover."

She followed him out into the garage. "I'm one of the most

responsible people I know, and look at the mess I made."

"You didn't make it. Ryan did."

"I can't blame this one on him. My decision has caused this problem."

"We'll get it worked out," Kevin said. "As soon as Austin knows the truth, his anger will mellow. If we craft it right, he'll turn his anger on the one person who deserves it, and that's not you."

"I hope you're right, but my son has a stubborn streak that has gotten him into trouble before. Look at the day he's had. My heart breaks for him." She headed toward the car, swiping at the tears streaking her face once again.

"You mean your brother?"

She grabbed the door handle and took a deep breath. "No, I mean my son."

8

JL AND KEVIN sped off the winery property heading for the city limits, searching for Austin. The rain hadn't abated, and the knots in JL's stomach tightened with worry. Austin was driving angry in bad weather.

Kevin reached over and laced his warm fingers with hers. "Back there...what you said...about Austin. Is he really your son?"

She sighed deeply, glancing out the window into the dark, rainy night. Never in her dreams had she believed she would ever tell anyone the truth. It wasn't her reputation she cared about. Every action she had taken over the past seventeen years had been to protect her son from the shame of her indiscretion.

"I was at summer dance camp the year between my sophomore and junior years in high school, and met a guy who was attending basketball camp at an adjoining campsite. We had sex the night before I was to leave. We made plans to see each other again, maybe going to the same college. Stupid stuff, but it was an attempt to believe that what we had done meant something, when in fact it didn't.

"Mom had all these plans for her only daughter to follow her on Broadway. When I discovered I was pregnant, abortion was out of the question. Mom hatched a plot to pretend the baby was hers. She and Pops talked to their lawyer, and they created a believable story that she was having a menopause baby. Since Mom was an excellent actor, everyone bought into it. She took time off from the theater, and I went to a private school in upstate New York for unwed mothers. We told everyone it was a performing arts school. When I went into labor, they came up to 'see a production at my school,' and took Austin home with them.

"Mom did tell her priest because she felt so guilty for lying. I was supposed to stay at the school for the entire term, but when she had the stroke, I came home. By the time she died, no one questioned the story. I stepped in and took care of my own child. All our friends and neighbors thought I was wonderful for making a sacrifice and giving up on my dreams. They thought I was a saint, but I was only atoning for bad judgment and contributing to my mom's death."

"Your mother had a stroke. It wasn't your fault."

"Try telling that to a seventeen-year-old unwed mother."

"What about her dream for you, to follow her on Broadway?"

That question was a sledgehammer to her heart. JL had failed her mother after all she had done to protect her. "The truth is I loved to sing and dance, but as a child all I really wanted to be was a cop like Pops and Gramps. Dancers," she said reflectively, "work hard, and are devoted to their craft, but cops put their lives on the line, and that's where I wanted to put mine."

"It sounds like you swallowed the Kool-Aid," Kevin said.

She understood the reference to the Jim Jones/Guyana tragedy only because she had recently heard a news report about the 1978 incident. "That sounds more altruistic than saying I wanted the car, a utility belt like Batman, and the authority to lock up bad guys."

"Oh, so that's the reason, huh?" he asked.

She rubbed the back of her neck. Kevin was digging to get to the heart of it, and he wasn't going to let her off the hook. She would spill her guts to him, not because he asked, or because her hands tingled when she was near him, but because of a deeper connection, a bond she couldn't explain or resist.

"Honestly, I wanted to be in the room with the cigar smoke and ball games, not in the kitchen trading recipes or breaking in a new pair of pointe shoes. I wanted to be where the action was. For a long time, I lived between two worlds, not knowing for sure where I belonged. Mom was pushing, and I put on the brakes."

"Did you think if you got pregnant you wouldn't have to be a dancer but you could still be a cop?"

"Whoa. Wait a minute. That's out of left field. I didn't intentionally get pregnant."

Kevin shrugged. "I didn't say you did. I was only asking a question." He pushed her hand aside, and his strong fingers massaged her neck from the shoulder to the base of her skull. "Do your brothers know the truth about Austin?"

"It was too much of a risk. My parents and I made a pact to never tell anyone."

"How about Ryan? Did you ever tell him?"

"No. I didn't trust him. I thought he would get drunk and tell Austin. I couldn't live with that fear."

"Why'd you tell me now?"

She held her silence for a moment, wondering the same thing. "It slipped out."

"Freud might have a different opinion of that."

"What? That I subconsciously wanted you to know? I live with the illusion of control, then in a rare moment I abandon the pretense that I am the master of my own fate and spill the one thing that can destroy me? That doesn't make much sense."

"The secret is your Achilles' heel, isn't it?"

"Maybe."

Kevin quit massaging her neck and pulled out of the lane slightly to see whether he could pass a slow-moving vehicle. Low visibility held him back. "I'm not judging you. Your parents did what they thought was right. Who knows if they were? Would you and Austin have been stigmatized in your close-knit community?"

"A friend of mine got pregnant the year before I did. She gave the baby up for adoption. All these years later, you can still see the sadness in her eyes. It would still be in mine, too. If I'd raised Austin as my own, instead of as my brother, he would have had a difficult time with the stigma. Growing up is hard enough without the added pressure of your parents' mistakes."

The car in front turned off the road, and Kevin sped up.

"If your mother got pregnant by a man other than your father, would you want to know?" she asked.

"No," Kevin said.

"Not even now? As an adult?"

"Not even now. And Austin is better off not knowing the truth."

She was glad Kevin agreed with her. If her mother had lived, they would have talked about Austin's father, but after she died, JL had held on to the secret, until now. Sharing it with Kevin took away the loneliness of living a lie. Once she had tried to talk to Pops about Austin's biological father, but he had shut down the conversation, telling her she dishonored her mother by discussing it. The pain of that discussion was still a knife twisting slowly in her gut.

"Who's Austin's father? Have you kept up with him?"

She had kept up with him, and she had bitten her tongue a thousand times over the years when her brothers criticized a shot he made or a foul that sent him to the bench, not knowing he was Austin's bio-dad. Even as supportive as Kevin was being, he didn't need to know the man's identity. "He's a power forward in the NBA, but I'm not going to tell you his name."

"You all but did. There are thirty teams, maybe fifty power forwards. It wouldn't take much effort to figure out his identity. When Austin starts playing on the college level, sportscasters will comment on his playing style, and other players he resembles. Comparisons will be made."

"I can't deal with that right now, and if we don't get him to the doctor, he might not have a career in basketball."

Kevin turned into the dorm parking lot and drove up and down the rows looking for the truck. "He's not here—at least, the truck's not."

She leaned her head against the headrest, closed her eyes, and pulled her bottom lip between her teeth, thinking, trying to get into his head. What would he do? Where would he go? "Would he have gone to Betsy's this late at night?"

"He could have gone anywhere. He might be sitting at a burger joint. The kid can eat anytime, anywhere. Let's wait here. Rest if you can. I'll stay awake."

"Park in the shadows over there." JL pointed toward a corner of the lot. "I don't want him to drive in and see us. We need to wait until he gets out of the truck before we approach him."

Kevin pulled into the parking space she suggested and put the car in park. JL unbuckled her seat belt and turned toward him. "Kenzie said you're not very good at keeping secrets."

That made him laugh out loud. "She said that?"

"What she actually said was that David called you a wee gossip."

Kevin put his elbow on the window panel and scratched the short beard stubble that had grown since his morning shave. "I got the reputation years ago, but I never shared information outside the family. I don't share anything now, but David perpetuates the myth."

"Why?"

"You'll have to ask him."

She took off her hat and ran her fingers through her still-damp hair, then turned the vent so the warm air hit her head. "David's not here. I'd like to know what you think. Besides, it takes my mind off why we're sitting in a high school dorm parking lot at two o'clock in the morning."

"David and I are close in age, but his experiences in Afghanistan aged him. He has expectations, and many times I don't meet them. We're stuck in a perpetual battle, with Elliott and Meredith in the middle. Since he and Kenzie got married it's not as bad as it used to be, but the tension's still there."

"David has nothing to do with this, and neither does Elliott's family, so I hope you'll keep this secret. No one else needs to know," she said.

He stared at her, eyes fixed wide and unblinking above a small, odd smile. "You know, maybe this blowup has created an opportunity for you to come clean about the divorce and his birth. Think about it."

She couldn't help but think about it, and she kept circling back to her mother. Keeping Austin's bio-parents a secret had been her idea, and JL couldn't undo her mother's planning and out her as a liar.

The inside of the Land Rover warmed, and she curled into her seat. Kevin's scent was on her skin, and she breathed him in. Eyes closed, she smiled. "I'm sorry we were interrupted."

He leaned over and kissed her. "I am, too. Try to rest. I'll wake you as soon as Austin drives in."

The quiet jazz playing on the radio lulled her to sleep.

A phone rang, jolting JL awake. She turned and twisted, staring up at the sky to see that it had just begun to lighten with the first shades of dawn.

"It's security," Kevin said, pushing the send button on the steering wheel. "Kevin Allen."

"This is Joe in security. We found the truck Austin O'Grady has been driving in the parking lot at the Welcome Center. He left his monitor on the seat. The truck has a flat left front tire, and the rim is bent. Looks like he ran over something. We're towing it to the garage for repairs."

Kevin put the car in gear and drove out of the parking lot. "Did he take a golf cart?"

"That's a negative, sir. All carts are in their charging stations."

JL put on her seat belt and patted her cheeks to wake up.

"Austin's been missing since one-thirty. I need you to check all the video feeds beginning at that time, along with the gate reports. Who came in and out and at what time?"

"The gate hasn't opened or closed since you left at one-forty-six."

"Then he's probably still on the property. We'll find him." Kevin pushed down on the accelerator, and the Land Rover quickly exceeded the speed limit. "We'll be there in twenty minutes."

"I'm calling Ms. Montgomery with a status report."

"Does she already know?"

"No, sir. Protocol says to call you first, then her."

"I'll call her."

"No, sir. I will." The guard disconnected the call.

Kevin scrolled through his contacts and hit Meredith's number.

"How much are you going to tell her?" JL asked.

"Only as much as I have to. The rest will have to wait." The call to Meredith went straight to voice mail. "I'll try again in a minute."

Kevin spun into a turn and sped down a two-lane road. The long stretch of road gave way to the rolling hills of the vineyards. He took the hills too fast, but she would have gone faster. The winding road threatened disaster when they headed into a monstrous curve with the rising sun in their eyes. Her stomach bottomed out. She gripped the door and the console and held on. The gray, thick clouds had rolled out, and Saturday morning was dawning with blue skies. An omen, she hoped.

Kevin hit the brakes and slowed the vehicle. As soon as he cleared the curve, he picked up speed again. His phone rang, and he hit the accept button on the steering wheel.

"Kevin, what happened to Austin?" Meredith asked.

"It's a long story. JL and I have been looking for him since one thirty. We're on our way to the security office now."

"I'll get dressed and meet you there."

Kevin turned into the drive leading to the back gate of the winery.

"I have to call Pops. He needs to know what's happened."

Kevin stopped and waited for the gate to open. "If he wants to come out, the plane is picking up David and the kids in Kentucky, and Charlotte and her crew in Virginia. The plane can go to New York, too."

She dialed Pops' number. "We have a situation here. Austin has disappeared."

There was a steel hard hiss in his voice when he asked, "How long ago?"

"Almost five hours."

"Is this related to your investigation?"

She hadn't made that leap, but now that her father had, she

couldn't rule it out. A sudden blast of fear churned in her gut. "I don't think so, but it's possible."

"I don't know what time I can get a flight, but I'll come as soon as I can."

"The Frasers have a plane in Kentucky bringing people out for the weekend. They can pick you up, too."

Kevin tapped her arm. "Tell him you'll call him back with details."

"I'll have to call you back, Pops."

She disconnected the call and listened in on Kevin's call.

"What time can you be at Teterboro Airport?"

"Two thirty eastern? How many passengers are we picking up?"

Kevin glanced at her and she said, "Just Pops."

"If your brothers want to come, there's room," Kevin said.

"I'll find out." She called her dad back. Pops put her on hold while he called her brothers. He returned to the call and told her they were all coming. "Connor, Jeffrey, Shane, Patrick, and Pops are coming. I hope there's room on the plane."

Kevin passed along the final count to the pilot and ended the call before parking in the lot at the security office. Meredith and Elliott were walking into the building.

JL stepped into the winery's command center. A dozen monitors flashed images of the buildings and vineyards. Two in the center showed live shots of the Wine Cave. The others were showing footage of the vineyards with a time stamp scrolling across the bottom of the screen.

"We found him running into the wine cave at one forty-five. We haven't seen him come out. We've got men searching, but so far they haven't found him."

JL stood in front of one of the monitors showing the inside of the cave. There were tables and chairs, a dance floor, and a bar along one side. "Can he get alcohol in there?" she asked. "I know it's a wine cave, but could he have opened a bottle or two, hid behind those barrels, gotten drunk, and passed out?"

"He could have gotten into the wine. He could have gotten

drunk and passed out, but he couldn't hide in there," Meredith said. "I should know. I tried several times as a teenager."

"What about the back part that you don't use?"

"Nobody goes back there," one of the guards said.

"You mean nobody goes back there, or nobody is supposed to go back there?" JL asked. "That's two different things." She glanced from one guard to the other. "That's what I thought." She headed for the door.

"Where're you going?" Kevin asked.

"To the cave. I'll need the keys to the doors."

"JL, wait," Elliott said.

She turned and glared at him. This smelled all too familiar, and she didn't intend to let anyone stand in the way of finding Austin.

"It will take a coordinated effort to search the maze of tunnels. No one has been in there for decades, possibly a century. We'll need a structural engineer and his team to lead the way. I won't allow ye to run in there unprepared. David will be here in a matter of hours, but he can start mapping a plan en route. I need ye to be patient. We'll find Austin."

"Great," she said. "You put your team together, but I'm going in now to take a look."

Elliott took a step forward and glanced down his nose at her. "No, lass, ye're not."

She took a step forward and glanced up, pointing her chin. "Dr. Fraser, I appreciate your concern, but this is a police matter—"

"—and ye have no jurisdiction," Elliott interrupted. "Ye reminded me of that yesterday."

JL whipped out her phone and flashed Detective Castellano's contact information. "I don't, but he does." She punched his phone number. When he answered, she said, "Detective, this is JL O'Grady. Austin is missing, and I believe he's in danger. He was last seen running into the Montgomery Winery's Wine Cave. Meet me there ASAP." She swiped the face of her phone, disconnecting the call. "Are we done here?"

She turned on her heel and headed toward the door. Men like

Elliott Fraser, wealthy men used to control, were nuisances. Fraser needed to stay out of her way. She didn't need his help or his interference, and once he understood his role and hers, they would get along famously. She hurried out of the security office, shaking.

Kevin ran after her. "What's going on with you?"

"I'm a cop, and there's a missing person who happens to be Austin. There's also a murder investigation going on. I don't know if they're connected, but I know it's a possibility. The best outcome for Austin right now is that he's lost. The worst…well…I can't go there right now."

"Come on. I'll take you over there."

She buckled herself in the passenger's seat and checked the rounds in her gun. Then she sent a text to Pops telling him what she knew so far.

He sent her a return message. *Call Napa detectives. You'll need local support. Be there soon.*

She pocketed her phone and said, "Tell me as much as you know about the cave and how each part is used."

He turned down another lane, taking the turn too fast and almost sideswiping the white plank fence. Within a few yards, he was back on the pavement, handling the transition from grass to asphalt with aplomb. She didn't trust many civilians behind the wheel, but she trusted Kevin.

"There are three parts to the cave system. The front part is where events are scheduled. We refer to that area as the Wine Cave. Behind the Wine Cave is the storage area where we store wine barrels for aging and crates of bottles ready for shipping. Over the past hundred years, the Montgomery family has used only a small portion of the cave system. It might go on for miles. No one knows."

"No spelunkers in the family? Not even David?"

"None, and David's claustrophobic. He can barely tolerate attending dinners there."

"Well, he won't be much help."

"You'll be surprised at what David can accomplish."

"We'll see," she said. "Tell me the rest."

"There's a thick oak door between the section where events are held and the storage area. A box with a combination code holds the key to the door. Meredith gave Austin the code because he goes back there on errands for her. Barrels line the walls for about fifty yards. Then there's another locked door. No one goes past the second door."

"Where's the key?"

"I have a key on my key chain."

"Why carry the key when no one needs it?"

"I inherited the keychain, but have never weeded the keys."

"When you gave Austin a key to the house, did you give him your key chain or a single key?"

"I gave him the key chain and told him to make a copy of the house key."

"If he forgot which one he was supposed to copy, he might have made copies of all the keys, which would have included the key to the second door."

"That's possible."

And, she was afraid, probable. What didn't make sense was why Austin would have done something so dangerous. It didn't fit his profile. "I can see Austin going to the cave to get ice for his hand and wine to drink away his anger, but I don't see him hiding in an unsafe area. If all the guards do is a routine cursory search, he could hide from them, but he couldn't hide from a thorough search of the premises."

"What are you getting at?"

"He went back there for a reason that had nothing to do with hiding or running away."

"Like what?"

"I don't know yet."

Kevin stopped in front of the cave entrance she had seen on the monitor. She jumped out and headed for the door, but turned and looked up for the camera, spotted it, and moved on.

"We have maps of the caves, but I've never looked at them."

"Good to know."

Another vehicle parked alongside Kevin's Land Rover. Elliott, Meredith, and two security guards climbed out and followed them into the cave. They walked through the front part of the cave until they reached the first oak door. One of the guards jumped ahead and used his key to unlock the door. He flipped on a light switch. Wine barrels lined the walls of a corridor that extended half the length of a football field.

They walked in tense silence until they reached another heavy oak door with black hinges.

"I don't think Austin would have gone beyond this door," Meredith said. "And where would he have gotten a key?"

"From me," Kevin said.

"I don't think he would have gone any farther, either. Not voluntarily," JL said.

The guard fumbled through his key chain, found the one he was looking for, and unlocked the second door. The door creaked open, and a strong, dank, earthy smell assaulted JL's nose. Drawing her gun, she carefully stepped over the threshold into chilling, impenetrable blackness. It couldn't be any darker if her eyeballs had been removed from her head.

She held out her arms, blocking those behind her. "Don't anyone move. I don't want the ground disturbed." She made a give-me gesture, wiggling her fingers. "I need a flashlight."

The guard gave her the light hanging from his belt.

The temperature dropped from one side of the door to the other by a good ten degrees. Her skin crawled, as if she had walked into a nest of spiders. She flashed the light along the high limestone walls that curved smoothly to the ground. The ceiling arched maybe twenty-five feet up to giant rock formations and bat roosts. Small, loose stones littered the floor. Her shadow dissolved into the surrounding darkness. Ahead, there was the sound of water dripping into water, but no echoing footsteps.

Multiple footprints had kicked pebbles aside and disturbed layers of dust. She squatted and directed the beam of light toward the floor. One set of prints was larger than the others. If she measured, she was sure the large, funky-looking treads would match Austin's sneakers. She walked farther into the cave, thirty feet or more, following the footsteps. A shiny object on the cave floor reflected light. She stooped and picked up a piece of fabric.

"JL, come back." Kevin's voice echoed in the cold darkness.

Emotion urged her forward, training held her back.

Biting down on her fear, not for herself, but for Austin, she turned and trudged out of the cave. Heart-wrenching despair swamped her heart, as much now as it had the day her parents carried her newborn away.

I'm not abandoning you, Austin. I'll come back. I promise.

She holstered her gun before anyone noticed how badly she was shaking. If Austin was going to survive, she had to muster every bit of self-control she possessed. And she wasn't sure if even that would be enough.

"Austin's in there. I followed his size fifteen footprints for thirty feet or more until I found this." She held up a ripped piece of fabric. "This was torn from his Nike running jacket."

Kevin examined the swatch closely. "How do you know it's his?"

She gripped the piece in her hand. "I bought him a reflective weather running jacket when I saw him in Kansas a few months ago. Call it a hunch. Call it my sixth sense, but I know he ripped this piece to leave me a clue. And it's not just any piece." She flashed the light on the jagged-edged fabric. "See. It's a reflective piece. He wanted to be sure I saw it."

She glanced back inside the cave. "There are people in there. I'm not a tracker. I can't read signs, but I can tell the difference in footprints. I saw three different sets. One large set and two sets about a third the size. The two smaller sets, both deeply embedded in the dirt, belonged to either overweight people or two people carrying heavy loads. Something is going on in there, and they've taken Austin. I don't know why, and I don't know where they are, but I'll find them."

9

JL, Kevin, Elliott, and Meredith returned to the Wine Cave entrance to find Hollinger directing two cops who were setting up barriers a few yards away. A police utility truck drove into the parking lot. JL's call to Castellano had resulted in a SWAT callout.

Four members of the team jumped out of the back of the truck, decked out in fatigues and Kevlar body armor. The ominous semiautomatic weapons glared in stark contrast to the brilliantly colored vineyards. Another truck arrived and disgorged four cops who joined the others.

JL accepted that there needed to be an organized, well-equipped force to follow Austin and his abductors, but the possibility of an engagement inside the cave was terrifying. Bullets could easily ricochet and kill Austin, especially if the perps tried to use him as a shield.

Hollinger advanced toward them, his lips compressed.

"I can't deal with his attitude right now," she said to Kevin. "If he wants any cooperation from me, he better be on his best behavior. If that's possible."

She and Hollinger glared at each other in bristling silence for a moment before he stepped closer. "Detective O'Grady, can I have a minute?" He wore no jacket or tie beneath his Kevlar. "Detective Castellano gave me your message. What makes you believe your brother's in there?"

She steeled herself to act professionally toward him, and handed over the swatch of reflective material. "Security has a video of him entering the cave at one-forty-five. There's no video of him leaving. I found this piece of his Nike running jacket about thirty feet inside the old cave system."

Hollinger fingered the swatch. "Sounds like he's run away."

She intensified her glare. This wasn't going well. "If you thought that, you wouldn't have brought SWAT with you."

He pulled a small plastic bag from his pocket and slipped the piece of fabric inside. "I read up on you, Detective, and familiarized myself with the Di Salvo drug cartel takedown. You believe we have a similar situation here, don't you?"

"Call it a hunch, but yes, I do."

"Look. I'm not as stupid as you think I am. I followed up on your comment about dealing with the Di Salvo family. My contact with DEA said there's been some chatter that a large buy is going down soon. It's possible the murder yesterday and your brother's disappearance are related." Hollinger glanced back toward the cave. "Tell me everything you know about the cave and any other evidence you have."

She wouldn't call it glowing acceptance, but at least fifty percent of Hollinger's hostility from the previous day had evaporated. She could work with fifty.

For the next several minutes, Meredith explained the layout of the cave and what history she knew, and then JL told Hollinger what she found in her short exploration.

"We need maps. Do you have any?" Hollinger asked.

"Old ones," Meredith said. "You can't rely on them, but I'll get them for you."

"I'll send a patrolman with you to carry them back."

The SWAT team marched toward the cave entrance, loaded down with supplies. The commanding officer said to Hollinger, "We need maps, if you can get them."

"We're going to get them now," Hollinger said. He then waved to one of the cops standing near the barriers and instructed him to go with Meredith.

"I want to go in with you," JL said.

"This is a SWAT operation," Hollinger said. "You know the rules. As soon as I have any information, I'll pass it along."

"Come on, JL," Kevin said, wrangling her toward the other side of the barriers. "There's nothing we can do right now but wait."

Elliott and Meredith drove away with the cops, leaving JL and Kevin behind. Waiting tried her patience, and she had never been one to sit on the sidelines. There had to be something she could do. While the police remained occupied at the cave, there were other angles to investigate. She just had to find those angles.

The cops huddled outside the entrance to the cave. She wanted to be part of the briefing, and it irritated her that she wasn't. Grumbling, however, would do no good. She knew the game. She had played it herself. Outsiders weren't invited in. "I hope they know what they might be up against."

"It's SWAT, not the Boy Scouts. These guys are trained," Kevin said.

"If the Di Salvos are involved, they might do what they did in New York and booby trap the cave. If that happens, we'll never get in."

"And they'll never get out," Kevin said.

"Exactly. And what does that mean for Austin?"

Kevin's jaw clenched and he turned to look at the cave entrance again. "Unless they're suicidal, why would they block their only egress?"

"In New York, they blocked the entrance as a distraction. We didn't know the cartel had already moved out. A remote set off the explosion. By the time the engineers dug through the blockage and we discovered the cartel wasn't there, they had set up business in a warehouse by the river. It took us weeks to find the new location."

"We know whoever took Austin is still in there," Kevin said.

"We don't have to worry about an explosion, then." An idea suddenly struck her. "If there is an explosion, my hunch tells me there's another entrance."

"If there is, Meredith doesn't know about it."

"We need to see the maps."

"I don't think you'll get a chance, unless Hollinger invites you into their huddle."

The rumbling of faint hunger in her stomach reminded her that Austin probably hadn't eaten since dinner. "Austin's got to be starving. He can't go longer than six to eight hours without eating. And his hand…" She stopped in mid-sentence.

Kevin squeezed her shoulder, sensing her fear. "We'll find him. His hand will be okay. He might need a stitch or two, but he'll be okay."

"How can you be so sure?"

"He's an athlete. He needs his hands. I doubt he put much force behind the punch. He wanted to make a statement, not injure himself."

She nodded, saying nothing, thinking hard and guessing even harder. "I hope you're right. Let's go talk to Meredith. In case we need a second entrance, it would save time if we already know the location."

They drove over to the Corporate Offices and found Meredith, Elliott, and the cop in a storage closet filled with furniture, file cabinets, paintings, and crates of whisky. In the corner sat a five-drawer, museum-style, flat file cabinet.

Meredith was thumbing through several clear archival envelopes. She pulled out two envelopes holding yellow maps creased with age. "These cave surveys were drawn in the late 1800s. There is no guarantee any of the passages are still open or even that they ever existed."

"Yes, ma'am. I'll tell Detective Hollinger. Is that all of them?"

"Yes, and please don't remove them from the envelopes. The paper is brittle and will crumble from handling them."

The cop headed toward the door, and JL itched to rip the maps from his hand. Unless Hollinger changed his mind, her position as a non-team member relegated her to the stands to watch and wait.

After the officer left, Elliott directed Meredith, JL, and Kevin into the conference room. On a large television screen mounted on the wall was the image of a ruggedly masculine man with dark, wavy hair and a three-day beard. JL recognized him immediately as the man in the picture in Kenzie's office.

So this was David McBain.

He seemed out of place in a swivel desk chair surrounded by a row of monitors. He should be climbing Mount Everest or skydiving from the fringes of space. A tight black T-shirt hugged biceps she wouldn't be able to wrap her hands around. Danger emanated from him like an angry black panther. If he and her brothers fought to prove who among them was the most alpha of the alpha males, David would win…barely, but he would scrape by. It would take a woman like Kenzie to tame a man like him, if it was even possible. More likely, it was a daily battle of wills.

A young woman rolled a cart loaded with pastries, bagels, coffee, fruit, and juice into the conference room. "That's fine, honey. Thanks. You can leave the cart here," Meredith said. "We'll serve ourselves. And please apologize to the staff for raiding today's pantry. After all the excitement yesterday, we might have a larger than usual crowd this morning."

"Call if you need refills," the woman said on her way out.

"The police will keep the gates locked again today," JL said. "It's an ideal situation. They can put officers at the gates and control the press and the crowds."

"I have to put workers in the vineyards. The harvest waits for no man," Meredith said.

"I'll talk to Detective Hollinger," Elliott said.

"He's not as difficult as he was yesterday, but he's still playing his hand close to his chest," JL said.

Meredith poured a cup of coffee. "Before we start, JL and I need a moment to use the bathroom. We'll be right back." She nodded toward JL. "We'll use my office."

JL didn't know what Meredith had on her mind, but it was obvious she wanted to have a private conversation. They crossed the hall and entered a corner office similar to Kenzie's. JL played along to see where this was going. The office was an elegant space. Any other time, JL would have paid close attention to the photographs and awards lining the walls, but not today.

"What's up, Meredith? I know this isn't about using the bathroom."

Meredith sipped from her coffee mug. "Look, I'm on your side. You probably don't believe this, either but so is Elliott. I need to know what happened. Why did Austin run away?"

If Meredith was on her side, she wouldn't be wasting time with a fake bathroom break. But she deserved an answer. Deserved the truth. Deserved someone to blame. The search for Austin was closing her winery for the day and costing her money.

JL hitched her hip on the corner of the desk and folded her arms across her chest. "In a nutshell, he walked in on Kevin and me and found us in a compromising position. Called me names, punched a hole in the wall, left the stair railing dangling, and peeled out of the driveway."

"Crap," Meredith said. "So he drove off, hit something that damaged the front of the truck, abandoned it, and headed for the Wine Cave to get drunk and soothe his anger."

"Sounds about right. But he might have gone for ice for his hand, too. What I can't figure out is why he didn't go inside the Welcome Center."

Meredith chewed the corner of her lip for a moment before saying, "Kenzie and Elliott have odd working habits. They often get up in the middle of the night and go to their offices or sit in the kitchen next to the Welcome Center. They would have discovered Austin. If he wanted ice and alcohol, the Wine Cave was the perfect choice."

"If he went to the Wine Cave, security would have seen him go inside. Why didn't they go after him?" JL asked.

"At one-thirty, the guards on duty would have been out checking buildings and gates," Meredith said.

"Do they have a schedule? Do they go out every hour? Why didn't they find his truck earlier?"

"The night supervisor makes up the schedule and passes it out when the shift starts. There is too much ground to cover every hour. They might be searching the buildings, the orchards, or the vineyards. Without a copy of the schedule, no one knows where security will be next."

"Do you get a copy?" JL asked.

"Kevin and I both do."

"When was the parking lot scheduled to be checked?"

"I'll have to look," Meredith said.

"I guess Austin thought he'd have better luck explaining his situation to a guard than to Elliott," JL said.

"I agree. Elliott would have asked too many uncomfortable questions. I have one for you that's also uncomfortable. What were you and Kevin doing? You're married. What kind of example does that set for Austin?"

JL could no longer escape the conversation she refused to have earlier. "Ryan and I split up last year, but he dragged his feet and wouldn't sign the papers until a few weeks ago. I didn't want Austin to know until the divorce was final. I knew he'd hold out hope for reconciliation. So until it was over and done with, I didn't want to tell him."

Meredith swore under her breath before taking a seat on the sofa. She sipped from her mug again before placing it on one of the coasters stacked on the coffee table. JL noticed for the first time the dark circles under her eyes. The woman hadn't been sleeping. JL bet Elliott and Kenzie weren't the only ones who woke up in the middle of the night and went to work. JL, too, had a history of enduring all-nighters, but hers occurred when she was in the middle of a big case, which only came along once every few months.

"Austin's a big boy, and I'm not referring to his size. He could have handled the news. I think there's a bigger reason."

Though it was clear Meredith wanted an explanation, JL fell into a stubborn silence.

Meredith leaned forward and rested her elbows on her knees. The fingertips of one hand bounced against the fingertips of the other. She had long fingers, manicured nails, and a few purple-blue veins leading to her wrists. Then they suddenly stilled, and JL waited for the next intrusive question.

"Were you hoping you'd get back together? Is that why you didn't tell Austin?"

JL eased away from the desk and joined her on the sofa, mimicking Meredith's body language with her elbows on her knees. She twisted the birthstone ring Austin had given her for Christmas a couple of years ago. She rarely took it off. "Ryan started cheating on me a year after we got married. I put up with it. I tried to give him more attention, but it didn't work. Finally, I couldn't take it anymore."

JL's pulse had been jumping up and down, but it settled to a quick, light thump. She could only imagine how fast Austin's was beating in captivity. If it had stopped, she would know. She could do nothing now except wait and confess.

"The reason I couldn't tell Austin the truth was because I wouldn't be around to help him deal with it. Dumb, I know. It's my nature to protect him. I did what I thought was best."

Meredith tilted her head to one side and eyed JL closely. "For him or for you?"

JL stiffened. Meredith had zeroed in on the one question she hadn't been willing to answer, even to herself. With her voice suddenly tight, she said, "In hindsight? For me."

Something flickered in Meredith's deep blue eyes. "You and Kevin met a few hours ago. Do you have a habit of jumping into bed with men you don't know?"

The question was a slap to JL's face, and it stung like hell. She didn't have to answer. She could get up and walk out of the room, but her feet gripped the floor, telling her she wasn't going anywhere.

"I don't know how to explain this, but it's more than that. I've been having weird sensations since I walked into the Welcome Center. Actually, since I saw the brooch your ancestor is wearing in the painting over the fireplace."

Meredith's mouth opened slightly, and her eyes slightly more. "Why? Have you seen it before? Or maybe one like it?"

"One like it, at least I think so. I was only a child. I was playing in my mother's jewelry box and I picked up this broken brooch—"

"Broken? How?" A cell phone beeped. It wasn't JL's. Meredith crossed the room and picked up her cell phone from the desk. She punched keys then set it down.

JL struggled to recall exactly what part of the brooch was broken. "A sliver of it was missing, like a slice cut from a cake."

Meredith's pulse beat rapidly at the open V of her running jacket. "What...color was the stone?"

If JL's focus hadn't been on Austin, she would have questioned Meredith about her intense interest. Instead, she wiggled her finger, sporting the ring from Austin. "My birthstone. An amethyst."

Meredith returned to the sofa and took JL's hands into her own. JL wanted to pull them away from her, but Meredith's hands were surprisingly warm and comforting.

"Listen carefully and remember what I'm about to tell you. The next couple of days will be difficult. The stress and danger will test your mettle beyond the limits of your previous experiences. Do not lose faith, even in the face of defeat. Remain strong, but don't be stupid. Act, don't react. And believe—always believe—love will bring you home."

JL blinked several times. "That's very prophetic, but what does it have to do with the brooch or with Austin?"

"I don't know. I was compelled to pass along that prophesy. My great-great-grandmother, Frances Montgomery, had the gift of prophesy that she inherited from her ancestor, Sarah Barrett, whom Kit met on the Oregon Trail. It's an interesting story. I'll tell you sometime." Meredith clambered to her feet, holding the arm of the sofa for support. "Let's get to work. We've got to find the back entrance to the cave."

"What makes you think there is one?"

Meredith looked at her with raised, expectant brows. "How else are you going to get inside?"

10

ELLIOTT SHOVED THE DOOR shut after Meredith and JL left, but Kevin kept his gaze fastened there until the click of JL's footsteps on the stone floor receded. Then he shot Elliott the full force of his glare.

"David," Elliott said abruptly. "Call back in five minutes." He clicked the disconnect button without another word, ripped off his reading glasses, and tossed them onto the top of the legal pad and file folders in front of him.

Kevin's senses quickened. What was going on with Elliott? Kevin had seen him angry hundreds of times, but in all the years he had known him, he had never seen him cut David off without an explanation.

Elliott leaned over the conference table, bracketing his notes with his weathered hands. The crow's feet—the only other visible fruit of age on the Scot—crinkled deeper at the corners of his dark eyes. Kevin wasn't standing all that close, but he could feel the heat radiating right through Elliott's polo shirt and starched khakis.

"What's up, Boss?" Kevin asked without a quiver in his voice.

A muscle jumped at the side of Elliott's jaw. "What happened?"

"Can you be more specific?"

His eyes telegraphed exactly how specific he intended to be. "Don't play games this morning, lad. All hell has broken loose around here."

Kevin shifted uneasily on his feet. He hated it when Elliott looked at him the way he was doing now. James Cullen had accused Kevin of giving him the same look. "You think I don't know that. Austin is like a—"

"—son?" Elliott finished the sentence, spitting the word out as his fingertips slowly crawled inward to form fists. "As ye are to me, he is to ye. Ye've done something to add to the hell going on around here. And I want to know *now* what ye've done."

Kevin ran his fingers through his thick hair. If he continued working day and night, drinking too much, and only catching snatches of female companionship whenever he could, he would be as gray as Elliott was within the next five years. He didn't want the gray, and he didn't want the lifestyle either—not anymore. He wanted JL in his life, and he would compromise and sacrifice to make that happen.

"This conversation needs to wait until later," Kevin said.

Looking highly disgruntled, Elliott said, "We're having it *now*."

Kevin raised his voice. "*Okay*. You want it now? Here it is. Austin walked in on JL and me. I'm not going to embarrass her by describing what he saw. He called us names, punched a hole in the wall, yanked down the stair railing, and squealed out of the drive."

"What the hell were ye doing messing around with Austin's sister? I thought ye understood she was *off limits*."

"I didn't get that briefing."

"She's married, damn it. I taught ye better than that."

"Yeah, you taught me how to screw everything in a skirt."

Elliott raised his hand. If Kevin had been within striking distance, Elliott would have struck him. "If she's married, she's off limits, and if she's family, she's off limits, too."

Kevin tsked. "And you've never screwed a married woman?" He'd never talked to Elliott the way he was talking now, not because he was afraid of repercussions, but because Elliott—with the exception of treating Meredith despicably one night many years ago—could never do anything wrong in Kevin's eyes.

"If ye've got a hair up yer arse, spit it out."

"This isn't about you or MacKlenna Corporation." Kevin sighed deeply. He had reached a crossroads, and whichever way he went, he would live with the consequences. "This is about JL and me. I don't know how to explain it. It's like I've known her all of my life. I've listened to stories about her for over a year. I admired her before I ever met her. And now that she's—" Kevin bit his tongue.

Kenzie said you're a gossip. Promise me you won't tell anyone.

Kevin made a conscious decision to honor his word to JL even if it caused an irreparable breach between him and the man he loved, the man who was more of a father to him than his own father had been.

"I care about her, and I'm not going to stop seeing her. I'll fly back and forth to New York. She can come wherever I am. We'll make it work."

"*She's married.* That makes her off limits. She's Austin's sister. Leave her *alone.*"

"Or what?"

"I gave ye a job with responsibility, and I can take it back."

"You gave me a job, and I can quit it. You obviously care more about Austin than you do me."

"Ye'd choose a woman over yer life here?"

"JL O'Grady is *not* any woman. She's the most exciting woman I've ever met." He took a deep breath and regrouped. "You have a son who will eventually take over the company. There's no long-range plan that includes me. I can start my own business now—"

"—Doing what?" Elliott interrupted.

"Did you even know I earned my CPA license?"

A dangerous smile curved Elliott's lips. "Did ye honestly think I didn't? Meredith said ye didn't want to announce it yet, and since ye hadn't mentioned it to me, I kept quiet."

"I can start my own firm. I have plenty of money, as much Apple stock as you have. I don't need this job."

"We've been together almost two decades. Ye'd leave now that we have plans to diversify, to grow the business into a billion-dollar company? Ye'll have a stake in that."

"With the ultimatum you've given me, yes. I'd leave. I'm not your son, Elliott. I'm the hired help."

"Ye're more than that, and ye know it."

"If I was more, you'd be happy for me."

"*Happy?* That ye've fallen for a woman ye can't have? Ye know we have plans for Austin. That makes him family. Makes his family part of our family. Hell no, I'm not happy at all. Ye're ruining yer life, and I won't stand by and watch ye do it."

"There was a time when *you* couldn't stand on your own, and I never left your side. I need your understanding right now." Kevin pointed his finger at Elliott and said, between gritted teeth, "I need you to trust me, and you can't do that, can you?"

"No, I can't."

11

JL AND MEREDITH returned to the conference room, but stopped short at the threshold. JL tasted tension in the air like smog on an LA street. Whatever had transpired between Elliott and Kevin left them both sour-faced and battle-hungry. She could easily picture them standing on a street in a low-budget western, hands poised over their holstered Colt six-shooters. The fastest draw was yet to be determined.

Meredith cleared her throat, and Elliott gave his wife a short shake of his head.

Kevin, red-faced, crossed the room, and wrapped his arms around JL tightly. The raw tension in his body nearly overwhelmed her already precarious self-control. His firm and possessive lips didn't sip at hers gently, and his beard stubble rasped her chin.

"Has there been any news of Austin?" she asked.

"None," he said, easing up on his embrace. "I hope the bathroom break wasn't too uncomfortable for you."

She kissed him back, letting their lips linger, not caring that Elliott and Meredith were both watching them intently. "It was fine. I'll tell you later." Her gaze flicked to his face. The flush had gone, the tension eased. "And you?"

He gave her an identical short shake of his head. Whatever had taken place during her absence was staying between the two men. She glanced from Elliott to Kevin and back again, seeing mirror images. Kevin must have practiced Elliott's moves until they became second nature to him.

"Let's get this planning session underway before David has to catch a plane." Elliott's testy tone didn't provide any coolant for the heated room. He tapped keys on his computer, waking the video screen, and David returned. One of the monitors at his desk showed the feed from the entrance to the cave. Two cops guarded the barricade, but there was no other activity, and no Hollinger.

"*Where is everyone?*" Elliott's deep, angry voice reverberated through the room. "Isn't *anything* happening there?"

"I've been watching the feed from inside the cave since yer last call. Do the police believe the shooter's in there?"

"Worse than that," Elliott said. "Austin has disappeared, and JL believes a drug cartel kidnapped him and dragged him into the old part."

"*Jesus Christ,*" David said.

JL moved to stand in front of the camera. "We opened the old door and found a mishmash of footprints in the dirt. Austin's running shoes have a unique tread. His shoes could have made one of the sets of prints. I intended to go in and do reconnaissance, but Hollinger, the lead detective, showed up and took over the show. I did find a swatch of fabric from Austin's jacket, so I'm sure he's in there."

"Didn't SWAT run into booby traps when they entered the cave in the New York case?" David asked.

"Yes. Two officers were wounded," she said.

"If I'm remembering correctly, there were three wounded by the time the case was solved," David said.

David's comment created an awkward moment for her. She didn't like to be reminded of the shooting. "Hollinger has reviewed the Di Salvo case file. He knows what happened in the New York cave," JL said.

"My camera is facing the opposite direction and I can't see a damn thing."

"Hollinger said he would let me know if he had any news," she said.

"Are you packed and ready to leave? We need you here," Meredith said.

"The kids and I head to the airport in an hour. And before ye ask, their manny packed their bags. If they don't have the right clothes, ye'll have to blame him."

"I'm sure they'll be fine," Meredith said. "If there's anything they need, we can get it here. What about Jack's crew?"

"He sent a text a few minutes ago. The Mallorys and McCabes will be on time for a change. Charlotte made hospital rounds early and didn't have any emergencies. The weather's clear, and the kids are all healthy, or almost. We should make good time."

JL fisted her hands and tapped her booted foot. A scream lodged in her throat. *Stop talking about the weather and packing. Austin is missing, and probably hurt and scared.*

"When Braham gets on the plane, query him for details of the cave," Meredith said. "He has knowledge that predates mine. It should come in handy."

"Oh, right," David said. "I guess he does have information from his *younger* days."

JL got the impression David and Meredith were speaking in code. Elliott stood glaring at the video screen with his hands on his hips, tapping his fingers, while Kevin was drawing a picture of the inside of the cave on a sketchpad—a very impressive, detailed sketch. Neither of them seemed fazed by the discussion, which meant she was the only one not in the loop, but she could make assumptions. The woman in the portrait was a MacKlenna/Montgomery/McCabe. Braham was a McCabe. Therefore, he had a history with the property, which logically would include the cave.

Kevin put down his pencil and looked up at the screen. "Hey, did you get my text about the pickup in New York? You didn't text back."

"Sorry. I was on the phone with the pilot when yer message came in. That's good news. We can use five additional bodies."

JL stepped forward. "Only four, David. Pops can advise, but he hasn't been an active cop in several years. He can't go in the field now. He could get hurt."

"I'll leave that to yer brothers, JL. I can't make any promises. If it was my kid, ye couldn't keep me from getting involved."

Me neither. But Pops wasn't going in, even if she had to handcuff him to the door. She and her brothers lived in fear of losing him to either a health issue or a perp from his past.

Meredith refilled her coffee cup and sat at the table with a notepad and pen. "We have another problem, David. The police took all the maps I had."

David swiveled in his chair, checking his monitors. "Those old surveys won't help the cops."

"How do you know?" Meredith asked.

"A few years ago I had our engineers digitize those maps, and after they studied them, they were convinced the surveyors' calculations were off."

"I never heard anything about their study. Did you, Elliott?"

"David might have mentioned it."

"And you didn't think I'd want to know?" She flipped her pen back and forth between her fingers, intently studying her husband, then she dropped the pen and turned her focus to David. "How could they tell the calculations were off?"

"Not sure," David said. "At the time it wasn't important enough for me to spend hours studying their report. Looks like I'll have to bring myself up to speed now. Historically, in the late nineteenth century, surveyors supervised the layout of caves and mines. They fixed boundaries and mapped the directions of tunnels using a compass especially made for use underground. The problem was that the large deposits of iron ore deflected the compass needle, making distances and bearings incorrect.

"If SWAT uses those original surveys, they'll discover the distances, angles, and even directions of the tunnels will be off enough that they could get lost or fall into enemy hands before they realize where they are. Following a good survey inside a cave is disorienting enough. With an inaccurate one, they'll be worse off."

"To be clear," Meredith said, "you have copies of the maps the police took from our storage?"

"To be clear, yes, I do. I also have better ones," David said. "When they digitized the surveys, they also did fieldwork and used sonography to probe the cave and determine the relationship of the cave to surface landforms."

"Why didn't you tell me?" Meredith asked.

"Mer, be thankful we have them instead of pissed ye didn't know," Elliott said.

Kevin pulled to his feet. "Look, it's my fault. I removed the study from your daily briefing. The engineers did the Wine Cave after they did the studies of the cave at Fraser House in Scotland. Considering all you had going on at the time—"

Meredith's finely arched brows lifted, and she said tersely, "You chose to protect me."

"You were recovering from histoplasmosis. I knew you would spend time studying the reports and consider going spelunking. When you got healthy, little Kit was born, the twins came along, and you moved on to marketing a new label."

"Where are the reports now?"

"In the file cabinet in my office, but the docs and pictures are on the server," Kevin said. "I've never looked at them and honestly forgot we had them."

"If I had had those reports, I might have put a renovation project in the budget, and this disaster might never have happened."

JL watched Elliott hover at Meredith's shoulder. He didn't engage. He was letting the two spar, but from his forward-leaning posture, he was prepared to jump in if Meredith needed rescuing.

Kevin pointed at her. "If it makes you feel better to blame this one on me, go right ahead. But in the last three years, you've had large capital improvements in the budget more important than renovating a cave you don't need."

"Kevin, sit down," David said. "He's taking the blame for me, Meredith. I didn't want ye to see the report. Kevin made sure ye and Elliott didn't. Now, if ye'll stop yer bickering, we can move on."

"I won't bother to ask ye why ye didn't tell me," Elliott said.

Kevin dug his fingers into the place where his neck and shoulder met; the muscles there, JL knew, were hard as wood beneath the skin. "Boss, you can't even keep Meredith's birthday present a secret from her."

JL almost laughed. If the situation hadn't been so damn serious, she would have.

"If I can have everyone's attention," David said. "I forwarded the reports to my team and instructed them to do a set of overlays, comparing the old images with the new ones."

"David," JL said, "is it possible the cartel, if that's who we're dealing with, has copies of the new surveys?"

He leaned back in his chair, folded his arms, and plucked at his whiskered chin. After a minute he said, "If the cartel is using the cave to manufacture illegal drugs, I can almost guarantee they have copies. They either broke in and stole them or, more likely, bought off an employee to steal them."

"How did the cartel know the plans were there to steal?" Meredith asked. "It's not like I go out and advertise my vendors."

"Really?" David asked. "How many sponsors do you have for the gala tomorrow night?"

"Crap," Meredith said. "Our engineering company signed on as a gala sponsor over a year ago. We even had a press conference for the announcement."

"There ye go," David said.

"Did the engineers mention a second access point?" JL asked. "There has to be one. We're all assuming the cartel has set up an operation in the cave. If that's true, I bet they have an escape route, and it has to be in an area of the property that isn't monitored by cameras."

"It's also possible a security guard looks the other way and also alters the video feeds," Kevin said. "Meredith's been suspicious of the security company for a while now. Maybe the cartel even owns it."

"They had to buy off a lot of people to keep this operation quiet," Meredith said. "I've run all over this property, and I haven't seen any off-road tire tracks. They're either sweeping them away, or only using the main entrance."

"Money's not a factor for them," JL said. "That brings us back to the possibility of a second entrance. Is there one, and if so, where is it?"

"We're looking. Hold tight," David said.

Elliott refilled his coffee cup, stirred in a spoonful of sugar, and said, very short-tempered, "For how long?"

David's fingers clicked across his keyboard. "We might have something this afternoon. Could be sooner."

"We don't have the luxury of time. Austin's been in there for hours now." JL's voice was sharp with agitation. "If they know who he is, that's he's an O'Grady…"

"Wait," David said. "It looks like…I'm not sure. I'll be right back."

To keep from flying off in a panic, JL dug her fingers into her upper arms like the teeth of a wolf trap.

Kevin whispered in her ear, his warm breath caressing her cheek, "Your knuckles are turning white. Breathe."

"I can't." She swallowed her heart, which had risen into her throat.

"We'll find him. We'll get him back."

JL wanted to believe, but knew Kevin was only offering comfort. To distract herself, she asked, "Tell me what happened in here earlier…between you and Elliott."

"I don't want to talk about it now. Later, we'll…"

JL's cell phone vibrated and warbled on the conference table where she had placed it. Glancing at the screen, she said, "It's Pops."

"Talk to him," Kevin said, and then mouthed the word "breathe" to her.

She nodded and took a deep breath before saying, "Hi, Pops."

"Any news?" he asked.

"SWAT has been in the cave thirty-five minutes. If they're sending reports back, I'm not privy to them. Although Hollinger did say he would notify me if there was any news."

"Where are you now?"

"The Frasers, Kevin Allen, and I are in the conference room in the Corporate Offices building. We're on a videoconference with David McBain in Kentucky. You'll meet him on the plane. He has copies of surveys made a few years ago, and we're looking for a back entrance to the cave."

"Give whatever information you have to SWAT. They're trained for this. You're not."

Her father's voice was barely louder than the beat of her own heart, but she heard him, heard every word, and knew, no matter what he said, if she found an opening, an opportunity to go in, she would take it. "Yes, sir."

"We'll be there in a few hours. Will you make reservations for us?"

She muted the call and asked Kevin. "Is there room at the cottage for Pops and my brothers? If not, they can crash on the floor in my room or stay at Austin's."

"There are three empty suites upstairs," he said. "Do they mind doubling up?"

"They'll be grateful for a shower and the corner of a twin bed."

"We can do better than that. Those suites each have two queen beds."

JL unmuted the phone. "There's room at the cottage. It's within walking distance of the cave. I'll see you this afternoon."

The call ended, and JL waited for David to return to the videoconference. Ten minutes became fifteen, and her agitation increased with every passing second. Unable to sit still, she crossed the room to the service tray and poured a cup of coffee. After taking a few sips, she returned to the chair next to Kevin and sat forward on the edge, tapping the cup with her fingernails.

Finally, after twenty minutes, David returned. "Remember that drone ye had security send up yesterday? My team made good use of the video. They overlaid those pictures with the surveys, and I think we found something."

"Where?" JL, Kevin, and Elliott all said in almost perfect unison.

"If it's an entrance, it's in the olive orchard. There are no signs that the vegetation around it has been disturbed. It lines up with a passage at the very far end of the cave. However, the elevation is twenty to twenty-five feet higher than the passage. It's too high to be used to bring people and supplies in and out. There has to be another entrance with a lower elevation, possibly on the far side of the ridge."

"Put it up on the screen," Elliott said.

David split the screen. He was on one side, and a picture of the terraced olive grove was on the other. JL recognized the running path up the hill. "That's close to where we ran yesterday."

Kevin crossed over to the screen and stabbed his finger at the bottom corner of the frame. "Austin found Salvatore here."

"If there's an entrance, I don't see it," Meredith said.

"My expert has a sophisticated system. He ran images through a time-lapse app looking for changes in the topography. This image was flagged."

JL did a visual grid search of the image until she spotted what she thought might be an opening in the terraced orchard. She tapped her finger on the screen. "Is this it?"

"I can't see where ye're pointing," David said. He drew a circle on the drawing. "It's here. Ye can only see a corner of the opening. Most of the day it's in shadow, but in the late afternoon, probably for only a few minutes, the corner is visible."

"That's what I was looking at," JL said.

Elliott stood behind Meredith and put his hands on her shoulders. "Kit and I built a hunting blind once. We came back the next day and couldn't find it. We thought someone had torn it down. It was in shadow, and even standing almost on top of it, we couldn't see it until the sun was just right."

"Do you think this is man-made?" Meredith asked.

"Hard to tell from here," Elliott said.

"How large is the opening?" JL asked.

"Three feet max," David said. "The total elevation is fifty feet higher than the elevation at the entrance to the cave."

"Are you saying the passage is twenty-five feet higher than the entrance to the cave, and this new entrance is approximately twenty-five feet higher than the passage?"

"That's correct. SWAT has a steady climb up and, if ye go in this way, ye'll have a steady climb down, or, more likely, ye'll have to rappel down."

"I trained in advanced tactical rappelling. I could use some help with hookups and gear, though. Otherwise, I'm ready," JL said.

"Kenzie is an expert. She'll get ye set up, but remember, going down isn't the problem. Coming back up is, especially if people are shooting at ye."

"I'm going in regardless," JL said. "I need supplies. If you'll direct me where to shop, I'll go pick up what I need." She snatched Kevin's drawing pad and flipped the page, then began a list of the items she would need: rope, helmets, lights, seat harness, guns and ammunition, knife, portage pack, food…

"*We're* going in," Kevin said. "The two of us."

"You're not," she said. "This is a police matter. You're a civilian. I won't allow you to risk your life. I won't take you."

"I'll follow you. Besides, you need me. I'm a trained paramedic with wilderness emergency medical training. We might be dealing with an immobile patient, hypothermia, or shock. You can handle the bad guys while I take care of the patient."

"I've got to leave for the airport," David said. "As soon as we're wheels up, I'll call back. But, JL, ye can't go by yerself. Take Kevin. He's as trained as anyone ye'll find in Napa's fire and rescue, and probably in better physical condition. As soon as we land, I'm sure yer brothers will want to follow."

The screen went dark. Meredith, Elliott, Kevin, and JL sat at the conference table in silence.

"I don't like the idea of ye going in, but I know I can't stop ye. My job is to be sure ye're equipped with the best caving gear on the market. I'll organize the gear. Kevin, go to the clinic and fix a red bag. Ye might be dealing with gunshots, so get what ye need. JL, I'll print out the surveys. From now until ye leave, ye need to study the passages and turns from all directions. Remember the passages don't look the same in reverse. I'd also like ye to make contact with Hollinger. Get a"—Elliott made air quotes—"professional courtesy update."

"Do you want me to tell him we're going in through a rear entrance?"

He swept his fingers through his hair in a quick, cursory gesture. "Ye don't know that ye are. An entrance exists, but ye don't know if ye can get through. I wouldn't pull Hollinger and his men off what they're doing without offering them something better. I recommend ye go in, look around, come back, and report what ye found. If ye find Austin, SWAT can go in after him. But honestly, I don't think ye're going to find anything."

"Then why help me?"

A muscle twitched along Elliott's jaw. "Because ye're an action person. Ye need to do something that makes ye feel like ye're contributing. I'd rather send ye and the lad down into a cave where the odds are low that ye'll find Austin—"

"Instead of going in through the front where the odds are high we could get killed." She had learned long ago to be careful and edit what she said when speaking to those in power, but right now she didn't care. "If it was just me, you wouldn't care, but you know Kevin won't let me go alone. You would rather we waste our time going in through the back with little chance of success. I get it."

The silence that fell between them was long and somewhat awkward. Finally, Elliott said, "I play the odds every day, missy. The best use of yer time is to rap into that cave and look for Austin. This isn't about who I'd rather see or not see navigating those passages. This is about seeing that ye"—he pointed at her—"do everything possible to rescue yer brother. When this is over, ye'll need to make peace with yer fate and not rail against it."

12

Jl rushed out of the Welcome Center and was met by cool temps and sunshine. The fantastic autumn weather did nothing to lift her spirits. Nothing could. Nothing would. Not while Austin was in danger.

Parked in the lot was a lone golf cart. She commandeered it for the short drive over to the Wine Cave, and used the time to prepare mentally for what she was going to do next.

Arriving five minutes later, she pulled into a parking space alongside the crowd control barricades fitted with flashing lights. A Napa cop stood behind the barriers, drinking from a Starbucks mug. The scent and taste of coffee had the power to jump-start her day, and although she had already had two cups, she wasn't feeling the caffeine jolt, yet.

"I need to see Detective Hollinger. He told me he'd let me know if he had any information. Have you heard from him?"

"Are you the New York cop?"

She nodded.

"He said if you came by, I was to let him know. He's in the cave. As soon as I can find someone to relieve me, I'll go get him."

"Is he at the command center?" She had been watching the video feed from the camera placed outside the door of the old part of the cave, but it had been installed facing away from the door instead of toward it, so she hadn't seen Hollinger or any of the other cops.

"Command center."

A loud rumble followed by a boom struck terror in JL's bones. She stared wide-eyed at the cop. "Did you hear that?"

The cop's unibrow raised and his face took on the pale cast of one instantly saddled with extreme fear. "*Earthquake.*"

Her breath hitched. "*No.* Not an earthquake. An explosion." Although a plume of smoke didn't bellow from the entrance, and no flames erupted, she knew instinctively the cave had suffered significant damage. She hurdled the barricade and bolted toward the entrance.

The cop ran after her. "Stop. You can't go in there."

She yelled over her shoulder, "Call dispatch. We need fire and rescue. *Now.* We might have several dead or injured." She sprinted through the door and ran the length of the front part of the cave. A few pictures hung askew on the walls, but none of the tables, chairs, or sofas had suffered any damage.

She flung open the unlocked door to the storage part and leapt over oak wine barrels that had rolled out into the aisle. A boiling cloud of dust was moving toward her, covering the floor and walls and barrels. She yanked up her sweater to cover her mouth. As she neared the second door, she sloshed through a wide red stream. The reek of alcohol mixed with the bitter smell of high explosives was as thick in the air as the rock dust.

Dozens of barrels had rolled into each other and smashed open, and the explosion had loosened rocks and clods of earth from the top and sides of the cave. The heavy door to the old section had blown off its hinges and crashed to the floor, buckled and splintered. The force had upturned tables and smashed chairs, sending computers and other equipment the team had brought in crashing into the walls.

There were no injured men. Matter of fact, there were no men at all.

"*JL.*"

She barely heard Kevin call her name above the roar of fear. "Back here."

He reached her, carrying a red trauma bag and wearing a mask over his mouth and nose. He hugged her. "Thank God you're all right. Where is everyone?"

She pointed to the old section. "They must all be in there."

"Here, put this respirator mask on. You've already breathed in too much of this contaminated air." He covered her mouth and nose. Once the mask was in place, he molded the nosepiece around her nose and tightened both straps. The mask was thicker than a surgical mask, but its purpose was to filter the air, not resist splashes of blood and bodily fluids.

"Help me find helmets and lights," she said. "We've got to get to the men." They righted tables and dug through upturned boxes of military surplus until they found helmets, lamps, and flashlights.

"All I've got is my Glock. I need another weapon. Do you see any?"

He pointed to a corner. "What's that over there behind the computers?"

She couldn't see until he moved the equipment out of the way, and her eyes lifted heavenward. "Thank God." She didn't have to open it to know what was in there. "It's a tactical ready bag."

Inside the bag, she found two automatic pistols and ammunition. Moving quickly, she loaded them and offered one to Kevin. He stared at the gun, then shoved it into his waistband, and she crammed the other into her jacket pocket. "I'll go first. The explosion likely killed or injured everyone who was in there. We might have to engage whoever set off the explosives. Follow my lead. Keep your helmet lamp and flashlight turned off. Got it?"

Standing in the doorway between the sections of the cave, he pressed his masked lips against her. "Got it. And we'll find Austin."

JL followed her search tactics training. With the flashlight on, she drew an imaginary line to her next point, then turned out the light and headed there, listening carefully, then doing it again and again. When her flashlight was on, she kept the light away from her body, using the light in a strobe affect at random intervals, making herself a harder target to hit. Instead of speaking, she used the beam of light to illuminate hazards in their path.

After fifteen minutes of creeping along the passage, Kevin tapped her shoulder and said in the suffocating opaque darkness, "I hear moaning."

She nodded, and they moved toward the groans that rose and fell, echoing off the walls with a haunting quality like a ghostly presence. A stronger, repugnant scent of explosives and blood replaced the dank, stale air. She stared into the darkness that pressed on her like a slowly closing fist, knowing her eyes couldn't penetrate it, but her heart did. Where was Austin? Would he be among the bodies she expected to find?

She swallowed hard and held up her hand for Kevin to stay put, then put a finger to her lips. With a gun in her right hand and flashlight moving strobe-like in her left, she stepped over debris. The dust was thicker here. The beam of light landed on a crumbled rock wall, solid, floor to ceiling, blocking the tunnel. Then bodies came into view. No one moved. She counted the bloody, dirt-covered bodies quickly. One, two, three, four…eight…nine.

"I found them," she said. "Turn on your lights. Hurry." She switched on her headlamp, and the corridor and the extent of the damage, both in life and property, came into full view.

She moved quickly from one man to the next, as did Kevin. She was surprised to find Hollinger among the wounded. One closest to the wall was dead. Eight others were injured. None of them was Austin.

"I've got four critically injured," Kevin said.

"What do you want me to do?"

"Fire and rescue should be here by now. Run back to the door and wait for them. Let them know we have eight injured, four seriously, and one dead."

"Austin isn't here," she said.

"We'll get him back, but let's do what we can for these men."

She squeezed his shoulder. "It won't take me as long to go back as it did to get here. If rocks start falling, grab whoever you can and get the hell out."

Using both her helmet lamp and flashlight, she was able to maneuver the rocky passage in under five minutes. By the time she returned to the blown-off door, six firemen had arrived wearing self-contained breathing apparatus and turnout pants and jackets.

"I'm Detective O'Grady. We have eight injured and one dead. Four of the injured are critical."

"I'm the company officer. Are you the NYC detective who jumped the barrier?"

"Yes, and Kevin Allen, the winery's CFO, is back there with the men. He's a paramedic, too, but he desperately needs help."

"Did you see any structural damage?"

"No, but scattered rocks and debris in the passage will prevent the use of gurneys. You'll have to carry the men out. The explosion caused rocks to pile and form a wall. I don't know how many went in, or if there are more on the other side of the wall."

"We have a report of eight members on the SWAT team and possibly two other police officers."

"And Austin O'Grady, age seventeen, went missing early this morning."

"That's the young man SWAT was searching for?"

"Correct."

"Are there any corridors off the main passage?"

"No. It's a straight shot, and it will take you about five minutes to reach the victims. Kevin desperately needs help. So let's hurry."

"Detective, we'll take it from here."

"Austin is in there…" Her voice cracked. She wanted to argue, beg to be included, but her throat had gone dry, and she knew there was nothing she could say that would change his mind. The firefighters and paramedics would need every inch of space to work on the victims. They didn't need her in the way. And Austin, if he was in there, was on the other side of the wall.

"We'll find him," the company officer said.

She checked the time on her watch. Elliott would be waiting for an update, but she wouldn't leave without Kevin. She paced outside the busted door for ten minutes. That was more than enough time for him to get out. Two more minutes and she was going back in.

After forty-five seconds, she moved to stand in the doorway. At the one-minute mark she set foot in the old part of the cave, and at the exact two-minute mark, Kevin came hustling out of the passage.

"I don't know if the four in critical condition will make it. One is in really bad shape."

They stood in tense silence staring at each other. Then she wiped black dirt from Kevin's face and asked softly, "Was it Hollinger?"

Kevin shook his head. "The detective will live to harass you again."

She drew in a deep breath, as deep as she could manage, then released it. Hollinger was a good cop. But where was Castellano? She rubbed her gritty, swollen eyes, promising herself she would keep it together. She had to.

"Let's get out of here. We've got lots of work to do," she said.

Kevin handed over the gun she had given him. She unloaded the weapons and returned them to the tactical ready bag. They left the cave, removing their masks while they exited through the front door. Elliott was among the dozen or more men and women milling around the barricade.

"We don't have any information yet. The winery is closed. Go home," Elliott said.

Meredith was behind the wheel of a golf cart. She waved, and Kevin and JL bounded over to meet her. "We've been watching the video. What happened?"

Kevin and JL squashed into the backseat, and he braced his arm around her shoulder. His presence comforted her, his body warmed her, and his resolve heartened her spirit.

Elliott climbed into the front passenger seat. "Let's go," he said, and Meredith drove out of the parking lot.

As soon as they were clear of the nosy employees, Kevin said, "The news is one dead, eight injured, one missing, plus Austin."

"Thank God he wasn't hurt," Meredith said.

Elliott turned in his seat. "Was there structural damage from the explosion? Could you tell?"

"The explosion dumped a wall of rocks in the passage approximately fifty to seventy-five yards into the cave. It'll take hours, if not days, to dig through," JL said. "The fireman said eight SWAT members and two other police officers were inside at the time of the explosion. We could only account for nine."

"Does that mean the other cop is on the opposite side of the wall?"

A sick feeling settled in the pit of her stomach. Could the missing cop be Castellano? What would his death do to his son, who had already lost his mother? "Whoever it was couldn't have survived the explosion unless he was well ahead of the group. Now he's either crushed, lost, or a prisoner."

Kevin reached for her hand and squeezed it tightly. She patted the top of his hand and gave him a tight smile. "You can't hide the doubt in your eyes. Don't let it take over your heart, too. We'll find them both," he said.

"David wants to have another conference call as soon as we get back," Meredith said.

"I have to shower first," Kevin said. "I've got blood all over me."

"We'll take you to the cottage. I want to check on the damages to the wall and railing and get the workmen started on the repairs before JL's family arrives," Meredith said.

The damage to the cottage was a reminder of the eruption that had taken place hours earlier, and she wouldn't be able to avoid telling Pops and the boys what happened.

Elliott pointed ahead. "Take the running path, Mer. I know ye don't like to drive on it, but it's quicker."

Meredith made a sharp turn and navigated a path similar to the one JL and Kevin had followed during their run the day before. Meredith stopped at a crossing and waited for a line of rescue vehicles to pass, one of which was a SWAT Hummer from San Francisco. She pulled in behind the last truck and drove for a short distance before turning off the lane again. The second path led through the woods to the back of the cottage. JL was dizzy by the time Meredith stopped whipping the cart in and out among the trees and lifted her foot off the gas pedal.

"Ye have thirty minutes to shower and change," Elliott said. "We have to be back in the conference room for a call with David."

Kevin and Elliott glared at each other in bristling silence for a moment before Kevin said, "Don't wait for us."

"I'll leave as soon as Meredith assesses the damage, but don't be late." Elliott's face was a mask of polite civility.

Kevin slid his arm around JL and gave her shoulders a reassuring squeeze. Even though the dread that had settled in her stomach was consuming, desire for him flared. That made the weight of her guilt, like a giant G pinned to her chest, an impossible load to carry very far.

Inside the cottage, Meredith hurried upstairs while Elliott sat at the kitchen table and scrolled through messages on his iPhone. Kevin swiped a dirty finger through a stack of mail on the counter, and JL grabbed two bottles of water from the fridge, giving one to him.

"I'm going to the shower."

He kissed her lightly, and she headed to her bedroom. Although she was out of sight, she wasn't out of earshot.

"I want ye to remember what our priority is." Elliott's tone didn't sharpen, but it had an undertone that made JL's shoulders rise to her ears, and she hugged the wall and listened. A foolish prick of tears stung, and she closed her eyes to hold back the impending storm.

Kevin's voice cracked as he said, "You don't have to remind me."

"Oh, but I do."

"Back off, Elliott. Austin's my only concern right now."

In a voice that was infuriatingly calm, Elliott said, "Then act like it."

13

TWENTY-EIGHT MINUTES LATER, JL and Kevin arrived back at the conference room, hair still damp from the shower. David was on the video screen, along with JL's father and her brothers. The author Jack Mallory was there, too. She recognized him from his book jacket picture. There was also another man, blond and green-eyed, whom JL had not met before.

"Elliott could have waited to place the call," Kevin said to her under his breath.

She had a sense that her presence and Austin's kidnapping weren't the only causes of the dissension between Elliott and Kevin, but she could take the blame for the lion's share. She crossed the room and stood in front of the video screen. "Damn, Pops. There's enough testosterone on that plane to keep it aloft without an engine."

"Hi, sweetheart. You holding up okay?" Pops asked.

Mallory adjusted the monitor so he was in full view. "JL, we haven't met, but just so you know"—he pointed at David—"McBain can keep this plane in the air with just what's pumping in his veins."

Except for David, all the men laughed.

A cat jumped up on the table, startling them all. "Where the hell did that come from?" David asked.

Huge green eyes below a mop of curly red hair peeked over the edge of the small conference table in the plane. "She's my kitty, Da.

I found her. Tabor sent her from Heaven so I wouldn't miss her so much."

David picked up what looked like a blue point Siamese cat and turned it upside down. "Henry, lad, sorry to disappoint ya, but yer kitty's got a penis."

An identical-looking child popped up on David's other side. "He's got a penis like me? Like Henry? Like yer wee one, Da? Where?"

Jack howled. "Robbie, you're my friend for life, buddy."

"Jesus, who's teaching those kids?" Elliott said.

Jack slapped David on the shoulder. "A wee one. God, I love it."

David glared at Jack, but it didn't quiet him. He only laughed louder.

JL knew firsthand that humor often defused tension in anxious cops. Looking at her brothers' faces, the stress lines of a moment ago had softened. If she did a serious assessment of herself, the knots in her stomach had loosened as well.

Henry remained focused on the cat, oblivious to the ruckus going on around him. "He's got a loud motor, too. Listen, Da."

David chucked the boy under the chin. "Take the kitty, Robbie. Ye'll have an anatomy lesson later."

"Can ye believe Tabor sent us a boy kitty? What was she thinking?" Robbie said to his brother.

"I dinna know, but he'll still be fun to play with, right?"

"Don't ye leave that cat here. James Cullen has been begging for a dog since Tate passed on. When it's time, we'll find a new pet, but not right now," Elliott said.

"Sometimes they select you," Jack said.

"That's a blue point Siamese," JL said. "I had a cat like that years ago. They're purry, furry, and very friendly. He'll make a good pet."

"Good. Ye can take him back to New York with ye," David said.

"No, Da, we're keeping him," Henry said.

"I have to talk to Elliott now. Take the cat to yer seat." Henry and Robbie trotted off and David turned his attention back to the monitor. "We're up to speed on the explosion and the number of injured and dead cops. That's a big hit for a police department. We've been debating whether or not to tell the Napa police about the other entrances."

"I vote no," JL said. "Whoever's down there will expect the cops to tunnel through. They won't know we've discovered other entrances. If we tell the cops, we lose the element of surprise. Kevin and I are going in now—"

"Do not engage, JL. It's too risky." Her father's voice sounded tired, and his strained expression definitely wasn't the friendly grin that greeted her at Sunday brunches.

"I don't intend to, Pops, but I've got to get a visual."

"JL, I'm Braham McCabe."

Ahhh. So that's who Mr. Green Eyes is.

"I'm familiar with the entrance ye're talking about," Braham continued. "There's also a second one on the other side of the hill. The one ye're planning to use goes straight down and is accessed only by a rope or ladder. It's the more difficult of the two to navigate. Both entrances lead to a cavern about a quarter of a mile in. There are a couple of side tunnels before ye get there. I've been down them. They're narrow, wet, and have low ceilings. It's a maze and easy to get lost in."

"Do the side tunnels go through to the cavern, or just the main tunnel?" she asked.

"I don't know. There's a fissure in a rock at the back of the cavern. It's narrow, and ye have to exhale to squeeze through. On the other side, a passage branches off in four directions. We didn't explore farther. It's possible one connects to the main passage somewhere in the maze."

"Don't get caught in one of those," said her oldest brother, Connor. "Those assholes will seal you up and we'll never find you."

"Thanks for the lovely thought, Connor. What was the cavern used for?" she asked.

"To my knowledge, it never was," Braham said, "at least not in the beginning, but Meredith might have family records that mention its use."

"How long has it been since you've been down there?" she asked.

David gave Braham that same quick shake of his head, and she knew she wouldn't get an answer, or one that would be of any benefit.

"A while," Braham said.

"You, David, and Elliott could have a convention of Scottish spelunkers," Connor said.

Jack laughed. "Take David off that list. He's claustrophobic."

Robbie popped his head up beneath David's elbow, with the cat dangling in his clutches. "What's claus…tro…bo…bic mean, Da?" Robbie said.

Henry butted in, pushing his brother aside. "Means Da doesn't like animals with claws." He flicked his hand. "Take that critter away."

"*Lincoln*," David yelled. "Entertain these two."

A kid about ten years old with beach-boy blond hair and thick bangs covering his eyebrows leaned over the table and rescued the cat from Robbie's clutches. "How much you gonna pay me, Uncle David?"

David pointed to the monitor. "Aunt Meredith and Uncle Elliott need our attention. Take these two toerags and keep them quiet until we land. Ye can send me a bill for yer services."

"I want a new ATV. Da said I have to pay half." Lincoln snugged the cat between his chin and shoulder, petting him gently. "Come on, Henry and Robbie. I'll let you play games on my iPad."

Elliott pushed back from the table, crossed the room to the video screen, and set his hands on his hips, elbows jutting out. His impatient body language was becoming familiar to JL now. "Let's get back to the cave. We're running out of time," he said.

Braham lightly roughed his son's hair, and Lincoln's freckled face lit up. "Okay, here's something else ye need to know," Braham said. "The echo effect in the passages is disorienting. If ye want to go toward the sound, wait until it stops, then go in the direction you last heard it."

"How clear are the passages? Are they difficult to maneuver? Any rocks, obstructions, anything?" JL asked.

"There's no way to know," Braham said. "The rocks could have shifted significantly since I was down there. Plan on rough terrain."

"The explosion littered the passage on the Wine Cave side with debris. We can probably expect the same on the other side," JL said.

"Meredith should have watertight hiking boots," David said. "Braham mentioned there's a waterfall down there, so it'll be wet and cold."

Meredith glanced up from her laptop. "Where's the water come from?"

"I don't know," Braham said.

Meredith directed her attention to Kevin. "Let's look into that later. We might be able to tap into the source for additional diversification."

"The rest of yer supplies, JL," David said, "climbing gear, headlamps, emergency rations, and flashlights, should arrive within the hour."

"I only have my—" JL was interrupted by a squabble among the children. Hearing the boys arguing reminded JL of her early years and fights with her older brothers. Nostalgia welled in her throat, and she swallowed back the tightening. Those same brothers had dropped everything and taken unscheduled time off to come help Austin.

"*Lincoln*," Braham yelled. "If ye can't keep those wee lads quiet, you'll lose yer pay."

"Yes, sir." He giggled. "Shhh. Ye're getting me in trouble."

When the little boys quieted, JL said, "I only have a Glock. Are there firearms here I can use?"

"Kenzie has a safe full of hunting rifles and handguns. She can fit ye out with another Glock and ammunition. Kevin's an expert shot, but he's a medical professional, and he'd never shoot a person."

Kevin's palms hit the tabletop, and he came up out of his seat. "You don't have to talk about me like I'm not in the room."

"Would ye shoot somebody, Kevin?" David asked.

Kevin's eyes weren't on the video screen. They weren't on David. They were on her, and they moved along her face, searching for a reaction—or approval, maybe. "I'll protect you with my life. If that means I have to shoot someone, I will. Without hesitation."

Her mouth opened, but no words came out. Instead, she took his hand and held it tightly. She had that kind of loyalty from the men she worked with. She had it from her brothers, too. To hear it from Kevin, though, knowing the personal sacrifice it would require to honor his commitment, shook her to the very core of her being. He sat and rubbed her shoulder gently, never taking his eyes off her.

After a protracted silence, Elliott asked, "What else do ye have on yer list, David?"

The question jolted JL back to the task. "If Kevin and I go in using the steep entrance, what are you guys going to do, Connor?"

"We're coming down your chimney," he said. "As soon as we get in position, David's calling the cops. SWAT will go in through the other entrance."

"How are we going to coordinate? Smoke signals?"

Chuckling, Connor said, "Good one, JL. McBain's taking care of that, too. He's a one–man military operation."

"I'm having a wireless miner lifeline telecommunication system brought up from San Francisco. The company is in Utah, but the sales rep is in California this week. He's making a personal delivery and should be on site within the hour. The system works on magnetic waves instead of radio waves. It's a two-way wireless voice and data communication system that allows ye to send and receive text messages."

"I'm tech-savvy, but this might be above my pay grade. I hope it's self-explanatory," she said.

"The rep will show ye where to set the antenna and how to use the communicator."

"Will the teams be able to communicate directly, or will we have to go through you?" Connor asked.

"Kenzie and I will have to relay messages," David said. "If we had time to install the system cave-wide, ye'd be able to communicate directly."

"Sounds like you've thought of everything," JL said, "except how we get Austin out."

"If he's in the cavern, we'll have to protect him when we go in so he doesn't end up as collateral damage, but he'll be our priority," Connor said.

Connor resembled Austin more than her other brothers. Although they all had auburn hair, she, Austin, and Connor had green eyes, and the others had light brown. It was hard to look at Connor now without bending double with even more worry and fear.

Kenzie entered and crossed the room to the video screen to stand next to Elliott. "Hey, McBain. I've been monitoring this conversation from my office. You're not planning to go down there, are you?"

"We took a vote," Connor said. "Anyone with children can't go. That includes Pops."

Kevin squeezed JL's hand. No one but Kevin and her father knew Austin was her son. If they had tried to cut her out of the rescue, she would have gone in on her own.

Kenzie put her arm around Elliott. "What do you think, Boss? Should that vote apply to authors, too?"

Elliott stroked his chin. "I'm inclined—"

"Forget it, Elliott," Jack interrupted. "I don't have kids. Don't plan to have any. I'm going. Period."

Kenzie glanced over her shoulder toward JL. "I'll be sure he goes with your brothers. They look like they can handle him." Then she turned back toward the screen. "McBain, give the detectives a heads-up about Jack."

"We don't have that much time, Kenz, but I'll do my best."

Jack pulled to his feet and said, raising his voice, "*Charlotte, I need your help, sis.* They're ganging up on me."

From somewhere off screen a woman said, "You're on your own, Jack. Besides, I'd probably agree with them."

Jack hung his head, shaking it back and forth. "After all I've done…"

Connor bumped shoulders with Jack and gave him the OK sign.

With a satisfied look, Jack relaxed back in his chair. "David, how many people you think are down there?" Connor asked.

"I've been reading the reports from JL's case four years ago, and, based on Braham's assessment of the size of the site, there could be a dozen, but there's no way to know for sure," David said.

"I disagree," JL said. "This isn't a high-traffic operation. A few people are slipping in and out. They've bought off a guard or two, possibly more, possibly the entire company. Even with that, they can't move a truckload of people in and out on a regular basis. I could be wrong, but that's how I see it."

"Now the alarm they set has been activated, they'll be breaking down the operation and getting the hell out of there," David said.

"Surely they know cops are crawling all over the winery. They can't leave from those entrances in daylight. They'll be spotted," Connor said.

"We have to assume they have a communication system and are getting regular reports from the guards on their payroll," Elliott said.

"Why do you think they killed Salvatore?" Meredith asked.

"Good question," JL said. "Here's a scenario. When Salvatore got a job here, it put Montgomery Winery on the cartel's radar. Later, when they needed a base of operations in Northern California, Salvatore's olive operation moved to the top of the list. He might have tried to shut it down. Whoever killed him screwed up and brought attention to the winery at a critical time.

"Hollinger told me his contact at DEA said there's word on the street that a big buy is going down soon," JL continued. "Since the passage is now blocked, they know they have to get out before the barrier is breached."

"But they don't know we know about the other entrances." Connor turned to speak to Jeffrey, Patrick, and Shane sitting behind him. There wasn't enough room at the table, so Connor, as the oldest, sat next to Pops. Which was good, because if they all tried to participate in the conversation, they would be more disruptive than the kids had been.

"Hold on a minute," Meredith said, swiping her finger across the face of her iPhone. "I just received an email from our engineering company in response to my query about the winery's surveys. It appears they had a system failure and lost several files. They only now discovered our surveys were among them."

"If David hadn't received copies before, ye couldn't get them now," Elliott said. "Interesting."

"Exactly," Meredith said.

"When did the failure occur?" he asked.

Meredith typed on her keypad. "I'll ask." He moved to stand behind her and looked over her shoulder. After a moment she said, "The second email says it occurred a year ago." Meredith sat back in her chair. "Those sons of bitches have been operating in the cave for possibly a year, and we haven't known about it. I want that security firm fired immediately and those guards escorted off the property or thrown in jail until this is over."

"Meredith, wait," David said. "We might be able to use them to our advantage. Hold off until I get there."

"David," JL said. "Pops might be able to help you. He has experience with security firms. He worked part time for two outstanding New York companies when he needed a second income. And besides, he'll need something to do while he's waiting for us."

David tapped his fingers again on the table, obviously thinking about the request. After a moment he said, "We'll get to work on it right after this call."

"Let's get back to the perps inside the cave," Connor said after a quick conference with his brothers. "Let's assume they're busting their asses to get out of there before the breach. Since we can assume they don't know we know about the other entrances, we should have the element of surprise."

"If Kevin and I go in to do reconnaissance, we should have an update by the time you guys arrive on site. As soon as the boys are ready to rappel in, David can notify SWAT and take them to the other entrance. That's assuming they haven't gotten through the blockage."

"The explosion could have caused significant damage in the rest of the cave, including the cavern where Austin might be held," Braham said.

"Unless they had a demolition expert who used the right explosives and techniques to block the path without causing structural damage, if that's possible," JL said.

"We're just guessing about all of this," Connor said. "We don't know the cartel is in there. We don't know if the other entrances go through to the cavern. We don't know for sure if they've got Austin. We don't know anything."

"We're making educated guesses," JL said.

"We've got six members of the NYPD with almost a hundred years of combined experience, plus Kenzie's and my military experience. If we're guessing, we're making highly educated ones," David said.

Kevin, who had been sketching the interior of the cave on his pad, asked, "How close is the blockage to the cavern where you believe the cartel has set up shop?"

"Based on your estimate of how far in ye found the injured cops, the cavern could be a quarter of a mile. Approximately the same as the two rear entrances," Braham said.

"So the plan is for Kevin and me to drop in, make our way to the cavern, find Austin, and then wait for everyone else to arrive," JL said.

Kevin made notations on his drawing of the distances from each approach to the cavern.

"Get a visual, but stay put until backup arrives. Got it?" Connor said.

"Got it," she said.

"What we're planning can't go beyond this call," David said. "If the perps get advance warning—"

"It'll mimic the thirty-second shootout at the OK Corral," Jack said. The men at the table, along with those in the conference room, all glared at him. "What?" He shrugged. "I'm just saying, from what I've heard about JL, she'll blast them all to hell in five seconds." He made a finger-gun hand gesture. "Bang. Bang."

"I'm sure they'll get a real bang out of it, Jack." Kenzie turned her back to the screen and said to Meredith, "He's losing it, and he's driving Charlotte nuts, too. We've got to find him a girlfriend—a real woman, not some bimbo—before he goes off the deep end."

"Good luck with that," Meredith said.

Elliott unclipped his monitor and slid it across the table. "If ye're wearing a monitor, leave it here. We can't keep our whereabouts a secret, but we don't need to advertise our locations either."

"Good idea." Meredith unclipped hers, as did Kevin and Kenzie.

"One thing to keep in mind," Pops said. "We might not be dealing with the Di Salvos."

"I don't give a shit if it's the Super Mario Brothers. If they've got Austin, whatever their name is, they're going down," Connor said.

"I just got an email from a contact in the DEA in response to my inquiry about the Di Salvos. Hold on, let me read it." A minute later, David said, "No information on the Di Salvos, but the Sinaloa Cartel is suspected of using a security company as cover for a meth and heroin operation near the Napa area."

"Not Sicilian, then? Mexican? That's who we're dealing with?" JL asked.

"Mexican organized crime has ties to Canadian organized crime. That makes California the corridor between the two," Connor said.

"I'm relieved to know it's not the Di Salvos," Pops said. "I'd hate to find out they're running the family operation from their jail cells."

"The Mexican cartel is just as nasty, Pops," Connor said.

"But they don't know the O'Grady name," she said.

There was a knock on the door. Meredith opened it and let Cate in. "There's a large delivery for JL. Where do you want it?"

"Wait a minute, JL," David said. "I want to be clear about this. By the time we arrive on site, if the engineers working for the Napa police haven't breached the obstruction to allow SWAT to advance, I'm letting them know the locations of the other entrances."

"You know they'll be pissed they weren't advised earlier," JL said.

"Yeah, well, I work for Elliott, and he wants ye to have yer chance. If SWAT goes in and Austin's killed, he wants ye to know ye did everything ye could."

JL stood, rested her hand on Kevin's shoulder, and said to Cate, "Send the delivery to the cottage. We'll tac up there." Then to Elliott she nodded, and to her family she said, "I'll meet you in the cave. Don't be late."

14

JAMES CULLEN COMPLETED his assignments, closed his calculus textbook, and sat back in his desk chair, crossing one leg over the other. A weird vibe had invaded the house a week or so ago, and he had yet to put his finger on its pulse, but it seemed to swirl around his parents. He knew his mom wasn't sick. She had her annual scan a few days ago, and her doctors announced she was cancer-free. So what was it?

He'd read an article in *Wine Digest*. The market was strong and so was Montgomery Winery's balance sheet. He didn't understand it completely, but Kevin had gone through the basics with him, and he understood the bottom line.

As for the horse business, well, it was always a gamble, but according to the *Thoroughbred Daily News,* the industry was thriving. His dad was happy about that.

Oil prices were down, his Apple stock was up, and his net worth, according to Kevin, continued to grow.

His investments should make him a millionaire this year. Granted, he didn't start from zero, but at thirteen, he was proud of the investments he had made since Kevin introduced him to the stock market. His biggest profits, though, came from the commodity trades recommended by Aunt Kenzie. Those were gambles, but so was the horse business.

On the surface, all might be well, but James Cullen's spidey senses were tingling, and tingling bad.

He shoved his fingers through his longer-than-usual hair, which had gotten so long his flipped-out sides covered his ears. He had promised his mom he would get a haircut before the gala, but that wasn't going to happen.

Austin's disappearance was only part of the reason for the weird vibe. His dad was withdrawn and had bailed on an overnight camping and rock-climbing trip the weekend before. He also skipped the past two training runs. That was unlike him, especially since they had registered for a Napa mini-triathlon in mid-November.

He had been short with Kevin, but that wasn't unusual. He yelled at Kevin more than he yelled at anyone else. His dad was a yeller, but not his mom. She was determined to make sure James Cullen didn't grow up imitating his dad's bad habit. His dad used to drink a lot and take prescription painkillers, but that was before he was born. James Cullen was glad he hadn't known his dad then.

Now that he stopped to think about his dad's behavior, James Cullen realized his dad was acting like Kevin said he used to act back then, when he took drugs. Kevin said he took drugs because he was in pain. If he was in pain now, it meant he was sick, because he wasn't injured like he used to be. The thought of his dad being sick scared the bejeebers out of him.

What were the odds of both his parents having cancer? He would Google that later, but right now he wanted to find out what was happening at the Wine Cave. He had tried earlier, but his mom was on a conference call, his dad was MIA, Aunt Kenzie had a Do Not Disturb sign on her door, and Kevin was with Austin's sister. Kevin liked her—a lot. James Cullen could tell. Kevin had that same look on his face he got when he drank wine from the reserve collection and smoked cigars—like nothing in the world could be better. Kevin had told him sex was like that.

James Cullen wondered if Kevin was having sex with Austin's sister. Next time he was alone with Kevin, he would ask. Kevin would probably tell him to mind his own business. That was his standard answer when he didn't want to talk about something personal. Kevin was like his older brother. He loved his dad and all, but he could ask Kevin stuff he couldn't ask his dad. If Kevin married JL, he might move to New York. If he did that, James Cullen would go, too.

He'd have all his high school requirements met by the end of his sophomore year and could apply to Columbia. With his 1495 SAT score, articles in junior entrepreneur magazines, leadership positions, and community service, he was a shoo-in to get accepted. Well, maybe not a shoo-in, but close enough, and he'd be fifteen by then. He didn't consider himself a prodigy, but he was really smart. He didn't brag about it, but everyone knew he was precocious. His parents and Kevin had balanced his advanced development with giving him social skills, athletic training, and a healthy dose of humility. His mom said that if he didn't have humility, none of his other gifts mattered. He practiced humility daily by putting the needs of others above his own.

He hadn't put anyone's needs above his own today, so he had better get busy. He wanted to mark the task off his list before lunch. His mom was an infamous list-maker and had taught him the skill, although he frequently lost the dang thing before he could check off all the items.

He turned on his phone. There was a house rule that when he did schoolwork, his phone had to be turned off. He didn't like being incommunicado, but that was the rule. If he broke it, he lost his phone for a week. A week was an eternity to a kid. He should know. He'd experienced an eternity twice.

An alert came across his phone. There had been an explosion at the Wine Cave, and fire and rescue was on its way. "What the hell?" The alert had gone out ninety minutes earlier. He had been in his bedroom doing his assignments and all hell was breaking loose. Usually if there was a news alert, his mom or dad would interrupt him, like they had earlier to let him know about Austin. His mom said if he stayed focused on his work, he wouldn't worry so much about Austin. It had sort of worked. But now two bad things had happened.

He dashed through the villa to the garage, grabbed his helmet, and sped out of the driveway on his ATV. When he arrived at the Wine Cave, he found the parking lot full of fire and rescue vehicles, an FBI Hummer, two SWAT trucks (one from San Francisco), police cruisers, and a command truck. A handful of police officers in SWAT gear huddled around a table with maps spread out. Several other police officers patrolled a perimeter protected by a sawhorse barricade.

He pulled alongside the barricade, and one of the officers approached. "I'm James Cullen Fraser. What's going on here?" He had expected the acrid smell of explosives, but all he could smell was the usual fermenting grapes.

The cop glanced around the parking lot. "Ask your parents."

"They're busy. Can't you tell me? I heard there was an explosion. Was anyone hurt?"

The cops exchanged glances and their pained expressions answered James Cullen's question. "I'm sorry for your loss, but I have to know if Austin O'Grady was among the injured."

"We don't have any information."

"Do you mean you don't have any information, or you don't have any information you can tell me?"

The first cop's guarded eyes narrowed. "We don't have any information."

"Right. Gotcha," James Cullen said with a shrug, deliberately nonchalant. "Hey, is Detective Castellano around? His son, Sammy, is a friend of mine. I wanted to play basketball with him today."

The other cop relaxed noticeably, as James Cullen had anticipated. His dad had told him once that if he tried to get information from someone who wasn't being helpful, then he should find a way to connect on a personal level. Nine times out of ten, he got the information he wanted.

"I heard he had to meet with the DA this morning to prepare for a trial that starts on Monday."

"Oh, right. Sammy told me his dad would be in court all next week. Mr. Castellano was lucky he wasn't here when the explosion occurred. He could have gotten hurt. Sammy would be..." James Cullen glanced down and cleared his throat.

The cop squeezed his shoulder. "Sammy still has his dad, but his dad's partner wasn't so lucky."

James Cullen's stomach did a flip-flop. "Hollinger was killed? Sammy thinks he's a great guy."

The cop squeezed his shoulder again. "Hollinger was still breathing when they carried him out."

James Cullen reached into his pocket for his phone. "I'll send Sammy a text about playing ball and make sure he's okay."

"Hey, don't mention any names in your text. Wait until the department releases the names to the media."

"Oh, right, sure. No problem," James Cullen said.

"Oh, and kid," the first cop said, fixing him with a serious gaze. "Your friend wasn't with the men they brought out."

James Cullen shuddered with relief. From the moment he had heard about Austin's kidnapping, he had been confident Austin would be okay. His mom had said being confident sometimes wasn't enough to get the job done. You had to have faith, too.

He had faith, and he had confidence. He also had an inner power. Not a sixth sense, or a seventh, eighth, or ninth exactly. It was more like a feeling, a Knowing he couldn't explain. He had talked to David about it once when they were fishing. David said it came from James Cullen's great-grandfather Fraser. David told him he was never to take it lightly or use it unwisely.

The weird vibe came from the Knowing. What he couldn't understand, though, was what purpose it served if he couldn't figure out what it was trying to tell him.

He left the Wine Cave behind and drove off toward the orchard to see whether there was any news of the investigation into Salvatore's murder. When he arrived, no one was there. The tarp they had erected remained in position, but there weren't any guards.

From the corner of his eye, he spotted a shadow moving through the orchard. He stopped the ATV and watched. What was it? A wild pig, a turkey? No, it was a brown, woolly bear or looked like one, a little one. A cub? He climbed off the ATV and approached slowly. The muddy animal dropped a recently deceased turkey at his feet. "You're not a bear. You're a dog."

James Cullen knelt, reaching out for the dog, who stood guard over his prey. He wasn't wearing a collar, but he wasn't unkempt, and from what James Cullen could tell through the woolly bear fur, he wasn't skinny. He had been cared for. He had either run away or been abandoned on the side of the road. The dog sniffed James Cullen from the toes of his boots, up his legs, to his hands.

"I'm taking you home with me, but you've got to leave the turkey here."

He got back on the ATV and patted the seat. "Come on, boy." The dog picked up the turkey. "Drop it." James Cullen patted the seat again. "Come on." The dog looked at the turkey, back at James Cullen, and back at the turkey. "Damn. Okay, bring it along." What was he going to do with a dead turkey?

The dog jumped up on the seat with the turkey in his mouth. James Cullen couldn't take the bird home, too, that was for sure. He would drop it off at the dumpster behind the lodge.

To avoid his parents, he kept the ATV on the running trails instead of the roads. If they discovered him driving around with a stray dog, they would be mad. If they discovered him driving on the trails, they would be pissed. He better not get caught.

When he reached the dumpster, he ordered the dog to drop the bird. "Sorry, boy, but this has to go." The dog let loose, and James Cullen tossed the turkey into the dumpster. "I'm going to call you Tater Tot in memory of our golden retriever."

Thinking about Tate always made him sad. Two years ago, he and his dad had stayed up all night with Tate because he was sick. When the sun rose, the aging dog had opened his eyes, whined as if saying good-bye, and quietly passed on. It was the fourteenth anniversary of his return from his Oregon Trail adventure, so he had lived longer than the usual life expectancy of a golden retriever. James Cullen's dad had said the trip to the past made him younger, and that's why he lived longer than expected. If that was the case,

James Cullen was taking his dad back in time as soon as he could figure out how to do it. At sixty-five, his dad needed to subtract a year or two from his age instead of adding one every year.

James Cullen drove home to find two golf carts in the driveway, which meant both his parents were there. They rarely drove their cars around the winery unless they had to go to Napa for a meeting. He left Tater Tot in the garage with a bowl of water and went to find his dad. If he could win over his dad, his mom wouldn't say *no way* to a new dog.

He entered through the laundry room into a quiet house and made his way down the hall toward the first-floor master suite. Loud noises—drawers slamming and unintelligible raised voices—came from his parents' bedroom. From where he stood in the hall, a sliver of their room was visible beyond the partially opened door.

"Elliott," his mom said, "I saw the missed call on your phone. Why was your urologist calling?"

Another drawer slammed, and the brass pull banged against it. "There's too much going on right now. It'll wait." His dad's voice was razor sharp. James Cullen had heard his dad use that tone with others, like Kevin, but never with his mom.

James Cullen backed up and tiptoed into the hall bathroom. He pushed the door closed, leaving barely a crack. His parents' voices, pitched low, reached him where he stood. He had never spied on his parents. All their kissing and groping grossed him out, but this was different. And he wasn't leaving until he found out what was going on.

"After all we've been through with my illnesses, you have to tell me."

His mom had been sick with cancer when he was born, and three years ago he and his dad had been afraid she had cancer again. Fortunately, it was the cave, not cancer, which made her sick. While she was sick, his dad had never left her side.

"What's wrong with you?" his mom asked.

"My PSA level is high enough that he wants to biopsy my prostate."

"How high? Four, five, six…what?"

"Ten," his dad said.

James Cullen's chest chilled with icy fear. He would Google *PSA of ten and prostate* to find out what they were talking about.

"Why didn't you tell me about your symptoms?" His mom's voice softened, and she sniffed.

Is Mom crying? He couldn't ever remember hearing her cry. This was serious.

"If you want a divorce—"

James Cullen sagged against the wall. *A divorce? Because of a PSA?*

"If I want *what?*" his mom said. "Are you crazy? I love you. There are many treatment options now. We'll find the best one. The best doctors."

"Are ye saying ye'll still want me when I'm pissing myself?"

"I'll never stop wanting you."

Now the gushy stuff starts. It's time to leave.

"It'll be hell to manage cancer treatments without Kevin's help."

Cancer? Without Kevin? No, this was the worst news possible.

"Kevin's not going anywhere. Isn't it time to be honest with him anyway? He needs to know you're his father."

James Cullen slid down the wall to the floor, pulled his legs into his chest, and laid his forehead on his knees. *Father? That would make Kevin my brother. He really is fam? That means Dad had sex with Mrs. Allen. OMG. Ugh.*

"I can't tell Kevin the truth until I talk to his mother. I can't blindside her," his dad said.

"She's the one who's kept you from being honest with him for all these years."

James Cullen could see his mom throwing shade at his dad. Her dirty looks could even make David cower.

"Kevin deserves to know the truth," she continued. "It's the same with Austin. He deserves to know JL is his mother, not his sister."

JL is Austin's mother. This is crazy.

"What JL does or doesn't do isn't our decision," his dad said.

"It'll all be different when she learns the truth about the amethyst brooch. She and Kevin are meant to be together."

Amethyst brooch. Will it match my sliver? Hashtag excited AF.

He'd heard enough. It was time to get out of the house before his parents caught him eavesdropping. He tiptoed out of the bathroom and down the hall. Before leaving, he unclipped his monitor and left it in the laundry room. He didn't want to talk to his parents right now.

He jumped back on his ATV. "Come on, TT. We're getting out of here."

He sped out of the driveway again with Tater Tot's ears flapping in the breeze, then turned onto a running path that snaked through the woods. The ATV bounced and heaved over the uneven path. Dumb to have picked the one trail his mom left in its natural condition to practice trail running. He grabbed the dog by the scruff of his neck to keep him from falling out. "Hang on, boy."

James Cullen's mind was a jumbled mess. If he had overheard the conversation anywhere else, he would have done an Onion check to make sure it was the truth. He tried to organize his thoughts like his mom taught him, so he could tackle them one at a time. To start with, there was a murder and Austin was missing. Next, his dad was Kevin's bio-father, and JL was Austin's bio-mother. His dad was sick with a cancer that made him piss his pants, and the amethyst brooch that might match his sliver of amethyst had shown up.

These news blasts were too big to tackle on his own. He needed his squad. Who could he trust with his fam's secrets? There was only one person he could tell. Time to T-up at Kevin's place.

"I know what to do," he told Tater Tot. He turned at the first crossroads and wound his way around the property until he reached the cottage.

James Cullen bounded up the porch stairs with the dog trotting behind him. He flung the door open, yelling, "*Kevin. Kevin.* Where are ya, buddy?"

"Stop yelling. I'm in the living room."

James Cullen ran to the back of the house to find Kevin kneeling on the floor, digging through ropes and hats and stuff. "What're you doing?"

"JL and I are going caving to find Austin."

"He's disappeared with the amethyst brooch, hasn't he?"

Kevin tossed a harness onto the sofa. "Where'd you get that idea?"

"I just heard my mom say everything will be different when JL learns about the amethyst brooch. That you two belonged together."

Kevin sat down, his elbows on his knees and his hands rumpling his hair. "Holy shit…" He glanced up at James Cullen, his eyes wide. "She has a brooch?"

James Cullen shook his head. "Yes, *but that's not all.*" He pointed at Kevin with his index finger. "*You're* my real brother. Not a fake brother like Aunt Kenzie and Aunt Charlotte are fake aunts. *You're a real brother.*" James Cullen jumped up and down, swishing his hands as if he were shooting baskets. "I just heard my mom say so. We're real brothers."

Kevin climbed to his feet, grabbed James Cullen's shoulders, and leaned in close to look him in the eye. "*Calm down.* You misunderstood. Your dad says I'm like a son, but I'm not a real one, so don't go spreading rumors. You know how dangerous they can be." Kevin shook him a bit. "Are you listening to me?"

"Yes, *you are* my for-real brother. I heard my mom. She said Austin deserves to know that JL is his mother and you deserve to know that Dad is your dad."

"*What?*" JL stood in the doorway, one hip cocked against the frame. Her skin looked pale, and her lips practically colorless. "What did you just say?"

"I know where Austin's gone. Well, I don't know *where* he's gone exactly, but I know how he got there. He went back in…"

"*James Cullen Fraser. Shut your damn mouth.*" Kevin's face reddened, and the veins pulsed in his neck. "You've got this all wrong." He went silent, and after a moment sat down hard on the sofa. So hard, in fact that the stacked gear bounced onto the floor. He tried to catch a helmet, but gave up and let it fall with the rest of the gear. "Listen to me carefully. Austin is in the cave with some bad men. This story isn't about a trip back somewhere, it's about what's happening here and now, and you need to calm down."

JL sat on the arm of a chair, her body sagging. "I don't understand what's going on here."

"It's simple. Kevin is my dad's real son and you're Austin's real mom. And Austin has disappeared because he went back in time like Aunt Kenzie and Aunt Charlotte."

"*James Cullen.*" Kevin's voice was forceful enough that it threatened to burst one of his bulging veins.

"*Don't yell.* It's true." Tears welled up in James Cullen's eyes. He refused to cry and took several deep breaths. "My dad's got cancer."

Kevin jumped to his feet. "*What?*"

"He has cancer that will make him piss his pants…" James Cullen swiped at his cheek. "And"—he stopped and sniffed—"he thinks Mom will want a divorce. Why would she want to divorce"—James Cullen's voice cracked, and he took another deep breath—"him when he stuck with her through breast cancer?"

Kevin scrubbed his face with his hands. "They won't get a divorce. I've never seen two people more in love, and if your dad was sick, after what we've been through together, he would have told me."

James Cullen put his hand on Kevin's shoulder. "He didn't even tell Mom. She had to drag it out of him."

Kevin picked the gear up off the floor and shoved items into his backpack, moving like a robot. "JL and I have to go now."

JL picked up her pack and shoved a bottle of water into the stretchy pocket on the side.

"Okay, but where do you think Austin went? The Civil War? World War II? No, Kenzie and Charlotte already went there. Maybe the Old West like Aunt Kit?"

Kevin looked at him a minute, then his eyes traveled to a spot behind James Cullen and grew distant. He had never seen Kevin cry before, but he thought he was about to.

"We'll talk about this when I come back." Kevin's voice was a dead monotone. "Do not repeat anything you just told me. Promise me."

James Cullen's breath hitched. "I promise."

The crunch of breaking glass resounded from the kitchen.

"What the hell?" Kevin said.

Fear grabbed James Cullen by the collar and shook him hard. "*Tater Tot.*" He dashed out of the room to find his dog wolfing down a Danish roll with a cream-cheese filling. Shards of glass from a broken serving plate covered the floor along with a dozen more rolls. James Cullen grabbed the dog around the neck and pulled him away from the glass.

JL picked up the rolls and tossed them in the garbage, along with the largest pieces of glass.

"Where'd he come from?" Kevin asked, patting the dog on the head.

"I found him in the olive orchard, but I can't take him home right now. Not after what I overheard. Mom and Dad would both tell me I couldn't keep him. Can he stay here until I figure out what to do next?"

"Put him in the laundry room. I keep a bag of food for visiting dogs in the pantry. Leave him food and water, but you have to clean up any mess he makes." Kevin pointed to the rest of the glass and the crumbs. "Including this."

James Cullen checked Tater Tot's paws to be sure he hadn't cut himself. "Do you know what kind of dog he is?"

"Looks like a standard poodle to me. They're smart, and they make good hunting dogs," JL said.

"Hmm. He was carrying around a dead wild turkey when I found him. I wonder... I'll look up poodles on the Internet so I can answer Dad's questions."

"He's a vet. I'm sure he already knows," Kevin said.

"Dad's a large-animal vet. He doesn't know much about dogs. If I want to keep Tater Tot, I need to be knowledgeable about the breed."

"Check the animal shelter website. His owner might be looking for him," JL said.

James Cullen hugged the dog. "He's not lost. He's abandoned. He's mine now."

"Just because you want it to be true doesn't always make it so." A quick flash of rage covered Kevin's face, and then quickly vanished. "Check the website. He's a healthy-looking dog. You need to find out who he belongs to."

"What about you, Kevin? Does your dad know you're Dad's son?"

James Cullen saw despair and something more written across Kevin's face, something buried deep, something that scared the crap out of James Cullen. "It's complicated," Kevin said. "We'll talk about it after we find Austin."

James Cullen took a second look at the gear on the floor. Kevin and JL were going back in time. He knew it, but why wouldn't they tell him? "If you're going to find Austin, what year are you going back to?"

Kevin put his arms through the straps of his backpack and adjusted it on his shoulders. "You've been told not to talk about the brooches, yet here you are doing what you're not supposed to do."

"But JL has the amethyst brooch. You know about the magic, right?" he asked her.

A veiled expression came over her face. "Hold that question until we get back," she said.

She acted like she didn't know what was going on, and that frustrated James Cullen even more. He wasn't a kid. He understood about life, stuff, and the mysterious brooches.

"Come on, Tater Tot." They headed to the laundry room. "You've got to be a good dog while we figure this out. I didn't want to let on to Kevin, but I'm scared. Cancer is a bad thing. A real bad thing."

15

AFTER JAMES CULLEN left the house, JL finished loading her backpack in tight silence. Her ears were still ringing from the boy's bizarre statements. She shook her head, wondering for just a moment if he had been hallucinating. Highly unlikely. His mind wasn't impaired. His problem was a sieve like mouth that allowed every thought to pass through unchecked. He wasn't aware that when he said inappropriate things, he hurt people.

If he were her son…

She shook off the thought. No need to go there. What pissed her off, though, was the revelation Kevin had lied to her. After promising he would keep her secrets, he had spilled them to Elliott. She couldn't forgive him for violating her privacy. Her fingers curled, and her nails bit into her palms as she resisted the urge to punch him. "I vote we table the questions we both have until we find Austin, but I do have one I need answered right now."

Kevin picked up the coiled rope and attached it to a loop on his pack. "If I can answer with a yes or no, I will."

"Braham's in his late forties. Did he go inside the old cave more than fifty years ago?" A sinking, twisting feeling wrapped around her throat. As outrageous as it seemed, she was inclined to believe Kevin would say yes.

"It's possible. Now I have a question for you. Why'd you tell Meredith about Austin?"

"*I didn't.* You told Elliott." She shoved her pack aside. "I'm using all the self-control I have to keep from using your abs as a punching bag." The shadow of strong emotion flitted across his eyes. "You broke your promise," she continued. "You did exactly what others have accused you of doing. You have a hole in your head and no off switch. Everything you know just pours out. Exactly like James Cullen."

Kevin fell silent as he sat on the sofa, arms propped on his knees, his large hands clasped. "I didn't tell him. I swear."

"No one else knew about Austin. If not you, who?" She could barely get the words past the constriction in her throat.

"I've never been surprised by the information Elliott and David can uncover, but this time I'm stymied." Kevin's anger was back, rising, smoldering behind his eyes. He couldn't conceal it now. "David has methods. And I feel as betrayed as you do."

"Yeah, you have even more reason than I do. You and Elliott look alike, but it never occurred to me you were actually related. My opinion of Elliott is now worse than it was."

"I don't blame you."

She slung her pack over her shoulders and adjusted the weight, relieved that Kevin hadn't betrayed her—but someone had invaded her privacy, and that pissed her off. "As long as it didn't come from you, I can deal with it."

Kevin jumped to his feet, his voice gravelly when he said, "I wouldn't do that to you."

She unclenched her jaw and relaxed her shoulders. "Where we're going, I have to be able to trust you."

The hunger and need in his eyes nearly knocked the breath out of her. "You can. I swear. We have to move past this. We can't let what James Cullen said come between us. We need to leave our anger here and deal with Elliott later."

"I can do that. Can you?"

"For you and Austin I can."

She managed a faint smile. "Then let's get out of here."

They each carried an armload of gear out to the golf cart in the garage, and every time they passed through the laundry room with another load, Tater Tot jumped up and barked. "Do you think he'll be okay when we leave?" she asked.

Kevin raked his fingers through the dog's thick coat from his neck to his tail. "James Cullen will come back as soon as he can. The dog won't be alone for long." He gave the dog another pat on the head, then closed the door between the garage and laundry room. Tater Tot whimpered and Kevin stopped and stared at the door leading back into the house.

JL tugged Kevin toward the cart. "Come on. The dog will be fine. He's safer here than he was running around loose, and someone else needs your attention more than the dog."

"I was thinking about what James Cullen said, but mostly I was thinking about Austin and how alone he must feel."

The fraying threads holding JL together were snapping one by one. *Snap. Snap. Snap.* If she lost her focus, she might as well sit in a corner and wait for the others to rescue her child. It wasn't that she could do it better. It was that she could do it now.

They climbed into the four-seater cart, and Kevin backed it out of the garage. JL reached behind her to hold onto the packs to keep them from bouncing out. "You'd think we were rappelling into the Grand Canyon with all this gear."

"David has over planned. We'll never use all this crap."

"Speaking of David..." Her hands trembled slightly as more threads snapped. She clasped her knees to still them. "Do you think he can really do the impossible?"

Kevin's dark brows drew together, as though the sunlight bothered him. It bothered her, and intensified the constant throbbing inside her skull.

"Meredith said once that David could do the impossible with one hand tied behind his back, but miracles took him a wee bit longer."

"A wee bit longer?" She snorted. "How does anyone inspire that kind of confidence?"

"When you meet him in person, you'll have your answer."

Her eyes moved slowly to Kevin, fixing on his face. "You make him sound like Superman."

"If he ripped open his shirt and flashed an S, I wouldn't be surprised."

Kevin drove the cart along the path they followed on their run the previous day. Life had changed drastically since they set out to investigate Salvatore's murder. As she looked back on the previous day, it was clear her turf war with Hollinger had been a harbinger of what was to come.

"Do you have a plan once we drop into the cave?" Kevin asked.

"I want you to wait at the drop point while I check out the passage. Once I have a visual and assess the situation, I'll report back. We'll text Elliott when we find Austin, then we'll sit tight and wait for the others."

"Correction: we go together or we don't go at all."

"Absolutely not. I'm not putting you in that kind of danger. There are dead and injured cops because of my stupidity. I'm not adding you to that list."

"You're not to blame for what happened in the cave."

"I don't see it that way. If I'd been honest with Austin, he wouldn't have run away. The cops wouldn't have gone in after him, and the dead and injured would be home with their families tonight."

"Maybe. Maybe not. I think the cops would have put it all together eventually and gone in to investigate. The result would have been the same."

"Not necessarily. They could have entered through the rear entrances," she said.

"As far as we know, they're not looking for another way in," Kevin said.

"I'm going in to get a visual. If SWAT can't get through the middle, David will give them the locations of the rear entrances. At that point, I have to be in a position to protect Austin."

"If we're inside the cave, SWAT will have to worry about us, too. Is that fair to them?"

"Nothing about this is fair." She checked her watch, cringing at how much time had elapsed. "Austin ran out of the cottage eight hours ago. We've been messing around for three hours making plans. Time's run out."

Kevin pulled to a stop near the top of the hill and rested his forearms on the steering wheel. "I don't have the experience you have. As I see it, though, we don't know for sure the drug cartel is in the cave, or even if Austin is there. If the cartel and Austin *are* there, we don't know if we can reach them. The passage could be blocked, and we're doing nothing more than chasing wild turkeys. I say let SWAT continue with their plans to breach the cave-in while we go exploring."

She liked his analysis, except for the part about Austin not being there. If he wasn't in the cave, where could he be? "We never called the dorm. What if he found another way back and has been in his bed asleep all this time?"

"That would be the best possible news. Call," Kevin said.

She dialed the front desk at Austin's dorm, and the door attendant told her Austin had called at ten o'clock to say he was spending the night at the winery, although he hadn't said anything to her or to Kevin. If Austin had called, the evening would have turned out differently. She knew the school allowed him to stay overnight at the winery as long as he called by ten, but still… According to the log at the front desk, he had not returned to the dorm, nor had he called again.

JL disconnected and slapped the phone against her palm, wishing the news had been different. "At least we thought of checking before we went caving."

"Let's find the opening while we wait for Kenzie."

Standing on the path halfway up the hill, JL turned and faced the top, orienting herself to the photograph David had presented in the briefing. "Eyeballing this, I'd say the opening should be between two and three o'clock." She pointed to her right and spotted an outcropping. "Do you see those rocks?" she said to Kevin. "Let's start there."

They hiked up the hill about thirty yards until they reached the outcropping. A jagged stone guarded the entrance. It was almost impossible for passersby to spot the opening in the muddy brown rock.

JL squatted, pushed the bushes aside, and glared into a hole barely wide enough for a person to crawl through it. She was tempted to throw down a pebble, but remembered Braham's warning about sound carrying underground. A pebble hitting the bottom might sound like an explosion.

"I need a flashlight."

"I'll get it. Hold on," Kevin said.

While Kevin trotted back to the golf cart, she stuck her head into the opening. One of Gramps's favorite sayings came to mind: *Consider the risks, anticipate the problems, and prepare for the unknown.* Had she done that? She sat back on her heels and thought a moment. Rapping into the cave was a medium risk filled with uncertainties, but her gut said it was the right action to take. Only time would tell whether her gut was right or wrong.

Kevin drove the golf cart to within a few feet of her and handed over the flashlight. She scooted in as far as she could, shining the light along the sides and all the way down to the bottom. Good thing she wasn't claustrophobic. She scooted back out. "It's made like a chimney. Five to six feet wide, maybe a five story vertical drop. Animal carcasses at the bottom. Looks muddy. The chimney opens into a passage. Sharp rocks on the sides, and they're wet. And…I hope you're not claustrophobic."

"I'm not. Not afraid of the dark either. Move over. Let me see." Kevin knelt and stuck his head into the opening. He took his time, then sat back and blew out a deep breath. "Poor kid. He's got to be scared shitless."

"The faith you have in David, Austin has in me. He knows I'm coming for him. I just hope to hell he doesn't brag to his captors that his brothers and sister are NYPD detectives."

"He might think you died in the explosion."

JL frowned and her entire body seemed to get into it, shoulders dropping. "He'll worry about that, but he knows Pops and the boys will come if I can't."

Kevin squeezed her neck, leaned over, and kissed her forehead. "He won't give up hope."

JL glanced back at the gaping hole, shivering. "Let's get the gear ready."

They unloaded the cart and stacked their packs next to the entrance, finishing just when Elliott arrived with Kenzie and a man JL didn't know.

Kenzie hopped out, grabbing a backpack. "What's it look like?"

"Best guess...it's a five-story rap to the bottom. I need help setting the anchors," JL said.

"That's why I'm here." Kenzie squatted, and using a flashlight, checked out the opening. "Do you want to find the other entrance and switch up with the guys?"

"We've lost too much time already," JL said. "Let's stick with the plan."

"Have you heard anything from David? What's their ETA?" Kevin asked.

Elliott approached the opening. "They're an hour out. I've ordered limos to pick them up. Yer brothers will rap here and come in behind ye. SWAT will come in from the other side."

"We don't even know for sure where the other entrance is. And, assuming we're dealing with the cartel, the drug dealers could have abandoned the cave by now," Kevin said.

"David considered that," Elliott said. "He hired a private security firm operated by ex-Navy SEALs. They're on the other side of the hill guarding the area and searching for the entrance. They also have an agent doing a deeper background check of the security company working for us, looking at clients, past associations, connections..."

JL shot an irritated glance at Elliott. "What else has he changed since we spoke last?"

"This op is fluid, JL," Kenzie said. "You know how that goes. David's waiting on your recon, though, to give SWAT the best intel possible."

"Then let's get on it," JL said.

The other man walked toward them, carrying boxes. "This is Bill Wilder," Elliott said. "He's from Miner Lifeline Telecommunications."

"We'll set the antenna first," Wilder said. "Once it's set and working properly, I'll give you instructions on the wireless senders."

"How long will it take you?" JL asked.

"I'll do it as quickly as I can," Wilder said.

"It'll take me fifteen minutes to set the anchors." Kenzie tested the rock outside the hole, found a flat, smooth section that would work, and then hit the rock with a hammer. "That ting sound means it's solid." She marked the spot with chalk. From the tool belt strapped around her waist, she produced a steel bolt a half inch in diameter. She mated the bolt with a climbing bolt hanger and screwed them together. "I spray-paint my bolts gray. They're very shiny when new, and I don't want the reflections picked up."

"Where'd you learn all this?" JL asked.

"Some of it in Cadet Basic Training at West Point. The rest I picked up from groups I rappelled with on weekends. I like rock climbing better, but I don't have time to do either one now."

Kenzie attached a masonry bit to a drill, put on safety glasses, and drilled a hole in the rock. The rock didn't chip, and she was able to drill a smooth, flat hole. After cleaning the hole of dust and debris, she hammered until the bolt was set in the rock. "I'd much rather find a solid tree to use for an anchor, but for this job, I don't want to depend on an olive tree."

While Kenzie worked on rigging the drop, Elliott and Wilder set up the antenna. JL and Kevin used the time to step into their climbing harnesses. JL checked the position of Kevin's harness, and he checked hers. "The waistband goes above the hipbones."

"I know, but it won't go any higher," he said.

"Loosen the leg loops a bit," she said. He loosened the leg loops and tightened the waistband. Then she checked the tightness again. "Lace up the loose straps and you're good."

He tugged on one of her loose straps. "Lace yours up, too."

She gave him a sly smile. "You're messing with me, aren't you?

You've probably rappelled more than I have."

He kissed her cheek. "I like it when you're in charge. It turns me on."

Wilder came over to them with two walkie-talkie-like devices. "These allow both voice and data communication, but I understand silence is necessary because of the echo. Type in your message here. There will be a delay of a couple of minutes before Dr. Fraser or Mrs. McBain receive your message, and another couple before you receive a reply. Be patient. The system will be working, but it's not instantaneous like your smartphones. Dr. Fraser will have a sender unit, too, and there are four more for the other team members. And here are extra batteries." He handed Kevin a package of AA batteries. "You should get twelve hours of continued use."

"We won't need that long," JL said.

Kenzie gave them last-minute instructions. "Watch for rocks. Don't engage. Backup will be here in about sixty minutes. Keep your head as high as possible. If you have a choice between crawling and crouching, crouch. Always keep your head up."

"I'll hit my head on the rocks," Kevin said.

Kenzie knocked on Kevin's helmet. "That's why you're wearing this expensive gear. Put it to use, even though your head is hard enough to withstand a hard knock or two. If you come to a trunk passage or to a room in a cave, you might have to choose which way to go. Estimate a level line from you to the place you're headed. It may take you over breakdown block—"

"What's that?" Kevin asked.

"Rock that breaks off from the ceiling and clutters the passages," Kenzie said.

"You may have to swing wide of a direct bee line, but the level line will require less energy to traverse. Pick out intermediate landmarks to head for to keep you straight on your course."

"Braham said there are passages, but he didn't know if they go through to the cavern," JL said.

Kenzie's lips pinched together. "Here's the thing, and I'll deny I said it, but…" She pulled Kevin and JL aside and out of Wilder's earshot. "Braham hasn't been in that cave in well over a hundred years. The earth could have shifted, opened some passages, and closed others. Don't take his memory as an absolute."

A hundred years? JL shook her head like a dog shaking off water. For right now, JL wasn't going to let that statement swallow up even one ounce of her focus.

"Here's one last piece of advice. Conserve your energy. Rest every muscle you can every chance you get. That will ward off fatigue and keep you alert. You're not used to using the muscles you'll use down there. Don't rest too long, though, or you'll get chilled. Hypothermia can quickly become a serious problem when you're caving."

Kenzie used two locking carabiners to attach the rope to the anchor, then handed the rope to JL. She gripped it in her right hand to control the tension off the breaking teeth. After double-checking JL's gear, Kenzie said, "You're ready to go. Good luck."

JL backed up to the edge, glanced at Kevin, and said, "I'll meet you at the bottom."

And then she was gone.

16

JL RAPPELLED INTO the damp, black abyss. When her feet touched the sticky mud floor of the cave, the bones of dead animals that had fallen through the hole crunched beneath her feet. She unhooked the climbing rope from the locking carabiner on her harness and tugged on the end so Kevin could hook up. While she waited for him to rappel down, she checked out the opening and the passage beyond.

The air was danker compared with the other part of the cave she had been in earlier, and there were twice as many long, narrow, finger like limestone formations hanging from the twenty-foot ceiling. Since she wasn't a caver, she couldn't remember which one was a stalagmite and which one was a stalactite, but both were inherently dangerous. She tapped her helmet and said a silent thank you for being the vertically challenged one in her family. Instead of being a duck-and-roll, the mission would be a duck-and-dodge.

Getting her head split open wasn't the worst thing that could happen over the next few hours. She had figured that one out already. It was finding Austin hurt...or not finding him at all.

She had been in the tunnels beneath New York City. The first trip down had been terrifying. The second trip, not so much. By the third trip, the anxiety, while still present, was completely manageable. What she had learned was to trust her instincts and depend more on her other senses than on her inability to see into the darkness.

There was a saying in her family that *some see darkness where others see only the absence of light*. She had never understood the saying until that third trip through the tunnels. Some people could live in the brightest sun and still see only darkness, while others could live in the dark, like Helen Keller, and see the light. It was all about a positive mind-set versus living in fear. She had tried to pass that philosophy on to Austin. This would be the test for him, and, no matter what happened, he would not come out of the cave the same young man who had gone in.

The crunch of boots on bones stopped her reminiscence. Kevin's headlamp flashed at her, and she lifted her hand to shield her eyes.

He plodded toward her, glancing around. "This breakdown makes the passage look like a junkyard."

"We'll be doing a lot of scrambling up and down rock piles and squeezing between blocks."

"And using up our energy," he said.

She pointed at the wall behind him. "What's that? It looks like graffiti."

Kevin brushed his gloved hand over the lettering. "It is."

JL stood next to him and read the inscription. "B MCCABE, C MONTGOMERY 1860." She glanced up at Kevin. "Either this is Braham's ancestor, or it's really true. He was here a long time ago." She snapped a picture with her phone. "This is for Kenzie, but who is C Montgomery?"

"Meredith's ancestor. Cullen Montgomery married Kit MacKlenna."

"The same Kit whose portrait is hanging in the Welcome Center?"

"The one and only," Kevin said.

"After we get Austin, we have a lot of talking to do. My list of discussion topics grows by the minute," she said.

He tugged her to him and kissed her. "And I want to have a long conversation with you. So be safe down here."

"Stay behind me. If shooting starts, stay down. I've been in shootouts before. I'm prepared for this."

He gave her one last hug. "I don't want to be a distraction. Do your job."

She shifted the hefty pack on her back, settling it just so. It was now eight hours since security had found Austin's truck. While she studied the terrain again, she realized reaching the cavern would take longer than she had anticipated.

Whispering, she said. "Send Kenzie a message. Let her know there's a lot of breakdown to scramble over. It will take longer to reach the cavern than we thought."

"Okay." Kevin grabbed the wireless communicator from his bag.

While he sent the message, JL sidestepped the fragments of a boulder that had fallen and shattered in the center of the passage.

He finished the message, put the communicator back into his pack, and for the next thirty minutes JL silently led them through the muddy cave and around the breakdown, using only one lamp on its lowest beam.

Sweating, she stopped to rest in their dark, alien world, and drank some water. A cave cricket crawled across her mud-caked boot. She glanced back in the direction they had come. Their footprints marked their path. No one would have a problem finding them. The walls along the passage consisted of gray and black rocks with white water lines. Had the cave flooded recently? Had the overnight rain seeped in? She didn't know, and that worried her. Austin had only worn a T-shirt and lightweight hooded jacket. If he got wet and was now in the cool, damp cave, he could be facing hypothermia.

"Have you heard the adage—*Take nothing but pictures; kill nothing but time; leave nothing but footprints?*" JL said, low-voiced.

"So far I haven't seen anything I'd like to take, and I hope I won't have to kill, but I'm prepared."

She linked her forearm with his and gave it a tight squeeze. "I hope it won't come to that either."

"How far do you think we've gone?"

"Maybe halfway. It's hard to tell. I'll have to dim the light soon."

"It won't be easy traversing this ground in the semidarkness."

"If my light's spotted, they'll shoot first. I'll use a flashlight like I did when we went in after the explosion. If I keep the light moving erratically, that will give us some protection." Not knowing where they were in relation to the cavern was a tightrope walk without a safety net.

They came around a twist in the passage and she stopped abruptly. "We have a problem. Turn on your headlamp." She turned on hers simultaneously, and clicked off the low beam flashlight. Slowly, she picked her way through the littered floor to a pile of rocks that completely blocked the passage.

How was she going to find Austin now? Her heart sank into her stomach, and she dropped to her knees. How had she reached this point—defeated by a cave, by rocky walls and a ceiling, by the highly polished pebbles on the floor? She grabbed a handful of damp, earthy-smelling cave fill, and the scent triggered memories of her mother's graveside service. She threw the dirt against the pile of rocks and willed her mind to separate the converging tracks. She couldn't think of her mother's death right now. Not when even the smallest possibility existed that she could lose Austin, too.

Kevin knelt behind her, wrapped her in his strong arms, and she wove her fingers between his—long and thin and surprisingly warm. His pounding heart thudded against the bones of her spine, and she sagged against him, shuddering, listening to the faint, eerie sounds of the cave and the skittering rats. If she had ever possessed a compass to direct her life, it had disappeared ages ago. There had to be some reasonable explanation for why she was here on the verge of hell's ghoulish darkness.

Austin had wanted to venture away from home for his last two years of high school to advance his chances to play at a top NCAA Division I school. Why here in Napa, as opposed to all his other choices, all other points on the damn globe? Why here, where his life could end so violently?

"SWAT will rescue him." Kevin's mumbled words were hot against her cheek, and the tears dripping from her eyelashes dried salty on her face.

"His captors…" she said, crying, "will use him as a hostage. He'll be in more danger."

"We can't give up." He squeezed her closer. "We have to have faith."

"I don't have any." She sobbed harder. "I never should have come here. None of this would have happened."

Years ago, after discovering she was pregnant, she had crumpled onto her bed, cursing the day she had left home for dance camp, wondering what would become of her—seventeen, single, Irish Catholic, and pregnant. After Austin's birth, after her parents concocted a fantastic story, after she fell madly in love with her child, she realized going to camp and meeting Austin's father had been the singular event that had catapulted her into an extraordinary life.

Like the sloped limestone ceiling hanging in decorative folds above her head, an event out of her control was crashing down, trying to steal her extraordinary life.

Kevin rubbed her shoulders, reminding her she wasn't alone, that someone guarded her back and cared for her in spite of her weaknesses. Drawing strength from a man was new for her, but she was doing it now, not only because she needed to, but because she trusted him. She depended upon and trusted her fellow cops, too, but her trust of Kevin was on a much deeper level. A man who would hold her and encourage her while sitting on the floor of a godforsaken cave would never stomp on her heart.

She swiped at her tears with the back of her hand.

He gave her a handkerchief. "Take this," he murmured in a rough, intimate voice she would dream about later.

She turned in his arms and looked up at him. "A handkerchief?" she whispered, and then realized it didn't matter. No one could hear them. "*Here?*" Her voice echoed in the inky blackness, harsh, and somehow mocking in the confines of the cave.

"Shhh." He pressed a finger over her lips. "Sound travels." He reclaimed the handkerchief and dabbed at both of her eyes. "Elliott told me years ago to always carry one, because women were impressed when you dried their tears."

"Have you done that often?"

"This is the first time. Is it working?"

"You've already impressed me. You haven't offered patronizing advice that if I stopped crying I'd feel better."

"I haven't been honest with many women in my life, but I'll never lie to you or give you false hope."

"We were an unstoppable force, but we met an immoveable object. Now I don't know what to do." She refolded his handkerchief and noticed the initials KBA. "What does the B stand for?

"Blane. I'd been working for Elliott for a few months before I discovered his middle name was Blane, too. I thought that was weird. Now I know why."

"I'm sorry you're hurting."

"I'm hurt and angry. I don't know if I'll be able to trust him again."

"What if Austin never trusts me again?"

"He will."

"Now you're patronizing me."

"No, I'm serious. He'll get over it."

The absolute matter-of-factness of his tone sent a shiver racing down her spine. "You're convinced he will, and convinced you won't. Why?"

His fine nostrils flared as he took a deep breath. "It's different. It's just different for me."

"That's bullshit."

"Maybe. But that's the way I feel."

"If the truth is an unstoppable force, and your inability to live with it is an immoveable object, then the constant battering of one against the other will give you sharp edges and turn you bitter," she said.

"Sounds philosophical," he said.

"Sometimes when you can't go forward, you have to move backward a bit."

"That sounds philosophical, too, but what good will moving backward do, unless you're retreating or quitting?" he said.

"I don't want to quit," she said. "I'd rather move one pebble at a time than give up. I don't know how long ago this cave-in occurred. A day, a year, a decade. My cave knowledge would fit within a tweet's hundred-and-forty-character limit."

"Well, here's a tweet for you: We don't have to quit, and we don't have to move all the way backward. Just a couple dozen feet." He directed his beam of light down the passage in the direction from which they had come. "What exactly did Braham say about other passages? Do you remember?"

She thought a minute. "There are several side tunnels. He'd been down a few. They're narrow and wet, with low ceilings. He didn't know if any went through to the cavern. He also mentioned a fissure in a rock at the back of the cavern that opened into a passage with more tunnels."

"It's possible one of those tunnels connects with one of the side tunnels off this passage."

"Braham sounded like he didn't think so, and if there is one, it could be blocked, too."

"He didn't rule out the possibility that one existed," Kevin said. "If we can't go through an obstacle, we can go around it. Water does, and maybe we can, too."

"But he called it a maze, and said it was easy to get lost in there."

"We have fluorescent yellow chalk to mark the walls. We won't get lost." His keen eyes challenged her. "Do you want to try?"

JL stood, keeping her light on the passage behind them. "If an event blocked this passage and others, it could also have opened another one up."

"Let's take the turnoff we passed and see where it goes."

She scratched her neck, wondering how much time they had. "Let's set a time limit. Say, twenty minutes."

"Agreed. I'll let Kenzie know what's happened and that we're taking a side passage."

While Kevin typed the message, JL attached a chalk bag to her belt and counted the pieces inside. Again, she couldn't depend on caving experience, but between what she had in her bag, and Kevin had in his, they had enough to get the job done. If they ran out of bread crumbs, she'd tear up her shirt and tie yellow ribbons around old rocks, pointing the way home.

The communicator set off a low beep, announcing a message had arrived. Kevin read it aloud, "Elliott said to return immediately. Do not take alternate route. Might be unstable."

"I don't remember Braham saying the passages might be unstable," JL said.

"He didn't. Elliott doesn't want us down here. I could see it in his eyes, but he knew he couldn't stop you. And if you were going, he couldn't stop me either."

"Send a message. Tell them we'll explore for another twenty to thirty minutes. If we don't find a connection, we'll come up."

Kevin sent the text. "Let's go. Waiting for a response will eat into our time."

They reversed their path, heading toward the side passage, climbing over the same blocks they had scratched and scraped themselves on earlier. Prior to entering the side passage, she gave Kevin a piece of chalk.

"Bread crumbs."

He grimaced. "I'm glad I'm not hungry."

She elbowed him. "It's for our return trip."

"I know." He gave her a teasing smile as he drew a heart and put their initials inside.

"I don't think that'll last a hundred fifty years."

"Neither will I, but what you and I have will last long beyond today."

She smiled. "You are a romantic, aren't you?"

"I am with you."

He finished the graffiti by drawing an arrow through the middle.

For the past few hours, her tension had spiraled to new heights. Mixed in with the tension was absolute terror for Austin. Surprisingly, Kevin had been able to de-escalate that tension, and had done it repeatedly. At first his attention hadn't been so obvious, but now as she thought back to what had brought them to this point, she realized he had either touched her, kissed her lips, or distracted her with something as mundane as sketching a heart on the wall.

How did he know to do that? He even drew little lines that made it look like the heart was beating. He tucked the chalk into his pocket and swept out his hand, gesturing for her to enter the corridor. "After you, my dear."

They left the heart behind and entered the passage, stepping over smaller pieces of breakdown. The walls seemed to close in on them. The six-foot wide corridor with an eight-foot ceiling narrowed to three feet and a ceiling that nearly grazed Kevin's helmet. It twisted left, then right, and then left again, and JL quickly lost all sense of direction. They could be traversing a perpendicular line, a parallel line, or God forbid, going in the opposite direction.

They reached the first turnoff and had a choice to make. Turn or go straight? It was a flip-a-coin moment.

"Let's stay in this corridor," Kevin whispered.

While JL drew an arrow with an H pointing in the direction of home, Kevin drew an X above the archway to the passage they decided to forego. He leaned in close, reminding her quietly, "We've almost reached our twenty-minute time limit."

JL returned her piece of chalk to the bag and looked at her watch. She wasn't ready to turn around, but they could wind around for hours in the maze and not accomplish anything other than worrying everyone topside.

Kevin wiped dirt from her face with his handkerchief. "I'll do whatever you want. Go another ten minutes or turn around."

She puffed her cheeks and blew out a breath of crappy indecision. "I have no idea what direction we're going in, do you? With all these twists…"

"I don't either. And I have an excellent sense of direction." Kevin peeled back the wrapping from a Power Bar without making a sound and took a bite. "I'm going to send Kenzie a text and tell her we're taking ten more minutes."

She kissed his cheek, whispering, "Good luck with that."

They didn't wait for Kenzie to respond. Instead, they continued down the corridor. When the message came through, they stopped to read it.

"Same as the last one," Kevin whispered. "Return immediately."

"Let's see where this corridor goes. If it leads nowhere, we'll turn around."

While Kevin typed a return message, JL rested on a block jutting from the wall and listened to the dripping water and scampering rats. She sensed every ounce of Austin's distress. Kevin put the wireless in his pack, and took a step forward, just as a new sound came echoing down the corridor. Her heart stopped, and maybe even time itself.

"Listen. What do you hear?" she asked.

Kevin whispered, "Something popping."

"Where's it coming from? Can you tell?"

He shook his head. "No."

"I can't either." Her heart fell into an erratic beat while adrenaline flooded her veins. She hurried back toward the archway with the florescent yellow X, dodging breakdown and the stalag-thingies hanging from the ceiling. "Hurry."

Kevin rushed after her. "What are we chasing?"

She put her finger to her lips. "Austin. He's popping his knuckles."

17

As soon as JL and Kevin ducked under the arch, the popping stopped. She did, too, jerking her head this way and that, trying desperately to pick up the sound again. *No*, her heart screamed. She bit her lower lip to hold the scream inside her mouth. Had she imagined the popping sound? No, Kevin had heard it, too. Right? It wasn't just her ears playing evil tricks. Her well-honed instincts told her Austin was nearby, which meant his kidnappers were, too. Treading quietly was essential, along with using the dimmest light possible to avoid giving away their position—a dangerous balancing act.

"Stay behind me," she whispered. "Keep your headlamp off. I think we're close."

He switched off his light. "Got it."

"Will you take my pack?"

He lifted it off her shoulders, brushing his cool fingers across her sweating neck.

Mentally, she went through a list. Her weapons were loaded—one holstered and one in her hand. Her belt held two easy-to-reach thirteen-round magazines, and she wore a bulletproof vest snugged between wicking T-shirts. Backup was unknown, but she and Kevin had the element of surprise, always a worthy ally.

Moving slowly, she sidestepped and climbed over the breakdown. When at last she neared an intersecting passage, a wedge of light angled across the floor from the right side. She raised her hand, signaling what she intended to do: move forward—alone.

Kevin tapped on her shoulder once to acknowledge the signal.

JL gave the flashlight to him, and with her free hand increased the tension on her gun to a nice firm grip, ensuring tactical accuracy, and moved toward the edge of the wall. She took a deep breath, and then another, while adrenaline surged. She flattened herself against the rough face of the wall and took baby steps so she wouldn't disturb the pebbles in the path. She ducked into the passage, into the light, and froze.

Ahead of her, maybe twenty feet, stood a wall with a fissure running down the center. Behind her, a dozen feet or so, the passage branched off into three other corridors. The scene was exactly the way Braham had described the cave's maze behind the fissure.

She cocked her head and studied the cleft. Since she wasn't a geologist or even a spelunker, she could only make an amateur's guess as to what had happened. It made sense to her that an event had caused the wall to split, and when the earth settled, instead of the sides lining up again, they had fallen out of alignment, and one side overlapped the other, creating a fissure several inches wide. True or not, she didn't care. She only wanted to find what she believed was on the other side—Austin.

A murmur of Spanish-speaking voices—definitely not Sicilian—filtered through the opening. She spoke Spanish, not fluently but enough to get by in New York City. The voices were too low and garbled to be intelligible.

She eased into the gap, flat against the wall. If she stood between the overlapping faces of the rock, her shoulders would brush the sides. Austin would be too broad-shouldered to fit facing forward, but he could shuffle through sideways.

She pulled her arms into her chest, gripping the gun, her heart pounding. She scooted to the edge and peeked out, finding herself in shadow.

Four male Hispanics, their backs to her, worked at a six-foot table, stacking bags of white powder. *Cocaine.* Large bricks of the stuff were stacked on the opposite end of the table, along with a set of digital scales and boxes of small resealable zipper storage bags. Four AK-47s were propped against the wall, and each man carried a weapon in a shoulder holster. Their movements were swift, yet efficient. If they had been expecting someone, they would have been looking over their shoulders. They weren't. Their heads were down, and they remained focused on their work.

Across from the table, on the other side of the thirty-foot-wide cavern, was a sleeping area with two cots, both empty. Breakdown littered the sides of the cavern and stalag-thingies hung from the ceiling and grew up from the floor, filling the cavern front to back and side to side. A pinball expert would find the approximately hundred-foot-deep cavern a challenging playfield.

Light from lanterns powered by propane radiated off the surface of the walls and ceiling, illuminating the center of the cavern. The jagged walls glistened as if they leaked icy water, and there was a slow-flowing waterfall on the side of the cavern near the kitchen area.

In a back corner, discarded with the trash, was Austin. He was on his side facing her. His jacket looked ripped and bloodied, and zip-tie handcuffs restrained his hands. A cut above his right cheekbone had bled down his face to his chin.

His chest had a slow and easy rise and fall. He wasn't passed out. He was sleeping. She knew that rhythm well, having pressed her hand on his chest while he slept as a baby and a toddler. And although she hated to admit she was that obsessive, she had checked his breathing as a schoolboy, too. He must have just fallen asleep, and that's why the knuckle-cracking had stopped. She would never again complain about that habit.

She slid out of her hiding place and returned to Kevin, who was waiting near the entrance to the passage leading to the fissure, gun in hand. She pantomimed to move back in the direction they had come. They picked up their packs and moved as quickly as safety allowed. When they reached the next passage, she dropped her gear, closed her eyes, visualized the scene, and ran a rescue scenario through her mind.

"Did you—" Kevin asked.

She held her hand in a stopping gesture, and Kevin silenced himself, allowing her mind to complete its visualization without interruption. A minute later, she said, "He's been roughed up, but he's sleeping. I'll draw a sketch, not as accurately as you could, but you can get a sense of the scene." Using a piece of chalk, she drew a layout of the cavern on the wall. It wasn't to scale, and the breakdown and stalag-thingies were randomly placed, but Kevin nodded that he got the gist of what she was trying to show. "I only saw four men, and they were here," she said, pointing to the table she had drawn.

Low-voiced, he asked, "How did Austin look? Was he cut or bleeding?"

"His cheek and lip are cut, shirt's ripped, but he's not writhing in pain. His hands are zip-tied in the front, and he's not cradling them as if one was injured."

"What's your plan? Walk in there and steal him?"

She weighed her plan and its objective with a critical eye. She couldn't go in with guns blazing and shoot the perps, even if that's what they deserved for kidnapping her child. The operation required a level head and stealth. First she had to wake up Austin and cover him while he escaped. Then she had to defend the retreat. It was doable.

"How long have we been down here?"

"Close to two hours."

"It will take thirty minutes to backtrack to the main passage to check on my brothers. Another thirty to get back to this point."

"We'll be able to move faster in both directions because we know where we're going."

She wanted to get Austin out right now—waiting was killing her—but she knew she had to give her brothers time to get there. "Let's go back to where you drew the heart and wait."

They backtracked, making better time, and reached the main passage.

"Send Kenzie a message and ask her why the hell my brothers aren't here."

Kevin typed a message. While they waited, they ate Power Bars. Five minutes became ten and ten became twenty. With each minute that passed, her initially bean-sized anxiety ticked up a notch. She curled and uncurled her hands, trying to keep them loose, and still no message arrived.

"It could be the plane. It could be the communicator," Kevin said.

"Could be both. What are the odds of that?"

"None that I'd bet on," Kevin said.

After forty-five minutes, JL stopped chewing her lip. She would come unglued if she didn't take action. "That's enough. I can't wait any longer. They've had time to get here, turn around, and fly back to New York. They've run into trouble, and for whatever reason, they can't get a message to us. I can't worry about them until after I rescue Austin."

She picked up her pack and slung it over her shoulder, cringing under the weight. She did a quick gut check, and Meredith's haunting words came back to her. *You'll be tested. Act. Don't react.* She wasn't reacting. Kenzie said the plans were fluid. It was now time for JL to act. Sparked with determination, she said, "Let's go."

Kevin grabbed his bag and they headed back in the direction of the cavern.

When they reached the place where JL had drawn the map on the wall she said, "Let's leave the bags here. I'll get Austin out, but after that we'll have to run like hell. Can we?"

"As long as we have the advantage of knowing the way out. If they know it, too, our luck might not last."

"I haven't seen any markings on the walls, stone cairns, or trash. If they've been this way, they memorized the route. One of the men was smoking, and I haven't seen any cigarette butts. Have you?"

"No."

"If they chase us, I'll take a defensive position here." She crouched behind a large boulder to check the vantage point. The spot, while not perfect, would provide limited cover for her while Kevin and Austin escaped. Standing once again, she said, "I'll cover from here while you get Austin out."

"I'm not leaving you behind."

An argument was pointless. If Austin's life were in danger, Kevin would listen to her. "Take only what we need. A knife to cut Austin's bindings and a helmet—"

"And my gun?"

"Both of them. Austin is an excellent shot, too. If you can't shoot at someone, you can shoot over their heads. That'll keep them ducking."

"What could have happened to your brothers?"

"I wish to hell I knew. Could Hollinger be holding them for some stupid reason? What'd Kenzie say to the last message?"

Kevin pulled the wireless communicator out of his bag and checked. "'Come back now.' Nothing since then."

JL looked at the face of the communicator. Her instincts had served her well while on the force, and they were jabbering now. She glanced at her watch. Her brothers weren't coming, Kenzie wasn't answering, and Austin needed help.

Kevin put away the communicator and withdrew two guns, a knife, and Austin's helmet, and set them aside. Then he held JL by the shoulders, pinning her in front of him. "I've only known you for twenty-four hours, but I've known Austin for more than a year. In some ways, you could be twins. You are a dozen steps ahead of me. Your instincts are talking to you. What are they saying?"

She shook her head. "I don't know. Something is off, way off. I don't know what it is. Kenzie told us to return, and my brothers are late. They're never late."

"Plans changed up top and they haven't bothered to tell us."

"That makes no sense to me, but I have to do what my gut tells me to do. Get Austin." She gazed into Kevin's eyes, hoping hers didn't show the fear gnawing in her gut. "I don't know how the change in plans impacts us, and honestly that scares me."

He pulled her closer, and the scent of him, the beat of his heart, and the warmth of his arms both eased and comforted her. In that comfort, her mind cleared away all distractions and singularly focused on the job at hand.

"We could be walking into a trap," he said.

"There are no surveys of this section, and we've seen no signs that anyone has been here since Braham and Cullen carved their initials. If the men holding Austin know we're coming, they won't expect us to come through the back of the cavern. I have to go in believing I'll catch them by surprise but prepared for a trap. That's all I *can* do."

She wanted to stay there in his arms, gazing up at him. She could die in the next few minutes and she would never know the absolute joy of loving him.

"Is that your gut instinct talking?" he asked.

"Instinct and experience."

Kevin gave her another squeeze and then released her. "I'm with you, Sugar. For this job, your instinct and experience are more than enough for me."

There was no more talking. He picked up the items he had set aside, and they quietly returned to the wall with the fissure.

She used hand signals to give last-minute instructions before picking up a handful of pebbles. Kevin gave her a thumbs-up, and they squeezed between the walls.

Austin had turned over in his sleep. She threw the smallest pebble at him, hitting him in the center of his back. He shot a look of annoyance over his shoulder, glanced around, shrugged, and rolled over again. She tossed another pebble, hitting him in the same spot. The hours she'd spent playing darts while crying in her beer were paying off.

The second pebble caught his attention. He sat up slowly and casually leaned against a crate, his eyes watchful. His movements were even and easy, non-threatening.

He knows I'm here.

Her heart swelled with pride, realizing he had actually listened to her safety lectures, which included things to do if he ever found himself in a life-threatening situation. Although he still hadn't glanced in her direction, his mouth tipped up slightly at one corner.

If she miscalculated, one or all three of them could die in the next sixty seconds. The adrenaline that had been pumping into her veins surged, and experience trumped fear. Her hands didn't shake, and her thought processes were clear and focused.

She would let Austin take the lead. Under normal circumstances, he was an exceptional problem-solver and cool under pressure. While he had done a lousy job showing those attributes after finding her with Kevin, by now he'd had time to reflect, and if that secret smile was any indication, he was back to his competent self.

His competence was evident in his body language—he was poised and ready. The same preparedness she had seen on the basketball court, she saw now. He was doing a mental rehearsal of the steps he intended to take, as if preparing for a free throw shot in the last seconds of a game.

"I gotta piss," Austin said. "*Mear*," he repeated in Spanish.

The men laughed. "*...pantalones de pis...*"

She couldn't make out exactly what they had said, but she thought they told him to piss his pants. That wouldn't sit well with Austin. He stood.

"*Mamacita, ayudar al bebé.*"

"*Siéntate.*"

"*Mear*," Austin said. He kept his eyes straight, never looking in her direction.

The sound of pebbles crunching beneath violent footfalls grew closer. A man with smoke and snake tattoos covering his arms approached Austin, pointing a Glock and shouting, "*Siéntate.*"

"I gotta piss. *Mear!*" Austin's voice remained strong but non-threatening.

The guard, a couple of inches taller than she, stepped in front of Austin, putting himself unknowingly between the two of them. She could smell Tattoo's body odor. She had smelled worse, but those men had been dead.

She glanced at Kevin, who was standing nearby, his face stony, but his eyes were wide and alert. She nodded and blew out a breath.

Ready. Go.

She cat-footed from the shadows. In less time than it took to snap a finger, the muzzle of her gun dug into Tattoo's scalp. She seized his firearm with her other hand. Hissing in his ear, "*Muevo y voy a disparar.*"

She tossed the weapon to Austin before putting her forearm across the man's throat and leaning on it. He tried to tear her strangling hand away from his throat, but she put more pressure on his windpipe. Not hard enough to make him black out, but hard enough to take the fight out of him. She might be shorter, but she lifted twice her weight in the gym, and used her strength now. She wouldn't be able to hold on for long, but she could give Austin the seconds he needed to escape.

She nodded at him to run, and simultaneously, she turned, dragging Tattoo as a shield while Austin made a dash toward the wall. When he did, rocks crunched beneath his weight and the sound caught the attention of a shirtless guard sitting at the table. He turned toward them and jerked a gun from his holster, but he hesitated to fire. She didn't, squeezing off a shot. The slug struck the man in the center of his chest, and he pitched forward onto his face. The other two upturned the table, sending bags of cocaine flying, and took cover. She swung the barrel toward the others, the gun roaring and bucking in her hand as she squeezed off shot after shot, finally emptying the magazine.

Kevin rounded the edge of the wall and fired multiple rounds. "*Move back.*"

While Kevin pinned the other guards down, she increased the tension on the chokehold and switched out her empty automatic for the other one with a full magazine, and fired again.

"Move back," Kevin repeated.

She backed up to the wall, got off a couple more rounds, then slammed the barrel of the gun into the base of her hostage's skull.

Kevin scooted through the wall, and she followed. "Hurry."

Austin, hands free of the restraints and wearing his helmet, stood off to the side with a gun raised, ready to fire. Kevin had seen to Austin's needs first before coming to assist her. She didn't have time now to reflect on how much that meant to her, but she would later.

"*Go,*" she yelled.

Kevin shoved Austin in front of him and hurried the teenager toward the side tunnel. "It's an obstacle course. Watch out for your head and shins."

JL reloaded while they ducked and dodged, moving as fast as safety allowed. They passed through the archway and made the turn toward the main passage. At the speed they were traveling, they could reach that point in fifteen minutes. JL stopped and listened for footsteps, but didn't hear any.

"How'd you find me?" Austin asked over his shoulder.

"I'll explain as soon as we get out of here. Keep moving," JL said.

He stopped. "I'm not going another step until I say I'm sorry and thank you."

Kevin pushed him forward. "Apology and thanks accepted. Now move your ass."

When they reached the main corridor and they still weren't being pursued, JL relaxed a bit, but that didn't stop her instincts from bugging the hell out of her.

"How much farther?" Austin asked.

"Less than a quarter of a mile. Let me see your hand."

"Why?"

"There was blood on the wall," she said.

"It's just a little cut. I didn't hit it that hard."

"Let me see it." Kevin examined Austin's hand and glanced at JL. "I should clean it and put a bandage on it. It'll just take a minute." He pulled a small kit from his backpack and cleaned the wound. "It doesn't even need a stitch. You got lucky."

"You sure did," she said.

"Give me some credit," Austin said. "I couldn't play with a broken hand."

She smacked his arm. "If you wanted me to worry, you accomplished that."

"I've got a lot of making up to do, don't I?"

"We'll talk about it later," she said.

Kevin put a bandage over the cut. "I'll clean it better when we get out of here."

JL glanced over her shoulder. "Let's do that before we have company."

All three of them could run a mile in seven minutes, but it took ten to reach the point where they had rappelled into the cave.

"Send Austin up first," JL said. "His harness is in my bag."

"How'd you get down here?" Austin asked.

"We rappelled down," JL said.

"I figured that, but where's the rope?"

Kevin and JL flashed their lights around the small chamber they had rappelled into earlier. The rope they had left dangling was gone.

"*Jesus Christ*. Where is it?" Kevin asked.

JL pulled Kevin and Austin over to the corner and whispered, "I've had a bad feeling about this." She handed Kevin her satellite cell phone. "I have reception in this spot. Call Elliott. I doubt he has my phone number in his contacts, so my name won't show up. If he doesn't answer, don't leave a message."

Kevin placed the call, but Elliott didn't answer.

"Wait a minute and then call David," she said.

When David didn't answer, either, she took back the phone and called her brothers and Pops. No one answered. She gave Kevin back the phone. "Try Meredith."

No answer.

JL's phone rang, flashing a number she didn't recognize. She showed the phone to Kevin. "I don't know whose number that is," he said.

"I'm not answering, then."

"Are we stuck here?" Austin asked.

She wrapped her arm around him and picked at his torn shirt. "Are you cut anywhere else?"

"Just my face. Am I going to have a scar on my cheek?"

Kevin looked at the cut closely. "Maybe a little one." He took out his kit again, and cleaned and bandaged the cut. "It needs a couple of stitches, but this will hold it for now." He slapped Austin's back and gave his neck a friendly squeeze. "A scar will give you character."

"Do you think a girl will be impressed if I told her I was abducted by a Mexican cartel and hidden in a cave with millions of dollars in cocaine?"

"Yes, she would, until she asked how you got out. You'd have to say your mo—"

JL punched Kevin in the ribs.

"I mean...your sister rescued you."

"Yeah, well, I think I'd rather say an undercover narc got me out."

"Do you want to try the other detective? Castellano?" Kevin asked.

She shook her head. "I don't trust anyone in the Napa Police Department. I'm sure they're not all dirty, but someone is."

"Call the state police or the FBI," Austin said.

JL thumbed through her contact list. The cops might have notified the FBI after the explosion. Should she start with them? Whomever she called could be the wrong person. She had to make the right decision. "I'm going to call Pete."

"Your partner's three thousand miles away. How can he help?" Austin asked.

JL studied his tired face. His voice was close to breaking. Adrenaline was leaving his body and reality was sinking in. He'd been in a gunfight that could have killed him, and now the rest of his family was missing. JL understood what he was going through, but she couldn't help him right now. Not until she found a way out of the cave.

"Maybe he can't, but my phone has only a thirty percent charge. How much do you have, Kevin?"

He checked his phone. "There's very little left. But I don't have reception here."

"Whoever comes to our aid will need to be able to communicate with us, or they'll never find the entrance. Pete can help by making calls." She dialed his number.

"Hey, *ragazza tosta*. How's the investigation?" Pete asked.

"It's taken a nasty turn. The cartel kidnapped Austin last night. The boys and Pops caught an early flight to come out here to help." Her sentences ran together she was talking so fast. "I don't know where they are now. No one's answering their phones."

"Slow. Down," he said in a stern tone of voice.

She took a breath. "We rappelled into a cave to rescue Austin—"

"Who's we?" Pete said too calmly for her patience.

Although irritated, she knew exactly what he was doing. Forced to pay attention to details, she had to focus. "Kevin. He works here. We rescued Austin in a shootout, but now we can't get out of the cave. The Frasers and their friends have disappeared. We have members of a Mexican cartel heading in our direction with assault rifles, and they aren't happy. I shot one and bashed another one in the head."

"How far did you rappel?" Pete asked.

"What difference does that make?"

"How far?" Pete asked again.

She glanced up at the entrance, remembering how far down it looked from up there—the same as a five-story building. "Fifty feet."

He whistled. "Can you climb out?"

JL flashed her light up the sides of the walls. "It's a class five climb."

"You need ropes and protection or a fall will be fatal, I got it," Pete said. "I went to training, too."

"Yeah, right. You bailed the same day I did."

While Austin listened to the conversation, he dug through JL's bag, coming up with a Power Bar and a bottle of water. He sat on the edge of a rock, gobbled down one bar, and went back for another.

"You'd probably get a quicker response if you called the Napa police or fire and rescue, instead of your partner three thousand miles away. Have you thought of that?"

"Don't be a jerk. Somebody is dirty, and it might be a Napa cop. I can't trust anyone."

"If I leave right now, flying commercial, I could be there in six hours. Can you hold on that long?"

"Against guys with assault rifles? No. And there's another problem…" She hadn't mentioned this to Kevin or Austin, but she'd seen the look on Kevin's face and knew he was aware of the change. "There's not as much light filtering into the cave as there was earlier. It'll be almost impossible to find the opening if you don't know where it is. Our phones are almost depleted, and we're running out of time, Pete. You've got to get us some help."

18

AFTER CONCLUDING THE CALL to Pete, JL did a quick assessment. She, Kevin, and Austin could be stuck for a while. Securing their position was paramount. Behind the wall, they were safe, but it could also block them in with no way out.

"Austin, stay behind the wall. If those perps find their way here, they won't be taking prisoners."

He moved back, chomping on his third Power Bar. "Where's James Cullen? You mentioned everyone but him."

"I'm sure he's with Meredith," Kevin said.

"He might have gone back to the cottage," JL said.

"I'll try him." Kevin used JL's phone and dialed James Cullen's number, putting the call on speaker.

"Hello," James Cullen said.

JL grabbed Kevin's arm as hope and possibility surged through her. "It's Kevin. Where are you?"

"In the laundry room with Tater Tot. Why?"

"Have you heard from your mom or dad?"

"I tried to call Mom, but she didn't answer her phone."

"This is JL. Have you seen or talked to anyone since we saw you last?"

"I went home, but no one was there, so I came back to the cottage to take care of Tater Tot. Why?"

Kevin punched off the speaker and held the phone against his chest. "I would ask him to help, but I don't want to put him at risk."

"What would Elliott do?" she asked.

Kevin rubbed a hand over his face, the stubble rasping against his palm. "He would depend on James Cullen to do his part."

"Give me the phone." She didn't put it on speaker because she wanted to hear the intonation in the boy's voice clearly, but she kept the phone close to Kevin so he could hear, too. If she heard fear in James Cullen's voice, she wouldn't use him. "We need your help. It'll be dangerous. Are you up for it?"

She could practically see him sitting up straighter; eyes alight, when he said, "Sure."

"Do you know where the security cameras are located on the property, and can you move around to avoid them?"

"I can't get around the cameras at the Welcome Center or the Wine Cave, but I can everywhere else. It's a game I play."

Kevin signaled to her to give him the phone. "I'm going to ask you to do something that could be very dangerous. You have to do exactly what I tell you. Can you do that?"

"I'm your man, Kev."

"I know you are, buddy. Now, look, here's the deal. A drug cartel has invaded the winery. We believe they're holding everyone hostage. You're the only one still free. You can't get caught."

JL put her ear next to the phone, and Austin moved closer, too. It was then that she realized he was shivering. She whispered, "There's a sweatshirt in my bag."

Austin dug through the pack again until he found the sweatshirt. He slipped it on over his jacket then returned to listen to the conversation.

The dog yelped, and James Cullen crooned, "I'm sorry TT." A loud bang followed and the dog barked. "Shi—"

Kevin tensed against her, and as close as she was to him, she could hear and feel his rapid breath rushing in and out. "James Cullen, what's going on?"

"I squeezed TT and knocked over the ironing board."

Austin cocked his head and scrunched his face. "Who's TT?"

"A poodle James Cullen found this morning," JL said.

"Where're my parents? Are they all right?"

Kevin didn't answer immediately, and instead looked at her, all hint of his teasing smile long gone. She had been listening for fear in James Cullen's voice, and now she heard it loud and clear.

"We don't know," Kevin said.

"Where's David?" James Cullen's voice held that tone that said he was afraid to ask, afraid of the answer, but more afraid of not knowing one way or the other.

Kevin's breathing halted briefly, and a lump of dread pinched JL's throat. The entire clan had absolute faith in David's ability to accomplish the impossible, and not knowing his whereabouts caused Kevin and James Cullen deep concern. Her, too.

"We don't know where he is either," Kevin said.

"What about Aunt Kenzie?" James Cullen asked.

"We believe she's with your parents," Kevin said.

"Did you find Austin?"

"Yes, he's with us," Kevin said.

James Cullen whistled his relief. "At least not all of your news is bad. So tell me what to do. I won't let you down."

JL tugged on Kevin's sleeve, and he pressed the phone against his chest again. "Let's see what Pete can do before we commit James Cullen. Right now he's our ace in the hole."

Kevin put the phone to his ear again. "Listen—"

"*No.*" James Cullen's voice blasted into the small space where Kevin, JL, and Austin huddled.

"Let him do it," Austin said. "He thinks fast on his feet, and he has the advantage of knowing every inch of the winery."

"I can do whatever you need," James Cullen continued. "You have to give me a chance to help. Dad would expect me to do what I could. So would David. This is a test to show I'm ready to go on an adventure. You can't deny me. You had you test adventure, Kevin. Give me mine."

"I wasn't thirteen." Kevin's voice came out sounding hoarse, and he cleared his throat. "James Cullen, this is a dangerous situation."

"I can do it. You have to let me."

Kevin glanced at JL, silently asking her opinion. Her mouth had gone dry as sandpaper. She grabbed a bottle of water from the mesh holder on the outside of her pack, and took a long swig. Pete wasn't in a position to help. The Frasers and JL's family had disappeared. Right now James Cullen was all that stood between a cold night in the cave and getting the hell out of the hole they were in. Reluctantly, she nodded agreement.

Kevin's eyes were fixed on hers when he said, "Okay, buddy. Listen carefully. The cartel is in control of the security center. They'll see you on the cameras. You have to avoid them. That'll be difficult in the vineyards. Take the running path through the orchard. Leave the ATV there until you are sure no one is guarding the hill. They'll hear the engine. The entrance to the cave is close to the top of the hill. When we rappelled down, Kenzie and your dad were there. I don't know where they are now, but a guard might be there instead. If you see one, run like hell back to the cottage."

"Got it."

"If no one is guarding the hill, then drive up the path. Stop when you're near the top, and take a sighting. If twelve o'clock is straight ahead, the entrance to the cave is about two o'clock. Drive to that spot. You'll see an outcropping. Kenzie drilled a hole in the rock and planted an anchor to tie off the rope. The rope should still be there, but in case it isn't, bring the coiled climbing rope and locking carabiners on the table in the garage. You'll need to secure the rope to the anchor and drop it down the hole so we can climb out."

"I've rappelled before. I know how to tie off ropes. Don't worry. I'll be there soon, and I won't get caught."

"If there's a guard, go back to the cottage and call JL's partner. She'll give you the number. Other than her partner, Pete, we don't know who we can trust right now. You can trust him. Do whatever he says."

JL gave James Cullen the number and disconnected the call. The battery was down to a twenty-five percent charge.

While they waited for him, JL gave the phone to Kevin and left to backtrack down the passage to see if anyone had followed them. Surprisingly, they hadn't. That meant the cartel was convinced their hostage and his rescuers were trapped in the cave with no one to come to their rescue. It also meant they had connections within local law enforcement agencies powerful enough to stave off concern for the Frasers, their employees, and their friends.

When JL returned to Kevin and Austin, Kevin was on the phone again. She stood close by to hear the conversation. "Where are you now, buddy?"

"Close, but I don't see the rock."

"Where are you exactly?"

"On the path at the edge of the orchard."

"Hold out your arm as if it was a hand on a clock. Straight ahead is twelve. Point your arm to two o'clock. You'll see an outcropping. Drive to that point. You're looking for a hole in the rock. But—and this is important—if you see anyone, get the hell out of there as fast as you can."

"There's no one here."

A few minutes later, a narrow beam of light shone down on them. "Kevin, are you there?"

"Yes. Are you sure it's safe?" Kevin asked.

"I see lots of footprints, but I'm the only one here."

"Is the rope there?"

"No, and the bolt Aunt Kenzie set in the rock is broken. It won't hold the rope now."

JL closed her eyes and dropped her head, cussing under her breath. The closest olive tree was twenty to thirty feet from the opening. If he used a tree as an anchor, the rope wouldn't be long enough to reach them. James Cullen would have to return to the cottage, and each additional trip put him at greater risk. She couldn't ask him to come back again.

"We'll need another anchor," Kevin said.

"I can tie the rope to the ATV's trailer hitch."

JL's head came up, surprised and alert. "Does he know how to tie off the rope so it won't slip?"

"David's taken James Cullen and Lincoln on survival camping trips, and I've taken them sailing. The boys know how to tie knots."

"Austin, you'll go first. Get into the harness quickly. If you get up there and see anyone, get the hell out. You can come back later for us. We'll be fine."

"No, ma'am. Ladies first."

She responded quickly. "Under normal conditions, yes, but this isn't normal. You're getting out of here. Now."

James Cullen yelled, "Rope." JL, Kevin, and Austin stepped aside as the rope spiraled to the ground.

Kevin helped Austin secure the harness and tie the end of the rope through the carabiner. When he was secured, Kevin tugged on the rope and a few moments later, Austin started climbing up the side of the rock wall.

JL held her breath as she watched him ascend to the entrance, and when he crawled through the opening, she exhaled her first deep breath since discovering he was missing.

"Your turn," Kevin said.

"No, I'll guard your back."

"Rope," Austin yelled, and the rope once again spiraled through the air.

"I'm going last. I'm the cop. I'm guarding *your* back."

Kevin grabbed hold of her harness and pulled her close, so close her breasts pressed against him. His grip didn't loosen; if anything, it tightened, and he kissed her more forcefully than any kiss he'd given her before. "I am not going up and leaving you behind." He tied a figure-eight knot and looped the rope through the locking carabiner. "Get your ass up that wall, and send the rope back down before those sons of bitches return."

"This is my job. I'm trained—"

He took her face between his hands and warm ripples of shock rolled over her, head to toe. "I don't give a damn how much training you've had, or how much training I don't have." Then he lowered his voice and said, "You're a mother, JL, and your son needs you up there more than I need you down here. Now, go." His hands were still on her face. His thumbs brushed along her cheekbones once, twice, before he stepped back and tugged on the rope. He lightly smacked JL's ass as she climbed up the wall.

You're a mother and your son needs you more...

She had always put Austin's needs ahead of her own, ahead of Ryan's, ahead of her family's needs, and they had all complained. Kevin understood, and she knew in her heart that even if she hadn't told him the truth, his action wouldn't have been any different. Kevin was an unsung hero, and she loved that about him.

As soon as she reached the top, Austin unhooked the rope and yelled, "Rope," before tossing the lifeline down for Kevin.

A few minutes later, he climbed through the opening with worry carving deep lines around his eyes and mouth.

"No one's around," JL said, reassuring him. "Except for the busted bolt anchor, you'd never know Kenzie and Elliott had been here."

"Elliott would never intentionally abandon us. Let's get out of here." Kevin shed his harness and untied the rope from the ATV hitch, quickly handing them to Austin. "You and James Cullen take the ATV back to the cottage. We'll meet you there."

The boys climbed on the ATV. Since Austin's legs were longer, he sat in front and started the vehicle.

"Stay alert," JL said. "And please be careful." When she realized she was wringing her hands, she stopped.

As the boys disappeared, Kevin said, "Your son was kidnapped by a drug cartel, but you were visibly more anxious watching him drive away on an ATV."

She turned to him, biting back tears. "They'll be okay, won't they?" She knew the tears she was fighting weren't because Austin was driving an ATV; they were because she had come so close to losing him. The high adrenaline levels in her system during the shootout and escape were now tanking.

Kevin laced their fingers and caressed her hand. "The boys know what they're doing. They're very safety conscious. So am I. Let's get out of here before our bodies try to recover from the adrenaline rush and we collapse from exhaustion. We still have a lot to do."

They settled their packs comfortably on their backs and did an easy jog down the hill. It was a different run than the day before. JL refused to let Kevin out of her sight. They ran together, side by side, as if they had been running partners for years, and knew each other's easy pace and push pace. They were running in hiking boots with thirty-pound packs, less water, Power Bars, and spent ammunition. She could continue the pace he set for a couple of miles, but the additional weight and heavy shoes would force her to slow down. After two miles, Kevin's breathing was only mildly elevated, but he slowed to match her breathing until they were once again in sync.

As they approached the vineyard, she asked, "You do know where the cameras are, right?"

Kevin pointed up ahead. "There's the first one. Let's circle around."

For the next two miles, they circled and backtracked until they reached the woods and were able to make up the time they lost. Knowing that Austin would be walking the floor until she and Kevin returned to the cottage, she tried to push herself, but Kevin held her to a slower pace.

When they reached the cottage, he pointed her toward the garage. "Let's go check our gear and reload."

She followed him through the outside door into the four-bay garage and broke into a relieved smile when she spotted James Cullen's ATV parked in the corner. The rope hung between two pegs on the wall, perfectly coiled.

JL dropped her pack on the worktable and unloaded the contents.

Kevin tossed his bag on the table, too. "I'll leave the other two guns in here, but I'll take the knife."

"Reload them first." She reloaded and secured both her weapons, one holstered on her leg, the other at the small of her back.

After reloading his two guns, he rummaged through a supply cabinet until he found a leather strap that he threaded through the notches in the knife sheath and strapped the knife to his lower leg. JL watched him go through his meticulous preparations. The flirty metrosexual she had met the day before had disappeared in the last few hours. From dashing through the cave and tending to Austin, his shirt was bloodied and mud-stained, and sweat streaked his hair. He was a mess, but sexier than hell.

Most of what had happened during the shootout had taken place so quickly that if she waited much longer to write down an account, she might forget some of the details, but she would never forget the part Kevin had played. He had emptied an entire magazine covering Austin's escape.

Kevin left both repacked bags on the edge of the table with the straps facing up, ready to grab and run. Satisfied with the preparations, JL drew her weapon and cautiously opened the door leading to the laundry room.

Austin and James Cullen were sitting on the floor, roughhousing with Tater Tot. She holstered her weapon, letting her breath out slowly. Austin jumped to his feet, and Tater Tot barked. "What took you so long? We made it back in five minutes."

Tater Tot jumped up on JL, planting his front paws on her shoulders, sniffing her. "Down."

Austin grabbed the dog around the shoulders, pulling him back. "Sit."

The dog did, and she patted his head, unable to resist his big brown eyes. "Good dog." To Austin she said, "We were on foot, remember?"

She removed the bandage on his cheek to see the cut in good light, her heart breaking that he would have a scar, albeit a small one, but obvious enough to be a daily reminder of what had happened. "We need to clean both cuts really well before they get infected."

"I'll take care of it," Kevin said. "Let's go upstairs. You need a shower, too."

"I don't have any clothes here."

"You can wear some of mine."

Austin turned up his nose. "Yours are too pretty."

"I thought you liked those black kung fu wicking pants."

Austin did a little muscle flexing. "On you. Not on me."

"Beggars can't be choosers. Move it." Kevin turned to JL. "Call your partner. We'll make plans as soon as I put a stitch in his cheek."

Surprise was not the word she would use. She was in fact, bowled over. "*You're* going to do it?"

"He's pretty good," Austin said. "I watched him sew up a cat once."

JL hitched her hand on her hip. "Putting a stitch in a cat isn't the same as putting a stitch in your handsome face."

James Cullen piped up. "He stitched Aunt Kenzie when she got shot in the head by that military intelligence agent the night before D-Day and Uncle David couldn't take her to the hospital. She doesn't have a scar."

Kevin scrubbed his face with his hands. "Your diarrhea of the mouth is stinking up the place."

Austin howled. "Good one, Kevin."

What the hell? James Cullen's stories sounded like a plot in a Jack Mallory novel.

James Cullen spread his hands, giving them an incredulous expression. "What'd I do? You're good at sewing people up."

JL gave her head a little shake. When she arrived at Montgomery Winery, she fell down a rabbit hole, and she hoped to hell there was a safe way out.

Kevin crossed his arms over his chest and leaned back against the washing machine with an expression of pure exasperation. He pointed a finger at James Cullen. "When this is over, we're having a long conversation about what's appropriate to talk about."

James Cullen spread out his hands again and bounced them up and down for emphasis. "JL has a brooch. She's part of the family. I'm not saying anything wrong."

"That's debatable," Kevin said.

JL met Kevin's grimace with a tight smile. Finding Braham's initials in the cave could be explained as belonging to an ancestor, but he would have mentioned the cave-in if he had been down there in the past two or three decades. James Cullen's bizarre statements were nonsensical, and, in fact, made the family sound like a cult. Of what? Witches and warlocks? If so, they could cast a black magic spell over the cartel. She didn't really think the Frasers were witches. Aliens, maybe. Something strange was happening here, but it wasn't evil. She knew evil. The cartel was evil, and it had infiltrated the winery's security.

The Napa Police Department had dead and injured cops. If the cartel had a cop in their pocket, the department would eventually expose the bad one. That created a dilemma for her. Because she didn't know who had connections with the cartel, if she contacted the cops she could put the lives of the boys and Kevin in more danger. She could contact the FBI or the California State Police, but before they barnstormed the winery, she needed more intel. Where were the Frasers and her family?

Kevin snugged her to him. "I'll take care of Austin. You call Pete."

She had lost the thread of the conversation, and all she could say was an indifferent *huh*.

"Call Pete," Kevin repeated.

A cold shudder of premonition flowed over her while she watched Kevin and Austin leave the room. Every decision she made from here on out had to be guided by what was best for Austin and James Cullen. The cartel believed she, Kevin, and Austin were stuck inside the cave. Telling even one person they had escaped risked revealing their whereabouts to the cartel. She couldn't take that risk.

When she glanced down at James Cullen, he was watching her, his eyes watering. She sat next to him on the floor and put her arm around his shoulder.

"Do you think my mom's worried about me?"

"Yes," JL said. "She's very worried, but you know what? I bet your dad is reminding her of how capable you are, and that you'll find a way to stay safe."

"Maybe I can rescue them, too."

"Where do you think they are? Is there a place at the villa or the

Welcome Center where they could be locked up?"

James Cullen scrunched his face. "Without windows?"

JL nodded. "That would make the best place. No windows and only one door."

"That rules out the basement in the Welcome Center. It doesn't have any windows, but it has two doors if you count the secret door near the stairs."

"How secret is it?" JL asked, riddled with curiosity. "Do most of the employees know?"

"Only my mom and dad. It's a family secret, and you don't tell family secrets."

JL covered her mouth to hide her smile. James Cullen must not have considered the bizarre stories of the brooches, or his dad's cancer, or Kevin's parentage to be family secrets. "Under the stairs, huh? Where does it come out?"

"Do you mean how can you get in?"

She rubbed his head. "You're one step ahead of me, buddy."

"If I tell you, you have to take me with you."

JL had to laugh at the absurdity of the whole situation. MacKlenna Corporation's CFO was stitching her son's face. A thirteen-year-old driving an ATV had just rescued her, Kevin, and Austin, and before today, she had refused to let Austin *ride* on an ATV, much less drive one. She had shot and probably killed a man and cracked another man's skull open. She would drown in paperwork later.

For now, though, she was sitting on the floor in a laundry room, stroking a poodle's thick fur, while her family and other people she had come to care for were being threatened and held captive God knows where. The bitter cherry on the top was that other than Pete, James Cullen, Austin, and Kevin, she didn't know who in the hell to trust.

19

WHILE JL'S PHONE charged, she stripped to take a quick shower. The number of bruises, scratches, and rope burns peppering her body horrified her. She must have bumped into more than one stalag-thingy, but there were no bullet holes. Nothing that required stitching by a CFO. It wasn't the thought of a needle that made her squirm, it was the numbing shot. She hated shots.

After drying and brushing her hair into a ponytail, she dressed in jeans and a T-shirt, and grabbed another pair of heavy socks from a drawer in the closet.

As she leaned to pick up her muddy clothes, she spotted splotches of blood on her shirt. It wasn't hers. It belonged to Austin or to the perp whose head she bashed. The feelings she had been holding at bay all day swamped her then. She dropped to the floor, pulled her knees to her chest, and rocked back and forth. She was tempted to take Austin and run, but she couldn't leave Kevin and James Cullen to fend for themselves. She had to protect the children at all costs. After all Kevin had done for her, she couldn't leave him either, and what of her family?

Where in the hell were they?

Being indecisive was so unlike her, but she couldn't risk making a mistake. Pete would want her to call for backup, but she was afraid she would ask the wrong agency for help. The major trafficking organizations represented the highest echelons of organized crime in Mexico. Their tentacles reached far into the United States. Money bought protection. The cartel had spent millions setting up an operation below the vineyards of Montgomery Winery. Part of the expense was buying off local authorities, and that made the situation terrifying.

Who in Napa and the surrounding counties had the cartel bought and paid for? The local police? State police? Someone had tried to kill her and Kevin by cutting off their escape. Not knowing who to trust was driving her nuts. She dropped her head on her folded arms and, after years of drought, tears poured from her eyes with an unrepentant ease.

I don't know what to do. Do I run and hide with the boys, or turn and fight the unknown?

She might be overthinking the situation. What if the answer was obvious, but fear was standing in the way of clarity? If that was the case, what was the remedy? She couldn't snap her fingers and make fear disappear. What was she afraid of happening? Making the wrong decision that caused someone's death or injury. She wasn't afraid at work, and she made snap decisions that impacted lives on a daily basis. So what caused the indecision now? Simple. She loved most of the people her decisions would affect, and she liked and respected the rest of them.

If Elliott, Meredith, and Pops could message her now, they would tell her not to worry about them; that her responsibility was to take care of the boys. If she could put them and Kevin in a safe place, she could go look for the others. Kevin would refuse to stay behind, though. The memory of him caught in the firefight, of bullets ricocheting off the rocks, pinging against metal chairs and tables, and the caustic bite of gunpowder burning the air, increased her tremors. Her legs would have crumpled beneath her if she had been standing.

"JL," Kevin called from the hall.

She reached for the towel bar for support and climbed to her feet, brushing away the tears. "Come in." She pushed the bathroom door shut. "Just a minute." Standing at the sink, she splashed cold water on her face, but she couldn't wash away the discoloration beneath her eyes. She gave up trying and walked out of the bathroom.

He was standing there, hands on his hips, hair damp from the shower. A delicious buttery-soft leather scent rolled off him. The edge of his short-sleeve T-shirt hugged his biceps, and while his faded jeans didn't have a crease, he was all class and model-worthy—a man she must have conjured up in a fantasy.

"Did you talk to Pete?" he asked.

She crossed the room to the closet to grab a running jacket. "Not yet. Did you talk to Austin?" She strapped on her gun, then slipped her phone and badge into her pants' pockets.

"He said he was sorry about the drama and the problems he caused." Kevin closed the distance between them and turned her to face him. He wiped the corner of her eye with the pad of his thumb, and the compassionate look he gave her just made the tears worse. He gave her a fresh handkerchief.

"I've got this open tap thing going on. I don't know why I can't stop crying." The soft cloth whispered over wet tears. "If you keep rescuing me, you'll run out."

"Then I'll give you the front of my shirt." For a few blissful seconds, his gaze held her in sensual bonds, with his dark eyes reflecting a timeless, almost mystical quality.

He lifted her chin and the tenderness in the pads of his fingers surprised her. The hot wonder of his kiss when his lips found hers—a touch at first, molding his mouth to hers, and then a sudden burst of hunger while his tongue slipped deep within her mouth, was amazing—a full-blown tongue-twining kiss.

The kiss ended, and she marveled at how powerfully she craved him now. Her face was mere inches from his. She memorized the slight part of his lips and breathed against them as he stroked his thumbs across her chin and along her jawline. He pressed his erection against her eager body. The kiss had been a prelude, a sample of what could follow, if only they had time and privacy to go where the passion led them. But they couldn't allow that to happen until everyone was safe.

She stepped back out of his embrace. "What else did Austin say?"

Kevin leaned back against the chest of drawers and crossed his ankles. It was hard as hell not to stare at the bulge at the juncture of his legs, and her glance kept flicking there.

"He was disappointed in both of us because you're married. I asked him if it would be okay if you weren't."

"You told him about the divorce? Oh God," she groaned. "Tell me you didn't."

Kevin held up his hands as if defending himself. "He's okay with it. He wasn't surprised."

"He loves Ryan."

"He might love him, but that doesn't mean he loves the two of you together. He doesn't think Ryan treated you very well, and he didn't know why you stayed with him."

"Why didn't he ever say anything?"

Kevin frowned. "He didn't want to hurt your feelings."

"We've been protecting each other?"

"You were both afraid the other person's love wasn't strong enough to withstand that kind of honesty."

She crossed her arms, bent double, and dropped into the nearest chair. Understanding what they had done to each other by remaining quiet caused her physical pain. "Did you tell him I was his mother?"

Kevin knelt in front of her, taking her hands in his. "That's for you to tell him later. After what's happened, I don't think he'll push back."

She looked away for a moment, blinking until the tears retreated. "What was it you just said about honesty?"

"You were both afraid the other person's love wasn't strong enough to withstand that kind of honesty."

Still feeling the bite of tears in her eyes, she gazed softly at Kevin. "Is your love for Elliott strong enough?"

Kevin blanched, and his hands, which had been lying still, tightened before he stood and stepped back. "Let's not talk about him. Have you called Pete?"

"I wanted to tell you about my conversation with James Cullen first. I asked him if there was a room close by where the cartel could stash his parents. He suggested the basement of the Welcome Center. He said there is a secret door, but he wouldn't tell me where it came out unless we promise to take him with us."

"He's his father's son, for sure." Kevin's jaw quivered and he cleared his throat roughly. "He's not the only one who knows where the entrance is located."

"You know, too? Where?"

"The door is set in the stone wall at the back of the old amphitheater. No one has used it for decades. Storage boxes could be blocking the door from the tunnel into the basement. I haven't been down there in months. Do you really want to go underground again?"

"Hell no, but we don't have a choice. We've got to rescue them, if that's where they are, and find out what happened to Pops and the others." It gave her the creeps thinking about going back underground, but finding Kenzie and Elliott would at least fill in a few gaps about the cartel and their sources. Together, they could decide who to call for backup.

"What about cameras? Are there any around the amphitheater?"

"That might be a problem." Kevin pursed his lips, thinking. "If we shoot them off the poles, they won't be able to see what we're doing."

"As soon as the cameras go out, security will know where we are." She thought a minute about what he was proposing. "I can take one out with my pistol."

"I wasn't planning on using your weapon. This caper calls for a BB gun."

"They'll still know where we are and can catch us on the way out."

"Not if we shoot out four at once. Call Pete. I have plans to make."

20

KEVIN HURRIED OUT of the bedroom without revealing any of his plan. She knew he would tell her later. Right now, she needed to talk to Pete. She pulled up her recent calls list and swiped his number. Three rings later, he answered.

"It's about time you called. Even the detective sergeant's pacing the floor."

She crossed the room to the window. The sun spilled through the panes, and the light and shadows made odd-shaped patterns on the window seat cushion. She reclined and closed her eyes, bone weary and hungry. "What did you find out?"

"I talked to DEA. They had an informant tell them a large buy was going down this weekend."

"Hollinger told me. DEA's not coming to the winery, are they?"

"Not until they hear from you. Where are you now?"

"At the cottage."

"How'd you get out?"

"Interesting story. I'll tell you later. The good news is that I have a lead on the Frasers' whereabouts. I'm heading there in a few minutes. As soon as I find out what happened to them, I'll call you back."

"JL, don't go in alone. You have to have backup. Let Drug Enforcement do it. You're lucky not to be still stuck in a cave."

She was silent for a moment, thinking through the enormity and possible futility of her plan. "If DEA barnstorms the winery, the

Frasers will be in more danger, and God only knows what has happened to Pops, the boys, and the others. They could have had mechanical problems or run into bad weather, or something could have happened to them once they landed. If I can get to the Frasers, I'll be closer to finding out what happened to them. I'm not grandstanding here, Pete. I have an advantage right now. No one knows we are out of the cave. I have to try another rescue. If I'm caught, bring in the cavalry."

"*Ragazza tosta*, you're scaring me."

"Look. What happens if I call the wrong people? What if the person you talked to has since talked to the cartel? My entire family might be in trouble. I have to make the right decision, and my gut's telling me to go after the Frasers now."

"I've never known your gut to misguide you. Do it and call me back. If I don't hear from you in two hours, I'm calling my contact at the DEA, and they're going in."

She disconnected the call, and before returning the phone to the charger, she set the countdown. Pete said he would make the call to DEA in exactly two hours, and he always did exactly what he said he would do.

There was a tap on the door. "JL, can I come in?" Austin asked.

"Sure," she said.

He stuck his head in the room. "Kevin said we're going to rescue the Frasers."

Something about that didn't sound quite right. She thought back to what Kevin had said, and she groaned—four cameras, four people. "He didn't tell me what he intended to do. Where is he now?"

"He and James Cullen went to the basement. That's where the gun safe is."

"Gun safe? Here?" Why hadn't someone mentioned that before? She could use another handgun and more ammunition. "How do you get there?"

"Off the kitchen. Come on. I'll show you."

JL followed Austin through the house and down the stairs. She found Kevin and James Cullen loading BB guns. "What else do you have in the safe? Any ammunition?"

"No. Kenzie has control over the *big* guns," Kevin said with a little eye roll. "These are for the boys to use during heavily supervised target practice."

"If you plan on the boys using a BB gun to shoot out a camera, then they'll be using the gun without supervision."

"That's true, but the MacKlenna Clan kids have been taught to respect guns and how to use them appropriately. Elliott and David would both approve of this plan. I know Austin has the same knowledge and respect for guns, but if you'd rather he not be involved, we can get by with three."

Austin turned his pleading eyes to her. "They've got Pops and the boys."

"We don't know for sure yet, Austin."

"You can't leave me out. You let James Cullen play a part. You have to let me. Besides, I'm responsible for this mess."

She hugged him. "I told you already, you're not responsible. They kidnapped you. Let me hear the whole plan, and then I'll make my decision."

Kevin grabbed paper and pen from a small courtesy desk where a half-eaten apple sat on a napkin. He drew a sketch of the amphitheater and the surrounding area. "Here's the door to the tunnel. Here is the camera. You have to take that one out before you enter the tunnel." He put an X to the east of her camera. "Austin will take out this one." He marked a spot to the west. "James Cullen will take this one." He marked another spot to the north. "I'll take this one. As soon as the cameras are disabled, I'll meet the boys back at the cottage. We'll remain there until you return, hopefully with Elliott, Meredith, and Kenzie, and possibly the rest of the gang who flew in this afternoon."

"And if they're not there?"

"Come back to the cottage, and we'll move on to Plan B."

"What's Plan B?"

He dropped his gaze and made an odd shrugging motion, and

then his brows drew together in thought. "I don't know, but we'll come up with something."

Although she found some absurdity in what they intended to do, she somehow found humor in it, too. "Okay. So show me how to get into the wardrobe."

James Cullen laughed. "I get it. *The Chronicles of Narnia*, right?"

JL smiled. "Right."

"The door is here." Kevin pointed to the door he had drawn on the sketch. "And the stone you need to push is here." He drew an outline around the location of the stone.

"Is it too high for me to reach?"

Kevin pursed his lips, thinking. "No, it should be eye level. Take a can of WD-40 just in case the door doesn't push easily. Like I said, it hasn't been opened, as far as I know, in a couple of decades."

"I'm surprised James Cullen hasn't been in there." She glanced at the boy. His face wore the imprint of guilt. "James Cullen, have you been inside?"

His head popped up.

"You've been in there, haven't you?" she said.

He pressed his hands together under his chin, prayer like. "Please don't tell Dad. He'll kill me. Lincoln and I went in last year, but we didn't go very far."

"So it wasn't hard to open."

"No, ma'am."

"What do you remember about the inside? Was the passage clear? Did it have an odor? Was it wet?"

"It smelled like grapes. But everything around here smells that way. There wasn't anything on the ground. It was dry and cool, but dark and, well..." He ducked his head again. "We were scared. We ran out."

JL touched his face with a sort of gentle cuffing pat. "I'm glad you went inside, and I won't tell your dad."

He visibly relaxed. "Whew."

Kevin handed her a BB gun. "I'll see to the boys then I'll meet you in the tunnel."

"We don't need you, Kevin. Go with JL," Austin said. "We did okay getting back from the cave."

"We should all go rescue my parents," James Cullen said. "We could be *The Four Musketeers.*"

"Look. I appreciate the offer, but it makes more sense for Kevin to stay with you two. If I get caught, I'll need someone to rescue me again."

Kevin's brow furrowed, and she traced the lines in his forehead with her fingertip. "This will be a grab-and-go. I'll be fine. And I won't worry about the boys, because I know they're with you. Do this for me, and for Meredith." All she could do was stare at him, and in the extended silence, tears pushed to her eyes.

Kevin used his handkerchief again and wiped her face. "I understand your logic, but I don't like it. I'll get the boys settled in a safe—"

She pressed her fingers against his lips. "Don't make this harder for me, please. Let's stick with the plan."

He kissed her, and his tongue was soft as it slipped into her mouth, and she tasted the apple he hadn't had time to finish. He enfolded her body in his arms and held her so close against him that she could hear his heartbeat. She willed him to comprehend the intensity of her emotions.

"Eck. Kevin," James Cullen said. "Get a room. After this is over, you two can go on *The Amazing Race* together."

"I know how you feel," Kevin whispered against her lips, "and I want to be with you."

Remembering where they were, she stepped back from him. She avoided looking at Austin, but he put his arm around her shoulder and gave her a squeeze. When she gained control over her swimming senses, she checked the time. Fifteen minutes had passed since she set the timer.

"It's time to go," she said. "Pete's calling in reinforcements in an hour and forty-five minutes, and I want to rescue James Cullen's parents by then, if we can."

"We can drive the golf cart to the tree that splits the path and move out from there. Is everyone clear about their assignments?" Kevin said.

The boys gave a simple nod, and James Cullen held out his hand, palm down. Austin slapped his on top, and then JL added hers. Lastly, Kevin's hand engulfed all of them. "On three, MacKlenna Clan. Ready? One. Two. Three."

"MacKlenna Clan," they all said in unison then high-fived each other. She and Austin weren't part of the clan, but coming together under a common banner seemed important to the boys.

JL picked up two BB guns and handed one to Austin. "You know how to use this, and you know when to use it. I trust you to use good judgment."

"Don't worry," Austin said. "I'll make you proud."

"You always do, son." As soon as the word slipped out of her mouth, she shuddered, and another round of panic burned in the pit of her stomach. She had protected the secret all these years, and at the worst possible moment, the unguarded truth slipped out.

Austin's arms went out as if he was blocking an offensive player's shot, and his big green eyes grew wide, but before he could say anything, James Cullen tugged on his arm.

"People have secrets. When this is over there'll be lots of explaining to do, including my dad and your mom, but right now isn't the time." He shoved Austin toward the stairs. "My parents need saving." But Austin's big feet wouldn't budge, and James Cullen slammed into his back.

Austin recoiled, outrage flashing across his face. "You're my *mom*? Not my sister?"

"Austin, this isn't the time to discuss it. The situation is complicated. Let's get through the next few hours, and then we'll talk. Okay?" JL said.

"If Pops isn't my dad, *who is?*"

She was unnerved by the question and wasn't prepared to deal with it, not now.

James Cullen's eyes widened and he glanced up at Austin in disbelief. "My dad didn't say anything about *your* dad. Who is he?"

Austin slapped his hand over James Cullen's mouth, and at the same time Kevin grabbed his collar, giving him a shake. "It's none of your damn business."

"But it is *mine*," Austin said.

She spun toward him. "*Not now.*" Her voice was more impatient than she intended. She was at the end of her rope and barely hanging on. If Austin bolted again out of anger or disappointment, she didn't have the energy to chase after him.

"I'm not budging from this spot"—he jerked his finger toward the ground—"until you tell me."

Kevin hiked his eyebrows at her, but otherwise remained stock-still and quiet.

Her muscles bunched tight in her shoulders. Austin's demand rattled her. She was tired of indecision and wasn't going to be held hostage by another uncomfortable choice. Either tell him or not. She pressed her fingers against her temples and then spat it out. "He's an NBA power forward, and that's all I'm saying right now."

Austin's jaw dropped. "NBA?" He exchanged glances with James Cullen.

James Cullen tugged on Austin's arm. "It shouldn't be hard to figure it out. How many power forwards are there?"

"Fifty at least," Austin said.

James Cullen's eyes were dancing. "But how many are white?"

"White?"

"You're not black or biracial, so there has to be at least one white guy," James Cullen said on the way to the stairs. "Let's go through the conferences. We'll start with the Eastern. Who plays for the Celtics?"

JL glanced up at Kevin. His hand squeezed her shoulder. The kneading felt so right, so warm, and was the exact thing she needed. She nestled close to him. "Austin doesn't even care."

"He's got a father who plays in the NBA. To him, that's better than having a bio-dad who's President of the United States."

"But what if his father doesn't want anything to do with him?"

"Then his father is an idiot. Come on. Let's take this one bird at a time."

21

INSIDE THE GARAGE, Kevin, JL, Austin, and James Cullen dug through the supply cabinet for camo gear. While they dressed, the boys dissected the team rosters of the Boston Celtics, Brooklyn Nets, and New York Knicks, and identified one possible candidate as Austin's bio-dad. They continued through the Philadelphia Sixers.

"Stop it," Kevin said. "You two have to focus on what we're doing. There is too much at stake. You'll have plenty of time later. Now get in the golf cart. I don't want to hear another mention of basketball until this mission is over. Got it?"

James Cullen saluted. "Yes, sir."

Kevin cuffed him behind the ear.

"You're right, Kevin," Austin said. "I am being selfish. I need to focus on the Frasers and my family. Not on myself."

JL shook her head. Had she really heard what she thought she had heard? She caught Kevin's grin. Yep, she had. An alien inhabited her son's body.

The boys dressed in camouflage and insisted on painting their faces with green streaks. She almost didn't recognize them. Their warrior expressions were an extension of the paint and camo. They were now hunters. They climbed into the backseat of the cart, holding their BB guns in two-handed carry positions.

If JL hadn't just survived a gunfight where she had probably killed a man, she would think she was heading out on a camping trip. This was real. The Mexican cartel had invaded the winery, and they weren't easily defeated in the best of circumstances. Her actions in the cave had upped the stakes and made their situation even more tenuous.

"I'll drop you three by the tree that splits the path," Kevin said. "Let's coordinate our watches. I have two-thirty. When I drop you off, we'll have fifteen minutes to get into position. You won't need that much time, so be careful while you wait. Make sure you're concealed. We'll blend in with our camo gear, but don't depend on that to keep you completely safe."

"You don't have your face painted, Kevin," Austin said.

Kevin grinned. "JL and I will skip the paint this time."

Ten minutes later, he stopped the golf cart at the tree. "Check your watches. In fifteen minutes, we'll shoot out the cameras. Then run like hell, but run carefully."

"If we can't get back to the cottage, where should we go?" Austin said.

"Stash your rifle, get off the property. Go down the road to the market and call a taxi to take you to Austin's dorm room. I gave you cash for emergencies. Whatever you do, don't get caught."

Austin hugged JL. "You be careful, too."

"We'll see you back at the cottage," she said.

"Be careful, JL, and tell my parents I can't wait to see them."

She hugged James Cullen, too. "I'll tell them, but please be careful. Don't take any chances. If you can't get your shot off safely, don't take it."

Kevin hugged James Cullen, and gave Austin a mock punch on the jaw. "Go get 'em."

After the boys disappeared into the woods, Kevin pulled JL into his arms. "Be careful, and don't take any chances, either. We have plans to make after this is over."

She melded against him, and her mind flashed back to Friday afternoon. She had looked away when Elliott hugged Meredith, jealous of the love they shared. She had silently prayed to have what they had. If she and Kevin survived the day, that kind of love might be possible for them, too.

Her hands slipped beneath Kevin's camo shirt, and her cool fingers warmed against the muscles that defined his chest. Underlying it all, an honorable heart beat strong and steady. "I know you'll keep the boys safe. Don't risk them for me. Do whatever you have to do."

Kevin brushed her face with his fingertips, and his warm breath fanned her cheek. "I'll be waiting at the cottage for you. Now, go get Elliott. I have a few things to say to him."

"I won't deny you that conversation." She kissed him, losing herself in the feel of his hot skin and hard body. The scent of him was wild and outdoorsy, and she wanted to drop to the ground and make love. She couldn't. Not now. She broke away and without looking back, moved silently into the woods. The *whirrr* of the golf cart motor receded while she moved farther away, weaving a path through the trees.

She jogged for ten minutes, following Kevin's directions. The sun finally broke through the canopy of golden leaves and she gazed down into a meadow with a gurgling creek along one side. The native stone amphitheater sat sphinxlike, alone in a painted field of fall flowers.

From her position at the edge of the woods, she estimated she stood maybe thirty yards from the back wall. Assuming she could find the turning stone quickly, and it turned as easily as James Cullen described, she calculated she could sprint to the wall and get inside within sixty seconds.

She glanced around, searching the trees until she found the camera mounted halfway up the meadow's lonesome pine. She nestled in among the underbrush at a point where she had a clear shot of the target and a direct path to the wall. She aimed the BB gun and counted down the seconds.

Precisely at three o'clock, four shots rang out. As soon as JL's target shattered, she dashed to the wall, counted the stones, and turned the one that opened the door. It moved on oiled hinges. She ducked inside and pulled the door shut, praying for the boys and Kevin. She sniffed. James Cullen was right. Everything smelled like grapes.

She quickly assessed her surroundings, beginning with where she stood on a four-foot wide landing. Ten steep stone steps led from the landing into the tunnel.

She donned her helmet and lamp, adjusted her backpack, and hurried down a cobblestone path, swimming through cobwebs. After an anxious five-minute walk, she reached the other end, having passed only a few cave rats along the way.

Sweat ran down the sides of her face, and she swallowed against a hard lump of fear. She didn't want to admit it, but she was scared of getting stuck in another damn cave. This one, while technically not a cave, was much more claustrophobic.

At the far end of the passage stood an oak-paneled door, wider than standard width, and over six feet tall, but there was no door handle. The door had to be pushed open, but how did that happen? She searched the ground. A sweeping arc was visible on the floor, indicating the door would swing in toward the tunnel.

Located on the right side of the door was a push-button light switch with white and black buttons. She pushed the white button, and a dim yellow bulb hanging above the door lit the end of the creepy tunnel. Dust tickled her nose, and spun in motes in the shaft of light from the bare bulb.

Below the light switch was a three-inch square door, also without a handle—possibly a peephole. If it was, she didn't want her light reflecting through the opening. She cut off her headlamp and pushed the black button, extinguishing all light before flicking open the small door. A rush of warm air hit the bridge of her nose, bringing with it an even stronger grape scent, and total blackness. She slipped on her night vision goggles and peered through the hole again.

Against the far wall, three people sat on the floor huddled together. Only a portion of the room was visible to JL, but from her vantage point, other than the occupants, this portion of the room was empty. If there were stairs, they weren't in her field of vision.

She closed the small door, flipped on her headlamp, and

searched for a way to enter the room. Her hand glided up and down the doorframe searching for a mechanism that would trigger a release. Nothing. She stepped back, studying the door from a distance. She pushed on the corners of the door—nothing. The middle—nothing. The bottom—nothing. The top—nothing.

What's the deal? It had to open. She snapped her fingers. "Abracadabra." That didn't work either. Knocking wasn't an option. The solution had to be there.

She cut the light and looked through the peephole again, then closed the little door and turned on her headlamp again. The peephole had scratch marks around it. She glanced at the arc on the floor. Maybe turning the frame caused the scratch marks. She gripped the sides of the peephole and flicked her wrist. When the little door moved, her heart almost leapt out of her chest. *Clever bastards.*

Before she gave it another turn, she cut the light and ran through her mental checklist: knives, guns, concealed body armor vest, and night goggles. The weight of the backpack would slow her down. She shed it, leaving it near the door, ready to grab on her way out.

With her weapon drawn, she gave the frame of the little door a final twist. A barely audible click told her she had indeed found the secret. She snagged the edge of the oak door, gave it a tug, and it opened without squeaking.

She entered, wearing her night vision goggles, and scanned the stone-walled room, which was about the size of a double garage. In the corner sat a square staircase leading up to a door on the first floor. A small sliver of light shone beneath the bottom of the door. There were no voices or footsteps coming from the floor above.

She approached the bodies, and was greatly relieved when she identified Elliott, Meredith, and Kenzie, and was even more relieved when each of them stirred. She went to Kenzie first and whispered, "It's JL."

Kenzie moaned behind her duct-taped mouth. JL peeled it off. "God, I'm glad it's you. I heard the click and prayed we were being rescued."

JL cut Kenzie's restraints and gave her a knife and flashlight before moving on to Meredith and Elliott to cut through theirs.

Meredith pulled to her feet, yanking the duct tape from her mouth. "Have you seen James Cullen?"

JL finished cutting Elliott's bindings, wishing she could leave him trussed up for Kevin to deal with. *You old coot.* "I left him a few minutes ago."

"Thank God," Meredith said.

"Have you heard anything from David and the rest?" Kenzie asked.

"We tried calling them, but no one answered their phone. I was hoping you knew something," JL said.

"David copied Elliott and me on a text to Kenzie. I received the message right before those men abducted me. He said the plane had landed, and two limos were waiting on the tarmac," Meredith said.

"I never received the message. It must have arrived after our phones were confiscated," Kenzie said.

"Let's get out of here before those bastards come down to check on us," Elliott said.

They hurried through the door and closed it. JL picked up her pack, and she led the way through the tunnel.

"Where'd you leave James Cullen?" Meredith asked.

JL couldn't tell her he was safe because she didn't know for sure. She fudged, saying, "He's our hero. He rescued Kevin and me from the cave. You should be very proud of him."

"But where is he at this moment?" Elliott asked.

"James Cullen, Austin, and Kevin should all be at the cottage. Each of us shot out a camera at the exact same time. North, south, southeast, and west of the tree that splits the running path. It was the only way I could get through the wall without being seen." A rat scurried over JL's boot and she jerked back her foot. "Damn rats."

"The amphitheater is west. The vineyard is north," Meredith said.

"The olive press is southeast," Elliott added.

"And the grape crushers are south," Meredith said. "Where did

James Cullen go?"

"He had the olive press and Austin had the grape crushers," JL said.

"Good," Elliott said. "Austin knows his way through the woods, and James Cullen has the shortest distance to go. They shouldn't have any trouble."

"There must be a bug in the conference room. Whoever is running this op knew our plans and systematically removed all the threats," Kenzie said. "If they knew what time the plane was landing, they could have intercepted the limousines, replaced the drivers with their own men, and taken David and the rest out of the city."

"They wouldn't have gone far," JL said. "In case they needed hostages, they would want our people close by."

"The kidnappers could have driven the limos into the Montgomery hangar and secured them there," Meredith said. "No one uses it but us. Plus it's isolated."

"There aren't any windows. We can go over there to look around, but we can't see what's going on inside," Kenzie said.

When they reached the door at the end of the tunnel, JL said, "Give me a few minutes to look around and make sure it's safe."

"How long has it been since the cameras were shot out?" Kenzie asked.

JL checked the time. "Twenty minutes."

"I don't think this old amphitheater would hold any interest. Security would be more concerned about the olive press and grape crushers. They would see this location as a decoy. We should be fine," Kenzie said.

"Let's go. I'm not staying down here any longer. David needs help." Elliott pushed open the door, glanced around quickly, and then proceeded toward the woods. They walked in single file, following narrow deer trails. JL took up the rear, constantly glancing over her shoulder. While they walked, Elliott peppered her with questions about Austin's rescue. After she finished her story, Kenzie described how she and Elliott were captured.

"A Napa police cruiser drove up the hill. We thought we'd have some explaining to do, but we weren't prepared for the treatment we got," Kenzie said.

"Were they bad cops or members of the cartel impersonating cops?"

"I don't know," Kenzie said. "They didn't talk."

Elliott held up his hand and everyone stopped. He put his finger to his lips, and JL listened carefully, but she only heard dead leaves rustling as squirrels scampered across the floor of the woods. Elliott waved his hand in a forward motion and they continued their trek through the woods.

"Why didn't they talk?" JL asked. "Because they couldn't speak English, or because they didn't want to converse with you?"

Kenzie gave a slight shrug. "Good question. I don't know. I asked questions. They ignored me. If I weren't pregnant, I would have been more assertive."

"They shoved us in the backseat of a cruiser at gunpoint," Elliott added, "and we ended up at the Welcome Center. Meredith was already in the basement."

"How'd you end up in the basement, Meredith?" JL asked.

"Two Hispanic men knocked on the door. I thought they were harvest workers. When I opened the door, they subdued me. Tied me up and carried me to the basement. A few minutes later, Elliott and Kenzie were dumped beside me."

"What happened to that Wilder guy?" JL asked.

"He left to relieve himself. Then just as the fake police arrived, we heard a gunshot. We didn't see him again. Probably another dead body in the orchard," Kenzie said.

"But why kill him? That doesn't make any sense."

"None of this does," Elliott said.

They broke through the woods, and JL spotted Kevin standing guard inside the cottage's screened-in porch. He bounded down the stairs with his brow creased in a worried frown.

"What took you so long?" he asked.

"We moved as fast as we could," JL said. "Did the boys have any problems?"

"Everything went perfectly," Kevin said.

Elliott, Meredith, and Kenzie rushed into the house, leaving JL and Kevin on the porch steps.

"I was scared something had happened to you." He reached out and touched her face, and her skin tingled in response. Then his warm fingers stroked beneath her chin and down her throat. In such a short time, his touch had become so familiar.

"If I'd been the one waiting…" She gave up trying to talk and kissed him. Her lips on his could tell him better than her stumbling words what he meant to her.

The door behind them opened, and when the sound of Austin clearing his throat got their attention, they ended the kiss. "Kenzie's anxious to find David, and I told her a beer would…you know…" He held out two Coors.

"Yeah, I know." JL snatched the icy cold beer and chugged it. Then wiping her mouth with the back of her hand, she said, "I need to wash up first, then we can make plans."

"Don't you need to call Pete?" Kevin asked.

"I want to talk over some more things with Kenzie first," JL said.

They entered the house to find Elliott and Meredith sitting on the barstools in the kitchen, while Kenzie raided the refrigerator.

"I've got to have something to eat," she said to JL. "Then we have to figure out how to help David."

"I have absolute faith that David will find a way to escape wherever he is," Meredith said.

"On his own he could, but he's got the boys and the others. He won't take risks with them," Kenzie said. "At least, not unless it's a life-or-death situation."

"Nobody's been hurt yet," Meredith said.

"Salvatore was murdered, the Napa Police Department has nine dead and injured cops, and we don't know what happened to Wilder," JL said. "We can't assume they won't hurt anyone else."

"If they're tied up like we were, what can they do?" Meredith asked.

"If David is anything like my brothers, they're already out of their restraints, only their captors don't know it yet."

"I'd like to know how," Meredith said, "so next time I get tied up I'll be able to free myself."

"Pops got the boys titanium escape rings for Christmas several years ago. There's a tiny hacksaw inside the band." JL set the beer on the counter. "I'm going to wash up. I'll be right back."

She hurried to the bathroom in the guest room and washed her face and hands. Standing in front of the mirror, she took a long look at herself. Twenty-four hours ago, she had been afraid to tell Austin about the divorce. Not only did he now know about the divorce, but he also knew she was his mother. To top it all off, the cartel had come close to killing him. They had also threatened the Frasers, and the whereabouts of the rest of the clan and her family were unknown.

Trouble didn't follow her, and rarely, if ever, did she step into it accidently. Now an unfathomable but extraordinary intersection of people and events was happening, and she, Kevin, and Austin were at the center of it. She had no idea why, but she sensed Meredith did. The woman had some inexplicable ability to know things—more than simply a mother's or a cop's intuition. Meredith's intuitive power—her subtle knowing—reminded JL of the mysterious perceptions her own mother had possessed.

She checked the time. Austin had a basketball game in four hours. Although he hadn't mentioned it, she knew it was on his mind, since there were several college coaches scheduled to attend. It was incredibly important to him, but until Pops, her brothers, and the rest were safe, she couldn't worry about the game. Actions had consequences, and because he hadn't mentioned the tournament, she believed he had received that message loud and clear.

When she reentered the kitchen, James Cullen was entertaining his parents with a slightly altered version of the great escape. There was no mention of the ATV he had used to pull Kevin, Austin, and herself out of the cave.

"Wait a minute," Kenzie said. "I watched one of the men who

captured us smash the metal loop I bolted to the rock. What'd you attach the rope to?"

Since Kenzie already knew the story, she was obviously messing with James Cullen. JL turned her head, hiding her smile.

James Cullen slumped his shoulders and squeezed his eyes shut for a moment, as if that would make his lie go away. "The ATV," he finally said with some reluctance. "Dad told me never to use the trailer hitch unless I was supervised, so I didn't tell that part of the story because I thought I'd get into trouble."

Elliott pulled James Cullen to him for a hug. "Ye did the right thing to get them out of the cave, but ye did the wrong thing lying about it."

"Judgment is important, and I didn't want you to use my mistake against me...you know...when the time comes." James Cullen's voice was so thick he seemed to have trouble squeezing out the words.

"When the time comes for ye to go on an adventure, everything will be used in my decision," Elliott said.

James Cullen's eyes brightened. "Did you hear Austin's bio-dad is an NBA power forward?"

Elliott's eyes blistered in their intensity, and a tic jumped at the corner of his jaw.

Kevin yanked James Cullen by the arm and stood the boy in front of him. "Your dad might think you've used good judgment today, but the jury is still out as far as I'm concerned. Your mouth is out of control. You have no filter. If my influence is responsible for that, I'm sorry, but it's time we both learned to keep our damn mouths shut. *Capisce?*"

James Cullen met Kevin's eyes stoically, and nodded.

"Go on and finish yer NBA project ye're being so secretive about." Elliott drilled Kevin with a look meant to peel hides, and the moment James Cullen left the room, Elliott demanded, "How'd the lad know that?"

An uncomfortable pause followed before Kevin said, "He heard you and Meredith talking a few hours ago."

Elliott's face reddened. "Is that all he heard?"

Kevin shook his head.

Meredith glanced at Elliott. "He overheard our conversation." Then to Kevin she said, "What else did he hear?"

Kevin's taut jaw quivered. "That you're my"—he made air quotes—"bio-father. That JL is Austin's bio-mother, and that you have prostate cancer."

Kenzie gulped and immediately positioned herself between Kevin and Elliott, slapping her hands together. "*Enough*. This will have to wait. We can't lose sight of what else is happening. My husband and my boys are missing. I'm not listening to any more of this shit until my family is safe. Got it?" She set her empty glass of milk on the counter with enough restraint to keep from shattering it. "The pregnant lady has to go pee again. When I come back, there better be a plan—a good one." She dashed off in the direction of the half bath in the hall.

JL wanted to applaud, but she also wanted to know how Elliott knew Austin was her son. She didn't dare ask now, though. There would be plenty of time later. She hoped. In the meantime, she would add the question to her growing list.

"Call Pete," Kevin said. "See if he's called DEA. We have to have help now."

JL placed a call to her partner and put the call on speaker.

"You just beat the clock by ten minutes," Pete said. "Did you find the Frasers?"

"I'm with them now. This call is on speaker. Pops and the boys, along with David McBain and his family and friends are still missing."

"Any ideas where?" Pete asked.

"Our last report was shortly after the plane landed. Two limos were on the tarmac waiting for the passengers. They haven't been heard from since. I'm going to the airport to check out the Montgomery hangar to see if there are any witnesses. It's possible they're being held there. If not, we have no leads."

"It's time to call in some help," Pete said.

"Let's think this through first," JL said. "Based on what I saw in the cave, the cartel has a lab set up and are processing cocaine-based bricks into an ingestible form."

"How were they getting the cocaine out?" Pete asked.

"In wine barrels," Austin said.

JL glanced up to see him standing in the doorway, alongside Kenzie.

"That's what those guys were doing," he continued. "They were stuffing bags full of white powder into wine barrels with red Xs on the sides."

"How'd they get the barrels out without anyone noticing?" Pete asked.

JL looked at Meredith. "What do you do with old barrels?"

"When they're worn out, I sell them to a barrel company. The same company had been buying them for decades, until this year—"

"Let me guess," JL said. "You're using a new company."

"If the same company has had a contract for more than two years, we bid it out to be sure we're getting the best price. The company usually gets their contract renewed, but this year, Barrel Restoration underbid our old contractor and got the job."

"So the barrels with the cocaine were carried off by Barrel Restoration."

"When I was abducted, the men were carrying barrels out of the old cave and stacking them alongside the other barrels," Austin said. "When they saw me, they couldn't decide what to do, so they took me with them."

A chill trickled down JL's spine. Austin had come so close to dying.

"JL, have you considered that you might not be dealing with the cartel after all?" Pete said. "You might have a local entrepreneur who wants a piece of the business. Barrel Restoration might be an innocent bystander who's being used to unknowingly transport drugs."

"I don't think they're innocent, nor do I think they're the main player," Meredith said. "Barrel Restoration was referred to me by our engineering firm. Since discovering they lost our surveys, I'm suspicious of them, too."

"If it's true a big buy is going down, then the barrels will be moved again. DEA will be in position to arrest the dealers and confiscate the contraband."

"If the engineering company has bankrolled the operation, then they'll be meeting with the buyer to arrange the transfer," Kenzie said.

"Isn't the engineering company a gala sponsor?" JL asked.

"Yes," Meredith said. "The president will be making a large donation to the Napa Boys' Organization, our principal charity."

"That presentation might be the signal for the buy," Pete said.

"We've got a little over twenty-four hours before the gala starts," JL said, "assuming you haven't canceled it."

"Not yet," Meredith said.

"Pete, we have to find David, his family, Pops, and the boys before we bring anyone else into this. If they're being held at the Montgomery hangar, Kenzie and I can search the premises quietly." JL glanced at Kenzie, and she nodded her agreement. "We're going over there. If our families aren't there, or it's too dangerous to evac them, we'll bring in other agencies."

"Be careful, *ragazza tosta*. Keep me in the loop," Pete said.

"What's all that noise?" JL asked.

"Oh…that…well, I didn't want to tell you, but I caught a ride on a friend's jet. I'll be there in a few hours."

"Here? In California?" JL asked.

"I wanted to be sure when this goes down that your back is covered."

"Don't kid the kidder. You're coming to drink wine."

"That, too. Hey, one more thing. I sent you a text earlier with the name of my contact at DEA. When you're ready to make the call, make it, but don't wait too long."

JL disconnected and hooked her phone to the charger on the kitchen counter. *Caught a ride on a friend's jet.* She had known Pete for most of her life. He didn't have friends with jets. She shot Kevin an edgy glance. "Did you send the plane back for Pete?"

There was a slight pink tint on his cheeks. "I thought…" He shrugged, "That Pete might…" He gave up and moved closer, placing his hands on her shoulders. "When you started shooting in the cavern, I was more scared than I've ever been in my life. Not for me, but for you. All I could think of was that I had to protect you. If one of my bullets killed one of those men, so be it. I couldn't bear the thought of losing you. Pete's been your partner for a long time. He's kept you safe. I can't protect you the way he can. It's not that I wouldn't do everything humanly possible, but because I'm not trained, I might make a fatal mistake."

Tears welled in her eyes. She couldn't hold them back, and they streaked down her face. Kevin wasn't a cop. What he had done in the cavern was done out of love. He had risked his life and put his moral code on hold to save her and Austin. She did truly love him. She touched his hair, his face, and gazed into his dark eyes as though to capture his image in this one moment. Her heart beat so fast it was sure to bruise her ribs.

"*Excuse me*," Kenzie said. "I hate to interrupt this tender moment, but we need to get the hell out of here. You and Kevin can pick this up when we get back, but right now, I'd rather go after my husband and children than watch you two eye-fuck each other."

"Watch yer' language, lass," Elliott said. "Although I happen to agree with ye."

JL unplugged and pocketed her phone. "Then let's roll."

22

JL discovered the BB gun safe wasn't the only one in the cottage. Behind a retractable wall in the unfinished part of the basement, David had stocked an arsenal that would fend off a six-month invasion. In all her years of police work, she had never seen a privately held stockpile of such magnitude. As she noted the types of armaments, one thing became very clear. The Frasers could withstand a six-month invasion using weapons designed for the eighteenth century to the twenty-first century. Most of the stockpile consisted of reproductions or antiques, valuable antiques, but why would the Frasers need guns used during the Civil War?

She would add that question to her growing list.

Kenzie loaded a duffel with handguns and ammunition. "Have you ever been in a tactical situation where you downed a barrier to take a room?"

"No. But I've come in right behind those who did," JL replied.

"This pump action shotgun has specialized twelve-gauge door-breaching rounds that can obliterate a door lock in seconds. You aim halfway between the lock and handle and the doorframe at about a forty-five-degree angle, as close as possible with the muzzle against the door. Most doors are breached with one or two rounds, depending on how many locks are on the door."

"Both the front and back doors have single locks," Kevin said.

Kenzie packed the shotgun in the duffel and zipped the bag. "Good to know."

Kevin opened a closet. "We need to change out of this camo gear. There are assault pants and shirts in here in different sizes."

JL slammed the door and faced him, hands on hips. "We? You're not going."

Kevin opened the closet again. "We've been through this before, JL. I *am* going."

JL glanced at Kenzie. "I don't think you can stop him," Kenzie said.

"Okay then," JL said. "You can go, but you're staying in the car." She searched through the closet and found men's small pants and a shirt that wouldn't swallow her. "Why didn't you open this room for us before we rappelled into the cave?"

"I asked David, but he didn't want you going in as part of SWAT. You were only observers."

"That doesn't make sense."

"It didn't to me either. You'll have to ask him why."

"I will, as soon as I rescue his ass."

"Don't you think we should call SWAT in on this?" Kevin said.

"No," Kenzie and JL said simultaneously.

"We don't know for sure our families are in the hangar. If they are, we only want to cause a distraction. David will do the rest," Kenzie said.

"We don't know how many guards they have," Kevin said.

"Doesn't matter." JL buttoned a tactical shirt over her vest and short-sleeve T-shirt. "I don't know David, but I know my brothers. If I can crack a window, they'll open it the rest of the way."

Kenzie hefted the duffel and handed it off to Kevin. "Wait outside while I change."

He stepped out while Kenzie stripped off the exercise clothes she had worn to the cave's entrance hours earlier. Standing in front of the closet in her panties and bra, she rubbed her hand in circles around her baby bump. A lump jammed in JL's throat, and she had to struggle to dull down the roar of her body's screams. When she had been pregnant with Austin, she had carried him in silence, never sharing the joy. Kenzie slammed the metal door to the closet, and thoughts of baby bumps deflated.

Kenzie adjusted the elastic slider waistband and tucked in the tail of her shirt. "I love how sexy these clothes are. I dressed out to seduce David once."

"Were you testing him to see which side of you excited him most—soldier/lawyer or mother?"

"Maybe." Kenzie did a quick throat clear to rid her voice of the huskiness that fear of loss puts in one's throat. JL knew the sensation well. It had been a constant companion the past several hours.

"David told me I could wear a flour sack and he'd still be turned on. He's a bloodhound, chasing my scent. He can find me anywhere. I call it radar, because he can zero in on the boys' location, too. He just knows. He waits on the porch for me because he senses I'm on the way home."

"Is that how he found you in London?"

"How do you know about London?"

"You told me that's where you met."

"Oh. Right." Kenzie wrapped her white-knuckled fingers around the mitered edge of the countertop. At the same time, a shadow wafted over her face as if she had gone to a dark place. Then she shook her head, and her lips curled up slightly. "He just knows things." Whatever funk Kenzie had fallen into swiftly vanished, and her eyes brightened.

She opened a wide, flat drawer lined side to side with an impressive array of fixed-blade weapons. "Pick your poison."

JL chose a dagger with a black Micarta handle, a blade length of five and a half inches, and a full, tapered tang. She held it, testing the balance. Perfect. She sheathed the knife and slid it into her pants' knife pocket. She knew how to fight with a knife, and how to defend against one, but so far in her career, she'd only used one to cut a rope. The goal for today was to survive it without adding more skills to her resume.

Kenzie unlocked a smaller cabinet and collected two M-3 assault rifles and ammunition. "I hope to God we don't need these, but I can't leave home without them. If you're ready, I am."

They found Kevin in the garage leaning casually against the Land Rover, drinking a bottle of water. The press of his fingers dented the plastic, almost bending the bottle in half.

JL's mind flashed back to the distinctive ways she had seen him in the past twenty-four hours: perfectly groomed, sweaty running clothes, out of the shower with damp hair and low-slung sweats, covered in cave dust, camo, and now tactical gear. Before now, if she had had to choose his sexiest look, it would have been the—out of the shower with damp hair and low-slung sweats—but he looked even sexier in tactical gear.

What did that say about her? What did that say about him?

Elliott followed JL and Kenzie into the garage. "Find them, but do not"—he pointed at the three of them—"put yourself in danger."

Kenzie kissed his cheek. "We'll bring them back, Elliott. Don't worry. Keep a watch out while we're gone. I don't think you're at risk here. But who knows?"

Meredith appeared at Elliott's side, and he put his arm around her, pulling her close. "Do ye have words for the rescuers?"

She gave them all a discerning look, and then scrutinized JL in a most uncomfortable way. "This time, whatever you do can't be undone. Before you step out, be sure your footing is sound."

There she goes again, speaking cryptically.

JL didn't roll her eyes, but an irritated burn started low and slow in her belly. Why didn't Meredith just spit out what was on her mind? She didn't wave, nor did she smile. What did JL want? That one was easy. She wanted a blessing combined with reassurance that they'd all survive the day, because believing love would carry her home wasn't enough right now.

Elliott pushed the button on the wall that opened the garage door, and Tater Tot came bounding in, followed by James Cullen and Austin.

"Damn," Kevin said. "The secret's out of the bag."

"Let's go. We don't have time to deal with it right now," JL said.

"Where'd that poodle come from?" Kenzie asked.

"We'll tell you on the way." He gripped the steering wheel and sped toward the winery's side entrance. When they arrived at the gate, he pressed the remote clipped to the visor. The gate didn't open. "Crap. When security changed the code, I didn't get the text with the new one."

"Maybe whoever changed it didn't want you to have it," JL said.

"The text is automatically generated and pushed out to a number of people every time the code's changed. It can't be overridden."

"Does this mean we trash the gate?" It had been a few years since JL had crashed through a barrier while in pursuit of a perp, and she wasn't anxious to update her resume with that skill, either.

"I have a key that should"—he lifted his eyebrows—"override the new code." He cast a look around before opening the car door. "Keep watch. There are cameras all around here." He moved rapidly, exiting the vehicle and reaching the gate's control panel, a metal box mounted on a stone post, in under five seconds.

She and her current partner, Pete, now had another thing in common. She, too, thought of sex every other minute. She had always wondered how Pete could focus on work and sex at the same time. Now she knew. The thought of having sex with Kevin gave her an edge. Kept her alert. Not a bad way to live, as long as you had a release. Pete did. He had an awesome woman in his life—a cop from another precinct.

JL kept her eyes peeled on their surroundings. "What do you make of the fact that no one's tried to stop us?"

Kenzie, sitting on the backseat and twirling the chinstrap on her helmet, said, "I've been thinking about that." She fixed her sight on something beyond the tinted window. "Whoever kidnapped Elliott and me and abandoned you and Kevin in the cave has probably left the premises. While that sounds promising, I wouldn't advise Elliott to come out of hiding yet."

"Because you believe they'll come back?"

"No. Because I'm pregnant."

JL did a double take. "If there's a connection there, it's broken for me."

"I thought I was the jokester." She twirled her index fingers. "Rewind that and let me start over. While I was lying on that stone floor, tied up like a calf in a tie-down roping contest, it dawned on me that if I hadn't been pregnant, I would have fought those men. I could have taken out one or two, but I didn't want to put my baby at risk."

"So if the enemy is still here, you don't think you'd be able to protect those who need protection because you need it yourself? Is that what you're saying?" JL asked.

"In a roundabout way, yes. Sounds cowardly, doesn't it?" She was silent for a moment and then said, "What's Kevin doing? I could have kicked the damn thing down with my combat boots."

"He's probably taking a leak."

"Did he drink a beer?" Kenzie asked. "If he did, that's exactly what he's doing. He's as bad as a girl."

"He did drink a beer, and you're not a coward. I don't buy that you wouldn't take a risk if you had to protect someone you loved. If you think back, you probably picked up a signal from Elliott."

"He and David have weird signals, almost like baseball players. They're subtle, though. David has taught me a few of them. Elliott twitched his finger. I might have interpreted it to mean stand down now. I don't know if he did, or if that's what I wanted to believe. I haven't asked him, and probably won't. He might not appreciate David telling me his secrets."

"It was good advice, even if you imagined it. Honestly, I don't believe you'd be here now if you weren't willing to take a risk."

"That's not complimentary of me as a mother to risk my unborn child."

"You're a soldier, Kenzie. You can't separate the mother part of you from who you are. I imagine David has harped on you about taking care of the baby while he takes care of you. Well…he's not here, and right now you have to do both, plus rescue him and your children. I believe he'd expect you to do what you're trained to do."

Kenzie tipped her head sideways a little, no more than an inch, but something in her eyes changed as if she had made a decision.

"David will exact a pound of revenge. You don't mess with him."

JL chuckled. "I bet you mess with him all the time."

Kenzie fired a smile at JL. It wasn't a paste-on smile, but a smile that said, yes indeedy, she messed with her husband. "If our families aren't at the hangar, where do we look next? Barrel Restoration?"

"That's the only other lead we have."

Kenzie picked at her bulky tactical shirt. "If we're going to snoop around, we can't go dressed like this."

"Let's see what we discover at the hangar and go from there."

The gate swung open, and Kevin signaled JL to move into the driver's seat and drive through to the other side. She scooted over and shifted the car into gear. Her eyes settled on the steely set of his jaw and his swagger. In a way, she had underestimated him, and he had risen far above his pay grade.

"Kevin's channeling McBain. I've never seen him like this. David will be proud of him. I know Elliott is."

"Did you know he was Elliott's son?" JL asked.

Kenzie racked the slide of her automatic, putting a bullet in the gun's chamber. "David's always suspected it."

"I'm surprised he didn't have their DNA tested."

"Oh, he did," Kenzie said. "The report is locked in his safe in an unopened envelope."

JL barked a laugh. "Seriously? He never read it? Curiosity would have killed me."

"No. He never did. Or, if he did, he's never mentioned it, and I think he would have." Kenzie's eyes took on a strange, focused look as if she were searching somewhere within herself. "This is just a guess, but I think David saw reading the results as an intrusion. He didn't want to invade Elliott's privacy."

"Having the test done was the invasion," JL said.

"I agree with you, and I would have argued that point if I had been in David's life then. He's always pushed Kevin. I think he saw Kevin's potential and wanted him to be successful and responsible."

"He wasn't responsible before?"

Kenzie racked the slide of a second gun. "He did stupid shit all the time, and Elliott let him get away with it."

"Out of guilt for not telling Kevin the truth. I can identify with that." Boy, could she. One of her big mistakes had been encouraging Austin's relationship with her scumball ex-husband. She hadn't been able to give her son his bio-dad, so she gave him the next best possible father, who hadn't been the next best at all. Why hadn't she seen that before this weekend?

She stopped the Land Rover on the other side of the gate and, after closing it, Kevin climbed back into the driver's seat. "Sorry. Had trouble with the override key." He put the car in gear and squealed out onto Montgomery Lane. "Have you two worked out a plan yet?"

"We can't blast our way into the hangar without confirmation that our families are in there. The airport authority will see it as a terrorist attack, and I don't want my ass hauled off to jail for committing a federal crime," Kenzie said.

"Short of lowering a camera through the ceiling, how do you suggest we get a visual?" JL said.

"I'll go in," Kenzie said.

"No, you won't," JL said.

Kenzie waved her off. "We've got headsets. We'll be in communication. I'll go in, acting like I work there. If the hostages are there, I'll say hit it. Kevin can crash through the main door, and you, JL, can blow the back door."

"Are you writing a movie script? You're dressed for an invasion. No one will believe you work there," JL said.

"David's waiting to make his move. I have to create a diversion. He'll take it from there."

"If all David and my brothers need is a diversion, blowing the back door will give them that. If you go in the front door, they'll use you as a hostage."

"Maybe," Kenzie said.

No way in hell was JL letting Kenzie go inside the hangar. Although she had graduated from West Point and done two tours in Afghanistan, Kenzie was now a corporate lawyer with rusty skills and a bulging belly. No freaking way.

After a twenty-minute tense drive, Kevin turned onto Airport Road. "The Montgomery Winery's hangar is a large box at the far end."

"Where's the plane?" Kenzie asked. "I don't see it. Do you think it's parked in the hangar?"

"It went to LA to pick up supplies for the gala," Kevin said.

"I thought it went to New York to get Pete," JL said.

"No, he's flying in on a friend's plane."

"You said you sent the plane. Now you're saying it's a friend's plane. Which is it?"

Kevin looked away from her for a moment and then looked back. "I hired a plane for him."

"*You what?* That had to cost a fortune. Why'd you do that?"

He shrugged. "I knew having him here would make you happy."

"And you spent thousands of dollars—"

Kenzie tapped her shoulder and JL turned in her seat. "Let it go. Kevin can afford it. The men in this family do stupid shit, but they do it out of love, or think they do. Ask Meredith about the Hogmanay Elliott put on at MacKlenna Farm just to impress her. He flew in special food from Edinburgh, booked Wynonna Judd to sing, and hired a company to bring up a Ferris wheel. Spent almost a million dollars."

"I hope she was impressed," JL said.

"She was until Elliott blew it."

Kevin pulled up alongside the hangar.

"Drive around to the back," Kenzie said. "You and JL can get into position. I'll come back around and pick the lock."

"That's not going to happen, Kenzie," JL said. "I'm not going to argue about it."

Kevin drove around to the back of the building, glancing up to look at Kenzie in the rearview mirror. "I'm siding with JL. You're not going in." He parked behind the dumpster and turned in his seat. "David will kick my ass from here to Kentucky, turning me into nothing more than a tumbleweed blowing across the prairie.

Spare me the indignity, *please*."

Kenzie huffed. "I'll take the shotgun and blow the door, then. That's all David needs. The guards will be disarmed before JL can get through the haze of smoke."

"Will the blast knock the door off the hinges?" Kevin asked. "If anyone is sitting nearby, they'll be injured."

"The blast will fold the metal door in and do minimal damage to the frame. The door should stay intact. The locking mechanism, the dead bolt, and the entry knob should all survive the blast. There will be minimal projectiles into the objective. As soon as the door is blown, wait ten seconds. Then go in."

"I wish we could see in. I'd feel more confident. Can't we drop a camera?"

"We could, but we'd have to drill a hole in the wall. The sound would put the guards on notice. Is that what you want?" Kenzie said.

"Maybe that'll provide the distraction David needs," Kevin said.

"He needs a big distraction. One that will cause confusion. The sound of a drill will only alarm them."

"Airport security won't respond to a drill boring a hole in a wall, but they will to a shotgun blast. They'll be swarming us in seconds," Kevin said.

"Are you saying don't do it?" JL asked.

"I'm not saying one way or the other," he said.

JL shook her head. Damn indecision. Here she was again. Do it or not do it, but do something. She did a gut check, but got nothing. "What does your gut tell you, Kenzie?"

"Are you kidding? It tells me to blast the damn door down."

"Your gut's overrun with hormones. I don't know if you can trust it," JL said.

"I'll give it the benefit of the doubt. Check your headsets," Kenzie said.

"Check," Kevin said.

"Check," JL said, jumping out of the car.

"Check." Kenzie exited the vehicle and stepped into JL's space, glaring down at her. "The love of my life is in there with my children, and I'm not going to stand here and argue about it." She grabbed the shotgun. "No more talking."

JL pressed her fingers against her earpiece, which was still vibrating with the echo of Kenzie's determination.

Kevin kissed JL on the mouth. His lips were warm, and the delightfully bitter taste of beer transferred to her. "We have a date tonight."

She smiled into the kiss. "Nothing will keep that from happening."

JL, with her assault rifle in the ready position, moved within a few feet of Kenzie, who stood near the door with the breaching shotgun. Kevin stepped aside. Kenzie blew the door with a powerful blast that rang in JL's ears. Kenzie pumped the shotgun and stepped forward, but JL moved in front of her.

"You're *not* going in." JL puffed out her breath, punched her arms out, ready to take a shot, and then proceeded through the haze of smoke and acrid smell of gunpowder. *"Police. Get down. Police. Get down,"* she yelled.

Her gut clenched at the striking tableau set out in front of her.

On her left, Connor, with duct tape still over his mouth, was successfully subduing a white male, mid-twenties. Ten feet away, Jeffrey had another white male, same age, in a chokehold. A few feet farther, Shane had wrestled a man in his mid-to-late thirties to the ground. He didn't need help, and neither did Patrick, who had his knee planted in the back of a white male, early twenties. There were no other guards. The O'Gradys had cleared the field.

In the corner, David was on the floor with the twins squirming beneath him. Nearby Braham was on his knees with his arms around a woman who was also on her knees. Between them, they cradled two children. Jack Mallory was covering the woman's back, and Pops was covering David's, creating double layers of protection for the children. All the adults had their wrists unbound, cut zip ties near their feet.

Magic rings, and sealing wax, and other fancy stuff. Or something like that…

Her brothers' titanium escape rings weren't magical, but they sure could cut through zip ties. "Clear," JL said into her mouthpiece.

"Damn. I thought for sure they were here," Kenzie said.

"They are. All OK," Kevin said.

JL turned to find him a few paces behind her. Hadn't she told him to stay outside? Maybe she hadn't. More likely, he chose to ignore her command, treating it as an option. She would deal with that later.

"Coming in," Kenzie said.

Connor yanked his prisoner to his feet. "What the hell took you so long, JL?"

"From the looks of it, you didn't even need me."

Kenzie darted past her and into David's arms. "God, I was so worried." She peeled the duct tape off his mouth. Twitching his nose was his only response to her peeling off the top layer of his skin. She then turned her attention to the children he sheltered. Tape covered both boys' mouths. She peeled away their tape, too. The kids didn't whimper, but they did twitch their noses in a copycat gesture.

"You missed it all, Mommy. We were having an adventure," one of the twins said.

"A cool adventure," the other one said. "We talked with our eyes."

Somebody is going to tell me what this adventure crap is all about.

"In ten more minutes I was going to create my own goddamned diversion." David kissed Kenzie with one of those movie-style kisses meant to melt the hearts of the women in the audience. JL turned away quickly, and then mentally rolled her eyes at herself.

Pops plodded toward her, stiff-legged, pulling the tape from his mouth. "If I had any jurisdiction, you'd get a promotion out of this." He swept her into his arms and hugged her tightly. "Proud of you, JL. Where's Austin?"

"He's at the winery. He's safe."

"Thank God."

Damn. Tears were burning her eyes again. She dared them to spill out. She wiped the back of her hand beneath her nose. "How'd you manage this?"

Connor, with a two-handed grip on his prisoner, shoved him forward. "We used Morse code."

"How? Did you tap on the floor?"

David and Kenzie, each holding a child, joined her and Pops. "They blinked at each other like this…" The little boy in David's arms pursed his lips and blinked his eyes rapidly. "Daddy taught me how to say I love you in that code. Cool, huh?"

"Yeah, buddy. That's really cool." JL smiled and tousled his hair. "You'll have to teach me how to do that."

The twins twisted in their parents' arms until they released them to join the other two kids.

JL's brother, Jeffrey, took possession of Connor's prisoner. "Where's Austin?"

"He's safe," Pops said.

"Good work, JL," Jeffrey said. Then, along with Shane and Patrick, the three NYPD detectives secured the four black-suited kidnappers' hands with the surplus zip-ties and corralled them in a corner, away from the children and the blown access door.

"We were waiting for a distraction. The blast was perfect. But waiting for it was nerve-racking," Connor said.

"When did you attack the guards?" she asked.

"We made our move a mere second before you blew the door," Connor said.

"How? Why then?"

"David gave the signal."

She pivoted toward David and Kenzie. "We didn't make any noise. How'd you know?"

"I told you he has some weird radar," Kenzie said. "He knew I was at the door."

JL shook her head and looked up to find David's dark eyes on her, soft brown and full of speculation. "You aren't going to tell me, are you?" she said.

"It's a connection I can't explain. Ask Braham. He has a similar one with Charlotte."

Baffled, she said, "If you can't explain it, I doubt he can."

"He's a lawyer and a student of the ancient Greek philosophers. He can give ye a logical explanation based on his rather unique understanding of the universe." David, waxing poetic, seemed out of character for a Scotsman/soldier type, but what little JL knew about the man came only from personal observations and his wife's pithy comments. She wished she had more time to understand what really made him tick. Reading his books might help. She would download one to her Kindle and read it on the flight home.

Two airport cruisers with lights and sirens came to a screeching halt outside the hangar near the blown door. From where JL stood, she had a clear view as four cops took cover behind the open doors of their vehicles. Using a bullhorn, a cop said, "Drop your weapons and come out now with your arms raised."

JL snagged Connor's sleeve. "Let's go have a chat."

"I'm coming, too," Pops said.

"We'll come with you," Kenzie said.

"We'll handle this." Pops used his commander's voice and Kenzie immediately stood down as if a whip had cracked over her head.

David's lips twitched, and he nuzzled Kenzie's ear. "Let it go, lass. Pops is giving us a minute together. Let's not waste it."

Kenzie's pissed-off expression vanished. She flung her arms around her husband's neck and they gave each other another movie-style kiss.

JL glanced around for Kevin and found him in the middle of the pack of children. The four munchkins, competing for attention, were jumping up and down. "We had an adventure," one of the twins said. Kevin's twinkling eyes roved from one child to the other, and he laughed.

The struggles over the last few hours had hardwired the sound of his voice to her heart, and his laughter ignited a spark inside her. Kevin raised his head, grinning, and the spark ignited a flame. She touched her tingly lips, longing to kiss him in the same passionate way Kenzie was kissing her husband. Kevin seemed to know that, and his grin spread and spread until his entire face lit up like the slots at Caesar's Palace. He hadn't won the jackpot. She had.

"Come on, JL," Connor said. "We've got some 'splaining to do."

She pried her eyes off Kevin. Then, with Connor and Pops, the three of them left the hangar with their arms raised, flashing their shields.

Walking out into the sunlight, she said, "I'm Detective JL O'Grady."

"Detective Connor O'Grady," her brother said.

"Retired Deputy Chief Lawrence O'Grady," Pops said.

The cop with the bullhorn asked, "What agency are you with?"

"NYPD," Pops said.

The cop tossed the bullhorn onto the seat of the car and approached. He snatched their shields out of their hands and inspected them. He gave JL a wary glance. "I saw an interagency bulletin about you. You're the detective Hollinger and Castellano met with yesterday while investigating the Di Salvo murder. Is there a connection here?"

"You'll have to ask the four prisoners tied up inside," she said.

An unmarked vehicle with a flashing light pulled to a stop a few feet from her, and the driver's door opened.

"Aw, shit," she said.

"Detective O'Grady. Are you in the middle of this?" Detective Castellano said.

"How's Hollinger?" she asked.

"He'll be fine in a few weeks."

"How was your trial prep?"

Castellano glanced at the door Kenzie had blasted open. "Did you do that?"

"We did what we had to do to rescue my father, Retired Deputy Chief O'Grady." She pointed to Pops. "And my brother, Detective Connor O'Grady. My other three brothers are inside with four prisoners." She glanced up at Pops. "This is Detective Castellano."

"I'm going out on a limb here," Castellano said, "but I doubt there's a simple explanation."

"Why did airport security call you?" she asked.

Castellano briefly glanced toward the hangar. "They didn't. I got a tip that something was going down at the Montgomery hangar."

Two more police cruisers came to a screeching halt behind Castellano's vehicle. The cops got out and joined airport security entering the hangar.

"My dad and my brothers, along with Fraser family members—nine adults and four children—flew in a few hours ago. They were kidnapped as soon as they landed and held here in the hangar."

"By whom?"

She pointed over her shoulder with her thumb. "Those creeps inside might have a better answer. Go ask them."

He pointed his finger in her face. "I'm asking you. Then I'll ask them."

Pops put his hands on his hips and hunched to get in Castellano face, boring down hard on the much shorter man. "You'll treat this detective with respect. She's done nothing wrong and has probably saved your ass." Then he leveled a glowering look at JL. "This is why there're so many interagency turf battles. Show a little cooperation."

She narrowed her eyes while she glowered back at Pops, but she quickly surrendered. Having a glower battle with the deputy chief had never been successful for her…or anyone else, as far as she knew. "My guess? It's the same people who blew up the cave."

"Dammit," Castellano said. "Murder. Kidnapping. What else?"

"Drug trafficking."

He removed his glasses and cleaned them with the bottom of his tie. They weren't dirty. It always annoyed her when she had to look people in the eye and they had smudges on their glasses. Castellano was stalling. She took a deep breath and let the crisp October air filter through her lungs.

"Do us a favor, Detective. Don't ever come back to Napa."

"Gee, thanks, Castellano. And here I thought we were on our way to a great working relationship."

He shoved his handkerchief back into his pocket and settled his glasses on his nose. "It takes two, O'Grady, to make a relationship work."

"I didn't come here looking for any of this." Once again, tears threatened to embarrass her. She would be damned if she'd cry in front of Castellano, or Pops for that matter. Needing a distraction, she took note of the adjoining runway. The wheels of a jet were touching down, and she wondered if it was Pete's plane. An emotion she couldn't identify folded over her like a down comforter on a chilly evening.

"Look. Here is the deal. At daybreak, I learned Austin was missing, and ultimately discovered he'd been kidnapped. A couple of hours later, Kevin and I were abandoned in a cave; Elliott Fraser and Meredith Montgomery, along with Kenzie McBain, were escorted to the basement of the winery's Welcome Center, where they were tied up and left on a stone floor in the dark. Then as soon as their airplane landed, those men," JL said pointing toward the prisoners, "kidnapped and imprisoned them here. Someone knew every step we planned."

"The police didn't," Castellano said.

"I'm not so sure. Whoever was running this illegal op had deep connections with the police and/or winery security. If I asked the wrong agency for help…"

"You should have called me."

She slanted her eyes at him. "Hollinger was severely injured, and you were in trial prep. That sounded too convenient for me."

"I was *conveniently* not there because you called me. It pissed Hollinger off. I knew you didn't trust me. That's why I made it a point to talk to you at the game."

"Speaking of the game, I need to call Austin. He has to get to school."

"Make it quick. You have a statement to make, and it's going to be a long one."

She stepped away from the group and called Austin. "Everybody's okay, buddy," she said. "We're talking to the police now. Ask

Elliott to take you to the ball game."

"You sure everyone's okay?" Austin asked.

"Yes. Pops, the boys, and I will get to the game as soon as we can."

"If you can't make it, I'll understand."

"We'll be there as soon as we wrap up here."

"What about Kevin?"

She looked inside the hangar to see Kevin still on the floor listening to the kids. The sight was enough to melt her heart. "He'll be there, too." She disconnected the call and rejoined Castellano and Pops.

"I went to the academy with Tony Castellano," Pops said. "Is he any relation to you?"

"My uncle," Castellano said.

"Good man. We worked together at the One-Five."

"Let's get this over with," JL said. "I'd like to see some of Austin's game tonight."

They returned to the hangar to find the clan hanging out in the two limos. Her brothers and Kevin were drinking beers. Mallory, Braham, and David were drinking from cups. The strong scent of alcohol told her they weren't drinking water or juice. In the second limo, Kenzie was reclining on the bench seat, and the woman she had seen with Braham was taking her pulse.

"What's wrong?" JL asked.

"She's lightheaded. With all the gear she was wearing, she probably got overheated." The woman reached out her other hand and said, "I'm Charlotte Mallory."

JL gave a slight lift to her brow saying, "Aka McCabe?"

"She was a well-respected surgeon before she went on an adventure and met my dad. That's why my mom's still a Mallory like Uncle Jack." The comment came from a child sitting opposite the women and clutching a cat.

"You're Lincoln, right?" JL said.

"I was named after the president," he said. "He was a friend of my dad's."

Charlotte shot him a mom's evil eye. He cleared his throat and brushed his long, blond bangs out of his eyes. "Just kidding."

JL pursed her lips. "Ah, well, it's nice to meet you, Lincoln, and your mom, too."

His mom was beautiful, a natural blonde with striking blue eyes who spoke with a Southern accent that could melt sugar. JL pinned her for late forties. She presented herself as a poised and confident woman, yet, she had an aloofness about her, similar to Meredith's. In no way would JL describe either woman as cold. JL sensed that Charlotte, like Meredith, would warm quickly once she had time to assess and evaluate. There seemed to be a strong bond between Charlotte and Kenzie, as if they shared an experience that had changed their lives.

How did JL know that? She just knew. Her intuition had always been an asset, but over the past twenty-four hours, her intuition had been amped up. If she had to explain her unexplainable knowledge, she couldn't.

A man made a low noise in his throat, and JL turned to check out who owned it—Castellano. "Detective, meet me over there by that table," he said.

JL eyeballed the area of the hangar where he pointed and nodded.

Kenzie raised her head. "I'll go with you."

"You stay here and rest. You can give your statement later," JL said.

"Okay." Kenzie lay back down and Charlotte placed the stethoscope's chest piece inside Kenzie's shirt.

JL stepped away. She was confident Kenzie would be fine with a *well-respected* surgeon tending her. She chuckled. How did these children become so advanced and mature? That question belonged on her list, too.

"Is she okay?" Kevin asked.

"Charlotte said Kenzie got overheated. I need to go talk to Castellano."

He took her hand and laced his fingers with hers. "I'm going with you."

"I don't need protection."

"I know you don't, but I may remember something that slipped by you."

Her inclination was to say no, but if what she read in Kevin's eyes was a reflection of what was speaking to his heart, she couldn't deny his need to be with her or her desire to have him there.

They sat down across from Castellano at a six-foot table with neatly organized tools and random machine parts. "Start with leaving the game last night and don't stop until you reach this place"—he thumped the tip of his finger on the table—"right here, right now."

She and Kevin took turns, picking up where one of them ended one segment of the story and starting another. JL took the lead when they reached the part where Austin interrupted them in Kevin's bedroom. She glossed over the intimate details, giving just enough to explain Austin's subsequent behavior.

When she ended their joint statement, Castellano said, "Mr. Allen, would you excuse us? I'd like to talk privately with the detective."

JL squeezed his leg, and smiled. "It's okay."

Kevin left the table and moved out of earshot, but he remained in her line of vision. He didn't take his eyes off her, and she barely took hers off Castellano. She picked up one of the black chauffeur's caps, checked the inside label, and then fiddled with the visor.

"Why the hell didn't you call me?" Castellano said.

"I told you. I didn't trust you." She tossed the cap onto the pile with the other three.

"Sorry. I don't buy it. What's the real reason?"

"That is the real reason."

"Still don't buy it. We connected when we talked. There was trust. You ignored it and put your life in danger. Put your friends in danger, too. You refused to ask for help. Why?"

While her eagle-eyed gaze remained fixed on Castellano, she clasped her hands and dropped them in her lap. "I don't know what you're after."

"You thought the Di Salvos were involved. You wanted to break them. Didn't you?"

She squeezed her fingers so tightly they tingled from a loss of circulation "It had nothing to do with them."

"A few years ago they almost killed you. You thought you had them all in jail, but you got here and believed they had set up a new operation. You were out for blood, determined to end it once and for all."

She refused to move, to scratch the tickle on her face, to drop her eye contact, to show any sign that he was getting under her skin. "You're wrong."

"You shot at least one man and bashed another one in the head."

She broke her tight clasp, slapped her palms on the worktable, and leaned forward. "It was self-defense." Out of her peripheral vision, she noticed Kevin had changed positions and now stood only a few feet away, ready to come to her aid.

"When this case is reviewed by the DA," Castellano said, "I don't want there to be any misunderstanding. Hollinger cut off your legs. I tried to reattach them, but you wobbled out on a limb all by yourself. You could have gotten Austin, Kevin Allen, and yourself killed in that cave, or when you barged in here, for that matter. I hope to hell your ghosts are dead now, because you should smell like shit, but instead you're wearing a big fat H on your chest."

"Tell me what you really think, Castellano."

"Get your ass out of here. And next time, pick up the goddamn phone and call me."

23

AUSTIN HIT A THREE-POINTER from his favorite spot, just to the left of the key, a spot where he rarely missed, tying the game at the buzzer and sending the last matchup of the tournament into overtime. Pro Prep took the lead to open the extra minutes with a steal and a layup by Austin. Both teams had ample chances to win, but Pro Prep walked away with the W, and Austin ended the tournament with a triple-double in points, blocked shots, and rebounds. If college scouts were attending the game, they had to have been impressed with his playing. She was.

The MacKlenna Clan and friends occupied most of the center section of the bleachers. Three Scotsmen, seven members of the NYPD, a *New York Times* bestselling author, a renowned surgeon, an international vintner, a pregnant, decorated vet and corporate counsel, five precocious children, and one multitalented CFO. With the exception of Pete, everyone had been through a terrifying ordeal that could have ended badly. From the smiles on everyone's faces, though, onlookers would have thought they had spent the day winery hopping. If there was a common denominator among members of the group, it was resilience.

JL, on the other hand, wasn't so sure she was as resilient as she had been. Kevin had entered her life and rocked her world, and nothing would ever be the same again.

Why now? Why here? Why him?

It wasn't the first time she had pondered those questions in the past thirty-plus hours. Her job, her career, her family, her community were all in New York. Kevin's life was with MacKlenna Corporation and the Frasers. Could a bicoastal relationship work for them? Could she leave her life in New York and move to Kentucky or Napa? They had a lot to talk about later.

On the way out of the gym, through a gaggle of gawking women—and who wouldn't gawk at a thundering herd of testosterone-reeking studs?—Pete spun on her, pulled her out of the stream of exiting fans, and directed her into a side hallway.

"What's up with you and Kevin? You were all but screwing each other during the game. It embarrassed even me."

"We were *not*," she said, lifting her eyebrows for emphasis. "And don't give me that crap. Nothing embarrasses you." Her cheeks heated. There had been that *one* time when her hand accidentally slipped between Kevin's legs. Now, in the hallway, she cleared her throat and said to Pete, "Absolutely nothing is going on."

"Don't bullshit a bullshitter."

"You said that so eloquently. Didn't you tell me at the airport not to come back without getting laid?"

"Yeah, but I didn't tell you to fall in love."

"I'm not in love." Her whole face heated with that one, too, and the flame of denial sucked the breath from her lungs. Pete's eyes focused on hers, and it took a long moment to recover the air she needed. "We've been through a traumatic twenty-four hours. When two people go through a do-or-die experience, they bond. Eventually the emotion burns off, and this will, too."

"Believe what you want, but you two have…synergy."

"Synergy? Really? What kind of word is that? Who are you? And what have you done with my partner?"

"Stop it. You know what I mean. Together you're stronger than you are individually. Don't let the job or your family come between you. After the shit you've been through, you deserve to be happy. He's good for you."

She smirked at him. "Why would you say that?"

"Because he's *not* a cop. He's a handsome dude with access to a jet and a cellar full of wine."

"You don't even drink wine."

Pete snorted. "I don't like the cheap stuff they sell in Jersey bars."

"So you want me to hook up with him because he's loaded?"

"No. I want you to hook up with him because you love each other."

Her head pounded from excessive stress and the high decibel level in the gym courtesy of screaming teenagers and over-the-top sports parents. She rubbed her temples, hoping for relief from Pete's questions and her untenable position.

"Come on. The others are waiting. I've said my piece. Just keep in mind that I heard recently they're hiring cops in California." He slapped his forehead. "Oh, my bad. You don't trust any of our western brethren."

She smacked his arm and stomped away. Under her breath she said, "He doesn't know what the hell he's talking about."

"I heard that," he said.

She shot a glaring look over her shoulder. "Oh, go to hell."

"Okay, but we'll be sharing seats on the same bus."

He laughed, but it wasn't just a gleeful chuckle. It was a guffaw. Loud and unrestrained. His laughter, and the fact that he always told her the truth were two of the things she loved most about him. If he hadn't been Connor's best friend, they would have hooked up years ago. Thank God they hadn't. She would much rather be his partner than his wife.

When she pushed through the gym door, the cool valley air smacked her in the face, bringing the scent of new wine. She took a refreshing breath. In the funky mood she was in, she might be able to get drunk on the air alone. She found Kevin waiting next to his car, parked in the principal's spot.

"If you hadn't been with Pete, I would have come looking for you. You okay?"

"I'm tired, hungry, and..." She pressed her lips against his. "...horny. Is there anything you can do for my condition?"

"Feed you, love you, and hold you while you rest."

"Damn, Allen. Please don't tell me that's another one of Austin's lines."

"No, Sugar. That's an Allen original, written just for this moment."

God, no wonder she loved him. "Don't call me sugar or spice or anything nice like that. I bet you've used those endearments with dozens of women."

"Nope. Just you. Never met anyone else so sweet."

"Good grief. Give me a break."

He kissed her again. "Come on. Let's go home."

She ran over to the other side, yanked open the door, and threw herself into the seat.

"Are you in a hurry?"

"Hell yes. I want to get in bed with you before I fall asleep." The car purred when Kevin turned the key, and so did she. "Hurry." He spun the Land Rover out of the empty parking lot, and she was counting how many minutes it would take them to get back to the cottage.

They were only a few blocks from the school when Kevin's phone rang. He pushed the accept call button on the steering wheel to put the call on speaker. "Kevin Allen," he said.

"This is Castellano. Do you have O'Grady with you?"

"I have one here listening to this call. The city is overpopulated with them tonight."

JL couldn't drag her gaze from Kevin's face.

Castellano laughed. "I've heard about you, Allen. You have a reputation in the valley. I hope JL's dad is watching out for her."

She grimaced at Kevin, mouthing, "Reputation?"

"*Castellano*," Kevin said, clearly irritated, "why the hell are you calling?"

"To give you an update. Do you want it or not?"

"Yes," she and Kevin said simultaneously.

"Thought so. We found the ex-Navy SEALs McBain hired to watch the cave entrance. The cartel had tied them up and left them in the cavern. Other than being pissed as hell, they weren't injured. The cavern had been swept clean, or rather the perps had attempted to do that."

She sat forward in the seat, visualizing the cavern and shuddering slightly at the image her mind conjured, along with the sensory memory of her trigger finger pulling, pulling, pulling, searing the semidarkness with bolts of lightning. She shook her head to clear it and rubbed her finger, freeing it of the memory.

"Did you find any bodies?" she asked.

"No, but the crime scene investigators found blood and trace evidence that indicated the cave was used as a cocaine lab, but no cocaine."

Kevin peeled his eyes from the road to glance at her and mouthed, "What the hell?"

She shrugged, then said, "What about Barrel Restoration?"

"We showed up with a search warrant, but couldn't find any barrels with red Xs."

"Shit," she said. "Did you check any other barrels?"

"Our warrant specifically said barrels with red Xs."

Kevin mouthed a what-the-hell again. "Get another one. Check *all* the barrels."

"I wish it was that easy," Castellano said. "We had probable cause that evidence of a crime would be found. It didn't pan out. The judge won't approve a fishing expedition."

Kevin ran a yellow light that turned red in the middle of the intersection. She clutched the door hard. If a driver had rushed the green, he or she would have hit their vehicle. "We'll be there when the store opens in the morning and buy every barrel they have," Kevin said.

"If the barrels were delivered there, they've been hauled off by now," Castellano said.

She pried her fingers free as they sped down a dark road illuminated only by their headlights. "You don't know that for sure."

"They could have been off-loaded at Barrel Restoration, loaded onto another truck, and delivered out of town. But, hey, if you want to spend a buttload of money on barrels you don't need, go for it."

The shadowy outlines of Kevin's face had coalesced into a portrait of a steel-jawed, sexually charged, and un-rockable man. "Check the owners of the engineering company. See if anyone owns warehouses or land where the barrels could be stored."

"We're checking, but no flags so far. Honestly, unless one of the kidnappers gives them up, we don't have a direct connection to anyone."

JL pounded one fist on top of the other repeatedly. Jumbled up in her logical mind were her thoughts, questions, and suppositions. She hoped her brain would sort itself and spit out a few brilliant answers, but she got nothing.

"What about bank accounts?" Kevin asked.

"We need probable cause for a subpoena. We don't have that either."

Almost as an afterthought, he asked, "Did you find Wilder?"

"The mine communicator guy? No. He found us. He showed up at the police station claiming he'd been kidnapped."

For the third time, Kevin mouthed, "What the hell?"

Remembering what a nightmare everyone else's escape had been, she asked, "I'd sure as hell like to know how he got away. According to Kenzie, shortly after he disappeared, she and Elliott heard shots fired. Ask Wilder if the kidnappers shot at him."

"Oh, yes, they did—to get his attention," Castellano said. "He said when he was forced into the cave he picked up a rock and bashed the guy's head. We didn't have any reason to disbelieve him, so we sent him on his way but told him not to leave town."

"That doesn't make any sense. Why wasn't he taken to the Welcome Center with Elliott and Kenzie?"

"I asked him that. He said his expertise was needed."

"Maybe," JL said, shoving another piece of data into her chugging-along computer brain. "But it doesn't sound right. Where is he now?"

"He's staying at the Napa Inn."

"He got a room in the priciest hotel in Napa on a Saturday night during harvest? That's impossible," Kevin said. "Even Elliott can't do that."

"I'll check it out," Castellano said. "Anything else?"

"What about Di Salvo's shooter?" JL asked.

"We don't have any leads. The four guards signed statements saying someone hired them over the phone and paid them in cash through a courier. They intercepted the original drivers and took their places. We found the four drivers tied up in an abandoned building at the edge of town. The guards were instructed to hold the hostages until six o'clock this evening."

"They were just going to let them go? Seriously? If they'd been masked, I might believe that. They had every intention of killing them." There was silence on the other end of the phone. "We're batting zero for two."

"Nice analogy, O'Grady. We'll do better tomorrow."

"I hope so," she said.

"Fill McBain in, will you? He left a message, but I haven't had time to return his call."

"I will as soon as we get back to the cottage. Thanks for the update," Kevin said.

"Tell Deputy Chief O'Grady, while you're updating the rest, that this looks like interagency cooperation to me."

She chuckled. "I'll tell him."

After disconnecting the call, Kevin lifted one hand off the steering wheel and massaged her neck. "It's almost over."

"Ten years on the force and I've never had a day like today."

"Not even when you were investigating the Di Salvos?"

"Even then." The massage lulled her and she closed her eyes. The next thing she knew they were pulling into the cottage's garage. "Let's make love before I fall asleep again."

"Not tonight," Kevin said.

"No? Really? After the day we've had. We're not?"

"I'm not making love to you until we've both rested and our minds are clear." He took her face between his hands and kissed her. "Don't forget Austin, your father, and four brothers are staying at the cottage."

"They'll be here tomorrow, too."

He kissed her before coming around and opening the car door for her. "I have something special planned. A place where we won't be interrupted."

"I like the uninterrupted part. We could camp out in a tent for all I care."

"Ah, trust me. This is better than a tent."

She opened the front door of the cottage expecting a clamor of excited voices tinged with accents from the Scottish Highlands to Staten Island. "Where is everyone?"

"Probably at the villa. It's way past the kids' bedtime."

"Oh." She was disappointed, but until she took a nap, she couldn't contribute to the discussion in a concrete way. Best to let Pops, her brothers, and Pete dive in. She would catch up later.

She led the way to her bedroom and sat on the edge of her bed. "I need to take a shower, but I'm going to close my eyes for just a second."

"Whatever you say, Sugar."

"Don't call me that," she mumbled. "You know it gets late early out here."

"It sure does, Yogi."

That was the last she knew until she woke hours later, fully dressed except for her shoes. Kevin hadn't undressed her. He had removed her shoes and covered her with a throw blanket, but left her fully dressed. She wasn't sure she liked that. Seriously? Did she want him to manhandle her while she slept? No. Then get over it.

Where was the non-manhandler now? Had he gone to the villa? Possibly. After she took a shower, she would track him down.

Pulsating streams of steamy water pelted her tight, sore muscles and worked out the aches and pains in her shoulders and legs. She worked out and ran long distances, so she shouldn't be so sore. Then she remembered she had climbed over cave rocks carrying a thirty-pound pack.

After towel drying her hair, she padded her way to the kitchen to raid the refrigerator, wearing the warm Turkish robe. She stopped in the doorway, tightening the robe's sash. Kevin and Pete sat on barstools poring over sketches and notes spread out on the counter.

Kevin stood, smiling. "I hope we didn't wake you." He kissed her lightly.

"You didn't. My stomach did."

Pete laughed. "Her stomach has to be fed every four to six hours or the growling will drive you insane. She complains about Austin eating so much, but so does she."

Kevin winked. "Nice to know."

"What are you two doing? It's the middle of the night."

"We started talking, and here we are," Kevin said.

Among the papers sat three empty bottles of wine. She picked one up and read the label. "That's not all you were doing."

"Talking and thinking out loud makes a man thirsty. How about an omelet? I don't cook much, but I can cook egg dishes," Kevin said.

"You can make omelets?"

"Sure. What do you want in it?"

"Cheese, green peppers, bacon, mushrooms. Whatever you have?"

He looked in the fridge. "Avocado, red peppers, jalapenos, spinach, apples, smoked salmon, tomatoes, Brie, feta, pine nuts."

"Whatever. Just make it easy for my stomach to digest." She glanced at the clock. "It's two o'clock in the morning. What time did I fall asleep?"

"About nine."

Five hours of sleep was about all she ever got. She should be more refreshed than she was. "You've been sitting here working and drinking since nine?"

"We weren't alone," Pete said. "David, Braham, and your brothers were here for a while."

"We divided up the work," Kevin said.

She pulled up a stool, and when she sat, the robe flipped open, flashing her leg. It wasn't intentional, but she couldn't help chuckling at Kevin's wide-eyed reaction. Now she understood why he hadn't undressed her. She folded the edge of the robe over her leg, smiling.

"What work did you divide up?" she asked.

"Trying to find a connection between Di Salvo's murder and the drugs," Pete said.

"Any luck?"

"David is tracing the money, your brothers and Pops are reviewing security tapes and patrolling the grounds, and Braham is guarding the villa," Pete said.

"I took your brothers with me to the security center when I fired the staff. They escorted them off the property. I have to admit, I was concerned when I gave them the keys to the ATVs and golf carts. They looked at each other with gleams in their eyes, and quoted lines from the movie *Top Gun*."

JL rested her elbow on the counter and dropped her head in her hand. "Don't tell me. Let me guess. *'I feel the need. The need for speed.'*"

"You know them well," Kevin said.

"Where's my omelet?"

He lifted a skillet off the hanging rack. "Coming right up."

She grabbed a glass from the cabinet and a bottle of orange juice from the fridge. Kevin came in behind her and picked up a carton of eggs and a handful of ingredients from the vegetable bin.

"You did everything I did, and I'm exhausted. Why aren't you?"

He cracked three large eggs into a mixing bowl and whisked them together. "You started off with a three-hour time deficit, and then you stayed up all night."

Pete laughed. "The truth is, he's tired, but he wanted to stay up so he could interrogate me while you slept."

She glared at her partner. "About what?"

"I've known you most of your life. Don't you think I have a few stories that…you know…the man you're in love with…"

She gasped and slugged him in the arm. "You didn't."

Pete rubbed his now-bruised bicep. "Yep. I told him everything he wanted to know."

She dragged her hands down her face. "You're an ass. Why don't you go home?" Then she gasped again. "Did you tell him what you told me when you dropped me off at the airport?"

Grinning, Kevin poured the eggs into the skillet. "I'm glad I could help you out. I thought we had something special, but it turns out I was just a convenient dick."

She picked up the bottle and threatened to bash Pete over the head. "Traitor."

Kevin took the bottle out of her hand. "Blame me. I bribed him."

She lined the bottles up in a row. "I can see that. Each of these cost eighty to ninety dollars. Am I right?"

"How do you know?"

"I'm a detective. I spent the last month preparing for this trip. After the day we had, I'd have been better off going spelunking than researching wine." She poured another glass of orange juice and sat next to Pete. "So what have you figured out so far?"

He pushed the empty bottles aside, collected the pages of notes, and stacked them together for her to read. "There's a common denominator that connects the cave and the hangar."

"My brain's not fully functioning. I can't play guessing games. Just tell me."

"David called the mining company during the flight to California. The company connected him with their sales rep, who was making customer calls in San Francisco. David confirmed that Wilder knew who was on the flight and the plane's ETA."

"So Wilder is in on this?" she said.

"David's doing a background check. He should have more by late morning," Pete said.

"He's trying to connect Meredith's engineering company to the wireless communication company through their client list," Kevin said.

"How's he doing that? I doubt there's a list on their website."

Pete gave her a subtle wink. "I didn't ask."

"You didn't, because you don't want to know the answer." She doubted plausible deniability would work here. "If he's doing anything"—she made air quotes—"questionable, I hope it doesn't compromise the investigation."

Pete shrugged. "It's not our investigation."

"Not officially. That's true." Glancing down the list on the top sheet of paper, she noted a question mark next to Kenzie and David's names, along with the comment *unique relationship*. Boy, was it. She had never seen anything like it. The question mark, however, triggered a thought she'd had earlier. "Do you know why Kenzie kept sending us messages to return to the entrance?"

"I asked her. She said she never sent or received a message," Kevin said.

"Damn. That means Wilder *is* involved."

"Tell Castellano to put a tail on Wilder," JL said.

"Already did," Kevin said.

"If his company has connections with mines all around the country, it's possible he's set up similar operations," Pete said.

"Did you mention that to David?" JL asked.

"He said as soon as he gets a client list, he'll check with DEA for high drug-related activity in the cities where the suspected clients are located."

"So what's the angle? Does Wilder work with local engineering companies?"

"Either that or he breaks in and steals copies of surveys for the mines he's interested in."

Kevin put a plate on the counter in front of her, and her mouth watered at the sight of a perfectly cooked omelet. "Looks delicious."

He refilled her juice glass. "If it's not, I'll make another one. Would you like champagne with your orange juice?"

She licked her lips and held out her glass. "A mimosa sounds wonderful."

He went into the other room, came back with a bottle of Champagne Krug Vintage Brut, and held it out in front of her.

"That's the 1988. It's too expensive. It's not a middle of the night mimosa."

He tapped his fingers against the bottle, obviously annoyed.

"How would you know?"

She glanced at Pete. "Two years ago?"

"Three," he said.

"We investigated a break-in at a high-end nightclub. A case of 1988 was stolen."

Kevin popped the cork over her objections. "Did you recover it?"

She put her hand over her glass. "Empty bottles and four drunk teenagers."

He swatted her hand away. "The bottle is open now, so you have to drink it."

"Drink it, *ragazza tosta*."

She glared at her partner, and he grinned, obviously enjoying Kevin challenging her frugal nature. *What the heck?* She offered up her glass and Kevin poured, probing her with a visual caress. She sipped, and the bubbles tickled her nose. "It definitely explodes on the palate with depth and complexity."

Pete almost fell off his stool laughing. "You wouldn't know depth and complexity from height and simplicity."

"Oh, don't be a jerk. I read up on the label while we were searching for the stolen bottles."

She finished the omelet and pushed the empty plate aside. "That was exactly what I needed. Thank you." She finished her second mimosa, and Kevin made a move to refill the glass, but she put her hand over the top of the goblet. "No more. I need to be clear-headed today."

He corked the bottle and put it in the fridge. "I'll fix you another one for breakfast."

"Sounds like the perfect way to start my last day of vacation."

"Aren't you going to stay and see this through?" Pete asked.

She tilted her head to the side, pursing her lips, considering her answer. "Castellano doesn't need my interference, and David will be working on the case, along with his international staff of thousands. If we have any bright ideas, we can call."

"I've never known you to walk out on a case before it's finished."

"This isn't our case, partner. Besides, have you forgotten what's on our desks? Nobody's helping us."

Kevin started the dishwasher then reached out for her. "I'm going to bed. Will you join me?"

"Where're you sleeping, Pete?" she asked.

Pete's eyes twinkled. "Kevin's room. He said he wouldn't need it tonight."

She appraised Kevin, whose eyes were sweeping over her. "Do you think you can keep me awake long enough for a good night story?"

With a cheeky grin, he said, "I'm up for the challenge."

24

WHEN KEVIN AND JL reached the guest room door, he said, "Wait. I wanted to do this when I first brought you to this door." He pinned her against the wall. Something wild and dark flared in his stormy eyes, and he kissed her. It wasn't gentle. It was possessive. He rocked his arousal, large and hard, against her, and she moaned into his mouth.

Breathless, she said, "I wish you had."

"I wanted to do this, too." He picked her up and cradled her in his arms. "I wanted you the moment I saw you." He carried her across the threshold and kicked the door closed. Balancing her in his arms, he locked it. "This time we won't be disturbed."

She tested the doorknob. "The house will have to be on fire before I leave this room tonight."

He crossed to the bed and laid her there. "It took every ounce of restraint I had not to kiss you Friday when I brought you in here."

"If you had, we would have ended up doing exactly what we're doing now."

"You think so?" His devilish gaze impaled her while he unbelted her robe, spreading it out on either side of her, leaving her naked and exposed and tingly and vulnerable. Then he whipped his shirt over his head and unzipped his pants.

"I know so."

In a very deft maneuver, he shed his jeans and boxer briefs and stood completely naked. A perfectly proportioned man with arms and legs and chest dusted with crisp brown hair. His well-defined quads caught her eye. *Liar.* It wasn't his quads. It was his dick. Slightly curving upward and very erect. Well above average in length. Not massive. Well-rounded. Perfect. She had thought so before, but there hadn't been time to, uh, focus on it, only to lick her lower lip in anticipation, which was exactly what she was doing now.

Standing over her, he stroked her with his fingertips from neck to pubic bone, slowly, erotically, teasingly, as if he had an infinite amount of time. From the wonder on his face, he intended to enjoy every tantalizing second.

"According to Pete, I was a convenient dick, a weekend lay."

Blood roared through her veins, and she squirmed when he brushed her knuckles whisper-soft over the tops of her breasts. "Go right on believing that." It was safer for her if he did. The moment quickly turned heady and bewitching, and she didn't want it to end—ever.

He lay down next to her, and the bed dipped only slightly beneath his weight. "I wasn't supposed to be here Friday."

"You weren't?"

He kissed the sensitive skin just behind the lobe of her ear, traveling down her neck and along her collarbone, leaving a trail of fire blazing on her skin wherever his lips touched. His mouth hitched into a sexy half-smile. "I was supposed to be in Kentucky. I'd planned to fly out with David and the rest, but I came Tuesday with Kenzie instead. I wonder if you would have found another dick to entertain you."

She made a move to rise. "I'm going to go kill Pete right now."

Kevin held her down by simply sucking her nipple into his mouth, and she forgot all about killing her partner. The sharp intensity of Kevin's attention accentuated the pulling and tingling sensation, running head to toe and back again. He dragged a lazy fingertip across the swells of her breasts.

"If I hadn't been here Friday, Austin wouldn't have caught us in a compromising position, and he wouldn't have stormed out to get kidnapped. None of the last thirty-six hours would have happened."

Her heart slammed in her chest. Fate had played a major hand even before she arrived in Napa. "I've been struggling with fate since I got here. Your changed travel schedule makes it even more difficult to understand. But I sort of like the idea of thinking this is our first time; that we didn't have that—to use the kids' vernacular—previous adventure."

His fingers trailed a path to her scalp, where he used long, sweeping strokes, massaging down to the base of her head, kneading the area with his thumbs. Her breath caught deep in her rib cage, and she arched her back, lifting her breasts up to him.

His fingers continued their erotic path and slid down between her legs, where he stroked, drawing soft circles on her clit, teasing her endlessly, while she lifted her hips slightly at the erotic touch.

"Friday, before our run, when I was stretching you out, all I could think about was making love to you," he said.

"You hid it well."

He slipped two fingers inside her and rocked back and forth. Damn if her toes didn't curl in sweet agony. She pulled her lower lip in between her teeth and dug her nails into the sheets.

"God, you're wet." Once again, he took a nipple between his lips and suckled her, delightfully so.

"I'm about to explode. You're torturing me."

"I want to watch you come."

It didn't take much more than the desire in his eyes and the velvet touch of his fingertips to give her an orgasm. "Don't blink, then, because…ah." She gasped. Her body tightened. Every muscle taut. Fighting for breath. For life. For now. For him. She was so close, and she trusted him to complete her.

He groaned. "Oh God. You're beautiful."

A blinding, earth-shattering orgasm swept over her, and she knew her fragile being would never be the same. He devoured her with his lips. The taste of wine, the fragrant scent of musk, and the steamy texture of his skin assailed her senses. Delicious and intimate. A thread of silk sensually tied itself around her heart, and for the briefest of moments, wouldn't let it beat.

I love you, Kevin.

He positioned himself between her legs and rolled on a condom. She took hold of his erection and guided him to her, and when he entered, he moaned while she stretched around him. Wanting him deeper, she gripped her legs high around the middle of his back, and he pulsed within her. She gazed up at him, then kissed him furiously, like a thunderstorm, a lightning storm, kisses raining from the sky, bursting with fire and sparks and resounding noise.

Again, ravenous desire filled her, and she sank into it and drowned in pleasure. His hips thrust harder with every stroke. He took her lips roughly, swallowing her cries as she came a second time. Then his orgasm hit, surrounding her, enveloping her, more powerful than anything she had ever known, and a savage roar tore from him as their releases merged.

All the danger and fear and anguish of the past thirty-six hours melted away.

25

JL AWOKE, STRETCHING. She sat up and surveyed the guest room and the view of the vineyards through sun-streaked windows. Her mind flashed through the past two days and then through the past few hours—a juxtaposition of absolute terror and absolute ecstasy.

She glanced at the other side of the bed. Empty. Her mood deflated, but when she remembered Kevin's promise to return, she smiled and hugged her arms close to her chest.

She had fallen asleep in his arms. Then, sometime around dawn, he had awakened her, and they made love again. Thinking about how delightful it had been to wake with him, she curled back into the covers. The pillow smelled of him and her, and both of them together.

A quick check of the time on the bedside table clock had her jumping to her feet. "What the…" It was after ten.

She snatched the robe off the floor and scrambled to the shower, not wanting to waste another minute.

She had only been in the shower a couple of minutes when Kevin, completely naked, surprised her with a smile, a wink, and a hard-on. Taking her hands out of her hair, he held them above her head, his body trembling, and he pressed her against the wall, kissing her deeply.

"We came so close to losing each other before we knew how great we are together." He kissed down her neck before capturing her lips. She returned the kiss, sliding her tongue into his mouth. This was more intense, more urgent and relentless, wilder and fresher, and he eroded her senses.

"You should have woken me up."

He slid his hands over her hips and grabbed her ass, lifting her. "I am now. Good morning, Sugar."

"Don't call me sugar."

She locked her legs around him, and he edged his erection into her, melding her body to his. With a guttural groan, he jerked her close with powerful arms, consuming her mouth with a kiss surely driven by the sheer will to possess her. Her back slapped against the tile wall as he thrust into her. The man knew how to make her hot and needy, and he was using that insider knowledge now, turning her mindless, boneless, and drugging her with passion.

His fluid hands glided along her soapy skin, a throbbing bundle of nerves, in an endless full-body caress that had her writhing against him. She trembled now, too, and she gasped, "I'm so close." It astounded her how fast and furiously he took her to the edge, leaving her breathless and mindless. The nipple he captured between his teeth was still tender from the last time he made love to her, but the tiny pinches of pain combined with exquisite pleasure only intensified the erotic sensations snapping through every synapse in her system.

She was on fire, sizzling.

This wasn't vacation sex with a hot guy. This was a mind-blowing, moving-in-with-your-guns-and-running-shoes-packed-in-an-oversized-suitcase kind of sex. The kind of longing Pete had said she would find one day; that she would live it, breathe it, and scream inside with it.

At the time, she had called him crazy.

Kevin's mouth roamed at will, no longer gentle, as he devoured her, ravenous against the smooth curve of her throat, the soft flesh of her ear. Their open mouths fused hungrily. How was it possible for her to want and need him so desperately, as if she'd gone months without him?

The tip of his tongue dueled with hers until he gave up and kissed her fully. No playful nips, but a full-on siege that allowed her to taste sweet berries on his mouth and lips and tongue.

The multiple sprays of pulsating water steamed up the shower, but their loving steamed up much more. Her mouth opened in a cry of pure need, and a choked sob came out. Sensations swamped her, and she went utterly mindless, her body acting all on its own. Her hips churned hungrily, burning for the release hovering just out of reach. Belly and thigh muscles contracted as Kevin stroked her in a deliberate rhythm until her cries of release echoed in her own ears and an orgasm rushed through her with exquisite pulsations.

She was living it. Breathing it. Screaming inside with it.

Kevin growled and moved rhythmically until he swelled thicker inside her. He buried his face in the crook of her neck while his entire body shuddered and a raw groan of ecstasy ripped from him. He slumped against her, and she slowly dropped her legs to the shower floor.

When her brain jump-started again, she said, between gasps for air, "That should...take the edge...off for the day. Don't you...think?"

His breath heaved as if he'd been running at a superhuman pace. "Are you kidding? I'm taking this hour by hour, and I've already missed out on four. I'll be coming for you at eleven."

She glanced down at him and swallowed hard. "You didn't wear a condom."

His heavy breathing picked up the pace again. "Oh God. Where are you in your cycle?"

"It's not God's cycle we should be worried about."

"If you get pregnant, I'll—"

She pressed her finger against his lips. "Shhh. I've been there, remember?"

"You won't go through it alone. Not again."

"Don't worry. I should get my period the middle of next week. But, you know, it's kind of hit and miss with you, isn't it?"

"Not usually."

"I'm not as worried about a pregnancy as I am other things."

"Oh, I'm clean," he said.

She turned her back to the spray and washed the soap out of her hair. "What have you been doing this morning?" She didn't want to waste time talking about unpleasant topics like unplanned pregnancies, or STDs, or never seeing each other again.

He washed her breasts and hips and stomach while she squirted conditioner into her hair. "You have a gorgeous body. Muscular in the right places. Soft in the right places. Wet in the right places, and…"

She glanced down at his dick, quivering against her. "Stop. Are you trying for a PR?"

"No, are you?" He held up one hand and then the other. "Shall we count the number of times you've screamed, 'Kevin, I'm coming?' It might not be close to a personal record for you, but it is for me."

"As Pete says, 'Don't bullshit the bullshitter.'" She couldn't tell if his face reddened from hot water, sex, or embarrassment, and she laughed. "We haven't gotten anywhere near your PR, but I'm willing to give it a try."

He reached for her, but she pushed open the shower door and stepped out. "But not without a condom."

He slapped his hands to his face and shook his head while his damn dick stood up and saluted her. "You're killing me, O'Grady."

She reached for a towel, but Kevin strutted out of the shower and snatched it from her. "I'll dry."

"How manly of you." She wrapped her hair in another towel, wondering how many times she had washed her hair in the past several hours. She snickered. Was she trying to *wash that man right out of her hair*? Nellie Forbush, eat your heart out. No, and it wasn't that her hair needed washing, either. She had showered so often because she couldn't resist the delightful sensation of the full-body multi-jet sprays pelting her body. This shower was one luxury item she would certainly miss.

Kevin dried her off and rubbed her with lotion. "Tell me what you smell."

She sniffed, thinking, then sniffed again. "Amber, brown sugar, vanilla beans. The scent is sinfully delicious."

"Now you smell sinfully delicious, too." He tapped his nose. "Your natural scent is highly erotic. I picked it up the moment I walked into the bar in the Welcome Center."

"You did not."

"Trust me. I did. I shouldn't mask your unique blend with artificial scents, but you need special attention today." He kissed her nose and her eyes, and ended with a long, lingering kiss on the mouth. "I thought I'd keep you naked in bed until time for the gala."

"Keep thinking that, buddy. I've got work to do. Playtime is over. I need to follow up on last night's conversations and find out where we are with the investigation."

Kevin dried off, folded the towel in thirds, and hung it perfectly on the towel bar next to the bunched-up one she'd left there previously. He folded hers, too. Men were quirky. She knew, because she had lived with plenty of them—Austin, her father, four brothers, and Ryan. Some folded towels. Some left them on the floor with dirty, smelly underwear and socks. Always socks, and never two that matched. She had a sneaking suspicion Kevin's socks would always match. He probably used those Sock Cop clips she'd seen at The Container Store on Lexington Avenue.

Wouldn't it be sweet to live with a guy who retained some of his early training?

Kevin's update cut into her crazy thoughts of men and their habits. "Castellano hasn't found the barrels. The kidnappers aren't talking. None of their guns is a ballistic match to the bullet from Di Salvo's head. The judge won't sign subpoenas for bank records, and Wilder hasn't left his hotel room."

She made a frustrated face. "Sounds like the case is progressing at warp speed. How about David? What's he doing?"

"Following the money trail. He's expecting reports in the next couple of hours."

"And Pete?"

"Haven't seen him. I heard he and Connor went to the cave."

She rocked back slightly and clutched her arms to her chest, dreading Pete and Connor's reactions to the conditions they would find there. "Connor will drop and Pete will kick my ass from here to San Francisco."

"Why?"

"Because we went down there without backup."

"But we thought backup was on the way."

"Doesn't matter. We should have waited."

"Hindsight is twenty-twenty, and he agreed to the plan."

"That doesn't matter either."

Kevin rubbed her bottom. "Don't worry, Sugar. I'll cushion your ass as it bounces down the highway."

"Don't...call...me...Sugar."

"Not even if I'm saving your ass?"

"Not even..." She didn't care if he called her Sugar. She would have had the same reaction with any term of endearment. It was all about the game, and she loved it. "What else do you know? What's Pops doing?"

"Salivating over the controls at the security center. He said to go there as soon as you could. I don't think you'll be able to drag him away. Elliott's already offered him a job to manage a security force."

"He'd never leave the city, and he has a part-time job taking care of his grandkids."

"I think he loves his new job, too."

"What?"

Kevin shrugged. "He didn't accept, but he said he'd consider it."

"Wow. Austin would love having Pops in California, and the warmer temps would be great for him. What's he been doing there other than drooling over the controls?"

"Studying the equipment and viewing surveillance tapes. Other than that, I don't know."

She slipped on the robe and moisturized her face. "I'll go over there. What's on your schedule?"

"Besides making love to you again?"

She rolled her eyes.

"I'm thick-headed, but I'm getting the message you need to work, and I need to leave you alone. I'll do that, but not for long. In the interim, I'm taking James Cullen, Lincoln, and the twins to get haircuts."

She blinked rapidly. "What? You're taking four kids—"

"To get haircuts. They listen to me, and they want to go riding this afternoon. If they don't behave, I won't take them."

"You're taking four kids horseback riding?"

"Yes, and I almost forgot. Meredith is taking Kenzie and Charlotte to the salon for facials and massages, and would love for you to join them."

A facial and massage in Napa might be cheaper than in New York, but it would still screw up her budget. If she was going to do that, she would rather spend the money on new clothes for Austin. "That's sweet, but I'll hang out with Pops." She opened the bathroom door and crossed the room to the clothes closet. "What happened with the dog?"

Kevin laughed, following her into the bedroom. "Elliott threw a fit until James Cullen told him the dog's name was Tater Tot, and he was Tate's namesake. Elliott got misty-eyed and hugged the dog. Then he really surprised me. He found Braham and Charlotte's little Kitherina, and together they gave the dog a bath and a checkup. Tater Tot got a clean bill of health."

"What about the cat the twins had on the plane?"

"Elliott gave him a checkup, too, and Kitherina named him Cooper. The Frasers have two new pets."

She pulled a clean sweater and jeans from the closets, thankful she had overpacked for the weekend. "Have you had a chance to talk to Elliott?"

"Saw him this morning. He said we had a lot to talk about later. He preferred to wait until after the gala, but he gave me a package and said he'd like me to wear it tonight."

"Wear what?"

"The Fraser tartan."

"Like a kilt? Wow. That is special. Are you going to?"

"I don't know yet. It'll make a statement, and I'm not sure it's the proper way to do it. If I don't wear it, though, he'll be disappointed."

Personally, she thought Elliott deserved more than disappointment, but she would keep her feelings to herself for right now. Instead, she kissed Kevin, and his tongue was soft as it slipped into her mouth. "Do what feels right," she said, before kissing him more thoroughly. She broke off the kiss when it dawned on her that they were both naked and she would never leave the bedroom if she didn't stop. Right. Now.

As if he'd had the same thought, he snatched a pair of boxer briefs off the chair and slipped them on. The underwear stretched, challenging the seams, to contain his engorged dick. She shook her head in an attempt to rein in wayward thoughts.

"What about Austin? Are you going to talk to him this morning?" Kevin asked.

She stripped her gaze away from his stretchy underwear and yanked up a pair of panties before she gave in to desire and kissed him again. "After I talk to Pops. He needs to hear from me that Austin knows the truth. Then we'll confess to my brothers."

While Kevin's eyes were eating her for breakfast, he asked, "How will they take it?"

She pivoted, turning her back to him, knowing it was the only way she'd ever get dressed because her eyes were eating him up, too. "They'll be upset. I understand that. They've been lied to for all these years."

"Does Pete know—about Austin, I mean?"

She racked the slide in her gun and holstered it. "I've never told him, but I don't think he'll be surprised."

Now that she was dressed, Kevin's eyes undressed her, lingering on her boobs. "You should go braless. Your breasts are amazing. My fingers tingle with the memory of stroking them."

She ran her tongue along her bottom lip, and then followed it with her finger, rolling and exposing the underside of her lip. "Isn't it time for you to take the boys for haircuts?"

A quick check of his watch had him glinting. "I have five minutes." His palms slowly grazed the sides of her arms. Then, they moved to her waist, and the gentle caress of his thumbs near her hipbones stole the last remnant of her resistance. He removed the gun and set it on the dresser.

"No one's ever disarmed me so quickly. Are you afraid I'll shoot you?"

"Hmm. Yes. I think your exact words were, 'If you won't let me come, I'll shoot you the first chance I get.' Am I right?"

"Kiss me, you devil, and don't stop until I do."

"What? Shoot me or come?"

"Let's find out." She kissed him fully, completely dreamy-eyed over a man with matching socks and the patience to take four kids horseback riding.

Save me, Jesus. I've fallen hard.

26

An hour later, JL wiped an I-just-got-out-of-bed-with-a-hot-guy smile from her face and steeled herself for an uncomfortable conversation. She walked into the security office carrying two cups of coffee and a bag full of cinnamon rolls packed by the wait staff at the lodge. As she had suspected, her father was the only one there. He reigned over his fiefdom from a leather command seat facing an array of monitors and control panels. He rolled his chair from one display to the other, adjusting camera angles. As much as Pops enjoyed music and the theater, he probably envisioned himself as a conductor setting tempo and beats, shaping the sound of an orchestra.

God had to love Pops' heart. She sure did.

She sniffed, wrinkling her nose. Earlier, when her mind had been so singularly focused on Austin, she hadn't noticed much of the room. The air had a clean, sanitized scent that worked well with the sleek, black lines of the equipment. One wall had a large, tinted window that overlooked the vineyards. The tint distorted the vivid colors, but it protected the equipment from the sun's rays and the staff's work from prying eyes.

She placed a cup of coffee on the table beside him. "Kevin said there was a coffeemaker here, but I thought it would be a fancy-schmancy machine and you wouldn't take the time to figure out how to make it work."

"You're right about that, sweetheart. Thanks."

She removed the scarf she'd tied around her neck, along with her leather jacket, and tossed them on the desk. In here, she didn't mind showing the imprint of her firearm holstered at the small of her back. "So what do you think of this setup?"

He uncapped the paper cup and blew on the strong, black brew before carefully slurping. "Hmm. Just what I needed." He reclined the chair to almost a forty-five-degree angle, but because his legs were so long, his feet remained flat on the floor. "I've seen pictures of places like this, but never thought I'd get a chance to take one out to the ballpark."

"In other words, you love it."

The chiseled lines of his mouth curled into a soft smile. "What's not to love?"

Her dad was handsome and in good health, and if the rumors about him were true, he did well in the romance department. There was no slope to his shoulders, and at sixty-four, he carried himself with the confidence of a much younger man. His short-cropped salt-and-pepper hair gave him a refined look that made women think he was aging like fine wine. Maybe that was why there were so many women's phone numbers on his contact list. While he and Elliott were contemporaries, they had lived much different lives. Their faces, however, had both aged well, and the beautiful wrinkles on the sides of their eyes screamed 'happy past and a great life.' Whether that was true for Elliott or not, she knew Pops had lived the life he wanted, married to his great love for thirty years.

"The question is," she said, drawing her mind back to the conversation, "do you love it enough to move out here?"

He set down the coffee cup, leaned forward, and placed his forearms on his knees. "I've lived in Pearl River my entire life. My friends and family are there. I buried your mother, God rest her soul, there. I have children who put up with me and grandchildren who think I personally hung the moon. Why would I ever leave?"

"Because you're retired and can do whatever you want."

"I'd be glad to help the Frasers temporarily, but I don't want the responsibility. I have a good pension and plenty to keep me busy.

It's different for you, JL. You're young and beautiful. You deserve more than starting every day wondering if you'll survive it."

"That's my life, Pops."

"Maybe, but I've never seen you glow like you are right now. I don't know if it's the air in California, or the company you're keeping, but you're happier than I've ever seen you."

She glanced at the monitor showing the feed from the front of the wine cave. Parked in the lot were cruisers, SWAT vehicles, and two trucks from a mining company. The barriers remained in place, and uniformed men and women hustled in and out of the cave. The site would remain a crime scene until the investigators removed the blockage, found the missing cop and determined the cause of the detonation.

Meredith and Kenzie had met with the investigators. The police agreed that, as long as the gala was located on the other side of the property, away from the orchard and caves, the presence of the guests would not compromise the investigation. Score one for the home team.

Pops reached into the bag for a roll and took a bite. "I was rummaging through drawers and found a CD without a label." He took a moment to chew, and she made fast circles with her hand, gesturing for him to continue with the story. "It shows your murder vic standing near the entrance to the cave you and Kevin rappelled into. It's not time- or date-stamped. Has anyone mentioned seeing him there?"

"How do you know it's the vic?"

"I read an online post about the murder. The article included his picture."

"No one's mentioned it. Can I assume he was alone in the video?"

"See for yourself. I'll queue it up."

The video came to life on the monitor directly in front of his chair. She watched the orchardist walk up the hill and stand close to the entrance of the cave, but he never moved toward it. "This doesn't prove he knew the entrance was nearby."

"It puts him in the proximity of the entrance. If the shooter was connected to the cartel, he or she probably saw Di Salvo's appearance there as a threat. Maybe there are other tapes, possibly one of him near the entrance on the other side."

"Did you find any other tapes?"

"There's a year's worth of surveillance footage stamped with time, date, and location. This is the only one not labeled, and the only one I've reviewed so far."

When Pops replayed the tape, something niggled at her. "Wait a minute. There are no cameras up there. Who taped this? And how?"

"Looks like footage captured by a drone," Pops said.

"David had the drone capture footage of the crime scene Friday afternoon. I'll have to ask who has access to the drone." She pored over the tape again, asking Pops to start and stop the video at points of interest. "I think we might have a motive. If whoever was processing the cocaine-based bricks into an ingestible form was operating out of the cave, he or she would keep up surveillance to be sure the operation wasn't discovered," JL said.

"Di Salvo could have noticed tracks through his orchard and followed them," Pops said.

"Makes sense. But why a mob-style hit?"

"To create a false lead. I doubt the Napa cops would have connected the shooting with the drug cartel if you hadn't put the idea in their heads," Pops said.

She patted his shoulder. "I came in here looking for answers, not more questions."

He glanced up at her, smiling, "You're a good detective. You'll put this case to bed before you leave tomorrow."

"Maybe, but this situation has created another complication."

"Anything to do with Kevin Allen?"

She sat in one of the other rolling chairs and pulled up next to Pops. "It has a lot to do with Kevin, but Austin's my immediate concern. He knows the truth now."

Pops nodded. "Good. You should have told him when you and Ryan split up."

"If I'd had the benefit of hindsight, I would have, but I mean he knows the truth. The *whole* truth." She closely watched Pops' eyes. The moment his brain understood the nuance of what she had said his eyes opened wide.

"You told him? That surprises me."

JL shook her head. "I didn't mean to tell him. It sort of slipped out after James Cullen overheard his parents discussing it."

"How did the Frasers know?"

"I'll ask them later."

Pops scratched his head, probably digging through his memory, checking for loose ends. Although the seventeen-year-old secret concerned Austin and her, and Austin's bio-dad, if the truth filtered out, the lie could tarnish her mother's memory, and Pops would never tolerate that.

"Did you tell Austin who his real dad is?"

"I only said he was a power forward playing in the NBA. Austin has probably figured it out by now, but he hasn't said anything. I'm going to talk to him today, but I wanted to talk to you first."

"He won't let it go until you give him a name."

She snatched her cozy circle scarf off the desk and kneaded it with her fingers. "I haven't talked to Chris since the last night of summer camp—the night I got pregnant."

Pops gave her a smile that turned down the corners of his mouth. There was a catch in his voice when he said, "It's a long-overdue conversation."

"Probably."

He lifted his wallet from his back pocket and dug out a sheet of paper. "Here's Chris' number. I've kept it updated through the years in case Austin needed him. The Warriors are playing at home this weekend, and Oakland's not that far away."

She threw the scarf down on the desk and pushed to her feet. "Why, for God's sake, would Austin need him? He has us."

"You're a cop. You know how fragile life is."

She didn't like this at all. She needed her mom. Was she looking down from Heaven? Did she know her only daughter was struggling and needed her wisdom desperately? Did she know JL's future, and how this would all play out? What would her advice be? Her strong shoulders had carried the weight of JL's tears all those years ago, and she needed them now. Struggling for composure, she bit back tears and glanced at the number. After committing it to memory, she handed the paper back to Pops.

"I've got it, but you keep it, too."

Pops reached for his jacket. "I have something else for you." He held an item in his closed hand. "I was packing yesterday morning, and I heard your mother's voice. She spoke with that tone that always got your attention. You remember?"

JL nodded. Pops had mentioned before that he often heard her mom's voice.

"I knew this was serious, so I listened with my heart. 'Lawrence,' she said, 'Get that old piece of jewelry out of the lockbox and take it to Jenny Lynn. She needs it.' I sat on the bed and thought about it. What would you want with a broken brooch?

"I finished packing and walked down the street to let the neighbors know I was going out of town. When I saw the church's silvery metal crucifix glinting in the midday sun, I went to confession instead. I told Father Paul about hearing your mother's voice. He said, among other things, that 'God speaks in many ways.' Whether that message came from God or your mother, I can't say, but I did what I was commanded to do."

He put the amethyst brooch in her hand. As soon as it touched her skin, it heated, turning her palm red. "Feel my hand, Pops. It's hot." He squeezed her hand. As the pressure of his grip tugged her to him, she no longer saw his strong, tanned hand, but her mother's delicate, satiny one. Tears flooded JL's eyes, blinding her, and huge sobs racked her chest. She cried like the teenager who had to confess her pregnancy to her mother.

"If Mom hadn't been under so much stress, worrying over me and Austin, she wouldn't have died. It's my fault."

"Shhh," Pops said. "Her death wasn't your fault. An unknown defect in her heart threw a clot and caused a stroke. It had nothing to do with you. You *never* disappointed her. She loved you dearly, and was so proud of you."

"She wanted so much for me, and when I got pregnant her dreams died."

"No they didn't, sweetheart. She only wanted you to be happy. She would have loved it if you had followed her on Broadway, but she would have been just as proud of you for choosing to be a cop. You never disappointed her."

"I disappointed myself. I spent all those years taking dance lessons, and I haven't put on a pair of tap shoes since the day I discovered I was pregnant. I should have been more responsible."

"Singing and dancing are in your blood. You'll never lose the gifts. And...we all make mistakes. How we manage them going forward is what matters. If you need forgiveness, ask for it. If you need to make a course adjustment, recalibrate. But God forbid, if you have to put out a fire and only have a bottle of alcohol, I hope you realize the mistake before you blow yourself up."

JL tried to chuckle, but could only hiccup.

"Do you remember what your mom used to say about crying?"

"I'll never forget it," JL said. "'Tears are only water. Roses can't grow without it, and neither can I.' Funny, but when she died, I stopped crying. I've cried almost nonstop since I arrived in California."

"If you've been crying that much, you should be as tall as Austin."

She knew, like Pops, that growth had nothing to do with height and everything to do with forgiveness, living comfortably in your own skin, and loving others. She was JL O'Grady. A mother, daughter, sister, cop. She smiled in a bubble of serenity at the thought that she was also a girlfriend. She had asked for forgiveness years ago. She just never believed that she deserved it. The loving others part drove her into police work. She didn't always get it right, but she tried.

"Early in our marriage," Pops said, "I'd walk in on your mom during her morning devotionals, and she always had tears in her eyes. I'd ask her what was wrong, and she'd say, 'God's passing along a little instruction and forgiveness, and every tear makes me a better person.' It must have worked, because she was the finest person I've ever known. When she died, she traveled straight up. No purgatory for her."

For more than seventeen years, JL had blamed herself for her mother's death and believed a horrible lie. A lie that had held her captive in a world of guilt and shame. Changing that belief wouldn't be easy. Change never was, but it would be easier than living that damnable lie.

The door opened, and the breeze *whooshed* in, carrying the strong scent of fermenting grapes. Pete and Connor trekked in, too, laughing. The keys Connor dangled in his hand resembled the key James Cullen used to start his ATV.

She slipped the brooch into her pocket before snatching a napkin from the paper bag to wipe her runny nose. "I'm not sure I want to know what you two have been doing."

Connor sat heavily in one of the chairs. "Working." His color was high and his breathing hard. He and Pete must have raced back from wherever they had been. Since Pete wasn't breathing as hard and had a stern look on his face, he must have lost the race.

Pete stomped across the room until he stood in front of her. He tenderly lifted her chin with the tip of his finger. "You can't hide from me, *ragazza tosta*. I've known you far too long. In all these years, I've never seen you cry. Allen hurt you, didn't he?"

Pete didn't dwarf her like Kevin and the men in her family, but she still had to look up to see his face. "No, and this has nothing to do with him." She repeated the statement to herself a couple of times, and instead of her heartbeat slowing, it picked up the pace. She could try to fool everyone else, but she couldn't fool her heart. Everything had to do with Kevin.

Pete's gaze remained steady on her. "You don't even cry over sad movies. What's up?"

"Long story, but I'm good now. Really."

"Then you no longer have my sympathy, but you definitely have my anger." He grabbed her shoulders and shook her, not too gently, but not roughly either. "*What the hell were you doing in that cave?*" He dropped his hands and fisted them. "That place is *worse* than the tunnels below New York City. I got evil vibes in there. Your life and everlasting soul were in danger."

"You're being a little overly dramatic."

He raised both hands and shook them. "*Overly dramatic? Me?* I'm the calmest man you know."

"You're first-generation Italian-American. That speaks for itself. Look, my son's life was in danger. What was I supposed to do?"

"I know Austin was in danger, but…what'd you say?" Pete plopped one hip on the desktop and crossed his arms. "Looks like you're finally admitting the truth."

"You knew?" JL said.

"We're sports fanatics. You can't watch Chris Dalton play without seeing the resemblance to Austin," Connor said.

"Their moves are dead on. The way they shoot the three. It's awe-inspiring," Pete said. "I think Austin even patterned his jump shot after Dalton's."

Connor raised his arms and made an imaginary jump shot. "*Swish*. No. He patterned it after mine."

"Keep on dreaming, *compagno*," Pete said.

"It was only a matter of time before Austin noticed the resemblance, too. We all knew that was why you didn't want him to play in California. The Golden State Warriors are right down the road. They were bound to see each other's pictures in the paper, or an announcer would comment on the resemblance."

"So you wanted them to meet?"

"No, we wanted Austin to have the best opportunities. We all talked about it and agreed it was worth the risk."

She glared at Pops. "We. You thought it would be a good idea, too?"

He shook his head. "I wasn't part of the conversation."

She should be furious, but she only had herself to blame. She caught her reflection in the only monitor not showing the video feed from one of the dozens of locations on the property, and she cringed. Her eyes were puffy little slits that gave her face a dull look. Before she saw anyone else, she would have to apply a few makeup tricks to brighten her eyes. No one would take a puffy-eyed detective seriously.

Pete picked up the bag of goodies and peeked inside. "I thought my nose smelled food. Spelunking made me hungry."

She snatched the bag out of his hands, and their gazes locked and held. "This is for Pops. The lodge serves food all day. Go get your own."

"Lighten up. We're on the same side. Remember?"

She gave a low laugh of self-deprecation. "I know. It's just been a rough couple of days." She gave the bag back. "Have at it."

Pete refolded the sack and set it back down. "Nah, we had breakfast at the lodge and plan to head over for lunch."

"You have cave dust all over you. Did you find anything in the cave the Napa cops missed?" Pops asked.

Pete flicked a business card onto the table. She captured it and read the card's contact information. "What the hell?" Chill bumps broke out on her arms, and she chafed them. "Wilder's? Where'd you find it?"

"Near the area where you said the cots were set up. I tripped over some small rocks…"

Connor flailed his arms, pretending a dramatic backward fall. "He fell on his ass."

Pete slung out his arm and gave Connor a backhanded slap in the chest. "If I hadn't, I wouldn't have found the card. Best guess is that it fell out of someone's pocket. Then the explosion loosened some rocks, and as they say…"

Connor thumped the card in her hand. "Look what's written on the back."

She turned it over. "Montgomery Winery gala."

"What we don't know," Connor said, "is if Wilder scheduled a meeting—"

"—or," JL interrupted, "someone else wrote the message on

Wilder's card and gave it to the contact to meet Wilder at the gala."

Pops had been listening with one ear—a talent JL had tried to duplicate during her years of raising a toddler and studying for exams—while still monitoring the caterers' movements at the party tent. "Or," he said, "the message has nothing to do with Wilder and the card was just a handy piece of paper."

JL, Connor, and Pete whirled on Pops, glaring.

Pops shrugged. "Just saying..."

"If he shows up at the gala, we won't let him out of our sight," Connor said.

"There'll be two thousand people in the party tent. Good luck with that," JL said.

"Two thousand, four thousand. Doesn't matter. We'll catch him," Pete said.

"I plan to drink champagne and dance with Kevin on my last night in Napa. I'll be off the clock, so coordinate with Castellano. Don't come looking for me."

In many ways, the weekend had been a journey to another world, a strange place for her. A place where people drank hundred-dollar bottles of wine and flew around the globe in private jets. In spite of the danger and almost losing Austin, it had been a weekend she would remember for the rest of her life.

She had spent hours with a man who rocked her world, and she had unloaded a ton of guilt she had carried for years, along with a secret that had haunted her relentlessly. Nothing would ever be the same again.

Tonight she would drink champagne and dance, and tomorrow she would feel lucky as hell to have met someone who was so hard to say good-bye to. If this thing with Kevin was only a weekend fling, she wouldn't cry because it was over, she would smile because it happened.

27

JL AND HER SISTER-IN-LAW had spent the last few weeks planning every detail of JL's dress, hair, and makeup for the gala. The one thing they hadn't included in their meticulous strategy to wow every male at the party was where to put her gun.

JL made a frantic call back to Pearl River. "Where am I going to put it?"

"It's been a while since you've had sex," her sister-in-law said, laughing "but I don't think even you could forget where to put it."

Exasperated, JL said, "I'm not talking about sex. I'm talking about my gun. Where am I going to put it?"

"You can't put it anywhere," Julie said. "If you wear it at the small of your back or strapped to your leg, everyone will see it. You might as well hug it to your hip."

"Why didn't we think of this before now?"

"I did, but you were so excited about the dress, I didn't mention it. For one night you can jolly well leave your six-shooter at home."

"It's not a six-shooter, and I can't leave it at home. I might as well go naked because that's exactly how I'd feel," JL said, not bothering to hide her irritation.

"Calm down. Pops and the boys will be at the party. They'll guard your back. Although from what I hear"—Julie laughed—"you've got that covered already. I can't wait to meet Kevin."

"He said he'd come to New York, but I don't know when."

"Jeffrey gave me the impression Kevin was coming home with

you."

"I don't know. We'll see." JL checked the time. In five minutes, Kevin would be waiting at the door. "Look, I've got to go. I'm going to try one more thing, and if that doesn't work, I'll leave it in my drawer. Watch me get shot again."

"Don't even joke about that. Stay close to the boys. I'll text Jeffrey and tell him to shadow you."

"He can't do that. They all have assignments tonight."

"Jeffrey said they found an offshore account in the Cayman Islands tied to Wilder. That's a good lead, right?"

"Yeah, but they haven't found out where the millions came from. He certainly didn't make that kind of money as a sales rep."

"Jeffrey said if David McBain joined the NYPD, crime would end in New York City."

JL laughed. "From what I hear, David carries a superhero ID card, and I don't doubt he deserves it. I think he straddles the legal line, though. I'm surprised Jeffrey isn't turned off by that."

"My husband has been known to straddle that line, too."

"I can condone roughing up gang rapists, but I cringe at hacking into computer systems."

"If a private security firm can ferret out information that will convict a murderer and drug trafficker without harming anyone else, I say join the ferrets."

"You're not a cop, Julie."

"I know I'm not, but your brother is. If Jeffrey is on board, I won't disagree with him." The steely timbre of Julie's voice told JL two things. Jeffrey not only admired David, but successfully sold his wife on the man's merits. Since Julie, like JL, viewed the world through a black-and-white lens, this was a monumental endorsement.

JL rolled her neck and shoulders, but the kinks were too tight and had set too deeply in the muscles. She didn't know which was more culpable: the contortions Kevin had put her body through, the weight of the pack her shoulders had borne, or the stress of the weekend. In a clipped voice, she said, "I don't want to argue. I just want to know what to do with my gun."

The echo of a crash came across the phone. "That's easy. Leave it at home. I have to run. Little J just threw a strike with his bottle and knocked out a lamp. The boy has a power arm like his uncle Connor. Call me after the party."

JL ended the call and pitched the phone onto the bed. Her face heated, remembering the cleaning staff had been stuck changing the sheets that morning. No one could have walked into the room without the musky scent of pure, hot sex burning their nostrils.

If she stopped to think about Kevin now, if she stopped to remember what he had said when they woke to the scent of fermenting wine wafting in through their open window, she would cry. With a feathering touch, he had painted her face with the tip of his finger. From her hairline down her forehead, over the bridge of her nose, across her lips to her chin, he never dropped his probing gaze. "On the pulse of a new day," he said, "let's turn our story into the best it can possibly be." Although she came close to accusing him of feeding her a new line, she hadn't, because she knew in her heart the romantic in him had written it for that moment.

Before she got maudlin, she turned her attention back to her problem and made a last attempt to strap the holster to the outside of her right leg. Satisfied with its placement, she shimmied into her dress.

Rrrrip.

A loud "fuck," came out on a *whoosh* of expelled air. She closed her eyes, refusing to look at what she had done. When she finally did, she almost threw up. Staring back at her was a two-inch gaping seam. "Why didn't I listen to Julie?" Too late now. What were her options? She had packed a pair of dress slacks and a silk blouse, but they would look awful at a formal affair. She collapsed in a chair and bit back tears that threatened to ruin her makeup.

Even if she had a needle and thread, she couldn't fix the rip. When was the last time she threaded a needle? Like—never. Why learn how when the laundry down the street could make repairs quicker and better?

"JL, are you ready?" Kevin said, knocking on her door. He turned the handle, but she had locked it, wanting to surprise him.

"No, I'm not," she said.

"I have orders to be there exactly at eight o'clock for pictures. I'll call and tell Elliott to wait a few more minutes."

"Don't do that. I don't want you to be late. Please go. I'll take the golf cart."

"Why is the door locked? I'm not leaving without you."

She stepped out of the dress and gave a discouraged sigh at the damage she had done. "I have a wardrobe malfunction and it will take me a few minutes to fix. So go on. I'll be fine." She had no idea how she would fix it. Maybe she could find some Super Glue.

"I'm good at fixing things. Let me help."

"I don't want you to see me or the dress until it's on."

"What'd you do? Pop a button? Rip a seam?"

"A seam."

"Leave the dress on the bed, and I'll fix it."

"You can sew up a dress?"

"Sugar, I just sewed up Austin's face, didn't I?"

Wearing a black pushup bra and panties and carrying her dress, she opened the door. "Okay. It looks pretty bad, but here."

His eyes widened and his gaze slowly dipped from her face to her body. He grinned playfully, touching the curve of her breasts. "God, you're gorgeous. You should go like you are."

Now it was her turn to ogle him. "My God. You'll turn every head at the party. I've seen lots of men in kilts in New York City at the Tartan Day Parade, but you're worthy of a part on *Outlander*." She reached behind his fur sporran and touched him. "Au natural. I'm impressed."

He kissed her. "If you're impressed, that's all that matters. Now finish getting ready and I'll be back in five minutes."

It took him fifteen minutes, but she didn't complain. He carried her dress neatly folded over his arm. "Let me help you get into it so it won't rip again."

"It wasn't that it was tight. I was trying to pull it down over my holster."

"Give me your gun. I'll carry it. If you need it, you'll be able to reach it quickly." He opened his sporran. "See? Plenty of room, but you won't need it. David has given everyone an assignment, and they will tail Wilder the entire evening. Our roving photographers will photograph everyone he talks to, and Pops will run the pictures through recognition software at the security center. If there are any hits, your brothers will detain the person. We'll find the buyer. Don't worry."

"What about the West Virginia mine? Did David learn anything from DEA?"

"They're investigating now. David has been working with Wilder's client list. Three other mines have matched his search parameters. One outside of Pittsburgh, another one in Colorado, and another one in Utah. He sent those locations to DEA, too."

"We have to catch the shooter, and whoever blew that passage and killed and wounded those cops."

"David's convinced we'll get him."

"I hope he's right." She slipped her gun inside Kevin's leather pouch and snapped it closed. "Now wait in the hall and let me finish getting ready. I'm almost done."

She sucked in her breath and shimmied into an exact copy of Princess Diana's figure-hugging, black silk *revenge* dress, and when the seam held, she let the breath go.

Julie had found the killer dress at a classic secondhand store in the Village. Then, while standing at the checkout counter, JL had spotted a reproduction pearl choker with simulated diamonds and sapphires, and Julie had insisted JL splurge. Paying off the debt she accumulated for this trip would take her months, but future sacrifices were worth the memories. So what if she couldn't buy a Starbucks latte every day?

She pulled her hair back at the nape of her neck and gathered it into a tight bun with multiple overlying twists. The style had taken her weeks of practice to perfect, but tonight she got it just right. Black suede pumps with four-inch lacquered heels were the pièce de résistance. Oh, how she loved living in New York City. If you knew where to look, you could find fabulous sales—Jimmy Choo shoes and designer dresses at a fraction of retail cost.

Before turning out the light, she did one last twirl in front of the full-length mirror in the bathroom. She had been to dozens of New York galas, but only as a working cop. This was so different. She was a guest this time, and while she was no expert, the image reflected in the mirror looked red-carpet worthy.

She shored up her confidence, turned out the light, and strode across the hall to find Kevin.

When his eyes met hers, he pressed his hand against his chest, and his mouth gaped open as if he'd breathed his last breath. "You're the most beautiful woman I've ever seen, not only on the outside, but on the inside as well." He held out his arm for her. "Let's go dancing, Sugar."

28

THE ENTIRE MACKLENNA CLAN and JL's family were milling around the Welcome Center when Kevin and JL entered the building. She hoped no one wanted to shake her hand. Rarely was she nervous, but right now her palms were sweating. This was a big deal. Even though Kevin loved the way she looked, she was worried that Meredith wouldn't approve of her dress, hair, makeup, or jewelry. If Meredith's eyes reflected her disapproval, JL would manage to survive the evening, but it would be her last Montgomery/Fraser event—ever.

"Here they are. Get into place. The photographer is on his way." Elliott, dressed in a kilt that matched the one he had given to Kevin, waved his arms like a yellow-jacket-clad ramp agent directing an aircraft to the gate. "Guests are arriving and we need to move to the tent. Let's get this picture taken." He took a position directly under the painting of Kit MacKlenna with Meredith on one side of him. He pointed to his other side. "Ye're here, Kevin."

David and Braham, also wearing kilts, whistled at Kevin. "Nice legs," Braham said.

"James Cullen, hurry. Stand here"—Elliott pointed—"next to yer mother."

The crisp pleats of James Cullen's matching Fraser tartan kilt swished as he swaggered through the Welcome Center and stood next to his mother, who looked gorgeous in a green tartan gown.

Pops, Austin, and her brothers—handsome devils in their rented tuxedos—relaxed nearby, sipping from champagne flutes.

When Meredith saw JL, she smiled and mouthed the word, "Beautiful."

JL wanted to run a victory lap, but fished her cell out of her tiny purse for a quick text to Julie instead. *Knocked it out of the park.*

As Kevin stepped to the fireplace, he fiddled with the fly plaid on his shoulder. "This won't stay put. I need a pin."

Meredith fiddled with it, too. "You're right. James Cullen, look in the kitchen for a pin, will you please?"

"I have one." JL reached into her purse for her mother's brooch. "It's broken, but I think you can drape the fabric over it so the broken part won't show."

James Cullen gawked at her brooch. "*Dad. Look.*" He poked at it with his fingertip, the way a child pokes at dead critters on the beach. He then cast a suspicious eye on JL. "*Where did you get this?*"

Pops skirted Elliott and Meredith and sidled up next to JL, leveling a withering glare at James Cullen. "It *belonged* to my wife," he said emphasizing the ownership. "Her mother gave it to her. It's been in the family for generations."

James Cullen's face blanched at Pops' tone; his lower lip quivered. "I didn't mean to be disrespectful, sir. You see, I have…" He stopped, reached into his sporran, and pulled out a sliver of silver and amethyst. "I have the missing piece."

A collective gasp went out among Pops and JL's brothers, while Elliott, Meredith, and David seemed curious but not particularly surprised.

"May I?" James Cullen asked before taking the brooch from JL. He tried to match his sliver to the brooch, but the sliver acted like a positive end of a magnet, which was repelled by the positive end of another magnet—the brooch. He tried again, pursing his lips with frustration. "It doesn't fit." He tried again, and when he couldn't get it close enough to the slot the second time, he glanced up, holding his sliver like a sacred totem and said, "It's the right size and shape, but it won't go in. Why not, Dad? Why doesn't it fit?"

Elliott bent over to be eye to eye with his son. "Mayhap the wrong person is trying, lad. Give yer sliver to Kevin and the brooch to JL."

James Cullen held tight to his treasure and cocked his head, glancing up at his dad. "If I can't make it fit, he can't either."

"This isn't yer story or yer adventure. Go on. Give it to him."

James Cullen tucked in his bottom lip. After a thoughtful moment he said, "Does this mean I'm like Mr. Digby?"

JL whispered to Kevin, "Who's that?"

"A solicitor in Edinburgh. I'll explain later."

Elliott smiled. "I think that's a perfect analogy. Why don't ye give yer sliver to Kevin and see what happens?"

James Cullen squared his shoulders and placed the sliver in Kevin's open hand. Kevin picked up the piece with his thumb and forefinger and slipped it into the brooch's pie-shaped gap. The brooch sucked in the piece as if magnetized. The stone crackled and popped and James Cullen jumped back, gasping. The brooch emitted a flash of brilliant purple light that consumed JL's hand in a dense, spherical burst of stars, a miniature fireworks display.

Kevin's head flinched back slightly.

JL's palm warmed but it didn't burn. Her mind filled with visions—of screaming men, of blood and tormented cries, of rattling swords and Gaelic words, of dying hopes and wasted lives, of caves and battlefields and warriors' cries—until her eyes glazed over and she fainted.

29

WHEN JL OPENED her eyes, Charlotte was hovering over her with a stethoscope's ear tips in her ears. She had the cold disk pressed against JL's skin just beneath the neckline of her dress. Kevin sat nearby holding a cold cloth on her forehead. JL glanced around and didn't recognize the low-lit room, although the furnishings were similar to those used in the Welcome Center. In the distance, a band played George Strait's "Cross My Heart."

Of all his songs, why that one? She had cried in too many beers over those lyrics. She tried to rise up off the deep-seated sofa, but Kevin, sitting on the arm, had other ideas. He pressed down on her shoulders. Good thing, because when she moved, her stomach did a tumble and roll, like being sucker-punched, leaving her defenseless. She was defenseless with the scent of him all around her.

Like the song, she knew in the entire world, she would never find another man like Kevin.

Charlotte smiled and removed the disk and the ear tips, letting the stethoscope dangle around her neck. "Welcome back. How do you feel?"

"Like crap. What happened?"

Kevin lifted the cloth from her forehead and exchanged it with a kiss that left her wanting more. "You're in the sitting room next to the Welcome Center, and you fainted."

"If he hadn't caught you, I'd be stitching up your head right now," Charlotte said.

JL touched the side of her head. The carefully twisted bun had come undone, but she wasn't bleeding. She could easily fix her hair. A scar lasted forever. She had enough of them, inside and out.

Elliott pulled up a chair and took JL's hand in his, holding it firmly, and she found comfort in the strength of his callused palm. "Ye saw something, didn't ye, lass? Ye had a vision, and it scared ye. I saw terror in yer eyes. If ye can remember, tell me about it."

JL closed her eyes and shuddered. She didn't want to go back there. Elliott was pressuring her the same way she had pressured crime victims to retell their painful stories. She didn't like it at all, but she knew it had to be done. What she saw, what she heard, what she felt would always haunt her unless she understood the vision.

"Bloody and more violent than anything I've seen in New York City. Fear. Terror. Screaming men. The clang of swords. Shouts in…I think it was Gaelic." She grabbed her breast with her free hand. "A woman was"—JL squeezed her eyes tightly, seeing it all vividly in her mind again—"in a cave. Someone stabbed her, and she was pregnant—"

"Who was she?" Elliott asked.

"I don't know. I didn't see her face. She was scared and bleeding." JL squeezed her breast as if trying to stop the blood. "She dragged herself out of the smoke. That's it. That's all I remember." JL shook her head. "No, wait. The vision ended there, but I know she got out. She survived."

Elliott leaned back in the chair, scratching his chin.

JL sat up and patted the seat next to her for Kevin to join her on the sofa, then directed a question to Elliott. "Do you know what the vision means?"

"Yer vision fits with the Fraser history."

"Who was the woman, Elliott?" Kevin asked.

A strange look came over Elliott's face. It was subtle, but JL saw a mixture of satisfaction and confusion. "She could have been the daughter of Gregory Fraser. If so, she's the lass who had James Thomas MacKlenna's illegitimate child in the mid-1700s."

Kevin jerked slightly. Even though JL's hand wasn't near his heart, she could feel the beat of its changing rhythm. "That's your direct line to the MacKlennas," Kevin said.

"According to Meredith's genealogy research team, that's correct," Elliott said. "Fraser House was partially destroyed during the Jacobite revolution. Sounds like the lass was wearing the amethyst brooch when someone stabbed her in the cave. She subsequently escaped the fire. James Cullen found the sliver in the cave at Fraser House. It must have been buried in the rocks for over three centuries."

JL pressed her fingers against her throbbing temples. "So I have a brooch that came through my family that once belonged to a woman who carried an illegitimate child, and Elliott is the direct descendant of that child. Seriously?"

"We don't know for sure yet, but I'd wager ye're a direct descendant of the lass."

"The ruby, sapphire, and emerald brooches are all linked to the MacKlennas," Charlotte said. "If this one links to the Frasers, it backs up the story your grandfather told David about the Keeper dispersing the brooches during the rebellion."

"How many brooches are there and who's the keeper?" JL asked.

"We don't know," Elliott said. "And there are a dozen or more brooches."

JL noticed the red tint on her palm. No blistering, though. "Why'd the fireworks go off?"

"Good question and I don't have an answer. There's an old family story floating around that something magical would happen when the ruby, sapphire, and emerald brooches came together. That hasn't happened yet. I'm afraid, lass, that we don't understand the full power of the stones." Elliott returned JL's brooch to her. "But yers is no longer broken."

JL passed the brooch to Kevin. "Here, you wear the lucky stone tonight."

"Elliott." Meredith moved away from the doorway, crossed the room, and sat on the other side of JL. "I've been standing in the hall with JL's family and Pete, trying to explain some of what's been happening. I didn't hear all of JL's story, but I heard enough.

"Based on the report buried under all the other reports on your desk," she said, glancing at Elliott, "the research team finally got a lead on the Fraser girl carrying James MacKlenna's illegitimate child. She died shortly after the baby was born. She had no other children. Whatever estate she had at her death passed to her heir. If JL's line traces back to the Fraser girl, then JL, Austin, her brothers, you, James Cullen, and Kevin are all direct descendants of that child. I hate to tell you, buddy, but your claim to being the last MacKlenna has been shot all to hell."

Elliott kissed his wife's cheek. "I've never been the last MacKlenna, except in my mind."

"I have another question," JL said. "Do the brooches have anything to do with the adventures James Cullen has mentioned more than once?"

Elliott nodded. "The stones have everything to do with adventures. I'm afraid James Cullen thought the amethyst would take him on one, but it took ye, Kevin, and Austin on one instead."

"I didn't even have possession of the stone until this morning. So I don't think we can either blame or thank the amethyst for the weekend's adventure."

"As I said, we don't fully understand the power of the stones," Elliott said. "We know they bring soul mates together. The ruby took Kit to Cullen. The sapphire took Charlotte to Braham. The emerald took David to Kenzie. And now the amethyst has brought ye to Kevin."

"Soul...mates?" JL asked.

Charlotte folded the stethoscope and put it in her medical bag. "My life is, was, and probably always will be in Richmond, Virginia. Braham's life was here in California in the late 1800s. When you think about crossing a century and a half, the distance from New York to California is a drop in the proverbial bucket."

A mystical sense of profound change taking place instantly replaced the tension headache bouncing back and forth between JL's temples. "You must..." Her voice came out sounding hoarse. She cleared her throat and began again. "...have gone through hell to work that out."

"Charlotte survived the burning of Richmond during the Civil War. Kenzie survived the Normandy invasion. Kit crossed the Oregon Trail in 1852 in a covered wagon. They all went through hell." There was a wide-eyed, purposeful attitude about Kevin as he said this, as if something monumental had clicked in his brain. "And we have, too," he said with a note of pride. "The brooches challenge people to rise above themselves. I hope I've exceeded what was expected of me. I know I've been forever changed by the past forty-eight hours, and..." He smiled that sexy grin she had first noticed. "I've found the woman I want to spend the rest of my life with."

Did JL hear him correctly? Life with him? The heady scent of him wafted all around her.

"The two of ye can work on that later without our interference. For tonight, we have a crime to solve and a party to attend. Tomorrow we'll debrief, and I'll answer as many questions as I can." Elliott kissed her cheek. "Welcome to the family."

Kevin helped her stand, then pulled her into his arms and kissed her deeply. They were alone in the room now.

"Will you marry me?"

She gazed into his eyes. "Charlotte said the distance between our lives was only miles, not centuries, but to me it might as well be. I'm just a cop from Pearl River."

"You're much more than that. And besides, you're my perfect foil."

"So I bring out your superhero qualities, huh?"

"Something like that."

She laughed. "We sound like the perfect duo."

"We are," he said.

"Let's wait and see how we get along when our lives aren't being threatened. We've been living on adrenaline, and that's skewed our reality. Let's take our time. In six months, if you still want to marry me, we'll talk about how we can make it work."

"One month."

"I'll compromise and agree to four."

"That's no compromise. I'll give you two," he said, nuzzling her neck.

A warm breath of air stroked the tender shell of her ear, and the low pitch of his voice resonated deep inside her.

"Three," she said. "One for each day of our adventure."

"Three it is. I'll be in New York City in early January to press you for a wedding date."

"Not New York. Let's go somewhere warm and sunny where we won't have any interruptions. We'll be bombarded with family if we stay anywhere near there."

"Deal. But I'm not waiting until then to take you to bed."

He eased his hands underneath her hair to cradle her head while he kissed her. His lips traveled down her neck to where the necklace fastened around her throat. Wild, fresh kisses eroded her sense of time and place. She tilted her head and cast her eyes to the side, giving him a coy, flirty smile.

"I can't wait even an hour."

He pointed with his chin. "There's a lock on that door, and a comfy sofa behind you."

"Do you think anyone will miss us?"

A throat clearing in the doorway got their attention. She turned to find one swarthy Mediterranean man and one Irishman with windswept hair and roguish green eyes leaning against opposite sides of the doorjamb.

"We hate to interrupt," Connor said, "but we need another set of eyes. You two can get a room later."

"We'll be right there," she said.

As soon as Connor and Pete disappeared, Kevin said, "Why do those two remind me of Starsky and Hutch?"

She rolled her eyes. "Because they think they are. Pete even has a red Ford Gran Torino. Thank God they aren't real-life partners. They'd drive the NYPD nuts."

Kevin looked longingly at the sofa. "Guess the cushions will have to wait."

"I'd rather make love in the big bed anyway." She straightened the fly plaid on his shoulder. "I want to try again to pin this on you, and I hope to hell nothing happens."

"I think we're safe."

She pinned it securely, and as Kevin predicted, nothing happened. The image of the bleeding woman flashed in JL's mind's eye like a burst of light, and a sudden rush of cold settled in her marrow. She shivered against him.

"You're cold."

His comforting arms embraced her tighter, and he kissed her, warming her instantly. She sighed, relaxing into him, and as she did, she traced the outline of the brooch. "You'll be protected now if anyone comes after you with a sword."

He laughed, and the deep rumble in his chest reverberated against her. "I don't think that will happen. I need to warn you, though. There is an inscription written inside the stone, or there should be. Whatever you do, don't read it aloud."

She glanced up at him. "Why?"

"Because I don't want to chase after you. I mean I'll chase you as long as it takes, but I'd rather run after you in this decade, not into another century. Do me a favor, and don't read it aloud unless we're holding hands."

Curious, she said, "Okay, but tell me what it says."

His strong fingers slid into her hair again to cradle the back of her head, and he slanted his mouth over hers for a sweet, deep kiss. "It's a Gaelic inscription about love and how it's not limited by time or space."

"Mmm. That's nice."

"The kiss or the inscription?"

"I'll start with the kiss." Her single-minded thoughts zeroed in on the softness of his lips, not the words on the stone, but then, like the good detective she was, the puzzle pieces fell into place, and the significance of the brooch being in one piece wasn't lost on her.

"For the first time in seventeen years, I feel whole again."

The next kiss he gave her was soft and possessive at the same time. It wasn't a hungry, devouring sort of kiss, but slow and filled with passion. "I'm glad." He traced the line of her throat with his lips, and she moaned, letting her head fall back to give him better access. "Because I love the whole of you."

The sound of a throat clearing came from the doorway and drew their attention again. JL recognized the clearing throat. Pete did it at least once every shift when she would stop to talk to a neighborhood grocer. She ignored it, hoping he would take a hint and go away. When he did it again, she glared at her partner.

"We're coming," she said.

Looking into Kevin's twinkling eyes, she considered her options. She didn't have any. Not really. Not that she could live with, anyway. Her family had flown to California because of her actions, and the perps had put their lives in danger. Finishing the case fell into her ballpark. Not because she had jurisdiction, but because they were family, and family deserved justice.

"Don't make me come back a third time," Pete said.

"Go away. We're coming. I promise," she said.

"You know I'm not a courage and love of danger kind of guy," Kevin said. "I normally advocate caution and prudence. Can you be happy with a man who's not out chasing bad guys?"

"Not only happy, but thrilled. And don't forget, you do have a superhero cape to use in emergencies."

"I'm burying it in the back of the closet. Now, let's go to the party and drink champagne."

30

THE GALA UNDER the tent for two thousand people didn't come with Port-a-Johns. Not at Montgomery Winery. Meredith had luxury portable restrooms, complete with multiple stalls, vanity sinks, hand dryers, mirrors, and attendants. Not one trailer, either, but several, and they all had long lines. JL gave up waiting. The line would be shorter at the restroom inside the Welcome Center. Before she went inside, she needed to tell Kevin where she was going. They had separated to use the facilities and designated a meet-up spot right inside the tent. She headed in that direction now.

She was short. Kevin was tall. Austin was taller, and she spotted him first—her spiky-haired son—waiting with Kevin. "Where's Betsy?" she asked, poking Austin in the arm.

He pointed with his chin toward the trailer JL had stood in line to enter. "She went to the restroom."

"Hope she has better luck than I did." JL leaned into Kevin, and he wrapped his arm around her. A minute didn't go by that she didn't touch him, kiss him, or think of him. Julie would call her pathetic. Maybe she was, but it felt so good, and so right.

Kevin nuzzled her neck. "Do you want to go inside? That line won't be as long."

"I will in a minute."

Austin had his hands shoved in his pockets, and he chewed on his lower lip, his eyes darting back and forth.

"What's wrong with you?" she asked.

He tilted his head, using it to point toward his right. "He's here."

"Who?" She stretched her neck to look around him. "Coach Calipari?"

"No. I mean yes. Coach is here, but…" Austin flashed his eyebrows. "*He's* here, too." Austin stepped aside so she could see into the tent. "Chris Dalton. He's talking to Coach Cal."

Although she had seen pictures of Austin's bio-dad all grown up, seeing him in person was—in Yogi Berra vernacular—*déjà vu all over again.* The lightheaded sensation she'd had earlier threatened her again. She cupped her hands and breathed into them.

"Your face is turning white," Kevin said. "And you're trembling and blinking back tears. Let's go. You don't have to talk to him."

"Wait. I want to know who invited him." She searched Austin's face and wasn't sure she liked what she saw there. A bit of guilt. A bit of fear. A bit of I-did-it-and-I'm-not-sorry. "*You* invited him?" So much for fainting. Now she was pissed.

Austin licked his lips while studying his feet.

"Look at me," she said. "What'd you do? Did you call him?"

Austin looked up and confessed. "We sent a fax."

She was aghast. Inviting Chris was beyond the pale, beyond anything outrageous Austin had ever done and just plain beyond being the right thing to do. "Why would you do that?"

"We talked about it—"

"We," she echoed her son. "Seriously?" She crossed one arm across her chest to support the other as she tapped a finger against her cheek. "Let me guess who belongs to the E in the We." Then she used that finger to poke Austin in the chest. "You're older. You should be setting an example, not encouraging James Cullen's adventurous spirit."

"Don't blame James Cullen," Austin said.

"I'm not. I'm blaming you."

He raised his hand in school-like fashion and said, "I'll cop to the fax."

"O…k…a…y." She slowly enunciated each letter of the word. "What'd the fax say, and who'd you send it to?"

"We faxed a party invitation to the Warriors' office."

"There's got to be more. Spit it out," Kevin said. "Or I'll go find James Cullen and shake it out of him."

"James Cullen wrote a note on the invitation that said if Chris would come, James Cullen would make a donation to Chris's *Boys without Fathers* charity."

"He lied to get Chris here?" JL said.

"He didn't lie," Kevin said. "James Cullen has a foundation. I had it set up for him as a tax shelter. He gives away a hundred thousand dollars a year to various organizations. Donating to Chris Dalton's charity would fit with his foundation's goals."

"Unbelievable. You two are a piece of work. So, what was the plan? What'd you intend to do once you got him here?"

"We didn't get that far. James Cullen said if Chris actually came to the party, we'd handle it on the fly."

JL shook her head, rubbing her neck. "What do you want to do now?"

"I don't know. Maybe you could say hello, introduce me, and tell him I'm a fan."

"'And, by the way, this is your son.' If that's what you had in mind, that's not fair to him or to me," JL said.

A voice from her past called her name. "Jenny Lynn O'Grady. Is that you?"

She turned, smiling. "Chris Dalton. Power forward. Golden State Warriors. I'm surprised you remember me. Good to see you." Her smile remained pasted on her mouth while other parts turned to jelly—like her legs. Kevin hugged her tighter.

Chris's eyes sharpened as they roved appreciatively from her face to her décolletage then back to her eyes. The fact that she was wearing a knockoff of Princess Diana's revenge dress wasn't lost on her. JL knew she looked fabulous, and she couldn't ask for more than that.

"Are you kidding?" Chris said. "You're not the kind of girl—I mean, woman—a man's likely to forget." He kissed her cheek and extended his overly large hand to Kevin. "Chris Dalton."

"My...fiancé, Kevin Allen," JL said.

After shaking Kevin's hand, Chris turned his attention to Austin. "You look like a ball player."

"I'm Austin O'Grady, sir. It's nice to meet you. I'm a big fan. I'm playing at Pro Prep. This is my senior year."

Austin stood about an inch shorter than Chris, but their chins, noses, the deep set of their Caribbean green eyes, and the soft curve of their lips were dead-on identical. What struck her most was the way they stood—head up, chest and legs and hands in the open position, their backs straight, confident. The cocky teenager she had met at summer camp had turned into a cocky man.

When JL glanced at Kevin, his stance was identical. If he'd had on khakis, he would have had his hands in his pockets with his thumbs out, confident and cocky, too. God love him. She certainly did.

"Good program." Chris's eyes roamed over Austin's face, his shoulders, and arms. "Where do you want to play college ball?"

"Kansas, Duke, Florida, UCLA have shown interest, but my eye is on Kentucky."

"Coach Cal is here tonight. I'll ask him to take a look at you." Before Chris stepped away, he leaned in as if giving JL a kiss on the cheek again, and said softly, "Call me tomorrow." Then, to Kevin and Austin, he said, "Nice to meet you." He walked away but suddenly stopped and turned back. "Are you still a cop in New York City?"

Her breath caught, and she opened her mouth in surprise. "Yes."

"I read an article in the *New York Times* shortly after you were shot during a takedown of the mob. The article mentioned your father and brothers, so I knew it was you. I called the hospital, but they wouldn't give out any information. I called every day until the paper reported that your doctors had moved you out of ICU. You deserved the promotion you got."

It had never occurred to her that Chris had thought of her after the night they shared. Maybe he deserved more consideration than she had given him. "Chris, thank you. And the answer to your unspoken question is, yes."

His eyes flashed from her to Austin, then back to her, and he smiled. "I'll be in touch."

Austin's eyebrows raised and his mouth fell open. In a shaky voice he said, "Chris wants to get to know me, doesn't he?"

JL wasn't afraid of what would happen next, of possibly losing her son to his bio-dad. She couldn't see any further than the moment. The single heartbeat of a moment. She had deprived Chris of years of enjoyment, of opportunities to teach his son the game of basketball, a game they were both passionate about, and so much more. She took a deep breath and shrugged a bit. Austin loved her, Pops, and the boys, and he always would. He was branching out now, and she couldn't hold him back.

"I think so, but you'll need to give him time. He knows where you are," she said.

"I've got to find James Cullen." Austin hugged Kevin and then her. "Thanks for telling him."

Austin hurried off, leaving her slightly off balance. She had imagined having that conversation with Chris hundreds of times, but in all her imagining, it had never gone so well.

Kevin took her hand. "Come on. Let's go find a restroom." He tightened his grasp and drew her closer, tucking her hand into the crook of his elbow. Moving slowly, as though caught up in a time warp, they threaded their way through an ocean of people. "You handled that well. I know it wasn't easy."

"Easier than I thought it would be."

"You know the part I liked best?"

She stopped and gazed up into his warm cocoa eyes. "No. What?"

"You introduced me as your fiancé." He cupped the side of her face. "I recognized your ulterior motive—that you wanted Chris to know you were attached—but I didn't mind that at all. I want to be attached to you and Austin. I love you both. And I'm not jealous of Chris Dalton." He captured her lips in a tender, lingering kiss, caressing her lips lightly with his tongue. "Come on. Let's go inside."

At the door to the Welcome Center, a man stopped Kevin, and asked, "Can I have a minute? I have a question I forgot to ask Elliott during our meeting at the bank."

"I'll go on," she said, pointing in the direction of the ladies' room. "I'll meet you right here."

"I'll just keep him a minute," the man said.

Kevin squeezed her hand, and she smiled. "I'll be right back."

When she reached the restroom, she found the line snaking down the hall, a good fifteen-minute line, which wasn't any better than the ones outside. She twitched her nose, thinking. Wait here. Wait there. There wasn't a line for the men's room. If she had been working, she would have had Pete guard the door, but that wouldn't go over so well with this crowd, and she wouldn't want to embarrass Kevin. She tapped her foot, remembering Kenzie and Meredith had bathrooms in their offices, and they had both offered free use of them. There definitely wouldn't be lines there. Thank goodness, she hadn't been drinking beer, or she would have peed her pants by now.

JL traversed the pass-through to the Corporate Offices and punched in the security code Austin had given her the day she arrived. The lights weren't on. She flipped one of the switches, lighting the hall with only the recessed lights. Enough to see where she was going, but not enough to light up the building and alarm security, currently monitored by her brothers and Pops.

Kenzie's office was the first one she reached. Kenzie had closed the door but not locked it. JL stepped inside and flipped on that switch, too. Instantly, adrenaline pushed into her veins and she reached for the gun she wasn't carrying.

"What are you doing here?" The last person she expected to see was Castellano. He was rifling through documents on Kenzie's desk. The hairs on the back of her neck tingled. She trusted Castellano, but her instincts had been wrong before.

"I...uh...Mrs. McBain said she'd leave an employee list for me. I thought since I was here, I'd pick it up."

"Why are you using a flashlight instead of turning the lights on?" JL asked.

"I thought I could get in and out without alarming anyone," Castellano said.

"How'd you get in the building?"

He put down the documents and stepped away from the desk, but JL didn't back down. "Why the third degree?" He moved toward her, keeping his body relaxed and non-threatening, but she watched his roving eyes and spotted a nervous tic along his jaw. "We're working the same case, aren't we?" he asked.

"I'm surprised to see you here, in the dark, going through Kenzie's documents without her permission."

He waved his hand, brushing off her observations. "The custodian was leaving. I showed him my badge, and he let me in." He removed his glasses and tucked them into his inside jacket pocket.

Castellano's explanation didn't pass the smell test, but until she could confirm his story with Meredith and Kenzie, she wouldn't challenge him on it. "I'll leave you to finish up what you were doing. Kevin's waiting." She turned to go, but Castellano rushed her and grabbed her arm. He didn't squeeze it, but his grip was tight enough that she couldn't walk away with only a tug. To break his grip would require a defensive move, and she wasn't ready to escalate the tension.

"Wait," he said.

Behind his eyes, his mind was working feverishly, searching for an out, and she had to give him one. Her gut told her Castellano wasn't a murderer, but his jitteriness and hesitation put her cop instincts on notice. He was dirty, and that pissed her the hell off.

"Let's go drink champagne," she said. "When we see Kenzie, I'll ask her about the list. How's that?"

He swallowed, and his Adam's apple bobbled in his throat. He released her arm, one finger at a time, as if waiting for the last possible second to let her go. "Okay. Let's go."

"What a cozy twosome. The troublemaker and the brother-in-law."

JL spun around to find Bill Wilder with eyes glaring, poised in the doorway with a wide stance and his chest thrust out. He had a steady grip on a nine-millimeter pistol identical to the one she had given Kevin to carry in his sporran. Her mind flashed back to the moment she had left Kevin at the entrance to the Welcome Center. Had Wilder overpowered him and taken her gun? No, she tossed that thought aside. She didn't have the only Glock in the world.

She shot a hot glance at Castellano. "Your brother-in-law? I never pegged you for a murderer and drug dealer."

Wilder stepped farther into the room. "Oh, don't blame Michael. He hasn't been *that* bad," Wilder taunted. "It was just that one time, right, old boy?"

Castellano stepped between JL and Wilder. "You've said enough, Bill. You need to leave."

"Not until I get the survey."

"It's not here. I looked."

"Maybe you didn't look as thoroughly as I will. Step aside."

"No. I won't let you do this. Not again. This needs to end. Now." Castellano lunged for Wilder, and the gun exploded. Castellano dropped to his knees then to the floor, blood spurting from his chest.

Wilder glanced at the body of his brother-in-law, tsking. He pulled another gun from his pocket. "Such a waste." He switched guns and pointed the second one at JL. "Sorry you had to watch this little"—he dropped his chin, glancing briefly at Castellano—"family squabble."

Time slowed, and she moved as if wading through an ocean of syrup.

If she did nothing, she would die. If she lunged at Wilder, she would die, too, but she would go down fighting. Austin would have Chris to direct his career, and she would die having known the depth of Kevin's love.

Wilder's eyes widened, his finger twitched, and she made her move. She ducked and plowed into him at the exact moment Kevin barged into the office and threw himself in front of Wilder and the muffled roar of his gun. The snap of bone, a violent curse, the thud of a bullet penetrating a body, the sting of excruciating pain all happened in a millisecond.

Wilder, a fighting bull, jerked to his knees, screaming curses and waving his gun. "You bitch."

The taste of metal seared her tongue and warm liquid flowed down her side. She was a red flag, daring him, and he took aim once again. Kevin was down, unmoving, and she could do no more for either one of them. Her lips moved as she silently prayed, *Hail, Mary, full of grace; the Lord is with thee...*

Her life flashed before her eyes.

A gun blasted, and she flinched, waiting for more searing pain that would precede her death. Wilder pitched forward, his face a rictus of pain. Behind him stood Pete. From his gun came the barest whiff of gunpowder and the final white curl, as if he had stubbed out a cigarette.

31

JL'S EYES POPPED open, but her mind lagged seconds behind. Cold. So cold. She was in a hospital, shivering. The scene was familiar right down to the tubes, beeping machines, antiseptic smells, a tolerable amount of pain, and Pete wearing a downcast face.

The face didn't match his gregariousness and sunny disposition.

Then it all came flooding back, and tears pushed into her eyes as fear roared into her chest. "Is Kevin..." The words caught in her dry throat. She couldn't ask. She couldn't go there. All she remembered was the caustic smell and the spray of blood. So much blood. His, hers, Castellano's, Wilder's.

Pete pushed to his feet and leaned over the railing. His arms rested there, and a small crease formed between his brows. He didn't make that face often, but when he did, he always had bad news. If she could prepare herself, she would, but she couldn't bear to hear Kevin was dead. He had taken a bullet for her, and she wasn't worth his sacrifice.

"You won't be able to run the New York City Marathon in a couple of weeks," Pete said, "but you'll live to run again. So will Kevin. You two can heal on a beach somewhere warm."

Relieved in body, soothed in mind, her mouth was dry, but she managed to ask, "Where is he? I want to see him."

Pete turned toward the glass door. "If you could sit up, you'd be able to. He is across the hall. Elliott flew in his parents. They're with him now."

"Parents?"

"I met them briefly. Nice people. They live in Kentucky."

"Austin?"

A smile flickered briefly across Pete's face. "Until five minutes ago, he never left your side. He went to the cafeteria to get something to eat."

"Must be feeding time." Her hand drifted down her side to the dressing near her hip. "What happened to me?"

"The bullet lodged in the fleshy part above your hip. It didn't hit anything vital. You were lucky."

"And Kevin?"

"The bullet fragmented when it hit the brooch. Pieces chewed up the pectoral muscle, broke his collarbone, grazed a rib, and lacerated the brachial artery. It was a five-hour surgery to put him back together. He'll recover, but it'll take a while to heal."

"Thank God." Thinking about the scar he would have, she wondered whether he would see it as a badge of honor or a blemish. She closed her eyes and drifted off to sleep again.

When she woke sometime later, she was in a room nicer than any hotel she had ever stayed in. Hand-blown glass on a shelf, hardwood trim, a sitting room off to the side with a full-sized sofa, not one of those vinyl loveseats she had seen in other hospital rooms, and a coffee bar. They had put her in the wrong room. Her insurance would never pay for this. Pete and Austin were on the sofa watching TV.

She still had to pee.

She rolled to her side and tried to push up. Austin hustled toward the bed. "Wait, I'll help you."

"I have to go to the bathroom."

He took her arm and helped her to stand while Pete grabbed the IV pole. "How do you feel?" Austin asked.

"Like I've been shot."

"Ha. Ha," Pete said.

She shuffled toward the bathroom, thinking none of this would have happened if she had only waited in line at the trailer. "Where's

Kevin?"

"He's supposed to be moved to his room before supper," Austin said.

"I want to go see him. Will you get me a wheelchair?"

Austin pushed opened the bathroom door and helped her in. "They won't let you go."

"They can't stop me." She squeezed Pete's arm. "Work it out, please."

He nodded and closed the door to give her privacy. When she came out, the wheelchair was waiting for her. "You can go in and kiss him, but you can't stay. If you give anybody trouble, they won't let you go back."

"What kind of trouble would I be?"

"As hot as you are for the guy, you'll probably try to climb into bed with him," Pete said. "Don't do that. They'll call security."

Austin held up a white robe like the one she had been using at the cottage. "Ms. Montgomery left a robe and slippers for you. I guess she figured you'd go see Kevin as soon as you could."

"That was thoughtful." JL slipped her arm into one sleeve while Pete snaked the IV bag and tube through the other one, a procedure they had followed four years earlier. She cinched the belt, then, holding her side, she slowly sat in the wheelchair. Austin lowered the footplates and put slippers on her feet. As they headed out of the room, Pops and her brothers arrived.

"We just came from seeing Kevin. His parents said he's tried to get out of the bed to come see you," Connor said.

"I better hurry, then. Pops, will you do something for me while I'm gone? The nurses made a mistake and put me in this big room. My insurance won't pay for it. I need to move before the hospital charges me an outrageous rate."

"I told Dr. Fraser you wouldn't approve, and he said he didn't care. If you move to another room, he'll have you moved right back," Pops said.

"He will, huh?" She made a decision right then not to waste precious energy fighting Elliott on this issue. Austin pushed her chair into the elevator, and they got off on the second floor. After Pete wrangled a visit for her, Austin pushed her into Kevin's room, leaving her there. The nurse lowered the bed so JL wouldn't have to stand.

"Mr. Allen's parents just went to the cafeteria for dinner," the nurse said. "They'll be back in a few minutes."

JL gave the nurse a weak smile. "I won't stay long." She would love to meet Kevin's parents, but not today. She didn't want to meet her future in-laws riding in a wheelchair.

Kevin's hand was cool to the touch. She sandwiched his between hers to warm them, and he lightly squeezed her fingers. When his eyes opened, she said, "You didn't read the rules, did you? You're supposed to put on your superhero cape *before* you jump in front of a speeding bullet."

He managed a short chuckle and then moaned. "I thought I could get by this one time," he said with a hoarse voice. "Next time, I'll wear it." He puckered his lips. "Kiss me?"

She leaned forward and so did he, and their lips met, but they couldn't hold the kiss. She collapsed back into her chair, her side burning from the effort. "We'll have a lot of time to make up for when we get out of here."

"They're supposed to move me upstairs in a couple of hours. Will you come visit?"

"They won't be able to keep me away. If no one's looking, I'll get in bed with you."

"I'd like that," he said.

She kissed his hand because she couldn't reach his lips again. "I love you, Kevin."

His lips twitched with an effort to smile. "Love you, too, Sugar." Then his eyes closed and he drifted off to sleep.

JL was quiet on the ride back to the elevator. The image of Kevin diving in front of Wilder's gun and taking the bullet meant for her would haunt her for the rest of her life.

"Did you know Dr. Mallory is one of the country's top trauma surgeons?" Austin said, interrupting her thoughts. "She has privileges at this hospital because her family spends so much time at the winery. She operated on Kevin, and another doctor she recommended operated on you."

"I'm glad she was here to work on him."

"Dr. Mallory said if Kevin had had to wait for the EMTs, he wouldn't have survived. She clamped off a spurting artery that kept him from bleeding out," Austin said.

That made her stomach curl, and she swallowed hard, trampling down fears that roared even louder now. Her hands turned clammy, and she clasped them together. As a distraction she asked, "What about Castellano?"

Pete shook his head, and his carefully coiffed hair bounced back into place. Pete was so put together he didn't need anything else to be camera-ready. It was so unfair. He and Kevin had a lot in common. "Castellano didn't make it. He died instantly."

"He was Wilder's brother-in-law," she said, licking dry lips.

"That's what Wilder said in his statement. He planned to pin Di Salvo's death on Castellano. You messed up his plans," Pete said.

She tilted her head as if trying to solve a puzzle, and she couldn't quite get the right angle to view it "So he killed Di Salvo? Why?"

"Di Salvo saw men go inside the cave and told security. Unfortunately for him, the security guard he told was the man working for Wilder. The guard killed Di Salvo. He was arrested late last night," Pete said.

"And before you ask," Austin said, "Di Salvo was a second cousin of the New York Di Salvos, but he wasn't part of their cartel." Austin wheeled her into her room, and Pops kissed her cheek.

"Do you feel better now you've seen Kevin?" Pops asked.

"Much better. I'll be glad when they move him into a room so I can stay with him."

"You've got to take care of yourself, too. You need rest," Pops said. "You haven't had much sleep in the last few days."

That was true, but she would sleep peacefully at Kevin's side. Switching tracks, she asked, "What about the cocaine? Any luck finding the barrels?"

"Wilder wouldn't give it up, but Pops found it," Pete said.

"How?" she asked.

"Get back in bed, and we'll tell you," Pete said.

Pops helped her to stand and remove her robe. "Okay, tell me." Hissing, she eased down on the edge of the bed. If she moved just right, she could avoid tugging on the incision. She grimaced as she lay down and pulled up the covers. It was several seconds before the rush of pain subsided and she could breathe again without hissing.

Pops' eyes watered. He might be a man of steel, but he bent double when his children were in pain. "I was watching the drone surveillance footage," he said, "and spotted a van on the other side of the road. Something clicked, and I looked at the winery's old plats. I discovered that when the highway was constructed, it cut through the property. The Montgomerys eventually sold off the acres on the other side of the road. That got me thinking that one of the tunnels might go all the way through."

"We went down in the cave," Connor said. "Took us four hours of twisting, turning, and backtracking. We were about to give up when we saw daylight. We came out on the other side of the road. Nature had hidden the entrance well. We wouldn't have found it if we'd been coming from the other direction."

She raised her eyebrows encouraging him to continue.

"The barrels were lined up along the wall. We called DEA. They took possession and said the street value is between ten and fifteen million dollars."

"What about Castellano? How'd he get involved in the first place?" she asked.

"It was all about money," Pops said. "When Castellano's son was born, he had severe health issues. The medical bills mounted. When a state senator offered Castellano a bribe to make evidence disappear in his son's DUI case, he took the bribe, and the court dismissed the case for a lack of evidence. Castellano told his wife what he did. She told her brother. When Wilder set up a drug operation in Napa, he blackmailed his brother-in-law to give him the heads-up if anyone became suspicious. After Di Salvo was killed, Castellano told Wilder about JL and her background."

"How did David get Wilder's name? Did that come from Castellano?" she asked.

"Purely a coincidence," Connor said, "and a timely one for Wilder. He didn't believe there was a direct passage from the entrance you and Kevin used to the cavern. He wasn't worried about you finding the cocaine, but he had to stall David and the rest of us. When Castellano discovered what Wilder had done, and that he intended to kill his hostages, he rushed to the hangar to rescue us."

"But that would have exposed Castellano," JL said.

"He did the right thing at his own expense," Pops said.

"What will happen to his son, Sammy?" she asked.

"Castellano's sister has custody. From what Hollinger said, the aunt has been a substitute mother to him and they have a wonderful relationship," Connor said.

"What about Austin? Why was he taken?" she asked.

"He was in the wrong place at the wrong time. Wilder would have had him killed with the rest of the hostages," Pete said.

"Wilder's responsible for the death of Salvatore and two cops, plus wounding eight others, kidnapping fourteen people, and intending to sell cocaine worth millions of dollars. If he's convicted, he'll receive the death penalty, won't he?"

"The DA took the death penalty off the table in exchange for a full confession and identifying Di Salvo's shooter. In the beginning, I don't think Wilder intended to kill anyone, but he did, and he'll have to face the consequences."

"And Wilder's buyer," JL asked. "Any leads?"

"Wilder didn't even know the identity of the buyer. They were supposed to meet at the gala at ten o'clock. David won't give up the search, though. He thinks the sellers Kenzie has been negotiating with might be participants, and that's why they were pushing so hard to do a land swap. He can't make a connection yet, but if one exists, he'll find it."

"Two more questions," JL said, "and then I'm going back to

sleep. How did Wilder get inside the building, and how was it that only one shot was fired, yet Kevin and I were both shot?"

"The security guard working for Wilder gave him the door code," Pete said. "As for the single shot, the brooch deflected the bullet, shattering it and changing its trajectory. Instead of Kevin's heart, pieces of the bullet headed toward his shoulder. One piece went straight through him and into you, lodging near your last gunshot wound. You now have parallel scars."

Pops lowered her bed and pulled the covers up to her chin, just as he had done when she was little. "If the brooch hadn't deflected the bullet, it would have killed him."

"Thank God he was wearing it. I guess it's broken again, though."

Pops chuckled. "No, sweetheart. It's barely dented."

32

AFTER JL'S VISIT with Kevin, she fell sound asleep, and other than visits from the nursing staff, she didn't wake up until early the next morning. When she woke and realized the time, she hung on to her IV pole and shuffled over to the sofa, where Austin slept with his bare feet hanging over the edge. She resisted the urge to rest her hand on his chest to check his breathing, the way she used to do, and instead shook him awake.

"Why didn't you wake me last night? Is Kevin okay?"

Austin rolled over, stared up at her, and grumbled, "What time is it?"

"Six thirty. You need to get ready for school."

He sat, lifting his shoulders in a faint shrug. "Pops told me to let you sleep. Take it out on him." Austin stood with the effort of an old man and stretched. "I'm getting a shower. Is there any food?" Grumbling about not getting enough sleep, he lumbered toward the bathroom.

She ignored his complaints and asked again, keeping her voice calm, "Where's Kevin?"

"He stayed in ICU another night."

She stalked Austin across the room, spilling her calmness along the way. "*Why?* What's wrong?" Austin was not a morning person, and she had learned years ago to let him wake up slowly. The blood had a long way to go from his huge feet to his brain, but this morning he needed to act like an adult.

"Uggh. He's okay. Don't yell at me. He was running a fever. Dr. Mallory wouldn't release him to a private room."

"That's all you had to say the first time, and I wouldn't have had to bug you."

"Stop worrying. I was watching your back while you snored."

"I don't snore."

"Yeah right. Tape yourself sometime. Look, if Kevin's fever's down this morning, he'll be moved."

"Thank you, and you're more than welcome to eat my hospital breakfast."

"Barf. I'll stop at McDonalds."

He waved his arm, shooing her away like an annoying fly, and closed the bathroom door. Within seconds, the ring of sliding shower curtain hooks and splashing water echoed off the tile walls and floor. She sighed. Austin's early morning communication skills carried a sense of the familiar that she found comforting in the midst of distress.

Needing an additional boost to start the day, she stepped over to the bar and made a cup of coffee. Stirring the brew, she stood in front of the window and sipped while dawn rushed toward morning. Her phone beeped with a text message. Austin had been monitoring her phone calls, and had left the phone on the table next to the sofa. She glanced at the phone's face, which showed a text from Pete.

Braham confirmed Kevin moved to private suite early a.m. After a run and breakfast, I'll come visit.

The water stopped, and after a couple of minutes, Austin walked out with a towel wrapped around his waist.

"Do you have clean clothes?" she asked.

"Only if you washed them," he said.

"Yeah, right."

He laughed, opening the closet door. "Meredith brought clothes for you, and just so you know, I packed my own bag."

She took her phone back to her bed and read get-well emails from friends while he dressed. "Pete said Kevin was moved to his room. I need to find out where."

"Look next door," Austin said. "Dr. Fraser pulled strings so you could be close. I'm surprised he didn't cut a door in the wall." Austin shoved books and clothes into a duffel and kissed her cheek. "Got to go. I'll be back after practice this afternoon."

JL ran her hands over her hair until tangles trapped her fingers. She glanced in the mirror, and her stomach roiled at the sight of the blood-matted knots. "Gross." She pushed the nurse call button.

"Can I help you?" a disembodied voice answered from the intercom.

"I want to take a shower."

"Someone will be right there."

Fifteen minutes later, a nurse came in, unhooked her IV, and added waterproof tape over her dressing. Then an aide assisted her into the shower. As the hot water pelted her head, streams of red streaked down her body. The gun explosion blasted her ears. The taste of sulfur coated her tongue. The hot burn of the bullet gripped her side. She was there once again, living it, breathing it, smelling it, and watching Kevin fly through the air, catching the bullet meant for her.

She sobbed into the hot, steamy water. She had come so close to losing the love of her life, her soul mate. If being shot twice in four years wasn't a sign, she didn't know what was. The time had come to hang up her shield. She could use her master's degree in law enforcement administration and work in another capacity.

A knock on the door brought JL back to the here and now. "Detective O'Grady, do you need assistance?"

She turned off the water. Making that odd double-breathing sound that comes after a hard cry, she forced out the words, "I'm good." She would be as soon as she could hold and kiss Kevin. That reassurance would move her mountain of fear and uncertainty down the sloping surface of her heart quicker than an avalanche.

A clean body, a new dressing, and a silky gown courtesy of Meredith, and she was ready to visit her guy.

She rolled her wheelchair into his room, overjoyed to see him sitting up and eating from a breakfast tray. She had to stop and breathe. Even after everything they had been through together, a bit of first-time jitteriness flitted in her belly.

"You look great," she said.

"I imposed on our trainer, Ted, to come over and help me clean up. He was glad to do it. It gave him some perverse pleasure thinking he'd get to bust my balls when I'm released to work out again."

"Thanks for telling me. If he offers his services, I'll politely decline."

"Meredith loves him."

JL rolled her chair to the bed. "That's enough of a recommendation, then."

Kevin pushed away the rolling table with the breakfast tray and patted the side of the bed. "I'll make room."

"I was hoping for an invitation." She stood and eased down on the bed. They were wounded on opposite sides of their bodies, and Kevin was still attached to his IV, so finding a comfortable position wasn't easy. When they finally did, she slipped into his arms and they shared a kiss. Although tentative at first, their passion quickly exploded into a deep yearning for a level of intimacy they hadn't reached until now. A yearning she had once feared, she now willingly accepted, opening her heart to all he had to give.

They stayed that way until they drifted off to sleep.

A chair sliding across the tile floor woke JL. "Hi, Elliott."

"How's the lad?"

"I'm awake," Kevin said, opening one eye. "With all the noise, you can't sleep around here."

"I told them I wanted rooms away from the nurses' station," Elliott said.

"I'm not talking about the hospital noise. I was referring to JL's snoring."

She covered her face with her hands. "Not you, too. Austin has already given me grief. Just for that, I'm getting up."

"I'm just teasing, Sugar. Don't go."

"Too late." She eased out of the bed and back into the wheelchair. "What brings you out this early, Elliott?"

"I wanted to talk to both of ye before everyone came by to visit this morning." He crossed his legs and folded his hands in his lap with his index fingers pointing out, like a horizontal church steeple. "I owe ye an apology for the way I acted. I didn't know JL was divorced, and I didn't want Kevin to fall for a married woman and make the mistakes I've made." Elliott tapped the points of his fingers, and JL heard in her mind the metrical ticks of her piano teacher's metronome.

After a short pause, he continued. "When I met yer mother, Kevin, she and yer father were separated, and had been for several months. She told me the marriage was over, and that she would never go back to yer father. We dated for over six months. I fell in love with her and encouraged her to file for divorce. I thought that was what she intended to do." Elliott paused again, but his fingers continued setting the pace of his confession.

"I had to fly to Scotland on business. When I returned a week later, she told me she and yer father had reconciled. I couldn't believe I was being dumped again. I took my broken heart and returned to Scotland. For several months, I traveled infrequently to Kentucky. I made all sorts of excuses, so no one would know what an ass I had been for falling for another married woman. Fortunately, Kit came into our lives then, and loving her filled the emptiness in my life.

"Fast forward to Kit's junior year in high school. She introduced ye to me at an equestrian event. Do ye remember?"

Kevin nodded.

"When ye told me who yer parents were, I knew ye were my son. Yer mother had told me she and yer father had been to dozens of doctors. All her tests came back normal. His tests showed a low sperm count and bad morphology and motility. They tried assisted reproduction, but she had never gotten pregnant.

"I encouraged Kit to invite ye to the farm to ride. I wanted ye close to me. Out of respect for yer parents, I never openly claimed ye, but I've tried to treat ye as my own. David's accused me of indulging ye, and maybe I have, but it's been out of love for ye.

"A couple of days ago, ye said there was no place for ye at MacKlenna Corporation. Ye're wrong. When I retire, ye'll take my place. I hope ye'll forgive me for keeping this from ye, but I did it for yer mother."

JL squeezed Kevin's hand, and he squeezed hers. "You're forgiven, Boss. You know I've always loved you and wanted to be just like you."

"Until Meredith came into our lives, I wasn't a very good role model."

Kevin grinned. "I thought you were. I had a great time emulating you. I do have one question, though. Does my dad know?"

"I'm sure he does. But I've never heard that directly."

"What about Meredith? Does she know?" Kevin asked.

"I told her before our wedding. She had already guessed the truth."

"Speaking of parents," JL said, "how'd you know I was Austin's mother?"

"When Austin came to work for us, David did a thorough background check. The story of Austin's birth seemed odd. The deeper David dug, the more we were convinced Austin was yer son. Finding his father took a while. We found the camp ye attended. When we couldn't match up any potential candidates, we looked at groups who used the adjoining facilities. When we discovered a basketball camp had been there at the same time as yer dancing camp, we knew we were on the right track. Austin is a fine young man. Ye've done a fine job with him."

"I think so," she said. "Did you hear Chris Dalton was at the party?"

Elliott chuckled. "It cost James Cullen twenty-five thousand dollars. Yes, I heard."

"What about your cancer?" Kevin asked.

"I consulted three doctors. They all recommend a wait-and-see approach. That's what I'm going to do. I'll be carefully monitored."

"Good," Kevin said. "I've been through several surgeries with you, and I don't care to do it again. You're a terrible patient."

"Aye. I was a bastard for sure." He uncrossed his legs and leaned forward. "There's another matter to discuss."

JL's heart stopped for a beat or two. She stiffened and waited for what she knew was coming. Elliott still didn't approve of her, and he was going to discourage her relationship with *his* son. If he thought he used to be a bloody bastard, he was wrong. He still was.

"I would like to offer JL the position of Senior Vice President of Global Security for MacKlenna Corporation."

What the hell?

"Even if ye and Kevin decide not to marry for some asinine reason, Meredith and I want ye to be a part of MacKlenna Corporation. We hope ye'll accept."

"Wow," JL said. "I wasn't expecting that." If she hadn't been sitting, she would have been now—smack on the floor.

"I'm also extending offers to yer brothers, Connor and Shane, and yer partner, Pete, to come onboard as Vice Presidents of Operations and Security. They will be carrying out yer global initiatives on a local level. Patrick wasn't ready to make a move. His offer will remain open. I have also extended an offer to yer other brother, Jeffrey, to join our legal team when he graduates from law school. And, I've offered Pops an advisory position on the board."

Flabbergasted, she had to take back her earlier opinion of Elliott. He wasn't such a bastard after all. "Why?"

Elliott sat back again, recrossed his legs, and picked at the knife-edge pleat in his pants. "Ye and yer family are good people. After the problems we've had at the winery, I don't want to hire outsiders to manage our security. Knowing I have ex-cops throughout the organization will give Meredith and me the confidence we need to move forward with our expansion plans. MacKlenna Corporation will be a multibillion-dollar organization within the next five years."

"I don't know what to say," JL said. "Can I think about it?"

"The offer will remain on the table until ye're ready."

"Has Pete said yes?"

"He and Connor are waiting on yer decision."

Elliott's phone beeped with a text message. He glanced at the face of the phone. Instead of responding to the message, he said, "Come in, Jack."

Jack stepped in, his face glowing. "Sorry to interrupt but…" He handed Elliott a photo, then one to JL and Kevin. "I was at a book signing the other day and saw a baseball book on the shelf. It looked interesting, so I bought it. An hour ago, I was thumbing through the pages and saw this picture. After I stopped shaking, I made photocopies and rushed over here to find Elliott."

"It's Ty Cobb sliding into third base. It's an iconic baseball picture. A game in New York, right?" JL said.

Jack pointed to a woman standing in the background. "Yes, and look at that face. Who does she look like?"

JL peered closer. "Sort of like Amy Spalding. She's been missing since…what? Friday?"

"According to the news reports, she met with her great-great-aunt's attorney for the reading of the will. Amy's inheritance included a residence on Riverside Drive in New York City. The police found her purse and cell phone there. There was no evidence of foul play. She just disappeared. I believe she found a brooch in her great-great-aunt's possessions and has gone back to 1909."

"That's a stretch, Jack," Elliott said.

"It's more than David and I had when he believed Kenzie had gone back to 1944."

"But ye knew she'd received a package from Solicitor Digby. In this case, ye don't have any evidence she received a brooch."

"No, but I have her face in a picture taken in 1909."

"I've heard Digby's name before," JL said.

"James Cullen mentioned him the other day. He's a solicitor in Edinburgh. He mailed Kenzie the emerald brooch and Charlotte the sapphire brooch. He has refused multiple requests for meetings with Elliott and David. We don't know where he got the brooches," Kevin said.

Jack continued, "Amy might be in trouble. Maybe, like Kenzie, her brooch won't bring her back either." He glanced at Kevin and

JL. "I'd like to go back to help her, and I'd like you two to go with me."

"Back to New York City in 1909? No way," JL said. "We've had enough adventure for a while. Kevin put his superhero costume in the closet. Besides, according to Yogi, 'No one goes there anymore. It's too crowded.' Pick someone else."

"That's just it. No one wants to go except James Cullen. That's not going to happen. So what do you say?"

"Bad timing, Jack. I'm looking at weeks of rehab," Kevin said.

"Good, I'll start making plans." Jack bounded out of the room leaving JL, Kevin, and Elliott staring at each other, mouths agape.

JL rubbed a hand along the back of her neck, trying to loosen the tension that had increased tenfold. "How do you make plans to go back to 1909? It's not like you can book a flight."

Elliott laughed. "Adventures take a while to plan. In the meantime, ye two need a long vacation at the beach."

"Looks like we're signed up for an adventure, Sugar," Kevin said.

"Don't call me Sugar right now." She rolled the chair's wheels back and forth—the wheelchair equivalent of pacing a room. What she really needed was an hour in the gym sparring with Pete. "Answer a question for me," she said. "How can you be excited about this, after all you've been through in the last few days?"

He pulled himself up with effort, grimacing as he did, and gazed into her eyes. "What we did scared the hell out of me, but we did it together. I'm stronger with you, partnering with you, than I've ever been on my own. If your brooch hadn't been broken, we would have met in the past. This trip won't be our story. It'll be Jack's. We'll just be along for the ride. Besides, there's no war going on, so it'll be safe. We'll watch some baseball. Eat some popcorn. Go to a few fancy parties. It'll be a piece of cake. What do you say?"

"There may not have been a war going on, but New York City in the early 1900s was a cesspool of crime."

"In that case, I'll be sure to pack my cape." Kevin's eyes twinkled. "Come on. We'll have fun."

JL put her palm to her forehead, shaking her head. "My great-grandfather's stories of Wild West shootouts on the streets of the city, widespread robbery, racketeering, prostitution rings, and the corrupt Tammany Hall political machine have always fascinated me, as has Diamond Jim Brady and Lillian Russell. Call me crazy, but those..." She burst into song.

"Little town blues are melting away. I want to be part of it! New York, New York!"

33

THAT NIGHT ELLIOTT climbed into bed and kissed Meredith squarely on the mouth. "After all these years, I love ye as much as I did the night I pulled a leaf from yer hair in Lou's library."

Meredith removed her glasses, smiling. "Why, Dr. Fraser, are you saying it was love at first sight for you? If so, I don't believe it. Lust at first sight, maybe."

He laughed and kissed her again. "Then I'm still lusting. Put those papers aside so I can ravish ye."

"Five minutes," she said.

He pulled the papers and glasses out of her hands. "Read them later."

"Before you ravish me, tell me about your conversation tonight with David. Kenzie said the experience in the hangar was especially difficult for him. Did he say anything about it?"

Elliott rolled over on his side, bent his arm, and propped his head up with his hand. "He drank. I listened. Kenzie is right. The lad had a hell of a time of it. He said he had never been so scared. If anything had happened to the twins, he never would have recovered."

Meredith mirrored Elliott but slung her leg over his hip and tugged him closer. "Kenzie wouldn't have either. What does David think of JL?"

Elliott's dick twitched against her. "He thinks she is highly competent, dedicated, level-headed, devoted to family, trustworthy…and a tank built to smash through obstacles. He also thinks the two of us will lock horns over everything, and he can't wait for the action to start."

"I can't either. I'm buying front-row seats. She is exactly like you, dear. Kevin doesn't know it yet, but he'll spend the next couple of years refereeing your battles until you trust JL enough to let go of the reins."

"I trust her now."

"Not with your power, you don't. You don't even trust me. You'll eventually give up control of the corporation to Kevin, but JL will hold the real power. You saw the brooch come alive in her hand. I don't know how this is going to play out, but if I had to guess who the next Keeper will be, my bet is on JL."

Elliott kept his gaze determinedly fastened on hers and considered her words. If his opinion mattered, he would have anointed David the Keeper of the Stones. He hadn't considered a woman for the job, although JL was certainly capable. "Ye, my dear, have an acute gift when it comes to judgment and understanding. If ye say it, I believe it."

"No, you don't. Not yet, but you will. Be warned, though, JL won't venture into the gray zone as easily as David has."

"She doesn't know how necessary it's been."

"If she goes back in time with Jack, she'll find out." Meredith kissed him. "Go kiss the kids good night, and then show me how much you're still lusting for me."

He kissed her long and hard, then patted her ass and left the bedroom.

James Cullen's room was located at the opposite end of the villa's second floor. Elliott opened the door and the scent of baby shampoo and adolescent body products hit him. James Cullen leaned more toward Kevin's approach, a product for every part of his body, and Lincoln leaned toward his dad's approach, which was to smell delicious enough to get the lass in bed with ye, and let nature take care of the rest.

The wee ones had insisted on sleeping together. James Cullen and Lincoln were asleep in the double bed with Tater Tot between them. Henry, Robert, and Kitherina were sleeping on pallets on one side of the bed, and Austin was on the other. Kenzie would deliver in four months, and if Kevin and JL married, Elliott anticipated they would have a large family. The next generation would be a fine group of lads and lassies.

Elliott kissed all the children, and, as he stood at the door to leave them for the night, Cooper scooted in between his legs and snuggled up with Kitherina. He smiled, and as he was accustomed to doing, he whispered, "Wherever ye are Kit, may God hold ye and these precious children in the palm of His hand."

About the Author

Katherine graduated from Rowan University in New Jersey, where she earned a BA in Psychology with a minor in Criminal Justice. Following college, she attended the Philadelphia Institute for Paralegal Training before returning to Central Kentucky, where she worked as a real estate and tax paralegal.

Katherine is a marathoner and lives in Lexington, Kentucky. When she's not running or writing romance, she's enjoying her five grandchildren: Charlotte, Lincoln Thomas, James Cullen, Henry Patrick, and Meredith Lyle.

Please stop by and visit Katherine on her social media sites, or drop her an email. She loves to hear from readers.

Website
www.katherinellogan.com

Blog
www.katherinelowrylogan.com

Facebook
facebook.com/katherine.l.logan

Twitter
twitter.com/KathyLLogan

LinkedIn
linkedin.com/in/katherinellogan

Pinterest
pinterest.com/kllogan50

Goodreads
goodreads.com/author/show/5806657.Katherine_Lowry_Logan

Google+
plus.google.com/+KatherineLowryLogan/posts

I'm A Runner (Runner's World Magazine Interview)
www.runnersworld.com/celebrity-runners/im-a-runner-katherine-lowry-logan

Email:
KatherineLLogan@gmail.com

Family trees are available on Katherine's website
www.katherinellogan.com/books/the-celtic-brooch-family-trees

* * *

THE CELTIC BROOCH SERIES

THE RUBY BROOCH (Book 1)
Kitherina MacKlenna and Cullen Montgomery's love story

THE LAST MACKLENNA (Book 2 – not a time travel story)
Meredith Montgomery and Elliott Fraser's love story

THE SAPPHIRE BROOCH (Book 3)
Charlotte Mallory and Braham McCabe's love story

THE EMERALD BROOCH (Book 4)
Kenzie Wallis-Manning and David McBain's love story

THE BROKEN BROOCH (Book 5 – not a time travel story)
JL O'Grady and Kevin Allen's love story

THE THREE BROOCHES (Book 6)
A reunion with Kit and Cullen Montgomery

THE DIAMOND BROOCH (Book 7)
Jack Mallory and Amy Spalding's love story

Future Brooch Books

THE PEARL BROOCH
THE AMBER BROOCH

And More…

If you would like to receive notification of future releases
Sign up today at KatherineLowryLogan.com or
Send an email to KatherineLLogan@gmail.com and put "Sequel" in the subject line

* * *

Thank you for reading THE BROKEN BROOCH
I hope you enjoyed reading this story as much as I enjoyed writing it.
Reviews help other readers find books.
I appreciate all reviews, whether positive or negative.

Author's Notes

Special thanks to my experts. These wonderful people are not responsible for any mistakes I might have made in regards to weaponry, police procedure, or forensics.

- Tom Biggers, President of the New York Police Department Running Club (www.nypdrunningclub.com/about)
- Retired Chief of Police Scott Silverii (www.silverhartwriters.com/about-scott-liliana)
- Retired homicide detective and forensic coroner Garry Rodgers (http://dyingwords.net).

Special thanks to my awesome beta readers: Lynn Wilson (www.campcripplecreektn.com), Nancy Qualls, Shirl Deems, and Theresa Synder (http://theresasnyder.blogspot.com), and to Andrea McKay (https://akaeditorial.com) for proofreading the final draft.

And special, special thanks to my fantastic editor, Faith Freewoman (www.demonfordetails.com), and to the best boyfriend in the world, Dr. Ken Muse.

Printed in Great Britain
by Amazon